GATEKEEPER

GATEKEEPER

A novel by

TERRY L. CRAIG

GATEKEEPER by Terry L. Craig
Published by Creation House
Strang Communications Company
600 Rinehart Road
Lake Mary, Florida 32746
Web site: http://www.creationhouse.com

Unless otherwise noted, all Scripture quotations are from the King James Version of the Bible.

The characters portrayed in this book are fictitious. Any resemblance to actual people, whether living or dead, is coincidental.

Library of Congress Cataloging-in-Publication Data:

Craig, Terry L.
Gatekeeper / Terry L. Craig.
p. cm.
ISBN 0-88419-597-X
I. Title.
PS3553.R24 G38 1999
813'.54—dc21   98-44579
                                                              CIP

9012345 RRD 87654321
Printed in the United States of America

To my beloved Bill

To my mother, Ethella, and my sister, Jo Ann

To Matthew and Daniel

CHAPTER ONE

HE HOPED HE WOULDN'T GET SICK. HE WAS ABOUT TO BE led into a hospital operating suite and didn't know how he'd react when he saw the real thing. News cameras were rolling, and bursts of light from still cameras flashed like assault weapons all around him.

Don Cole wanted to appear intelligent, poised, and focused. He had gotten only five hours of sleep on a bus and had a minor headache going.

How do people with families do this? he thought. He was glad to be single. He had seen too many "campaign wives." They were either hard as nails or overwhelmed and shot down in the first couple of months. Without a wife or children he was free to devote every waking moment to the race. And as a candidate for president of the United States, Donald Larson Cole hoped to take advantage of every "photo op" he could get.

His trusted friend and campaign manager, Bob Post, had arranged this visit to a hospital just outside Cleveland, where some of the latest medical breakthroughs were being put to use. Don thought it was a great idea to have his name mentioned in the same sentence as "cure for cancer," "breakthrough in diabetes," or some other medical miracle. The quality and cost of medicine still ranked as hot topics, and he wanted to jump right into the fray, a leader fighting for premium care at less cost. Caring for America.

Now he was about to witness a new type of surgery that represented years of research and the latest developments in technology—a revolution in medicine. He had seen it on film, but now he would soon see it in person, with the press watching. He could feel a trickle of sweat run down his back. Maybe this hadn't been such a good idea.

I am calm; I am focused, he thought as the volleys of light bombarded his eyes. To his relief, all the cameras and microphones suddenly turned in the opposite direction as Dr. Damian Walsh, who was to perform the operation, entered the room.

"Dr. Walsh, is this your most famous spectator?" asked one of the reporters, referring to presidential candidate Cole.

"Well, yes, but to tell you the truth, the Surgeon General would probably make us more nervous," he replied with a smile. A brief flutter of laughter floated through the assembled press.

"Mr. Cole is about to witness a surgery that challenges what have been the confines of medicine for more than a century," the doctor said. "In addition to the technological components, known collectively as 'the capsule,' we use a process that has taken years to perfect. These are joined with special training techniques for surgical teams and give the patient the benefit of all that modern science has to offer.

"The capsule can be used anywhere electricity can be generated. And once the patient is in the capsule, sterilization of medical personnel attending the patient will no longer be required. In some cases, where there is modem link-up, the doctor could be in New York and the patient could be in a capsule in Miami!

"Mr. Cole and the preselected members of the press will observe the removal of a cancerous tumor. At the end of the operation, written handouts will be made available to the press, and a brief time of questions and answers will be permitted.

"And now, Mr. Cole, shall we proceed?" Dr. Walsh said, motioning toward the doors.

Don took a deep breath as all of the cameras and microphones swung with a single motion back to him. He nodded with the look of someone who was ready for business and headed for the doors.

He proceeded across the room and followed Dr. Walsh through the doors with the selected reporters quickly closing in behind them. All of them were still wearing their street clothes.

Don's eyes were drawn to a large, transparent cylinder on a wheeled support structure that dominated the center of the room. It was bigger and rounder than a coffin, but that was what came to mind as Don looked at it for the first time.

The patient inside the cylinder, a middle-aged man, remained completely visible. Cole noted the wide band of opaque plastic material that was stretched around the man from his shoulders to the end of his rib cage, and the other wide bands circling his hips, legs, and forehead. The bands both covered him and held him down to the narrow shelf that ran through the center of the capsule.

Just like a mummy, Don thought.

What looked like a diving mask covered the man's eyes and nose, and a breathing tube was taped in his mouth.

A group of small, but powerful, lights and a small camera lens were suspended above the patient from a rod that ran the full length of the capsule. The lights could be moved along the rod to illuminate any area below.

Two sets of gloves, which fit the hands to well above the elbow, sat on either side of the capsule. They could move lengthwise along the capsule in a slot that maintained an airtight seal.

"The patient in the capsule," Dr. Walsh began, "is 'Mr. X,' and I will ask the media, once again, not to photograph his face. Mr. X, a Caucasian, is forty-seven years old and has worked in construction for twenty-nine years. During recent tests a tumor was discovered in his colon, and today we are going to remove it."

The doctor nodded to three people waiting near the capsule, and they moved to their posts around the patient and inserted their hands in the gloves.

"Everything inside the capsule has been sterilized, and all the instruments we should need are on a shelf beneath the patient, in front of the nurses."

Some of the spectators moved to the other side to gain a better view.

"If an unanticipated need arises, sterile instruments can be loaded into the air lock at the end of the capsule, the end sealed, and then opened on the inside by a nurse and placed on the shelf or handed to me.

"Much of the surgery will be done with lasers, so loss of blood will be minimal. Any flow of blood will be suctioned out of the capsule with this hose and deposited here, where, in some cases, it can be cleaned and recycled back into the patient," he said as he pointed under the capsule to a container.

"As you can see, there is virtually no chance for the spread of germs to the patient or from the patient. I can stand here in my street clothes along with all of you and maintain a cleaner environment around Mr. X than if we had all scrubbed up.

"With the latest in robotics and communications, even complicated operations can be performed by doctors who are not even with the patient. They can receive a live feed from the camera above and manipulate robotic arms that will mimic every move their hands make when fitted with computer-monitored gloves.

"The applications—on the battlefield, in remote locations, and small towns—are endless!"

Dr. Walsh had missed his calling as far as Don was concerned. He kept everyone so entertained, he should have been an actor. He filled the room with impressive medical chatter while removing a tumor! This guy was good.

Once outside the operating room, Don felt back in his own element. He would let Dr. Walsh have a few moments in the sun (hospitals and doctors always appreciated the right kind of free publicity), then he would give an interview. Don had studied health reform and had well-crafted statements on AIDS, the patient's right to die, abortion, and a dozen health-related issues that could be the kiss of death to his campaign if he were not careful.

He came to the podium with a memorized statement. When he finished giving it, he would accept a limited number of questions from the assembled media.

Bob, his campaign manager, held his breath and prepared to watch the sparring begin.

"As we have seen today," presidential candidate Cole began, "the world of medicine stands poised at a gate leading to a new echelon of excellence. A whole new realm where not only the length of life is increased, but the quality of life as well.

"But passage through this gateway and others beyond it is not guaranteed. It's an exploration, an uncertain pilgrimage, and it will not be without cost. If we are to venture into this new realm, there will be a price to pay in dollars and lives. Today we have seen dedicated men and women who have devoted themselves to this new era of medicine. How far can they go? Not much further without money.

"The current administration has seen fit to cut the funds for medical advances time and again while continuing to finance such things as 'police actions' on foreign soil and refurbishing the Oval Office.

"If elected, I pledge to search for every creative way possible to give the scientific and medical communities what they need to make our lives, the lives of our parents, and the lives of our children better." Don Cole looked around at the sea of hands as reporters vied for the privilege of shooting loaded questions at him. *Let the war games begin,* he thought, and pointed to a man in the front row. "Yes, you."

The man stood and said, "Mr. Cole, in recent months the public has been made aware of projects that are exploring brain cell manipulation and hormonal, gene, and chemical therapies in order to 'rejuvenate' the elderly and make their latter years more productive. If they succeed, would you be in favor of raising the age at which one can receive retirement and medical benefits?"

Whoa! Let's just start with the hand grenades, why don't we, Don thought. "Well, thank you for asking that. Actually," he cleared his throat, "I am aware of some of the advances being pursued in geriatric medicine. If you look, I think you'll see I have an excellent track record of supporting programs to benefit those over sixty-five.

"As some of you know, my father died of Alzheimer's disease three years ago, and my mother suffers with painful arthritis every day. If anything could be done to restore someone else's father in the future or make my mom's life better, you bet I'd be all for it. As for retirement and medical benefits, what intelligent person would address that before the situation was actually on the horizon?"

Bob Post smiled. If Cole didn't want to argue, no one could get him to do so. He fielded questions with an intelligence and grace that were certain to make him the next president of the United States.

Always wanting to leave them hungry and noting that the press conference had gone on for about ten minutes,

Bob gave Don the cue to wrap it up. Cole gave him a slight nod of acknowledgment, but he decided to take one last question from an attractive female reporter in the third row. She stood, and as she spoke, the room grew quiet.

"Mr. Cole, I have just finished a lengthy investigation of this medical facility and am prepared to prove that in another building scientists and doctors from this hospital are conducting human cloning and genetic experimentation. They are engaging in *interspecies* engineering—specifically chimpanzee/human. Should they be allowed to do this? Where do *you* stand on this issue?"

Don Cole blinked. For a moment, he thought he could hear his own heart beating.

Bob grabbed his assistant and whispered, "Who is that woman? Find out immediately . . . is she a crackpot or something? And get hold of our legal . . . "

After a moment of silence, Cole looked right at the woman and started to laugh. It was contagious, and soon others were laughing, too, as if the whole thing had been some sort of joke for a network comedy show. He regained his composure and said, "Well, I guess that's about all for today." He held both hands up to say good-bye to all, stepped away from the podium, and moved off into a side room.

Bob leaned over to his assistant again. "Never mind."

Within minutes all of the reporters had packed up and left. All but one. She waited until Cole and his entourage appeared and approached him. He breezed right by her and kept moving.

"Why did you do that to me?" she yelled after him.

He stopped and turned.

Bob Post stepped in front of Cole quickly. "Steady, boy; she could be taping this whole thing, just waiting for you to trip up."

Don looked at her again. She was lovely, but obviously a loose cannon. "Listen, ma'am, this was my show, not yours."

"My name is Linda Posner. I asked you a question, and you laughed at me."

"You didn't really ask me a question. You spewed out some possibly libelous dribble and then waited for attention. You're lucky I laughed. Maybe you'll be able to keep your job. If I'd answered you by any other means, you'd be in big trouble right now. This way no one took you seriously, and you're off the hook."

Her eyes narrowed. "Every word I said was true, and I was willing to prove it."

"Sure," he chuckled. "And you planned on holding your own press conference after mine?"

"It's the truth!" she exclaimed, fighting back tears.

Cole walked up, stood almost toe to toe with her, and looked down at her. *She's so young,* he thought. *Was I ever this young?*

"Listen," he said softly, "it's not about the truth; it's about power. You haven't got any. Go out and grab little fish first, then the bigger ones. Grow up, or the sharks will eat you without a second thought."

He turned and left the building.

When they were outside, Bob asked, "Do you think she was telling the truth?"

Don looked at the surrounding buildings. "Who knows? She very well could be. Just consider the possible motives. Eventually, corporations might have to stop using Third World children and prisoners to do their slave labor for them. What better replacement than someone who has the strength—and possibly some of the skills—of a human, but no 'human' rights? Scary thought, isn't it?"

CHAPTER TWO

SPECIALIST 5 JOEL LEVINE WOKE UP AND LOOKED AROUND. The aircraft had begun to make a different sound. Still in the belly of a C-130, they made their way to an undisclosed location in Africa along with several other transports carrying troops and equipment. After two days of flight, Joel figured they had to be nearing their destination.

A voice over the speakers told them to prepare for landing, and the plane leaned into a turn. Joel checked his harness moments before the descent began. He didn't suffer from "flight fright," but he didn't like it either. At this point he just hoped they were finally "there"—wherever that was. He heard the landing gear going down and felt the aircraft slow as the drag of the gear decreased their airspeed. A bump signaled that the gear had locked in place. The sounds of the engines changed again, and he heard a bang of contact with the ground and felt the slam of full brakes, full reverse. Everyone pitched forward; the cargo strained against its nets as they braked to a stop.

Must be a really short runway, he thought.

The plane made the turn off the airstrip and taxied to a parking area where it would be unloaded. The door finally opened, and warm, humid air rushed in.

For most of them it was their first classified assignment and their first time out of the country, so they were more than a little nervous. Most of the soldiers were younger than twenty-three years old. Even though they had received twenty weeks of training prior to this mission, the super secrecy of it filled them with both excitement and fear.

In addition to the basic combat training, they had learned special survival techniques for the terrain and climate they would now occupy. A booklet of health warnings passed out to each soldier contained words that would scare any reasonable person.

They would be expected to set up a small garrison to hold a strategic piece of ground against any enemy. What little they knew they were forbidden to share with family, friends, or even other soldiers who were not part of their unit.

Another announcement came to disembark and assemble in formation to the east of the aircraft. Levine and forty-three other soldiers exited the aircraft and got their first look at what would be their new home for an unspecified time. Joel looked around. *So this is Africa,* he thought.

They were somewhere in central southern Africa, but they were not told the exact location. There was an escarpment to the east and peaks in the distance to the north. The aircraft obstructed the view to the west, and only trees could be seen to the south.

Obviously, the landing site had already been prepared by someone who had cleared the bush and leveled the ground for a makeshift runway, but the only other evidence of previous human occupation was a small shack nearby. That was about to change. In fact, within three hours the entire landscape would be transformed.

Vehicles, equipment, and other troops would be unloaded from a string of aircraft. They would hear the steady roar of engines well into the night.

After they had set up tents and taken an ordered rest, Joel could have sworn he heard men talking in a different language outside his tent. He had not slept well in the sticky atmosphere; he would have quite a time getting accustomed to it. Another problem was his mosquito net. He hated that net. It seemed to cut off the flow of air to his cot. In the weeks to come, he would wake up several times during each night and just stare at it. The temptation to throw it off his cot was almost more than he could bear at first, but Joel knew the possible consequences of even one bite from an infected insect—malaria, dengue fever, filariasis, chikungunya, and a host of other unpronounceable diseases that could be transmitted by flying insects. The net would have to stay.

Then there were ticks, lice, and fleas that transmitted everything from Congo-Crimean hemorrhagic fever to the plague. And the water. Just by wading through fresh water one could get parasites that could pass right through unbroken skin. And you didn't even want to think about what might happen if you drank it untreated.

Joel remembered standing in line weekly to receive shots for cholera, hepatitis, typhoid fever, and other diseases—often with the nurse laughing and saying, "Boy, is *this* going to make you sick!" But Joel didn't mind. He wanted protection. Even now, just about all he could think of were the things for which there was *no* prevention, no cure. He resolved to keep his net on and to put on repellent at every opportunity. He tried to recall where the iodine (emergency water sterilization) pills were in his duffel bag and vowed to keep some in a pocket at all times until he left Africa.

For the next week a flurry of activity around the new airstrip produced tents, small buildings, and barbed wire fences at an incredible rate. Latrine facilities were dug, and a small field hospital was established. On the seventh day, they did not rest. They put row upon row of concertina wire around the encampment. Throughout all this, Joel's unit and the others were kept as separate entities, discouraged from exchanging all but the most crucial conversation with anyone outside their group.

Joel was certain they would be seeing action soon.

CHAPTER THREE

DOCTOR GEORGE GRANT AND HIS WIFE, EDWINA, SAT IN the restaurant, giving the outward appearance of a very well-to-do black couple. He was dressed in an expensive charcoal suit; she, in a lovely red dress. Together they made a handsome couple.

Actually, they did not often dress up this way, nor did they make a habit of dining out in expensive restaurants. They lived in a modest, pleasant three-bedroom apartment and only had one car, a lifestyle they chose so their finances could be used at their storefront clinic—which they hoped would become one of the best equipped in New York City.

The business had just reached its six-month milestone and was prospering—a cause for a minor celebration, they reasoned. They had worked very hard, but they were still stirred by the challenges that came through the door daily. Although they treated middle- and upper-income patients in the storefront clinic, they also cared for the poor and homeless (mostly out of a motor home, which they co-oped with two other doctors). It had been their dream for many years, and now it was a reality.

Tonight was a night to celebrate their success and to enjoy a little taste of the fruits of their labors. He reached across the table and squeezed her hand. She looked up from her menu and smiled.

He mouthed the words, "I love you."

A couple at another table saw this and smiled at them. "Dr. Grant," Edwina said, "you keep that up, and you won't get your dinner."

"That a promise or a threat?"

Edwina rolled her eyes, smiled, and looked back at her menu. "I don't know about you, but I'm starved. You can tell me how much you adore me after dessert."

"So you'd just cast me aside for a steak, would you?" he said in mock horror.

She didn't look up. "Actually, I was thinking more in terms of prime rib."

"Ooooo," he said, as he picked up his own menu. "Maybe we should wait until after dinner to discuss our mutual admiration for each other."

"You got it, babe," she said as they looked into each other's eyes and smiled again.

Later, at home, they cuddled up on the sofa while he rubbed her feet.

"You know, 'Wina, in a year, we could be doing really well if we keep this up."

"And there's only one thing that would make it all perfect," she said.

He stopped rubbing one foot for a moment and kissed the top of it. "Not yet, honey. Not yet."

"Not even next year?"

"We can talk about a baby then."

She sighed. "Oh, George. When I see all those women who have so many and don't want them, my heart just aches. Please, George. Let's give it some thought. It takes so long to adopt; maybe we should get on a list now."

" 'Wina, I want one too, but next year will have to do. We're this close to getting the right staff, the right equipment, everything. The clinic will need to be able to run without you so that you'll have time for a baby. Don't worry, honey; there'll still be some when we get to it."

"Promise?"

"I do."

CHAPTER FOUR

MAJOR ROSS HAD BEEN PART OF A LAST-MINUTE SWITCH OF personnel in the secret mission to Africa known as Operation Reclamation. General Rappaport had opposed the change, but a superior insisted. Ross was one of three people who held a key to the building in the southwest corner of the camp referred to as the "Cookie Jar," and only the three key holders knew what was inside it. The small building, which had a wooden exterior to make it look like a shack, was actually constructed of concrete and six-inch armor plating. It was guarded at all times by at least three sets of troops from at least two different countries. There were to be no unauthorized "hands" in the Cookie Jar.

Major Ross arrived on the fourth day of the mission with a key and a valid code. Lieutenant Colonel Tobin and Colonel Gronov—the other key holders—were not happy about this, but they had to yield. They would not risk discussing this matter over any lines of communication. Possessing a key and a valid code constituted permission to enter the Cookie Jar.

Major Ross was not a major. He was not even in the military. Ross now approached the building, gave the correct code word, and was escorted by two armed soldiers to the entry portal. He placed the key in the lock and entered the command code. The seal on the door released, and Ross entered, leaving the two guards who would stand outside the door until he exited.

Once inside the first door, Ross closed it and looked around the anteroom. It was about the size of a walk-in closet. On his left was a shelf containing familiar instruments.

First he selected a DD-650, a small, computerized, direct-reading dosimeter made of hard plastic, which was about the size of a hand-held calculator. Mounted on the wall next to the shelves sat a metal, toaster-sized box with a slot in it. He placed the DD-650 in the slot to activate it, removed it from the slot, then set the dose rate alarm and clipped it to his belt.

Next, Ross selected a Pocket Ionization Chamber, or PIC. The metal instrument looked like a fat ink pen with a lens at either end. The manual device measured gamma radiation. It was primitive, but it would do the job when many of the fancier things failed. He held the lens up to his eye and cocked his head back to let the overhead light shine into the other end. It was at zero. He clipped it on the front of his shirt.

Finally, he took a pair of paper booties and a pair of white, cotton gloves from the shelf and put them on. He walked to a round hatch in the floor that looked like the ones used on submarines. It had a wheel with a knob on it so it could be turned quickly if necessary. He inserted a key next to the hatch and punched in a different command code. This was a failsafe, in case one of the guards outside obtained the code for the outer door. The seal on the hatch made a "shoosh" noise, and he turned the wheel to open it.

He peered down into the well-lighted room below, then descended the ladder to it.

CHAPTER FIVE

EDWINA GRANT SAT DOWN AND EXHALED WITH A LONG sigh. She put one foot and then the other up on the chair in front of her. Every bone in her feet cried out for mercy. She had been standing all day and was certain she couldn't go another step.

"I know I promised you I'd lose fifteen pounds, but I've been busy, OK?" she said to her feet.

Right now, all Edwina wanted to do was to put her feet into something cool. She closed her eyes and pictured herself wading in a cool, babbling brook. The voice of her husband broke her reverie.

"Was it you who left that anonymous note on my desk asking me to take you dancing tonight?"

She closed her eyes again and moaned.

"No? It must have been Olga then."

She smiled. Olga was an old Russian woman who, every day, fancied she was dying...but would probably outlive everyone. Edwina suddenly imagined George in a tux with a red cummerbund and Olga in a flowing black gown with a rose clenched in her dentures as they tangoed with a walker between them. She laughed.

"You think it odd that someone of Olga's stature would find me attractive?" he said, raising an eyebrow. He looked young for his age, muscular and still without a wrinkle.

She laughed again. "I love you, George."

The door suddenly flew open. The frame of a large man exploded into the room. "Get a move on, Doc! Kid with a broken leg! Kid with a broken leg! Let's go!" Ricky said as he waved his arm like a traffic cop.

Ricky, their EMT and all-around assistant, never ceased to amaze them with the variety of things he knew. Having grown up in one of the city's worst slums, Enrique Ruiz was the son of an Hispanic mother and an unknown father. He had been given few opportunities as a young man outside of joining a gang and becoming a criminal—both of which he freely admitted.

George had heard that the missing half of Ricky's left-hand middle finger had been blown off by a gun. Were it not for Ricky's own disclosures, George and Edwina would have found it impossible to believe that this kind, happy individual had led such a dreadful life.

The only thing that made the Grants a little uncomfortable was what effected his "transformation." Years before they met him, Ricky had been drawn to the ministry of a large, nearby church where he had gotten "saved." Not the quiet kind of thing that happened in the hushed sanctuary of an old and hallowed church, but the jump-up-and-down-shout-"hallelujah!"-grab-strangers-by-the-lapel-and-yell-"let-me-tell-you-about-Jesus!" kind of saved. This was Ricky's only flaw as far as they were concerned. They were happy his life had turned around, but every so often they had to ask him to tone it down a few notches.

At six foot four—and so spirited—Ricky could be intimidating. They told him that his kind of religion wasn't everyone's cup of tea and he needed to respect that. On the other hand, he seemed so intelligent and caring that both George and Edwina thought it a pity he hadn't had the chance to become a doctor. They even toyed with the idea helping him through medical school.

"Hop to it, you guys!" Ricky shouted as he bolted back out of the room.

George quickly followed as Edwina pulled her feet from that cool, babbling brook and stood up. She winced a little and then hobbled out of the room.

A child lay strapped on the gurney. George tended her as Ricky questioned the woman who was with her.

The little girl was visiting the city for the day with her mother. She was nine years old and profoundly deaf. As she exited a cab, she neither saw nor heard a special delivery courier on a bike and stepped into his path. She fell, pulling the man and his bicycle on top of her, probably breaking her leg in the process. It had happened near the door to the clinic; Ricky, who happened to be standing outside, heard the sound of a bone breaking.

"I'm sure it's busted," he said when they got outside the room. "I heard the thing snap."

X-rays confirmed Ricky's diagnosis, and the leg had to be set. Later, as they put a cast on her leg, George noticed Ricky using sign language to talk to the girl. A slight smile came to the pale, little face. George and Edwina looked at each other.

"Where did you learn sign language?" George asked.

"Oh, I don't know much. I picked up a few books about it in the library, that's all. I always thought it was cool, and I figured it might come in handy sometime."

Edwina shook her head and patted Ricky on the shoulder as she left the room.

"Hey, 'Wina! Ready for dinner?"

Edwina looked out to the waiting room and saw Rosalinda Sanchez, her former college roommate and one of her closest friends. She rushed down the hall to give her a hug and suddenly remembered they were supposed to go out to dinner together.

"Oh, Rosa! I'm so sorry. I completely forgot about dinner. We had a last minute emergency . . . Can you give us just a few more minutes to close up?"

"No problem."

"Did you have any trouble getting here?"

"No . . . in fact, your directions were perfect," Rosa said and then hugged Edwina again. "'Wina, I have the best news. I got the job! I just found out this afternoon!"

"Oh, how wonderful! Do you know what this means? The dynamic duo can fly again!" Edwina said as she grabbed Rosalinda's hand and spun around. She looked up to see Ricky watching them and felt a little silly.

"You sure seem revived," he said wryly.

"Ricky, this is my dearest friend, Rosalinda Sanchez. She has just moved here, and I'd like you to meet her."

He stepped forward and put out his hand. "Yes. A lovely rose indeed. Happy to meet you. And now, if you will excuse me," he said, shaking Rosalinda's hand and then turning to Edwina, "I will help Joan close out our paperwork for the night so we can get out of here."

As soon as he left the room, she turned to Rosa and whispered, "I know this is not what we planned, but could we order out and go home with dinner? My feet are killing me."

"Of course! Why not? It's not the food I came for—it's the company."

"You're still the best, Rosa . . . Could I ask one more favor? Would it be OK if we offered Ricky a ride home? We've kept him so late tonight . . . "

"Certainly."

Once they were all in the car and on the road, Edwina realized they would have to pick up the food before they dropped Ricky off. She felt bad about this because she didn't know if he had anything decent to eat at home.

"You know, Ricky, I just realized we'll be picking up a large order of food on the way to dropping you off. Can we invite you to supper?" Ricky, sitting in the front seat with George, looked back at the two women. He seemed suddenly embarrassed.

"Uh, no. That's OK . . . I, uh, have stuff planned."

"Come on, Ricky," George pleaded. "They'll have a hen party all night, and there isn't even a game on for me to watch. Come hang out with me."

"Well . . . "

"It's settled then," Edwina said. "Drive on, Dr. George, and don't spare the horses!"

The conversation around the Grant's dining room table buzzed pleasantly for most of the meal. But during dessert things started to sour.

Rosalinda had been hired by the Department of Heath and Child Welfare and would soon be in an office just blocks from the clinic. As she described her job, she spoke of her desire to change the way things were in the neighborhood.

Ricky just smiled at her.

"What are you smiling at?" she said. Was he somehow mocking her?

"Nothing in particular," he said, but the flash of perfect white teeth grew wider.

That smile displeased her, and those dark eyes seemed to look right through her—even though these features were the only things she found even remotely attractive about him. Trying to appear calm, she raised her glass to her lips. Then she set it down to say one more thing.

"Well, all these people are having all these children, and then they just abuse them or let them run wild. I'm saying that the government is going to start holding them more accountable."

"What do you propose people should do with their children? Put them in programs? Government-sponsored clubs?" he countered.

Rosa didn't like his tone. He seemed almost twice her size, but she was not going to let him intimidate her. "I propose that, yes, parents avail themselves of good neighborhood programs, that bad parents should lose their rights to parent, and that the older kids who are beyond saving be removed from influencing other kids."

"You an only child?" he asked, with the smile flashing again.

"Well . . . yes. But what does . . . "

"Rich kid? Parents made lots of money when they came from Cuba and gave little Rosa the best of everything?"

She steamed inwardly.

He slowly reached across the table and pointed to a crucifix on a chain around her neck before speaking again. "That mean anything to you, or is it just a piece of expensive jewelry someone gave you?"

"I'll have you know I was *raised* in the church!"

"Meaning exactly what?" he continued, his gaze fixed upon her.

She was so frustrated she couldn't think of anything to say.

"I'm not trying to be rude to you, Rosalinda," he said in a calm voice, "but let me tell you something. I've been to hell and back, and it wasn't some 'program' that saved me. It was *God*. By your standards, I was unsavable, but God saved me. People don't need more police agencies; they don't need more programs—they need Jesus. Nothing short of that will make a difference that lasts this long," he said as he held his thumb and forefinger about an eighth of an inch apart.

Rosa reached for her glass again and knocked it over. The contents quickly fanned out over the table and dripped onto her dress. She stood, her face burning hot, and said, "I think I need to use the restroom. Excuse me."

"If you will excuse me, also," Ricky said as he stood to his feet, "I think I should be going home. Thanks for dinner."

"Here, I'll give you a lift." George offered.

"No. Really, I have some things I need to do, and I'd like to walk and clear my head. The station's not far from here."

"You're sure?"

"Yeah. Thanks for dinner. It was . . ." Ricky hesitated a moment. "Really good . . . food. Uh, thanks."

George and Edwina were left in the dining room alone.

"Gee, that went well. Got any other big plans for the evening, dear?" George asked.

"Actually, I think they kind of liked each other for a while there."

"Yeah," he said, chuckling. "If they'd liked each other any better, there probably would have been a homicide." They laughed about it until they heard Rosa returning.

"Rosa," Edwina said as she stepped back into the room, "I'm sorry about your dress. I thought you could spend the night in the guest room. Tomorrow's Saturday, and there's a good dry cleaner just around the corner. You can wear one of my 'skinny' outfits, and we can drop off your dress. How's that sound?"

Rosa looked as if she wanted to say something, but not in front of George. Realizing this, he got up from the table.

"Well," he said, "I think I need a shower." He kissed Edwina on the cheek. "Be out in a while."

As soon as he was out of earshot, Edwina repeated her apology. "I'm really sorry about your dress."

"*You* didn't do anything," Rosa said, as she started picking up dishes and stacking them. "Just who does that guy think he is anyway?"

Edwina joined in the dish-stacking routine. "Well, he's just Ricky. He can be a little intense, but he really is a nice man. George and I don't know what we'd do without him. He may not be much to look at . . . "

"What happened to his finger?" Rosa interjected.

"Oh, that." Edwina cringed a little. "I think someone shot it off."

"No." Her friend's eyes widened.

"Yes."

"It figures. He looks like the kind of guy who gets into trouble."

"Honestly, Rosa, he's a nice guy."

"He sat there all evening and insulted me, and he's a nice guy?"

Edwina stopped cleaning a plate and looked at Rosalinda for a moment. "He didn't insult you all evening. You just made assumptions about what he was thinking."

"Are you defending his behavior?"

Edwina stopped, looked at her again, and smiled. "Really got under your skin, eh?" She headed to the kitchen with a stack of dishes.

Rosa followed her but said nothing for a few minutes. Edwina scraped the leftovers into the sink and turned on the garbage disposal. When it was quiet again Rosa asked, "Do *you* think I'm a spoiled person?"

Edwina raised her eyebrows and thought a moment. "How can I answer such a question? If I say 'no,' you'll think I'm just saying that because you're my best friend," she said as she hugged Rosa. "If I say 'yes,' you'll probably throw me off the balcony." They both laughed. "Seriously, I think you misunderstood Ricky. And I don't think you are any more spoiled than I am—whatever that's worth."

CHAPTER SIX

DONALD LARSON COLE STEPPED INTO HIS HOTEL ROOM, exhausted. He felt as if he'd been campaigning for president since he was able to walk. And the election was still nine months away. Intellectually, he knew he would make it, but his body would take some convincing.

He had been to a breakfast, a brunch, two lunches, an afternoon tea, and a dinner. He had rubbed elbows, kissed babies, signed autographs, and given speeches.

When Don retired to his hotel room, he left strict orders. He wanted no calls, knocks on his door, or disturbances of any kind unless it was a "life-or-death" situation. He wanted nothing but peace and quiet.

He left the lights off in his room because his eyes were tired. There was enough light coming through the glass doors for him to get around the room without bumping into things. As he looked outside, the balcony seemed to invite him to come out and stand in the cool night air. He went to the glass doors and opened them.

Ah yes, Don thought, stepping onto the balcony, *if only I could spend the night out here.*

He walked to the railing so he could view the lights of the city below. *What city is this anyway? Oh yeah,* he remembered, *Seattle.* The candidate took a few deep breaths, letting his mind wander as he relaxed. A voice behind him jarred him back to the present.

"Good evening, Mr. Cole."

He started to turn, but someone pressed up behind him, shoved him against the railing, and stuck something sharp against the middle of his back.

"Remain quiet and very still. This blade is razor sharp, and if I struggle with you, it might slip, sever your spinal cord, and . . . " Don felt a sharp sting as the tip of the man's knife penetrated the skin on his back. He sucked air between his teeth but did not cry out.

The intruder put his foot against the shin of Don's leg and pulled it back. Don grabbed hold of the railing to keep from being knocked off the balcony. "That's right, keep both hands on the railing, and we'll do just fine. I apologize for the way I've had to sneak up on you, but this is the only way it could be done. I only want five minutes of your time, sir, and then I will leave as quietly as I came." He pulled the knife away just enough to ease the pain.

"How did . . . ," Don began.

"I get up here?" the man finished his sentence. "Let's just say no one saw me come in, and no one will see me leave. Just listen to me, OK?"

"You have my full attention," Don said, trying not to sound shaken. His heart pounded out of his chest. In addition to his own security, the Secret Service was supposed to be guarding him. His own campaign people occupied the entire top two floors.

How did this man get in my room? Or was he waiting on the balcony? This is the penthouse—is the guy a climber? The man's voice interrupted his flow of thoughts.

"We can be anywhere at anytime. There is no place that is too high, too deep, too hot, too cold, too sacred, too secure. In fact, tonight's visit is just a small demonstration of our . . . shall we say, capabilities."

"And this 'we' would be . . . ?" Don's mind leaped through the list of wacky groups that splashed into the news on a regular basis.

"We are not terrorists, Mr. Cole. We are also not right-wing extremists, or a cult, or some screwy little group that has headquarters in some podunky little town in Arkansas. Many of us have served or are serving this country in numerous government and military capacities. And we have seen too much."

Don broke in. "So? I haven't been elected. And even if I were president, what do you think I could do for you?"

The stranger poked him with the knife again, making him jump. "Listen, we know what you are. A politician. But you haven't been part of the 'beltway' group. You're a one-term governor. That puts you pretty much out of touch with what's going on in D.C. Your partner is a waste of skin, but we know there's no love lost between you and Lawrence.

"Bottom line, we believe you are clueless as to what is really going on—what's about to happen."

"About to happen?" Don felt another rush of adrenaline.

"Yes."

"This country, its government, its military, and its infrastructure are more divided than is widely known. There are two distinct powers emerging. We represent one side, and they are the other side."

"Of course, and you are good and they are evil, right?" Cole couldn't resist the sarcasm.

"Scoff if you want. Both sides are dead serious. You will have to assess your situation very quickly. The other side intends to bring such economic and social chaos that the loss of personal freedom and national identity will be a small price to pay for the peace and security they will offer.

"Mr. Cole, the group I represent hopes for a peaceful resolution, but it may come to something more unpleasant."

The intruder paused and waited for Cole's response.

"So why are you talking to me?" Don asked. "I'm in no position to help you, and according to you, I'm clueless. Why are you telling me all this now? If you're planning some sort of coup, why let me in on it? I'm certainly not about to storm the White House with you."

"Because," the stranger answered, "you are our last hope of making the transition back through the established channel of election to office. There need be no bloodshed."

"Bloodshed?" Cole said. "Who are you people? Do you think you can just take over the government?"

"Listen, I know this all sounds like a second-rate movie, but after tonight, we hope you will believe us. As far as taking over the government, you'll soon find out that someone already *has.* We're sharing all this with you in the hope that you'll realize we are telling the truth and will join us when the time comes.

"The enemy already has a timetable in place. If we do nothing, they will win. If you resist them without our help, they will simply eliminate you. Right now, they have left you out of the game because their candidate is already occupying the office, and they have little fear that you will win."

"Gee, thanks," Cole said.

"But," the intruder said, "*we* are dealing you into the game. We are going to assure your victory."

Don felt a hand sliding up the front of his shirt. The hand dropped something in his pocket, and the stranger continued, "I have just placed a disk in your pocket. Before you view it, I want you to know that the enemy will kill for it, so don't plan on sharing it—*with anyone.*

You are new to this. You have no idea who is on your side and who is not. This disk will give you a glimpse of some of the players and some of the pawns they are using.

"Soon we will release the contents of this disk worldwide, and it will devastate the president's campaign. He will certainly lose the White House and may yet be impeached. We will try to time the release of this information carefully, so there is opportunity for the scandal to unfold, but not enough time for them to get out the smoke and mirrors. The other guys thrive on confusion. And you, Mr. Cole, unless you die or do something unbelievably stupid, will be the next president of the United States.

"As long as things go well, we will restrain our forces until you are in office. If you decide we are telling the truth, we can work together. We are giving this disk to you now as a good-will gesture."

"Holding someone at knife-point could hardly be seen as a good-will gesture," Don said.

"I want you to know we could have killed you at any time today. I also want you to know," he said, pulling the knife away from Don's back, "that we're not bent on killing *anyone*, but we will do whatever it takes. We had to meet you like this, Mr. Cole. We had to do it in a way that *no one* would know you had been contacted. It is as much for your safety as it is for ours. You don't really know who your enemies are. You'll see, sir. You'll see soon enough. When it's clear the president's a goner, they'll come courting you, too. But after tonight, your eyes will be opened."

"What makes you so sure I won't decide to go with the other side?"

"Well, I suppose you could. But we know you better than you think. Your dad was a hero in combat, and he suffered with the wounds from it the rest of his life. You still have the Silver Star they gave him in a little pouch in your briefcase. We're hoping it's more than just a memento of your dad. We're hoping you still care about the things your father risked so much for.

"We are the kind of people who are still willing to risk something for freedom. We *will* win America back, whatever it takes . . . My time is up, Mr. Cole. We will contact you again soon."

"Who are you?" Cole said quickly, thinking at any second the man might whip out a rope and leap off the balcony.

"We are known as the Army of the Quick and the Dead . . . I am going to leave you alone with your thoughts once again, but before I do, I want you to look at your chest."

Don looked down. A small red dot glowed on his chest.

"See that red dot? It's a laser sight. A fellow patriot has a high-powered rifle trained on you." He leaned closer to Don's left ear and said in a confidential tone, "You know, Mr. Cole, you really should wear the bulletproof vest you were given." Then the intruder stepped back from him and said, "If you should try to leave this balcony or even turn around for at least one minute, he'll drop you where you stand. I want you to count out loud, slowly, backwards, from sixty to one. Begin now."

Don kept his eyes on the small red dot and counted quietly, "Sixty . . . fifty-nine . . . fifty-eight . . . "

CHAPTER SEVEN

DANIEL INGRAM SAT ON THE EDGE OF HIS BED. HE REACHED over to his nightstand and picked up the pad of paper and a pen. He'd had another dream, and he wanted to write it down before he forgot it. Since he was wide awake, he slipped off the bed and went to his study. He didn't want to wake his wife, Anne, so he closed the door before he turned on the light. He sat at his desk to write what he'd seen.

He'd been the pastor of a church in New York City for almost two decades. He'd seen God's faithfulness through the years and had realized success in the tasks God had entrusted to him. But recently he'd begun having dreams again. They were the kind of dreams that could get a man labeled a fanatic and cost him his friends and ministry if he dared to repeat them.

Many "prophecies" had been spoken regarding the turn of the millennium. Many people focused their fears on events that they were told would surely come to pass. Although there *had been* wars, large natural disasters, some frightening setbacks in the fight against disease, and major financial crashes that sent many of the "middle class" below the poverty level, *none* of the "world-*ending*" events predicted came to pass. America hadn't split in half. World War III had not broken out. No asteroids had come along and blasted the earth to space dust . . . The turn of the millennium came and went, and whether they wanted to or not, humanity survived. Even the loss of some of the globe's largest computer systems could not stop the world from turning. People were poorer and hungrier—but they were tired of "dark" predictions. They were ready to set their sights on a new, brighter era.

For several months now Daniel had been having the dreams. At first, he argued with the Lord, saying no one would listen. Then he pleaded, saying the ministry that had been built on years of hard work would be destroyed. The reputation for which he had worked so hard would be ruined. However, the dreams continued, along with the command to write and tell them. Daniel soon came to the place where he knew both his work and his reputation were nothing without the God he served. He began to write the dreams and to share them with others as God directed.

Daniel's hand trembled as he began to pen the words. He'd seen the destruction again, and he knew this was no mere nightmare. To him it was as real as if he'd just lived it. He moved his hand as fast as he could, knowing that details would fade if he did not capture them now. He came to one particular place in the dream. This he'd been told *not* to write. Daniel stopped momentarily, then moved on to other details.

He described whole cities abandoned, without inhabitants, and other cities destroyed. He saw multitudes killed by some deadly pestilence, and many others crying out for an end to the suffering. The Mississippi River flowed as red as blood with not a living thing on either side—not even a tree or a blade of grass—for miles. Finally he saw the earth as from space. He could see it rotating slowly. It began to spin faster and faster, then wobbled on its axis. Then all was dark, and he had awakened.

He wrote what he heard. "For the word of the Lord has come to many. I have spoken to My people early and late, but they would not listen to Me. Although I have consistently sent them prophets, My servants, they have not listened. The prophets came saying, 'Turn again now everyone from your evil way and wrongdoing, that you may dwell in the land your fathers gave you. Do not go after other gods to serve and worship them, and do not provoke the Lord to anger with the works of your hands.' But to their own hurt, they have not listened to Me.

"They have ground their heels on the face of the poor. They have ignored those who are sick or in prison. Adultery, drunkenness, greed, and perversion are all named openly in my house. They are reading their horoscopes, calling mediums, seeking out the dead, angels, and the Queen of Heaven. All these are things that I have said will provoke Me. But My people have said, 'What harm will it do?' 'Does He really see?' or 'He has not given me what I want; I will seek the help of another.'"

Scriptures came to mind, so Daniel looked them up and wrote them in the notebook:

"Jeremiah 23:20: 'The anger of the LORD shall not return, until he have executed, and till he have performed the thoughts of his heart: *in the latter days ye shall consider it perfectly* . . .'" Daniel underlined the last words with a note to himself to "study this," then continued, "Jeremiah 23:23–24: 'Am I a God at hand, saith the LORD, and not a God afar off? Can any hide himself in secret places that I shall not see him? saith the LORD. Do not I fill heaven and earth? saith the LORD.'

"Jeremiah 25:34–36: 'Howl, ye shepherds, and cry; and wallow yourselves in the ashes, ye principal of the flock: for the days of your slaughter and of your dispersions are accomplished; and ye shall fall like a pleasant vessel. And the shepherds shall have no way to flee, nor the principal of the flock to escape. A voice of the cry of the shepherds, and an howling of the principal of the flock, shall be heard: for the LORD hath spoiled their pasture.'

"Jeremiah 7:20: 'Therefore thus saith the Lord GOD; Behold, mine anger and my fury shall be poured out upon this place, upon man, and upon beast, and upon the trees of the field, and upon the fruit of the ground; and it shall burn, and shall not be quenched.'"

Daniel stopped writing. Tears filled his eyes. "O God, I will write, and I will tell, but take this pain from me. It is too much for me. I beg for Your mercy. We have sinned against You, but I beg for Your mercy. Stay Your judgment yet a little while. Help people to hear Your voice calling out to them. Send a faithful Gatekeeper . . . one who will stand in the gap, O God, that this nation would not be destroyed from the earth . . . lest the enemy rejoice and say that You could not save us. For Your own name's sake, Father, send Your word yet another time and help Your people to hear. Let Your servant come and reason with You."

Words came to him again, and he wrote them down. "I will speak once again, but this time with shaking. When this people awaken and seek Me, I will hear them and give them a place of refuge. Already, I have found one to stand in the Gate with Me, to hold back the tide for a season. I will send you this Gatekeeper. He will not be of your choosing, but Mine. A man who has no wife, no child, whom I will set apart for Me. When I send him to you, anoint him. Though he will not understand fully at the time, obey My command to you. He will rise up and will stand in the Gate for Me, and I will use him mightily. Pray for this man, for his enemies are great in strength and number."

CHAPTER EIGHT

DON COLE COUNTED ALL THE WAY DOWN TO ONE. THE
small dot of red light suddenly disappeared from his
chest. He took a deep breath and hesitated a moment
before turning to go back into his room, feeling rattled.
Was he safe anywhere?

How could this man have gotten into his room or onto
his balcony without being detected? Was this just a one-
in-a-million phenomenon carried off by a couple of
screwballs? Was it possible that the guy was one of the
agents assigned to "protect" him? He said they were in all
sorts of "government and military" jobs. What if there
really was a large group of them within the government?

Should he run to the door and inform his "guards" of
the intruder on his balcony? Might one of them be the
very man himself? Or could they be on the "other" side?

As soon as he entered his room, he closed and locked
the glass doors. He pulled the curtains, felt his way over to
the nightstand, and clicked on the light. He sat motionless
on his bed. Although he was scared, something told him

to wait and at least consider his options for a moment. Whatever he decided to do, there would be no turning back from it.

I could tell them that there had been someone out on the balcony but not tell them about the disk.

The disk. He took the object out of his pocket. Maybe he could view the disk first and then decide what to do. But then how would he explain the time lapse between the time of the intrusion and the time he reported it? Even now, the seconds were ticking away.

The fact remained that either man could have killed him on the spot—but didn't. Don didn't know if it was curiosity, ambition, or intuition that drove his choice, but he knew he had to see what was on the disk before he could decide what to do next.

A pain in his back reminded him that he had been injured. Cole put the disk in the drawer of the nightstand, went to the bathroom, and removed his shirt. He saw blood around a small slice in the fabric. He put water on a washcloth and turned to view his back in the mirror. After washing it off, he saw that it was a very small cut. He went back to the bedroom and retrieved the disk, then walked to the living room portion of his suite.

Energized by adrenaline, he opened up the computer, turned it on, and put the disk in place. Should he run it now?

He had thought the room was totally "secure," but now he had his doubts. *Oh well,* he thought, *was any-place else going to be any more secure?* He pressed the button and his screen lit up with an image.

The picture was strange. It took Don a few seconds to realize it was the view from a "fish-eye" lens, which takes in a wide scene but bends it. Later, he would come to the conclusion the "camera" must have been on someone's glasses or somewhere on their head, seeing everything the person was seeing—although somewhat distorted.

The beginning of the video was shot in what was probably the president's limousine. The people sat in a small, dark enclosure that had a lot of upholstery, and everyone was jostled around occasionally.

President Clarence "Sonny" Todd sat in the center, facing the person with the camera. Vice President Victor Bartlett and Secretary of Defense Ernest Schollet sat on either side of the president. Although his voice could be heard several times, only the right hand and dark trousers on a right knee were visible on a fourth man who sat to the cameraman's left. The cameraman never spoke, but he occasionally received acknowledging looks from the three men facing him in the vehicle. Schollet spoke first.

"The only thing we need to do is make sure we all have the same story."

"He's right, Sonny," Bartlett chimed in. "As long as we have a plan from the very beginning and stick to it," he said as he looked at the fourth man and the cameraman, "we can stay in the clear. Just saying national interests are at stake won't cut it anymore. We need a specific plan here."

"Might I suggest," the fourth man said, "that for Operation Reclamation we don't use national forces. What about international?"

"How will we sell it to the folks?" the vice president said with concern.

"You know how unstable some of those countries in southern Africa are. What if a huge war was about to take place and the troops were just going there to prevent it? It would be low-key, small clusters of troops over a wide area."

"Enough said," the president stated. "We will communicate about this again later. Ernie, get some numbers together and an estimate of the time frame," he directed Schollet.

"Yes sir, I can probably have them in twenty-four hours."

"You know how to contact me," the fourth man said. "I'll be in D.C. all week."

A short, blank spot on the video was followed by another scene. This one showed the president and Schollet seated at a table. The camera might have been inside a wall or in an object at one end of the table.

President Todd and the Secretary of Defense discussed papers the Secretary brought to the meeting covering the estimated numbers for Operation Reclamation. He spoke of several hundred "troops," but only two dozen "weapons."

Cole knew they weren't discussing mere guns or missiles.

Another blank space in the video followed and then a view of a military encampment. The time, day, and date appeared in the upper left-hand corner. Only a week had elapsed since this footage had been shot. The lighting was dim; the sun must have been close to setting. The person with the camera panned an airstrip. An unidentified male voice said, "This is the runway." The view tightened to an object held in the hand of the man with the camera. "This is the exact location in southern Africa." Don had toyed with the idea of being a pilot in years past and recognized the object in the video as a GPS, or Global Positioning System, a device that worked in conjunction with satellites to give the current, exact location of the user—anywhere in the world. Don looked at the numbers on the GPS screen as they came into focus in the video. He got out a piece of paper and jotted down the numbers. He knew the numbers would fix the location somewhere in southern Africa.

The man with the camera went to a small, well-guarded building in the camp, surrounded by two fences and a host of guards. An armed soldier at the gate saluted. He asked for authorization and identification. By now, Cole could tell the camera lens must be located on the man's chest—maybe in a button or in his ribbons. The guard had saluted and called the cameraman "sir."

"Bingo!" Cole said, pointing to the screen. "He's an officer."

The officer proceeded under armed escort to the door, produced a key, and entered a code in the keypad. He shielded his right hand with his left so no one could see the code he used. The outside of the building looked like a windowless wooden shed—a building incapable of withstanding a moderate storm. But when the officer entered the small building, it became clear that the exterior was just a facade. The small interior was concrete block, well lighted, and lined with shelves. The cameraman put on several devices, gloves, and paper boots, then opened a hatch in the floor and climbed down a ladder to another room. This room was considerably larger than the one above it. Shelves containing what appeared to be oversized metal suitcases filled one end of the room. The man went to the closest case and pulled it from the shelf. He placed the case, which had no exterior markings, on a table and opened the four latches around the rim.

Inside the case, there appeared to be a small, disassembled missile and a softball-sized object with the well-recognized, three-bladed radioactive symbol on it. He picked up a stack of cards, loosely connected at one corner with a small-gauge cable, and held them in front of the camera. The top card had "ERW & Badger Rocket—Assembly and Firing Instructions" on it. Cole stopped the video. An ERW, or Enhanced Radiation Weapon, was, in essence, a small hydrogen bomb made for the purpose of killing every living thing within a small area—but leaving all the structures and weapons intact.

Pretty handy if you wanted to kill a bunch of people but keep their stuff. Was Todd out of his mind? How could he ever justify the use of nuclear weapons?

If this video was the real thing, it really would put him out of office. The environmentalists he so often claimed to represent would have his head on a plate, not to mention the international community. Cole pushed a button and continued watching.

As the officer flipped through the stack of cards, English instructions and simple pictographs could be seen on them. He replaced them in the case and pointed to a serial number on a metal tag imbedded in the foam surrounding the devices. He closed the case and proceeded to the next one, and the next, until he had opened twenty-four boxes. Each box contained similar objects with different serial numbers.

But what if this video was a fake? Computer imaging technology could make anything look real. How could anyone prove there were nuclear weapons already deployed for use in Africa?

As Cole began to watch the next segment, a knock on his door startled him. Another knock followed, and he knew he must move quickly. He retrieved the disk, stuck it in a drawer, and shut off his computer. He ran to his room, grabbed his robe, and rushed to the door.

Don stopped just short of the door, took a breath, and rumpled up his hair. As he opened the door, he slumped and squinted his eyes. Bob Post and Jason, an aide, waited in the hall.

Jason looked anxious. "I told him not to disturb you, Mr. Cole."

Bob rolled his eyes. "Tell him you won't fire him, Don."

"I won't fire you," Don said blankly.

"Now, invite me in and tell him to go away."

"It's OK, Jason. I'll see you in the morning. Thanks," he said, opening the door wider for Bob to come in.

Bob went straight to the couch and plopped down. He started babbling about something, but Don's heart was still pounding and his mind leaping. He couldn't absorb any more for a moment.

"Sorry to get you up," Bob was saying, "but listen, we got a major break tonight. The Small Business Coalition has voted to go ahead with the national boycott! We've got to work out a strategy tonight before the press conference in the morning. Joe's already writing some spins on it." He picked up the phone. "I can get Trina up here . . . " He sat the phone back down. *"Hel-lo!* Bob to Don, Bob to Don, come in, Don." He waved his hand back and forth rapidly in front of Cole's face.

Cole snapped back to the present and looked at Bob.

"What I said was that the Small Business Coalition . . . "

Don needed a moment to think this out. "I gotta go to the bathroom. I'll be right back."

What am I going to do? He thought as he closed the bathroom door. He ran some water in the sink and splashed it on his face. *Think, man, think! What if Todd really is going to use ERWs? How would anyone ever prove it before he actually did it? The serial numbers. We would have to have some sort of access to the logs to prove those were valid numbers, and we would have to prove those weapons were in fact missing from the stockpiles . . . Do I want any part of this?*

Bob knocked on the bathroom door. "I'm calling room service. You want anything?"

"No," Cole said as he looked at himself in the mirror. "Don't call anyone. We have to talk first, Bob."

There was a momentary pause. "Sure. OK."

Bob had been his friend for twenty years. If he couldn't trust Bob, he couldn't trust anyone . . . and what would be the point of going on with any of this? He made a decision.

Don came out of the bathroom and sat down in a chair facing Bob. "Something has happened. I don't know what to do about it, but something has happened . . . "

His friend leaned forward. "Yes?"

Cole looked at his watch. "About thirty minutes ago, I went out on the balcony to get some air. A man was out there with a knife."

"What?" Bob said loudly as his eyes widened.

Don held up a hand. "Let me finish. He said he was part of some group, and I know there were at least two of them, because the other one had a gun on me."

"What?"

Don held up a hand again. "Obviously, they didn't kill me . . . He said they had to contact me this way because it had to be secret. He gave me a disk to watch on my laptop, and that's what I was doing when you banged on my door."

"What?"

"Would you stop saying 'what' every time I say something?"

"You mean you had a breach of security like *that* and you're just sitting in here, calm as you please, looking at a computer disk, and you're not going to tell anyone?"

"First of all, I am not calm. I probably won't sleep for days. Second of all, you should see what's on the disk. If it's the real thing, Todd will be blown right out of the water. He might even be impeached."

"What?" Bob said as he stood up.

Don gave him an exasperated look.

"Sorry," he said and sat down.

"These people have real clout, whoever they are. And they can obviously 'bug' any place. They could be watching us right now, for all I know. But they gave me this disk, and they hoped I would watch it tonight, so they must be pretty sure *Todd's* people don't have the room bugged."

"So what's on the disk?"

"Come over here, and I'll show it to you. I haven't finished watching all of it myself, but I'll start it over, and we'll watch it together."

It seemed that President Todd was involved in a plot to seize strategic points in Africa. If it went according to plan, this seizure would give the appearance of protecting the sovereignty of individual African governments from a bloody war. Bob and Don watched the disk again.

After two and a half hours, they decided they would tell no one about the visit or the video, but they would begin a casual investigation of international troop movements in Africa and determine if U.S. forces were indeed involved. They would see if they could find a way to locate the serial numbers of U.S. ERWs and use those to track down their actual location. And they would be sure to discuss this in 'coded' terms in the future, even when they were alone.

CHAPTER NINE

RICKY RUIZ TOOK THE SUBWAY HOME AFTER WORKING ALL day at the storefront clinic. He walked to his small, sparsely furnished apartment and was surprised to see a young man sitting on the floor in front of his door. It was Kendrick.

Kendrick Lockhart was in a gang and in trouble with the law when Ricky first met him on a basketball court over a year ago. The sixteen-year-old had tried to pick a fight with him. Ricky ignored his threat and talked to him about God.

"I know you will find this hard to believe, but God is telling me that you really want out of the life you're living. He says you've already done some time and you are about to stand trial again. You're scared, but you don't know what to do. That so?"

"You know me?" Kendrick said, stunned.

"Not until now. But God called you by name before you were ever born. You want help, or you want to concede the game and go home?"

"Well," the young man said as he looked both ways and then moved closer, "what if I did? Want to get out, I mean."

"There's only one way," Ricky said as he looked around, leaned closer, and then pointed up. "Jesus."

The boy waved his hand and blew air between his lips as he moved back. "Oh, yeah, yeah. And you want me to sing in the choir, right?"

"No. I want you to give your life to Jesus. You're throwing it away right now, and soon you'll be dead or in jail. Why not try giving your life away and have a chance to live on the edge in ways you never imagined?"

"You sayin' you can keep me out of jail?"

"I'm not saying anything of the sort—you may have to pay for things you've done. I'm saying that *wherever* you are, as of this moment, your life can be different. It won't be suddenly all perfect, but it can be suddenly good . . . It's like going from being a slave to being a free man. Slaves are driven. Free men still have troubles, but they also have choices . . . What do you say, kid? How about, if I win this game, you come to church with me? Or is a big boy like you scared of what might happen to him in a church?" Ricky said as he began to bounce the ball.

Ricky won easily and dragged poor Kendrick to church.

The church service caught Kendrick off guard. It was held in a renovated building that didn't have the look of any church he'd ever been in. He saw many people his age and others who didn't look like the "churchie" kind of folk he expected. The music was pretty good, too.

When the pastor spoke, he sounded as if he knew Kendrick's whole life. He talked about being free, too. By the end of the service, Kendrick thought about "giving his life to Christ," but he changed his mind. Ricky said nothing else about it, saw that he got home safe, and gave him a card with his number on it just in case he wanted to talk again sometime. Kendrick started to throw the card away and then, on an impulse, put it in his pocket. After a few days it all seemed kind of dumb, so he threw the card away.

A few weeks later, they met on the basketball court again. They played another game with the same stakes, and this time Kendrick won.

Ricky shook his hand. "Good game. Maybe we can play again another day." He picked up his towel and started to leave the court. "See ya' around."

"That's it? You're just going to go?"

"Yeah. What did you have in mind?"

"You wanna play another game?"

"Sure." He said as he threw the towel back onto the bench. "Same stakes?"

"Yeah. But if I win, you gotta come to the place I say and meet my people."

"Sure."

"You'd have to come tonight,"

"No problem."

There was no fear in his eyes. Kendrick couldn't figure him out.

Ricky lost again, but the young man had second thoughts about taking him to meet the others.

"It's OK. You don't have to go with me," Kendrick said, hoping Ricky would back out.

"Actually, I'd like to meet the folks."

"Folks? I meant my gang, man, my gang," the boy said as he shook his head. "I thought you were from around here. Maybe it's better if we just call it quits."

Ricky smiled. "No. Really, I'd like to meet your gang."

Against his better judgment, he took Ricky along to a meeting place—a corner where anyone with a "visitor" was required to stand and be approved before proceeding. By this time Kendrick was jumpy and wanted to find an excuse to call off the meeting.

Someone he thought he recognized from a rival gang drove by, and Kendrick started to flash him a gang sign. This was The Dogz turf and rivals had to be fended off, or it would be perceived as weakness. Ricky's huge hand shot out, engulfed Kendrick's hand, and held it down.

"Not a good idea, Ken. Look across the street."

The young man looked over and saw then six members of The Razors. Since this corner sat on the border to The Dogz' territory, the young men across the street were not trespassing.

"Let go of me, man," Kendrick said as he wrenched his hand away. "They'll think we're gay or something." Angry, he kept his hand at his side nonetheless. *How did he know what I was going to do? How did he know who those other guys were?*

A limousine cruised by and stopped around the corner from them. Two black men emerged from the back, looked around, and nodded to someone inside the vehicle. A larger, bejeweled black man emerged. Kendrick recognized him as Jacky D, the leader of another gang that had a truce pact with The Dogz.

Jacky D didn't even look at Kendrick, but suddenly held out his arms to Ricky and called out, *"Raton!* Is that you? Man, where you been?"

Ricky stuck out his hand and Jacky D slapped it. "Well, as you can see, I still get around."

Kendrick's mouth fell open. *Raton. He's friends with Jacky D, and his name is Raton?*

"You gettin' serious with the menfolk across the street or what?" Jacky D said, as he nodded his head toward The Razors. "Need some help?"

Ricky smiled. "Nah. We were just about to go somewhere."

"Need a lift?" Jacky D asked.

Ricky looked at Ken as if to say, *Well, what about it?*

Kendrick needed some time to think. "No. You go on. Tonight's not a good night for me. Better go on without me."

"Sure? Don't want you to think I slid out of a deal."

"No. I'll, uh, see you later."

Ricky wanted to give him another card with his number on it but thought better of it, given the present company. Instead, he said, "That's right, next Wednesday. On the court. I'll bring the ball." He looked Ken in the eye.

The young man seemed to catch on and nodded.

Ricky left with Jacky D, and the following Wednesday he waited for an hour at the court, hoping Kendrick would show. He had just about given up when Ken arrived.

"Ready to play?"

"Sure," Ricky said, tossing the ball to Ken. "Same stakes?"

"No," he replied as he began to dribble the ball. "I'll just go with you."

Kendrick gave his life to Jesus that night, and Ricky was right. It wasn't suddenly perfect, but it was suddenly good. Ken had many problems to face, but Ricky convinced him that—one by one—God would deal with those things.

Over the next year, "things" did come up, one by one. First there was Kendrick's trial for grand-theft auto. He hadn't stolen the car, but he was a passenger in it when the cops pulled them over. Because Ricky and some of the people from the church testified on his behalf, the judge gave him two months in Juvenile Hall and two years probation—instead of sending him straight to prison. And there was the matter of his membership in The Dogz and his occasional use of drugs. Each had a season of its own to be dealt with, followed by a few months of relative calm. Kendrick was getting his life on track and growing stronger in his faith every day.

So Ricky was surprised to see Ken sitting here on his doorstep.

"Hey, what's up?" he said, putting a hand on Kendrick's shoulder.

The young man shook his head. "I can't believe it, Ricky. I'm in big trouble."

"Why? What's happened?"

"Some of the guys from The Dogz boosted a car today. They saw me walkin' down the street and yanked me into the car as a joke. They got around the corner, and the cops started chasin' us. They kept going till it was outta gas and then jumped out and ran."

"What did you do?"

"I ran. What else could I do? And they know it was me! They've already been to my aunt's house looking for me. They're not going to believe me. I'm going straight to jail if they catch me!"

"Come inside, Kenny. We have to talk," Ricky said as he opened the door to his apartment. Ricky knew Kendrick would have to turn himself in.

"I know you're scared, but if you run now, it will never stop. We're in this together. You and me and Jesus. Just tell the truth."

Kendrick's eyes filled with tears. He looked like a man, but he was still just a kid.

"I've been here before, Ken," Ricky said as he patted his shoulder. "Trust the Lord. No matter what happens, you will live to see it turned to your good."

Ricky called other members of the church, and at seven the next morning, several men gathered at Ricky's house to pray and then go with them to the police station.

As it turned out, Kendrick was remanded to Juvenile Hall, and a hearing was scheduled for the following Monday. The police caught the other boys later that week on Saturday night. They all claimed that Ken had stolen the car and they were just joyriding with him.

At the courthouse early on Monday, Ricky met with his friend Steven Lenwick, an attorney who agreed to represent Ken in this "informal" preliminary hearing.

Steve and Ricky sat in the main lobby of the courthouse and discussed what would happen in the hearing. A woman walked by, and they looked up. It was Edwina Grant's best friend, Rosalinda. Ricky excused himself and caught up with her.

"Good morning, Rosalinda," he said as he came alongside her.

When she turned to see who was addressing her, her face suddenly tightened. She wanted to say, "Oh, it's *you*," but decided to keep her cool.

"Good morning. Here to fix a ticket?" she asked as she began to walk faster.

"Actually, I was just wondering what would bring *you* here. Court case?"

"Yes."

"Are you here to punish bad parents or to remove an incorrigible child from society?"

She stopped and turned to face him. Even with her four-inch heels on, he stood nearly a head taller. She tilted her neck and looked him squarely in the eye. "I have a job to do, and yes, sometimes that means removing bad kids from society. I'm sure you'd like to leave them all running loose, but I don't happen to agree with that philosophy. Now, if you will pardon me, I have an appointment."

She turned and walked away.

Ricky returned to Steve, and soon it was time to meet with Kendrick before the hearing. They were both allowed to see him behind closed, guarded doors.

As Kendrick entered the room, Ricky could see the fear on his face. He hugged him. "You're going to be OK," he said.

Kendrick smiled weakly and sat down.

Steve had already interviewed Kendrick at Juvenile Hall and just wanted to settle a few last questions with him.

"OK, Ken. I have gone over this, and I feel that the fact that you turned yourself in is a plus. However, the other three boys are still saying that you actually stole the car."

"Yeah," he said as he shook his head. "I never should have tried to leave The Dogz. No one ever really gets out. That's what this is all about, you know. They got word to me in Juvie. I'll never be free."

"So you're saying that you want to be part of The Dogz again?" Ricky asked.

"No, I don't want to. I hate them. But what can I do? I was stupid to think I could get away."

"You want to see stupid?" Ricky said as he stood suddenly. "I'll show you stupid."

He took off his jacket and unbuttoned the cuffs of his sleeves. He yanked off his tie, then started unbuttoning his shirt. "I don't let many people see this, 'cause I'm ashamed of it, but I can see you need to look at something more stupid than telling the truth." He pulled off his shirt, and both Ken and Steve stared wide-eyed at what they saw.

So much scar tissue covered Ricky's torso that there was almost no unmarred skin visible. His flesh looked like a moonscape full of pock marks and bumps of twisted skin. Ricky pointed to each scar. "This is a bullet hole. Bullet hole. Knife, knife, knife. Razor, razor. Chain, pipe. Knife, cigar . . . " Then he turned around, and it was even uglier than the front. "This," he said, pointing to a mass of gnarled flesh pulled over his shoulder and half his back, "is boiling water; over here we have the exit of two bullets, more chain, and various sharp implements . . . " He turned and held up his left hand, "Bullet shot my finger off . . . I don't want to go on, but I could. Hopefully you get the point, Ken. Most of what you see is the stupidity of being in a gang. If you want to go back to The Dogz, maybe we can compare our mutual good looks someday, you think?" He leaned down to look at the young man. "Becoming a Christian was the smartest thing you've done in sixteen years, Kenny. The next smart thing you did was realizing you weren't one of The Dogz anymore. You can be a free man in Christ, Kenny. A free man, no matter *where* you are . . . even in jail. Don't you *ever* forget it."

He put his shirt back on, picked up his coat, and left the room.

"Do you wish to change the statement you made at the police station in any way?" Steven asked after a period of silence.

"No. I told the truth; I don't need to change it."

"Good."

Ricky went to the hearing room. As he came through the door, he saw two people were already seated. A man and a woman. He had known it when she walked by. Rosa was assigned to Kendrick's case and would be present for the hearing.

When she looked up and saw Ricky, she frowned.

"It figures," she said without introducing him to the man next to her.

Ricky tried to sound upbeat. "What figures?" Then he turned to address the man seated next to her. "I'm Enrique Ruiz."

"That you were trying to get something out of me in the hall there," she continued.

"What do you mean? I just asked you what you were doing here."

"And then you said, 'Are you here to punish bad parents or to remove an incorrigible child from society?' You knew I was on this case and wanted to somehow effect the outcome . . . that was very disingenuous of you."

Ricky whistled. "'Disingenuous.' Let's see now. Disingenuous . . . dishonest . . . not straightforward. Kind of like using fifty-cent insults on someone when you think they have a ten-cent vocabulary?"

Her face flushed red.

"Look," he quickly added, "I'm already sorry I said that. This kid really needs a break. Can we just declare a truce for today?"

The man with Rosa stood and smiled, "Sounds like a good idea to me. We accept." He stuck out his hand. "Carl Price. D.A.'s office. I'm new. I talked to Rob down at the office about this case, and he thinks very highly of you."

Rosa said nothing.

Carl looked at both of them and spoke again. "Actually, I was about to tell Ms. Sanchez— obviously you've met—that we have some new testimony in this case that should settle the matter this morning."

The conversation stopped as Kendrick, his parole officer Bill Johnson, and Steve entered the room. Before they could be seated, the judge arrived, and introductions went around again. Bill and Steve sat on either side of Ken. Ricky sat behind them.

Carl spoke first. "Your Honor, I think before the hearing continues I should submit this testimony. As you know, a police officer, Reginald Davis, was injured during the pursuit in this arrest. He was unconscious until late last night. He gave us a statement this morning, and here are copies of it, Your Honor," he said as he handed one to the judge, one to Rosa, and one to Steve. "Officer Davis was the one who initially gave chase. What the young men in the car didn't know is that he had been following them for several blocks before initiating that pursuit. Officer Davis has submitted this sworn account of it. He states that he witnessed the defendant here, Kendrick Lockhart, being forced into the car after it was stolen."

"Praise God!" Ricky said. He put his hand on Kendrick's shoulder.

Kendrick exhaled and slumped forward onto the table in front of him. He didn't want anyone to see the tears in his eyes.

The judge looked over the statement and then said, "This statement will be entered into the court record. Now, to the business at hand. This hearing was to decide the status of Mr. Lockhart's probation. Given this evidence, Mr. Lockhart will be released on probation again." He turned to Kendrick. "Look at me, young man."

Ken wiped his face and sat up. "Yes, sir."

"You understand that you are still on parole regarding your prior conviction?"

"Yes I do, sir."

"All the terms and conditions still apply."

"Yes, sir."

"In addition, I would like to bring to your attention, Mr. Lockhart, that it was a policeman who came to your aid in this case. I hope you appreciate that fact."

"Yes, Your Honor, I certainly do."

"You realize that even though you will be released from charges in this case, you will be called to testify against the other defendants."

Kendrick's shoulders sagged a little. "Yes sir, I do."

"Case dismissed."

When they all stood, Ricky hugged Kendrick, then shook hands with Bill and Steve.

Ricky knew it would be a few hours before the young man was actually free to go. He said he would call Kendrick's aunt with the good news and then wait for him while the paperwork was processed. He hadn't eaten yet, so after he finished with the phone, he went to find the vending machines. When he found them, he realized he had no change. One machine did take bills, but the "use correct change only" light was flashing. He stood there a second with the money in his hand.

"Oh, well," he said to himself.

"I have change," a female voice said, and a small hand offered some quarters. It was Rosalinda Sanchez.

He smiled down at her. "Thanks."

She poured the quarters in his hand, and he gave her the dollar. "You're welcome . . . and I apologize."

He raised an eyebrow.

"You know. What I said. I'm sorry. I was mad because you were assuming I was there to do something heartless to that boy."

He put money in a machine and made a selection. He said nothing more as he opened the package and took a bite. Even after he swallowed it, he was silent.

"Well, I wasn't, you know," she said. "I was just here to check into all of this. That's part of my job. He doesn't live with his parents, and his aunt only has temporary custody . . . she wasn't even here."

"She's got asthma; she was on oxygen all last week, and she has three small children at home. I just got off the phone with her," he said.

She felt like an idiot. *Cut your losses and leave,* she thought.

"I need to get to another case," she said. "Say hi to Edwina and George if you see them later."

"Didn't you want something?" he asked as she turned to go.

"What?"

"You were here at the machines with change. I assume you wanted something to eat or drink."

This man must think I'm a nitwit!

He realized he had embarrassed her. "I just happen to have fifty cents. Want something?"

Later, when she recounted the incident to Edwina, she felt horrible all over again.

"I just *got* this job, and they threw fifty-two cases in my lap! There's no way I could know everything about all of them."

"So what did you do?" Edwina asked.

"I just shut up and let him buy me a soda. I have never felt so inefficient, so ill-tempered, so . . . stupid. Every time I leave his presence, I want to have my tongue cut out! Why does he do that to me?"

Edwina decided to keep her thoughts to herself.

CHAPTER TEN

DONALD LARSON COLE SAT WITH HIS CAMPAIGN MANAGER, Bob Post. Two weeks had passed since the encounter on his balcony with the intruder, and Bob was still trying to locate someone he knew he could trust with the questions they wanted to ask about nuclear weapons. Meanwhile, they had contacted Jay Rider, Bob's friend who worked in the Pentagon. He checked into troop deployments in Africa and reported that there had been several teams of special forces trained and sent to southern Africa to work with a multinational contingent there. When he reported back to Bob, Jay said, "I don't know what they're doing, or why you want to know about it, but trust me, you'd better leave it alone. I went out on a limb for you here, but I won't push this any further."

When Bob and Don discussed the subject, they referred to it simply as the "research" Bob was doing. If Todd became aware of his position, he might be able to cover his tracks before he was caught.

Another factor was Don's ability to claim innocence if someone accused him of helping to manufacture the scandal. Although extremely curious to see how it all played out, he did not want to be actively engaged in exposing Todd's secret plans. The visitor on his balcony never voiced the expectation of Cole doing anything. The purpose in informing him of their plans was to make sure he was prepared when it all unfolded, and that's what Don intended to be—prepared. While he planned, he would watch for "developments." If the Army of the Quick and the Dead managed to bring Todd's presidency to an end with the exposure of the truth, he'd be ready. For the time being, however, he was not about to count his chickens before they hatched.

Given his vivid imagination, it was hard to escape the feeling of being watched and heard all the time. For the first few days after his encounter on the balcony, his fear bordered on paranoia. He had a hard time discussing future campaign plans at meetings, thinking they might be tipping off their opponent by exposing their strategies. It was hard to rest with the feeling that someone sat at a screen somewhere, observing him.

One morning, after a week of this, Don realized he had had enough. He had just gotten up after too little sleep. As he stood brushing his teeth, he looked at himself in the mirror. His hair looked as if he'd stuck his finger in a light socket, and he had enough toothpaste around his mouth to look like a rabid dog. *I wonder what they'll do with* this *film footage,* he thought. Suddenly, something in him snapped. It could *not* be allowed to rule everything he did. He would not discuss the disk, but all other business would proceed as normal. He had to have open communication with his workers, or he would lose the race.

After he finished dressing, Trina knocked on his door to give him some messages and then walk with him to a scheduled meeting. Because she knew he loved chocolate chip cookies, she brought him some from a nearby bake shop.

As soon as he saw the small bag with a cookie shop label, he grabbed it. "Are these for me?"

"Why, yes. And you're welcome," she said, watching him bite into the first one.

"Thanks," he said with his mouth full of cookie. He put his briefcase under his arm and stepped out into the hall. She closed his door as he reached into the bag for another cookie and popped the whole thing in his mouth.

"I thought you might like them," she said.

When they got to the elevator, he reached into the bag for the last cookie. "Hey," he said holding up half a cookie, "what happened here?"

"Service charge," she said casually, stepping into the elevator. "If you want three *whole* cookies, send Avery. He doesn't eat sweets."

At the hotel conference room, they met up with Jason and others who were doing some investigation of government programs to be proposed for the elderly.

Don and running mate Lawrence Cunningham were both slated to address several large groups of retired persons in the near future, and they needed to be aware of the latest developments.

Several new advances claimed to slow the aging process. Medical studies conducted in other countries and summaries of the research were now being circulated widely. Some of the findings were said to be nothing short of astonishing. President Todd hoped to be the first to ask for legislation that would bring these "miraculous" advances into the health care system of America. To be seen at the forefront of this issue would be a major boost to his lackluster record with seniors—who were becoming a larger slice of the voting pool every day.

Bob, Lawrence, and Don seated themselves with the others in the conference room while Trina passed out several stacks of printed material for them to go over later.

"Oh joy," Don said, "just what I wanted—a ream of statistics to read."

Trina gave him the look.

Don ignored her. The only child of Joe and Eva Cole, Don had been taught to speak his mind. Although they made every effort not to spoil young Donald, his parents did encourage him to be himself and to stand up for others who were not as privileged. They were pleased when he decided to pursue a life in politics, even though many considered it to be a dirty profession. With his strength of character and keen mind, they were convinced he would make a lasting difference in society.

Now, as he sat in the conference room looking over the studies on aging, he thought of his father. He wished his father had stayed healthy and lived longer so they could have spent more time together. Don's mind went back to a vacation he and his father had taken when he was only eleven. Joe had spent a great deal of money to get them to a remote lake for a weekend of fishing. Don still treasured every memory of it. To this day, the smell of water, fish, and fuel could transport him back to that time. He could still see himself fumbling with the bait while his father chuckled . . . he could feel the excitement of reeling in the first big fish while his dad excitedly called instructions to him. He laughed to himself, remembering that in his eagerness to grab the fish he had dropped the rod in the water as the fish came alongside the boat.

"Something here amuses you?" he heard Trina say.

"Sorry. I was just remembering something, that's all." He cleared his throat and looked at her. "You have my full attention now. Fire away."

"Well," she began, "these are the statistics and summaries that Todd's people are going to make available. I will try to give you a synopsis, but it would be good if you could familiarize yourself with them in greater depth later."

"We were able to obtain this video of planned commercial advertisements. There will be an all-out media blitz with these ads when Todd makes the big push to bring all this propaganda into the system here. Every effort will be made to have these medical advances working their way through Congress before the election. If they are shot down in the legislative process, he can say it was Congress that held things up.

"When Todd goes public with this, the party will begin a systematic campaign on national and local levels to release these positive advertisements in conjunction with news bites about the procedures." Trina paused, picked up a television remote, and looked at Jason. "Dim the lights," she said, then sat down as the video played.

Don watched as the screen lit up with the smiling faces of a handsome, white-haired couple. The camera pulled back and framed a physician at his desk with a stethoscope around his neck. He briefly described the couple, who appeared to be in their sixties but were actually in their eighties. The physician spoke about "a new breakthrough in medicine that would virtually halt the aging process" in some people and give "dramatic results" in others who underwent "regeneration" with the technique. This was followed by another video with different people but the same basic message. There were other, less medical-looking clips of elderly people riding bicycles, running on the beach, eating romantic dinners. Then, to Don's surprise, he saw several news clips that had well-recognized newscasters giving glowing reports about "regeneration."

"OK, Jason," Trina said. He turned on the lights as she stopped the video. She turned to look at Don and Lawrence. "This is just the tip of the iceberg, guys."

"How are they planning to bypass the approval process? Isn't someone going to say there needs to be more testing?" Don asked.

Trina nodded. "That's a good point. The problem, as I see it, is that virtually no one is prepared to stand in the

way. The results of this regeneration therapy and some of
the other things they propose are so dramatic that they
expect the seniors to clamor for it. Their whole approach
will be, 'It has already been proven to work in other
countries; what have you got to lose?' I've even heard a
rumor that they will give special incentives for those who
will sign away their entitlements for the treatments.
Anyone willing to do so will be hailed as a 'brave pioneer'
in the advancement of medicine for those in the future, so
even if there is a downside somewhere, they can say that it
was for science."

Don had heard brief reports about these medical
advances, but he was truly surprised by the speed with
which they were being proposed as permanent parts of
the health-care system. He had a bad feeling about this.

"What can we do to slow this down a bit?" he asked.

Trina had Jason pass out more papers. "The advancements being touted were tried in other countries—mostly
China and Europe. The profiles I gave you when you
came in are filled with glowing reports of the results. But
according to *our* sources, there *are* some big problems.

"First of all, these tests were not performed in a
manner that would conform to the testing standards in
this country. Several prominent scientists and medical
doctors," she said as she moved around the table to where
Don sat and pointed to a list of names on the first page,
"have expressed deep concern over the quality and objec-
tivity of the testing. The second point to note is that the
results of the tests are not completely listed. Third, the
possible and actual long-term effects of these procedures
are not revealed in these summaries, which are being
made available to the public. Apparently—and I'm still
trying to get my hands on the documentation—in a sig-
nificant number of the patients, even though there was an
increase in physical capacities, there was a dramatic
decrease in mental function. In essence, they would be
physically healthy and useful for light manual labor, or

'mindless' tasks, but not much else. The scientists and doctors I have listed here feel that at least ten more years are needed to fully address all the questions raised by these new techniques."

Don scanned the sheets in front of him. Although his father was alive when Don was elected to the office of governor, Alzheimer's disease had taken his mind; he never comprehended what his dear son had accomplished. Don's thoughts flashed back again, this time to a day he had visited his father several years ago. The older man's mind had deteriorated to the point that he no longer knew his son. A picture of his father with a frightened look, saying "Who are you?", suddenly came to mind. The memory stabbed at him. How anyone could seriously consider doing something to people that might take their minds was more than Don could fathom. "This is *horrible*," he muttered.

"You're right. But if someone doesn't stop Todd," Trina continued, "our seniors are about to become guinea pigs. They will be told they are getting the 'cutting edge' in medicine and living facilities. It will be the next step in 'orchestrated medicine.' Under the new system, 'alternative health care' will be the bywords . . . and if Todd gets his way, they won't have any alternative."

Don looked up from the papers. "Good work, Trina. This is excellent. You and the others in research deserve a pat on the back. I'll try to go over this immediately. Time is apparently of the essence, so we're going to have to run with the information as soon as possible. Any suggestions?"

"We might find some allies in the people who market health care and vanity items to seniors," Lawrence said, thinking aloud.

They all looked at him.

"Hey," he said, "you're going to need all the help you can get. And in this fight, you're going to need some friends who have money *and* clout with the media."

"He's right, you know," Bob said. "This could end up being a bare-knuckles fight. We'll take all the help we can get."

Don said nothing and sat back in his chair. He had never liked or trusted Todd in the first place, but now it wasn't just a case of differing political views. He was convinced that Todd would do anything to achieve his goals. Nothing was sacred, not even life itself! Don shuddered to think of what the man might "accomplish" if he were given four more years in office. He looked at Bob and said, "Is there nothing this man wouldn't do?"

Trina noticed the look they exchanged and filed it away for future thought. But for now, she had other things to do. "I propose," she said, "that we immediately contact the doctors and scientists opposing this. We need to get our hands on all the data we can. If legislation is proposed, we will be ready to take it to the airwaves and to Congress."

Don looked at her. "Do it. We need an all-out assault on this."

CHAPTER ELEVEN

EDWINA AND ROSALINDA WALKED DOWN THE STREET TO the clinic. After a wonderful lunch together and a few moments of window shopping, it was time to get back to work.

As they neared the corner where each would go her separate way, Rosa's beeper went off. She took it off her belt and looked at it.

"Oh, boy. I guess I'll need to come in and use your phone, 'Wina. This could be an emergency."

"Come on, girl."

They walked the short distance to the clinic. As they entered, they could hear the sound of a man humming somewhere in the back.

Joan, the receptionist, was on the phone. Edwina waved to her, then turned to Rosa. "You can use the phone in George's office."

As they walked toward the back, the sound of the humming grew louder. At first, Rosa thought it was George, but near the open door of an examining room,

Ricky suddenly emerged with a bag of trash. He nearly bumped into Rosalinda.

"Excuse me!" he said and moved to the other side of the hall.

"Hi, Ricky," Edwina piped up from behind her friend. "What are you doing here? I thought you were off today. Where's George?"

"Henry called and said he couldn't do the van today, so George took it and asked me to be here until you got back, in case we had an emergency. He just called about five minutes ago. He should be here in less than an hour."

Rosa let them go on talking and went into George's office. She had no intention of saying anything that could be used against her. She had endured two more encounters with him since the courthouse and emerged without making a fool of herself. She didn't want to spoil her record.

A moment later, Edwina joined her in George's office.

"Yes . . . I understand . . . Wilbur Bordeaux. Wilbur? People still name their kids Wilbur? And where is he? And the officer's name? De la Cruz . . . " Rosa wrote the details in a little notebook. "OK . . . I'll go right there . . . Yeah. Bye." She hung up the phone and turned to Edwina. "We've got a girl in the emergency room. It's not one of my cases, but the guy who handles this one is out of town. I'm going to have to interview the family and look at the home conditions. Know how to get here?" she asked, showing Edwina the address.

"Well," Edwina said, "If you go to the station and get on the . . . "

"Remember, I have wheels now!"

"Oh yes, I forgot. Well, gee. You know I never drive anyplace." She went to the door. "Hey, Ricky, come here a sec, could you?"

Rosa gave her an exasperated look and whispered, "What on earth are you doing?"

"Ricky knows how to get anywhere. Trust me. He's the best one to ask."

Edwina grabbed the notebook out of Rosa's hand and showed it to him when he came into the room. "Know how to get there from here?"

"Sure. Why are you going there?"

"Not me. Rosa."

Rosa turned away from Ricky to give her friend a look that said a very sarcastic *thanks*. She tried to sound casual as she turned back toward Ricky.

"I have to interview somebody there."

His eyebrows came together in a frown. "This is no place for a woman alone. You're not going alone, are you?"

"Well, yes and no. I'm supposed to meet a police officer there."

"It isn't a place for a woman *or* a cop," Ricky said.

"How would you know that?"

"I grew up there. You sure you need to go there?"

"Well, as I said, an officer is supposed to meet me there and . . . " She caught herself wanting to give more details than necessary and reminded herself that this is what always got her in trouble. "I just need directions, please."

"They couldn't bring this person in for questioning and let you interview him there?"

"We're not necessarily trying to prove anyone did anything. Believe it or not, I'm not out to 'get' people. I just need to talk to the family and look at the home conditions."

"The cops couldn't interview them and then tell you what they said?"

"You really don't want me to go down there, do you? I have to look at the home. You think I'm not capable? A novice? This isn't my first job, you know. I've been in slums before."

Ricky seemed very ill at ease. "I'm not saying that you don't know what you're doing, OK? What I am saying is that you don't know what you're doing in *that* neighborhood."

In spite of his obvious reservations, he gave her directions, "Study them *now*. Don't be seen looking at them or a map when you get there. You never want to look lost, OK?"

He left the room for a moment.

Edwina patted her on the shoulder "He just doesn't want anything to happen to . . . "

He suddenly returned to the room.

"Did what I said scare you?"

She wanted to straighten her back, look him in the eye, and say no, but she knew that would be a lie. "Yes, frankly, it did."

"Good." He looked at Edwina. "Now that you're here, am I free to go?"

Edwina shrugged. "Sure."

He looked at the floor "If you'll let me, Rosa, I'll take you where you want to go."

"You're on."

"I'll get my coat," he said and started out of the room. "Oh. Leave your purse here. We'll come back for it when you're done."

"What about money, my license, my ID?"

"I have money. If you don't have any pockets, I'll carry the other stuff for you," he said as he disappeared through the door.

Edwina looked at her friend and smiled. "See? He's really very nice. Really. Will you be back in time for tonight?"

"In *plenty* of time. I should be back here before five. I'll have time to go home and change. Bertrand can pick me up at 7:30, and we'll see you guys at the theater at 8:30. Just wait till you see him, 'Wina, he is so . . . "

Ricky returned wearing an old jacket. "OK . . . Could you leave the earrings and the necklace, too?"

She opened her mouth to say something and thought better of it. After putting the jewelry in her purse, she slipped her license in the small ID pouch and placed it in her coat pocket. "Let's go."

"We're taking the subway."

"But I have a car," Rosa said.

"Government car? With government paint job and tags?"

"Yes."

"We're taking the subway."

The walk to the station was a short one, and soon they were on their way to her appointment.

As they sat on the train, she noticed him looking intently at many of the people getting on and off.

"Why do you do that?" she asked.

"Do what?"

"Stare at people like that."

He smiled at her. "Do I stare at people?"

"Yes, you do."

"I don't mean to stare at them. I just see them differently maybe."

"Differently. Like how?"

"Like they are people. Each one has a name, memories, sorrows, aspirations . . . " He stopped and looked down.

"And you care about all those things?"

"God does. I just want to see them with His eyes. It's kind of hard to explain. Maybe I don't do it very well."

"No. Really, tell me," she said. The train rolled into a station and everyone lurched forward as it stopped.

He remained quiet until the train started rolling again. He leaned toward her a little. "You see that lady in the sideways seat by the doors?"

She looked and saw a middle-aged woman sitting with a bag of groceries in her arms. "Yeah."

"Now, just look at her a moment. It's OK. She doesn't see us."

Rosa looked back at the woman. Ricky continued, "Just study her for a moment. Look at her eyes. She looks so sad. She looks tired, too. Her clothes are kind of worn. Not a lot of disposable income, probably. Look at the shoes, though. Real ugly shoes, but she probably paid a lot for them. Real comfortable. She spends a lot of time on her feet. Could be a nurse. Wedding ring on the right hand. Widow. Very little in the bag. She's probably going home to eat alone. No. I take that back. She has a cat. See? Can of cat food in top of the bag."

She looked at him while he was looking at the woman. "You're very good at this."

"Wait, wait. OK. See the kid standing up there? Don't look at me. The one with the purple jacket? Look at the way he's standing there. He's real ticked off about something. See how stiff he is? Look at his left hand all balled up in a fist . . . "

She turned to look at Ricky again, and he stopped his description of the boy. "Sorry. Just a habit."

"And this is what you did to me the first time we met?"

"Well, yeah, I guess. I didn't mean to make you so mad. Really, I didn't. You made me nervous, and then you got so bothered it *was* kind of amusing. And then I saw things in you."

"I made *you* nervous?" she said as she let out a little laugh. "You were amused by the fact that I was . . . 'Things,' what do you mean 'things'?"

"God just tells me things about people sometimes. Like if they need help or encouragement."

"So why did you say those mean things to me?"

"I wasn't intending to insult you," he said as he looked past her into the darkness of the tunnel outside the window. "I'm just direct. Life's too short for games, Rosalinda." The train started squealing to a stop again. "The next stop is ours."

She looked around for her purse. "Oh, that's right. I left my purse at the clinic."

They got off at the next stop and walked up the stairs to the street level.

"We want to go this way," he said as he pointed to their left. "Where are you supposed to meet the cop?"

"In front of the building. He'll be in a car."

Ricky looked unhappy about this.

"Something wrong?"

"It's just that there's always a lot of tension regarding cops around here anyway. And now things have gotten especially strained."

"How so?"

"You'll see."

They hadn't gone far before they met a few of Ricky's "friends." Some of them were old and toothless, some were just toothless, and many of them smelled bad. Barely a tree or blade of grass grew anywhere, but the street was littered with a lot of trash and broken glass. Many of the buildings had rusty porches and fire escapes barely clinging to them. Graffiti was scrawled or sprayed on every surface.

Then, as if they had crossed an invisible line of demarcation, they passed several clean, painted buildings. Trees and small gardens grew in the vacant areas around them. Several women with wraps around their heads watched as children played in a small but clean playground. It was almost like an oasis in the desert.

"What happened here?" she asked.

"Vital Union."

"The religious group?"

"Yeah."

"It looks as if they've done wonders for this place. This is incredible."

"Yeah."

"You're not impressed, I gather."

"Nope."

"Why not? From what I have heard, even though they're a little strange, they have managed to turn people's lives around. Just look at this. If this isn't proof, I don't know what is."

"Then you don't know what is."

He was starting to make her angry again. "Well, thank you!" she said. "You always seem to know when I'm being stupid, don't you? Please enlighten me, O wise one."

He shook his head.

"No! Don't start the Mr. Silent game with me again. What were you going to say? C'mon, say it!"

"It's just that this," he said, with a sweeping motion of his hand, "really is an illusion. It may *look* better than government assistance, but it's not. It's just another form of slavery. Most of the people in this neighborhood are second and third generation assistance beneficiaries. Assistance is gone, so what comes next? The gangs get bigger, they make treaties to strengthen their hold on the same people who were captives to poverty under welfare. Gangs have their own businesses now, their own set of laws, and their own system to protect, so they abuse those who might escape or disobey.

"Then along comes some religion that paints buildings and plants gardens, and makes a place for kids to play. They cater to the same victim mentality. The same need to be told what to do. They have their own laws, their own businesses, and their own system to protect, so what do they do?" He pointed to men on the corner, each of whom had a staff about five feet long. All of them wore gray. "They abuse the slaves who disobey."

She thought a moment. "Well, aren't you religious? Don't you expect people to live a certain way? I don't see any evidence of a church making any difference here."

"You're right. It should be to our shame. My church has shelters and halfway houses downtown, but one church can only do so much. The truth is, only God's plan can change people in a place like this."

"So why doesn't He do it?"

"Change things? People have a free will, Rosalinda. And it's easier to stay a slave than it is to become free. It's easier for nice folks to let people like you and like them," he said, nodding to the men on the corner, "keep things 'under control' than to come down here, pray for God's plan to set captives free, and then do it."

She could see his point, but she resented her job being thought of as a useless solution. "You know, there would be a lot more dead children if it weren't for people who do the job I do."

"I appreciate that. But it's not enough. It will never be enough, Rosa, as long as people choose to live like this."

They walked past the men on the corner, who watched them intently. Once again, they crossed an invisible line and stepped back into filth and decay. She heard the crunch of glass with each step as they walked the next block. An eerie tension hung in the air.

"Can you feel them staring holes through us?" Ricky said.

"Yes."

"Things are really tense right now. The Vital Union is taking over gang turf. It could get really ugly. That's why I didn't want you coming down here." Ricky approached an old, black man seated on a metal framed chair on the corner. "Hey, Ralph."

The old man looked up from his paper. "Raton? That you?"

Raton? she thought. *His nickname is Rat? Wonderful.*

"Yeah, it's me," Ricky said.

The man folded his paper and set it on the ground next to a can of beer. "How you been, man?"

"I've been just fine, Ralph. I want you to meet my friend, Rosalinda."

Ralph looked her up and down. "How'd an ugly boy like you get a girl that looks like her?"

Ricky just smiled. "We wanted to go up a few more blocks. You seen Greenie around anywhere?"

"No. But it's early; maybe he's just not up yet. You want me to tell him you're looking for him?"

"Nah. I'll just see if I find him while we're walking around." He shook Ralph's hand and then put his arm around Rosa. "Say hi to Vera," he said to the old man as they walked away. Ricky leaned down and spoke softly. "Ralph is a lookout. Putting that paper on the ground was the 'OK' signal. If he hadn't put the paper down, we would be in serious trouble. Just keep walking. I hope I'm not embarrassing you, but they sort of need to think you're mine."

This miffed her a little. Like she was someone's property. In fact, whenever she was with him, she was so bombarded with new thoughts and feelings (most of them uncomfortable) that it took days to sort through them all.

Being with this guy is like being on a roller coaster. As soon as you get over one thing, there's something else to consider, she thought.

Soon they approached the building where Rosa's interview was scheduled. A police car sat next to the curb in front of the building. Small groups of people clustered on balconies and near the vehicle, just loitering. And watching.

Ricky and Rosa approached the car, and she leaned down as they came close to the driver's side window. The officer rolled down the window as she got out her little pouch, produced her ID, and showed it to him.

"Officer De la Cruz? I'm Rosalinda Sanchez. You ready to go in?"

"Yeah," he said and shut off the engine.

"You have the necessary papers?"

"Yeah," he responded and reached for a clipboard. He got out of the car and locked it, turned and sized up Ricky.

"This is Ricky Ruiz. He wanted to make sure I got here safely."

"Darn right," the cop said as he looked around. "I don't even like to come in here without my partner, but he's sick today." He shrugged as if to say, *What else could I do?*

Ricky looked at Rosa. "I'll wait out here."

"By the time this is done, it'll be four o'clock and my shift will be over. I can give Ms. Sanchez a lift," the policeman offered.

"You could? That would be great," she said and then looked at Ricky. "So, I guess you're off the hook. Thanks for the tour."

Ricky was being dismissed, and he knew it. He stuck his hands in his jacket pockets. "Yeah. Sure. No problem." He watched them walk up the stairs. He'd had a bad feeling about this ever since he'd seen the address in her notebook. Should he stay and watch? No. She'd be even angrier if she thought he was following her around.

He headed back toward the station but only got about a block away when he met his old friend, Greenie.

"Hey, Greenie. How's it going?"

"Ricky! It's doin' great. Come on down to my place and have a cold one with me," he said as he put an arm around Ricky.

They walked to a not-so-bad looking building and sat on the front steps. Greenie sipped a beer, and Ricky had a glass of water. They talked about old times and the changes coming to the neighborhood.

"Yeah, man. Between the porkers and the non-porkers we're really gettin' the squeeze," Greenie said, referring to the police and the Vital Union, who forbade eating pork. "Makes a guy just want to move, you know?"

"Where you going to go?" Ricky asked.

"You got out. I could, too."

"The only real way out is the way I got out. You ready?"

Greenie chuckled. "You kill me, Raton. You ever give up?"

"No."

The sound of a phone ringing interrupted their conversation. Greenie popped a small cellular out of his pocket and flipped it open. "Yeah," he said into the receiver.

Ricky could hear an excited voice coming from the earpiece.

"Oh yeah?" Greenie said as his eyes got wider.

Ricky figured it was time to head home. He stood up and started to wave good-bye, but his friend suddenly jumped up and put his hand on the receiver and looked at him. "Wait! *Wait!* Something's happened. Hold on!" He took his hand off the receiver again and said, "Yeah, I wanna know. A cop . . . " He put his hand back on the phone and spoke to Ricky. "You just leave a cop someplace?"

"Yes, and a woman," he said, his heart pounding. "What happened?"

Greenie spoke into the phone again. "So which one got stuck? The cop . . . Is he dead? Is a woman there? Yeah, Raton's woman . . . Where is she now?"

Ricky held his breath. *Why didn't I listen to You, Lord? Why did I leave her there?* He hit himself in the head with his fist. *Oh, God, please don't let anybody hurt her.* "Yeah, I wanna know. OK." Greenie closed up the phone and put it back in his pocket. "The cop is dead in the alley behind a building over there," he said, pointing in the direction where Ricky had left them. "The woman's not there, but Casey is going to call me back."

CHAPTER TWELVE

PRESIDENT SONNY TODD HURRIED DOWN THE CORRIDOR
to the "secure room." Vice President Victor Bartlett had
come into the Oval Office and, with facial expressions and
hand signals, expressed the urgent need for a meeting in
the secure room, four floors below.

President Todd moved quickly through his next
appointment, the Arbor Day Foundation, and canceled
his appointments for the rest of the morning.

As Todd hurried down the hall, he tried to appear calm
and collected. A Marine at the door of the secure room
saluted him and stepped away. Sonny opened the door
and went right through the small anteroom and into the
secure room. He shut the door. Bartlett was already
there.

"Anyone else coming?" Todd said without a greeting.

"Ernie may come later, but we shouldn't wait for
him."

Todd went to the far wall and flipped two switches.
Lights came on over the switches that indicated the room

was secure from listening devices. Even so, Todd was
uneasy about meeting there. They almost always met in
places selected at random, outside the White House.

Bartlett got right to it.

"It's really hit the fan, Sonny. I mean it. We are in for
it if we don't think of something fast. Ernie got word
this morning that the Quick and the Dead people have
tapes of some of our meetings regarding Operation
Reclamation. They plan to blast them onto the Internet
any minute."

Todd sat down, listening.

"They're going to hang our hides on the highest tree,
Sonny."

"Wait just a minute, Vic. We're not dead yet. Have you
called him?"

"Who? Yosef? He's the one that sent word to Ernie."

"And he has no ideas?" Todd asked. His eyes kept
moving around the room as if the answer were hidden
there somewhere and he might spot it any second.

"Ernie was trying to get a secure line to him.
Meanwhile, he thought we should know so we could be
considering our position."

Todd pounded a fist on the table near his chair. "I
knew this was going to happen! I just knew it. Yosef let
the Quick and Dead have the stuff. We didn't go along
with that satellite software and the other deal they
wanted, so now they're going to let us go down . . . Well,
I'm not going alone, Vic, I tell you that. I will not go
alone, and I will not go quietly."

A beep indicated someone was at the door. Victor
jumped up and went to open it. When the door opened,
the secure lights went out.

"Ernie!" Victor almost shouted. "Come in, come in. Is
anyone else coming?" he asked, closing the door.

Secretary of Defense Ernest Schollet looked intently at
the lights as he shut the door behind him. Victor went to

the switches, turned them off, then on again. The lights came back on.

Ernie walked to the desk in the room and opened his briefcase. He removed a disk. "This, gentlemen," he said as he held it up, "is our problem."

He took out a laptop computer and booted it up. The three men gathered around the screen and watched the seventeen-minute show. Todd and Schollet repeatedly swore as each new scene unfolded, exposing more of their plan. Virtually every detail was there, from their very own lips. When the video stopped, the three men looked at each other.

"We're dead," the president said as he walked away, throwing up his hands.

"No, we're not," said the Secretary of Defense.

Todd spun around. "How so?"

"First, the weapons are already on their way back home, so it will be their word against ours. Second, Ross is the one who got us in the limo and in the Cookie Jar. He's still in Africa and has no reason to think he's been discovered. Yosef has a plan that will take them all down and make us stars again. We're going to pounce on them."

"With what?" the president asked.

"Why, the truth of course," Schollet said.

Todd and Bartlett exchanged slow, puzzled looks.

"We'll tell the press about our plan to save the governments in Africa from Chango forces. Meanwhile, we make sure to send the medical equipment for a viral 'front-line outpost.'"

"Then what?" Todd said as he made a motion for Schollet to go on.

"While the brave, international forces are maintaining freedom in Africa, there could be an outbreak of a deadly virus. We would document evacuation of several 'victims' to Fort Detrick. This alone, given the panic over such things, should be enough to capture public attention. If the Quick and the Dead ever convinces anyone the weapons were really there, you can say that the weapons were merely a fail-safe should it appear that world health was compromised."

"But then wouldn't we have to bring Detrick in on this?" the president asked, referring to the military base where victims of a "plague" might be taken.

"Not if the victims were really infected," Schollet said matter-of-factly.

Todd and Bartlett sat in silence as the full implication of what the secretary said soaked in.

"Listen," Schollet said, as his right hand went up, "not one scientist in the whole world has been able to figure out the intricacies of how some of these viruses spread. That's how plagues happen. The next worldwide epidemic could be breeding in Africa even as we speak."

Within hours, they had formulated a plan. They would temporarily halt Operation Reclamation. Originally, they had planned a fake ambush of international forces by the rebel group, Chango, which would then precipitate the fighting. Now, the ambush would still take place, but it would be a virus, not rebel forces, that overtook the soldiers.

As the three men hashed out the details, they realized this was even better than the original plan, because now they could say the rebels had possibly done it and then "disappeared into the African bush." The plague would create a need to "cordon off" sections of southern Africa and would limit travel while a quarantine was enforced. They could decide later on if one outbreak was sufficient or if more of these isolated incidents were needed to accomplish the goal of controlling the precious mineral resources in that part of the continent.

Todd and Bartlett agreed that Schollet should be given the go-ahead with the plan. Yosef would be contacted and given approval for his part in the deal. Before they withdrew from the secure room, they came to another unanimous decision: Ross, who was obviously a spy for the Quick and the Dead, could not leave Africa alive.

Within two days, the plan was in place. Orders would be sent to the selected site.

CHAPTER THIRTEEN

RICKY RAN AS FAST AS HIS LEGS WOULD CARRY HIM, CALLING out to God the whole way. He reached the building first and was surprised a crowd hadn't gathered. Apparently, whoever found the body must have only told Greenie so far. Ricky dashed through the alley and around to the back of the building. Two men stood over another man who lay on his stomach in a pool of blood. It was Officer De la Cruz. The men next to the body turned when they heard the sound of someone running up behind them, and one of them reached for a weapon.

"It's me. Raton," Ricky gasped as he put both hands up. He stopped running, bent forward, and put his palms down on his knees, trying to catch his breath. He could hear Greenie coming up behind him, swearing the whole way.

"Man! What'd you run like that for? The guy's dead, man," Greenie panted.

Ricky straightened up and walked over to the two men near the officer. "The woman. Where's the woman?"

"She ain't here. We came back here and found him, that's all."

"Somebody around here has to have seen what happened," Ricky said as he looked at all the facing balconies and windows.

Four more men came around the corner to the back of the building. Ricky recognized two of them and nodded.

Greenie spoke to them. "Any of you know what happened to the woman?"

"What woman?" they said, almost simultaneously.

"OK," Greenie said. "Get a search going. What she look like, man?"

"About this tall," Ricky said as he held his hand at his shoulder. "White Hispanic. Shoulder-length dark hair, brown eyes, wearing a beige pantsuit. And a scarf around her neck."

Greenie waved them on, "Go! We only got a few minutes before somebody calls the cops. Hey!" He called after one of them. "Casey, get on the scanner. We gotta know how much time we got." He turned to Ricky. "You know once the cops get here nobody will have seen or heard a thing . . . Let's go, man. We can be looking. I have the phone if anyone finds anything."

"Just wait a sec, Greenie. I'm so rattled I'm not thinking straight," Ricky said, then stood perfectly still. *God, You know where she is, even right now. Please help me find her. No matter what. Please,* he prayed silently. *You said that if I acknowledge You in all of my ways that You will direct my paths.* "Father," he said aloud, "You are Lord, even over this. You knew our ways today even before we woke up. I'm looking to You."

"Come on, Raton. Let's get going," Greenie said, nervous about being found in the vicinity of a dead cop.

Ricky thought he heard a rustling noise nearby and held up a hand to signal for silence. The sound came again. This time they both heard it and started looking around. Ricky realized the sound was coming from the large dumpster behind the building. He looked over the top of the bin. Rosa lay sprawled inside. The bags around her rustled as her weight made them shift around in the bin. She didn't move at all.

Greenie had been looking in the other direction, and when he turned, his friend was gone. "Ricky? Hey, man. Where'd you go?"

"Here. I'm in here."

Greenie walked to the bin and opened the small sliding door on the side to look in. He saw Ricky among all the garbage bags, gingerly stepping around Rosa. He planted one foot on either side of her and bent down to feel for a pulse in her neck. "Thank You, Jesus," he exhaled as he put his hand up to his heart. "She's still alive."

Her eyes opened, and she looked confused. "Ricky? Is that you?"

"Yes, *mi corazón,*" he said as he crouched closer. "Are you OK? Can you feel your legs and arms?"

"Yes. Why?"

"Does your neck hurt? Can you move?"

"No, it doesn't hurt. Yes," she said as she moved a little and lifted up her head. "I can moo . . . " She put her head back down. "My head. Oh. My head really hurts." She held her hand to her head then pulled it away and looked at it. "I'm bleeding."

He reached down and carefully felt the top of her head. "Oh, yeah. Somebody really popped you on the head, all right." He checked her eyes to see if the pupils were the same size and then held up three fingers. "How many fingers am I holding up?"

She thought a moment. "Three?"

"Anything else bothering you?"

"Yeah. Why does it smell so bad here?"

He beamed at her. "Probably," he said as he reached down and pulled a white, floppy string out of her hair, "because you have an onion in your hair. I don't know how to tell you this, but you're in a dumpster."

"No."

"Yes. You sure nothing else hurts?"

"Yes."

"OK. I'm going to pick you up as carefully as I can. Just say if I'm hurting you, and I'll stop, OK?"

"OK."

He gently picked her up and passed her through the door to Greenie, who sat her on the ground while Ricky hopped out of the dumpster.

Someone nearby coughed. The two men froze and looked at each other.

Ricky bolted to the body a few feet away and lay down next to him with his face almost touching the officer's face. He reached over and felt the man's neck. "He's alive, Greenie, he's alive! Call an ambulance *now!*"

Rosa sat on the ground with her back up against the dumpster, dazed.

Greenie shook his head. "You crazy? I can't do that. I shouldn't even *be* here."

"Hey," Ricky said, displaying the hand with half a finger shot off. "You owe me something. And I want it *now.*"

Greenie swore and dug into his pocket for his cellular phone. "Here," he said and slapped the phone into Ricky's hand. "You call. And I want that phone back, Raton!" he yelled over his shoulder as he ran off.

"Rosa. Rosalinda," Ricky said, rushing to her. "Listen to me. I know you don't feel good, but you gotta help me now. It's really important."

She managed to focus on him as he helped her up and walked her over to where De la Cruz lay. "Sit right here," he said. She plopped down. "Good. Now you're going to have to play nurse here. OK?"

She nodded.

He rolled the officer over, toward her. "Oh. Not good," he said. He pulled off his belt and put it around the man's arm to make a tourniquet. "Rosa, I need you to remind me to loosen this occasionally. Can you do that?"

He opened the policeman's shirt. "Not good at all." He saw two bleeding wounds—one on the man's chest; the other, just above the navel. Ricky looked around, quickly took off his jacket and shirt, folded them, and placed them over the wounds. "OK, now we're to the nurse part, Rosa. I need you to press hard on these two places right here so I can call for help."

She leaned forward and put one hand on the shirt, the other on the jacket.

"That's great. You're doing great," he said as he dialed the phone. "Yes, I have an emergency . . . My name is Enrique Ruiz. I am an EMT with a medical emergency. Yes. A wounded police officer and an injured woman." He gave them the location as he cradled the phone between his shoulder and his head so he could use both hands on the officer. "The officer's name is De la Cruz. He's unconscious and has multiple stab wounds. An artery in his left arm is probably severed, and he has a possible punctured lung. They need to hurry, or he won't make it."

"Ricky?"

He stopped talking and looked at Rosa. She stared at him, her face pale.

She put a bloody hand on his right shoulder. "You're hurt," she said as she looked with confusion at all of the scars. "All over."

He took her hand and put it back on De la Cruz. "No, I'm OK."

She started to shiver. "I'm cold, Ricky."

He was speaking into the phone again. "Yes. I also have a female patient with a head injury. She's going into shock." He put the phone down and placed two fingers on her neck to check her pulse. "I know you're cold, sweetheart, but I can't help that just now. Just stay with me, Rosalinda. Stay with me. It's important. Even if you're sleepy, c'mon, I need you, Rosa," he said. "Hear those sirens? They're coming for us. Just hold on. They'll be right here."

Within minutes, seven police cruisers and two ambulances screamed onto the scene, and a crowd of onlookers quickly gathered. The EMTs loaded Officer De la Cruz into the first ambulance and Rosa and Ricky into the other. The sun was almost setting as they pulled up to the hospital.

When they wheeled Rosa away to the x-ray room, Ricky realized his knees had been cut by broken glass as he worked on the policeman. One of the cuts required stitches.

George and Edwina rushed to the hospital as soon as they got the call. Ricky was in the waiting room with a blanket wrapped around him when they arrived.

"Are you all right? Where's Rosa?" Edwina said as she hugged him.

"I'm fine. They x-rayed Rosa. She has a concussion, and they are keeping her overnight, but she'll be fine. The cop is still in surgery."

"Here are the clothes you wanted," George said as he handed a bag to Ricky and put a hand on his shoulder. "You want to clean up first? I'm sure we can get you to a shower."

Later, as he stood in front of the sink and looked in the mirror, Ricky could still see Rosa's bloody hand print on his shoulder. His mind replayed the scene. *"You're hurt,"* she said as she looked at the scars. *"All over."* He closed his eyes and moved away from the mirror.

After he showered and dressed, he went to get an update on De la Cruz.

"He's still in surgery. You the man who found him?"

"Yes."

"His wife is in the surgical waiting room. She wants to see you."

Ricky walked to the waiting room and found a woman alone, on her knees, in front of a chair.

"Mrs. De la Cruz?"

She turned quickly. "Yes? You have news?"

"No. Nothing yet. I'm Ricky Ruiz. I found your husband."

She grabbed his hands and held them up to her cheek. "Oh. Thank you, thank you. God bless you."

"Are you a Christian?"

"Yes."

"So am I. Would you like to pray together?"

"Oh yes." Her eyes filled with tears.

An hour later, Ricky entered Rosa's hospital room with a tired smile on his face. Rosa appeared to be sleeping. George and Edwina sat in chairs on the opposite side of the bed.

"Any news?" George asked.

"He's still critical, but he's out of surgery and stable."

"Thank God," Edwina said.

"Yes, thank God," Ricky said as he moved to the bedside and slipped a hand around Rosa's hand.

She opened her eyes and smiled slowly. "It's you again. Where have you been?"

"I had to wash up. How are you doing?"

"My head hurts, and I feel drugged up, but other than that, OK." Just as she was finishing the sentence, she looked over to the door. "Oh. Hi there."

Ricky turned and saw a handsome man standing in the doorway with a large bouquet of flowers.

"This a private party, or can another guest come in?" the man asked.

Edwina looked from the man to Ricky, then to Rosa. "I had to call and tell him we weren't going to make it to the theater tonight."

The man walked into the room. "I've heard of finding excuses to get out of a date before, but this is going a bit far," he said with a smile. Ricky moved away from the bed and watched as the man leaned over and kissed her on the cheek. His smooth, blond hair was slicked back. He wore a very expensive suit and shoes. The smell of his cologne wafted through the air as he hovered over her a moment and moved her hair around on the pillow. "Are you OK?"

"I'll be fine. Papa always said I had a hard head. First time it did me any good." She noticed Ricky again. "Bertrand? I want you to meet a friend of mine. Ricky, this is Bertrand Warner. Bertrand, this is Enrique Ruiz."

The two men shook hands briefly.

"Nice to meet you," Ricky said and then looked at everyone. "I really need to go home and get some sleep now, so . . . "

George nodded his head. "Actually, Rosa, we should all leave and let you rest. Can we give you a ride, Ricky?"

The three of them said their good-byes to Rosa and left the room while Bertrand leaned down and kissed her on the cheek again and spoke to her in a soft voice.

Ricky made a quick phone call while George and Edwina went to get the car. When he exited the hospital, he could see Bertrand Warner getting into a black Mercedes Benz. He stopped and watched the man for a moment, then put his hand on his chest and sighed.

Chapter Fourteen

Lieutenant Colonel Tobin read the orders that would set the operation in motion. He had been ready to implement the plan two days earlier but had been forced to put everything on hold. A crew of special technicians had arrived on an aircraft, along with a coded message for Tobin and Colonel Gronov that included a change of plans. The contents of the Cookie Jar were to be replaced with equipment that was on the plane. The exchange was to take place while Major Ross was away from the base on a "mission."

Under no circumstances could the exchange be discussed with anyone in the base camp. The technicians who had come with the equipment were to be housed separately from the other troops. If anyone requested access to the Cookie Jar after the exchange, they would be denied "pending verification of orders." Officials informed Tobin and Gronov that the new equipment consisted of a stash of "essential" medical supplies and that the *old* "equipment" in the shack was being moved to a "more strategic location."

Prior to coming to Africa, they had been told that several rebel military groups had united with the intent of taking over a large portion of southern Africa. This new "army" of rebels and murderers, who called themselves Chango, would then attempt to hold the world hostage by controlling the minerals that all of industrial society needed. They would dole those minerals out as they saw fit—at a price of their own choosing.

In the past, the Arabs had banded together to cut back the world's oil supply—dramatically raising both their own status and the price of oil. Within a short period of time, governments that thought them scarcely worthy of notice in the past suddenly courted them with abandon. Some of the Arab leaders were depicted as good guys by the Western world—moderates in favor of progress. Others were portrayed as evil psychotic zealots. Regardless of how either group was perceived, each was now feared and respected.

Now, it was rumored this group called Chango felt their time had come. It was their turn to have the wealth mined out of African soil. It was their turn to be respected, courted, and feared.

As intelligence of this spread to industrial nations, a covert, multinational operation had been planned. This force, under the direction of General Rappaport and others, would secure mines and other locations perceived as targets of Chango and keep "stability" in the governments of southern Africa by "protecting" them. Lieutenant Colonel Tobin had envisioned a few skirmishes, the loss of a few soldiers, peace restored, and a quiet promotion.

The multinational force had spent weeks setting up this and other base camps, and then doing reconnaissance of the surrounding areas. Their targets had been located. Those in command had analyzed every aspect of the operation to ensure that the plans, made months ago, were achievable. The general had personally checked to see that every detail had been dissected, every contingency planned for.

The operation would start with a trip to a nearby village. Several would be on a routine mission and be ambushed by Chango forces. This would provide the excuse necessary to begin hostilities. The multinational force, superior in weapons and ready to defend strategic targets, would have won speedily.

One of the reasons Tobin had been selected for this assignment was that his superiors knew they could rely on him. His perfectionist nature ensured that he would follow orders to the letter. The men and women under his command for Operation Reclamation had been hand-picked and specially trained. But minor changes had been made at the last minute. As he reviewed these changes, Tobin felt growing apprehension.

After surveying the equipment in the Cookie Jar and evaluating the man in charge of the recently arrived technicians, he realized he couldn't delay the mission any further. He had received the orders. The only thing he could do now was send the expendable soldiers on the trip to the village.

Hathaway and Ross had been summoned, and they sat across from Tobin in his office.

"Hathaway," Tobin said, "I need a few men to go on a joyride to the eastern village. Can you spare some men today?"

"Yes sir," Hathaway responded. "I have several men who could go. Lieutenant Dustin, Specialist 5 Levine, and Captain Koslinski, who's on loan to us today from the Russian troops."

"Are you sure you can spare these men?" Tobin said, emphasizing each word.

"Definitely, sir," Hathaway said.

Hathaway and Ross knew that joyriders were likely to be ambushed. They also knew that this joyride was starting with special orders from on high. Tobin let them draw their own conclusions. Why Ross was to be informed of these orders when he had been excluded from the exchange of the materials in the Cookie Jar, Tobin wasn't sure, but to cover himself he would do what he was told.

"It's settled then. Have the soldiers prepare to leave the camp at zero nine thirty. Any questions?"

"No, sir." Hathaway and Ross said simultaneously.

"You're dismissed."

Ross and Hathaway stood and left the office. As they stepped outside, a wave of steamy heat engulfed them.

"Ahhh! Life in Africa." Hathaway said and made a face.

"You pick those men yourself?" Ross asked as he surveyed the grounds around them.

"Oh, yeah. The Russians have let us use Koslinski before. A worthless drunk. Dustin's a bad egg, and Levine . . . " Hathaway said as he leaned a little closer to Ross. "What can I say? One less Jew in the world, eh?"

"I get it." Ross said. If only Hathaway knew. Ross's grandfather came to America from Europe. Wishing to escape persecution, he had changed his name from Rosenberg to Ross.

The two officers parted company. Hathaway went to inform the three "lucky" men that they would be going on a joyride—a trip to a nearby village supposedly for reconnaissance, but considered by the men to be a chance to goof off.

Before the joyride set off, Ross received a secret communique updating the situation: He had been discovered, and the contents of the Cookie Jar had been exchanged for other items. Drastic changes had been made in Operation Reclamation—changes that had already been implemented in the village.

Soon Koslinski, Dustin, and Levine were assembled at the jeep. Of course, Levine would be the driver for the mission. The thought of having to drive that pig, Dustin, around really galled him, but nothing could be done about it.

An order to go into the village for reconnaissance meant Koslinski and Dustin would probably get drunk, or find some women, and leave him to babysit the jeep. Upon further thought, however, Levine realized this was better than digging ditches or cleaning the latrines.

As they headed over the bumpy road into town, Dustin and Koslinski sat in the back of the jeep, told coarse jokes to one another, and made rude remarks about how Levine stunk of bug repellent. Levine tried to keep his mind on driving.

The moment they entered the village, they knew something was wrong. Not a person was in sight. The abandoned streets gave the impression of a ghost town. The buildings, an odd mixture of newer concrete block and old shacks, appeared to be abandoned as well. Normally, all the windows and doors would be open for circulation of air. People would be sitting or standing in the shade, doing roadside business. There was an eerie emptiness here.

After they had traveled a hundred yards into the village, Koslinski leaned forward and spoke to Levine. "Stop the jeep."

Levine brought the vehicle to a halt.

They all just sat there for a few moments. Dustin and Koslinski drew their weapons.

"Pull over here," Dustin said pointing to the right.

Levine pulled to the side of the street and stopped again.

Dustin and Koslinski managed to raise the camp on the radio and asked for instructions, hoping they would be ordered to return to camp.

"Investigate with caution," came the reply.

The two officers decided to leave Levine in the jeep with the engine running. They would stick together and slowly move about the immediate area, covering each other.

Levine panicked. He was a sitting duck in the jeep, just waiting for someone to come along and shoot him. They had never practiced this scenario in training camp.

Koslinski and Dustin worked their way behind the nearest building to their right. Still not a soul in sight. They came back to the front of the building, crossed the road, and went behind another building. Levine watched them as they disappeared again.

They rounded the corner of a shack and entered a small alley running behind the buildings on the main road. Dustin thought he could see someone or something about a hundred feet away. It looked as if someone was lying in the road. He could only see what he thought were legs sticking out from behind barrels. Dustin poked Koslinski in the back.

"Look. Up there. That someone's legs?" he whispered.

"I think so."

They crept forward until they were within twenty feet of what they were now certain was a body in the alley. Was it a trap? They moved even slower, looking around for any evidence that someone might be planning to ambush them. Droplets of sweat broke out on their brows.

Flies swarmed over the area. Obviously, this was a corpse. They inched forward with caution. As the body came into full view, they noticed the back door of the building was open. The men glanced at each other. Koslinski moved to the side of the door and stood with his back to the wall, ready to fire into the building if necessary. They no longer concerned themselves with the body of the man in the alley. Regardless of what had happened to him, he could do them no harm. Of much greater concern to them was who may have killed the man.

Dustin crouched behind the barrels, and the flies were all over him. He signaled to Koslinski, who bent down, picked up an empty bottle, and threw it through the open door.

Nothing happened.

Dustin joined Koslinski behind the building. "Think we should try to go in?" he whispered.

Koslinski nodded, then moved in front of the open door with his weapon at the ready. Nothing happened. He stepped into the structure. It was pitch dark inside, and he had to wait a moment for his eyes to adjust. He heard a noise on the far side of the room and jumped. It took a few seconds for him to realize it was a wooden shutter. A small oscillating fan whirred overhead, and each time it sent air over the shutter, the shutter moved and creaked. Dustin came up behind him.

"Nobody's in here," Koslinski said, and then he realized he was mistaken. On the floor, in the corner, lay the body of a small woman. "Open that," he said as he motioned to the shutter. He walked over to the body and kicked the bare foot of the woman. As more light flooded the room, they could see the woman clearly. Though covered with flies, they could see she had been bleeding from the eyes, nose, and mouth.

Koslinski holstered his weapon and bent down to roll her over. No wounds were apparent.

"No! Wait! Stop!" Dustin said. "Don't touch her! She's got some sort of plague or something!"

It was too late. Koslinski had already grabbed her arm. He let go quickly and jumped back from the body. Dustin jumped back from Koslinski.

"Don't touch me!" Dustin yelled. "Don't touch anything!" He looked around the room and saw a half-empty bottle of whiskey. "Here, wash with that."

Koslinski grabbed his wrist with his left hand and held it out at arm's length as if he could cut off the circulation or keep the "germs" as far away from the rest of his body as possible. "Help me, help me!" he screamed.

Dustin unscrewed the lid on the bottle and stepped back from it.

Koslinski grabbed it and poured it over the contaminated hand.

"What should we do now?" he asked.

"Let's get back to the jeep!" Dustin said. "Don't touch anything with that hand. We'll go back, and they will know what to do!"

They could not get the front door open, so they ran out the back, past the body, and down the alley. Dustin emerged on the main road first and stopped. Koslinski came up behind quickly and stopped also. They looked to the right and to the left. Levine and the jeep were nowhere in sight.

They began the journey back to the camp on foot. Koslinski showed signs of illness first, so Dustin put an increasing distance between himself and the infected man. By the time he realized he was also infected, darkness had fallen and the Russian trailed far behind.

Dustin was still alive when they located him the next morning, rambling incoherently about Levine taking off without them. He screamed with terror at the sight of people in biohazard suits who looked like spacemen surrounding him. They loaded him into a sealed container and took him to the base camp. They would have transported him to Fort Detrick, but the virus was so fast-acting that he died within an hour of his rescue.

CHAPTER FIFTEEN

IT HAD GROWN DARK, AND SHE COULD BARELY SEE TO read. Sara Reisling turned on another light. As she did so, she realized the need to get up and stretch for a while. She had been grading test papers and homework for almost two hours. She had already changed to her sweatpants and sweatshirt, and her sandy blond hair was pulled back in a ponytail.

As Sara got up, a large, brown dog ambled over to greet her. "Hello, Mr. Moo," she said as she patted his head. "You ready for some dinner?"

He cocked his head to one side, looked intently at her, and then wagged his tail. He probably was clueless as to what she had actually said, but she liked to believe he was a very intelligent animal who understood every word she said. She had come home from work one day and found him on her doorstep, waiting for her as if he belonged there. He was a handsome animal, probably part golden retriever, and she figured he was lost.

In the following days she tried to locate his owner, but no one ever claimed him. Meanwhile, she let him come inside. The nights could get very cold. By the second week he was there, it was if he had always been her dog. Whenever she left or came home, he would howl, announcing her departure or arrival to the entire neighborhood. He often sounded more like a bawling calf than a dog—hence "Mr. Moo."

"OK then," she said, "what's it to be tonight? Strawberries and cream?"

His eyebrows came together.

"No? How about tomato soup?"

He sat down.

"Oh, I know. Chunky Bits?"

His tail wagged slightly.

"Chunky Bits it is!"

She walked toward the kitchen, and he followed. As soon as she opened the cupboard where she kept the pet food, a cat appeared out of his hiding place and started making a figure eight around her legs, rubbing his head, the entire length of his body, and his tail on her shins.

"First come, first served, Peaches. No butting in line."

Peaches meowed loudly.

"Complaining won't help you. You'll just have to wait your turn," she said as she reached down and scratched the top of his head.

Mr. Moo barked.

"Gosh, Moo. I'm getting it!"

She fed the dog and then the cat. As she put the pet food away, she realized it was time to feed herself. She opened the refrigerator and stared inside. Nothing in there seemed to be calling her name, so she closed the door and wandered around from room to room for a few minutes. The apartment was a wreck. She knew she ought to spend some time cleaning it but couldn't bring herself to do it.

Maybe, she thought, *I should check on Mrs. Mueller first.*

She had lived in a tiny apartment in Mrs. Mueller's home, in a northeastern Denver suburb, for two months now. When she first moved to Denver, she had shared a larger apartment with a friend, Rita. Rita decided to get married, and Sara was suddenly looking for a new roommate or a new apartment. Finding this place had been a blessing for her. She needed a cheap place to stay, and Mrs. Mueller, an elderly widow, needed a good tenant who would give her help around the house now and then. It was a perfect match. Sara only had one sister and had always been a tomboy. Since her dad had taught her how to fix simple things around the house, she was pretty handy.

Sara locked her door before she walked around to the front of the house. She knocked at Mrs. Mueller's door and saw the curtain in the front window move as she waited for a response.

"Come in," Mrs. Mueller called out.

Sara opened the door and entered the small house that contained hundreds of little knickknacks on old doilies and small shelves. The house always had a certain smell she couldn't quite identify. An attic smell maybe. Today it smelled like baked chicken in an attic.

Mrs. Mueller sat in her favorite chair in front of the TV. A game show was on, and she muted the sound of it when Sara came in.

"Hi!" Sara said as she went over and hugged the woman. "Just thought I'd stop in and see how you were today."

"Would you like some chicken?"

"Actually, I'm not that hungry right now. But don't let me stop you from eating."

The old woman waved a hand at her. "Oh, you could eat something. Henry and I used to have a nice dinner every evening. Linen tablecloth, napkins. It was just something we did. When you live alone, though, it's just not worth the trouble. You sure you're not hungry?"

Sara smiled. "I'd love to have dinner with you. Can I help with something?"

"Well, let's see," Mrs. Mueller said, rising from her chair. She walked slowly toward the kitchen and stopped in front of a hutch. "You could get those plates in there. Flatware's in the kitchen."

Sara got two plates out of the hutch and set them on the table before following Mrs. Mueller into the kitchen. The oven was open, and a beautifully baked chicken sat on the rack.

Sara moved to the stove. "Here, I'll get that. Where do you want it?"

"Just put it on top."

"Boy, this is a big chicken. Who were you planning to feed anyway?" Sara asked, looking at the large bird.

"Well, I don't know. I went to the store and just wanted a whole chicken. Henry loved chicken. Today would have been our sixty-second anniversary. I just had to bake a chicken."

Sara took off the oven mitts and gave Mrs. Mueller a little hug. "How many years has it been since you lost him?"

"Fifteen next March. The first few years went real slow. Now they just seem to fly by. I look at all the stuff they come up with these days and say to myself, 'What would Henry think of that? Boy, wouldn't he be surprised to see that?'" She seemed deep in thought for a moment.

"Do you have any pictures of him?" Sara asked.

"Would you like to see them?"

"Sure I would."

"Well, after dinner we'll look for some."

They ate dinner at a table set for company, complete with linen tablecloth and napkins. Sara told Mrs. Mueller more about herself, and Mrs. Mueller spoke of Henry.

Henry Mueller had married Edith Bowden when they were both just twenty-three. He had been in the Navy and was trained to work on boilers. When he got out of the Navy, he continued to work on large boilers and eventually got the job that brought them to Denver. They never had children, but Edith had no regrets. She was unable to bear children, and Henry wasn't that crazy about them anyway. They had had many wonderful years together.

After dinner, Mrs. Mueller got out old photos and served coffee. Sara looked at the pictures and asked questions.

When the evening ended, both women were a little sad. Mrs. Mueller had forgotten how much she missed having company—and how much she missed Henry. Sara missed her family.

They parted company, and Sara went back to her tiny apartment. She wrote a short note to her parents and then went to bed.

CHAPTER SIXTEEN

TRINA WATSON ADDRESSED PRESIDENTIAL CANDIDATE Donald Cole, Lawrence Cunningham, and all of the campaign staff members who had gathered for the meeting.

"Important news has reached us this morning. Congressional hearings have been scheduled on the subject of regeneration. The buzz I get says that if there is little or no public opposition at the hearings, it's going to be a done deal."

Don couldn't hide his agitation. Since he started reading some of the medical research surrounding this new procedure, he had become convinced it was a bad thing. With certain hormonal, gene, and chemical therapies, "old" people were said to be miraculously regenerated. But the more he looked into this technique, the more convinced he was that this was simply a way to strip people of their social security and medical benefits, while at the same time making them "useful" workers (taxpayers) again. "We can't let them get away with this," he said, shaking his head.

"Well, unless we act quickly, we lose any chance of rebuttal," Trina responded.

"What have we got in the arsenal so far?" Bob Post asked.

Trina looked at the notes in front of her. "Not much. It seems as if two of our four prominent scientists who had dissenting opinions have died. And get this—three of our five physicians have perished as well. I don't know about any of you, but I find that rather interesting."

Don felt a knot growing in his stomach. "Do we have any means of contacting the remaining scientists and doctors?"

"I have my secretary on it as we speak," Trina said.

"How about you, Lawrence? You get any response from the pharmaceutical, medical equipment, or cosmetic companies you contacted with this stuff?"

"Yes," Lawrence said, shrugging, "but most of them will not go on record as being against regeneration. They figure it would make them look too bottom-line oriented. The negative rebound would affect sales. Most did say, however, that they would be willing to fund party advertising against regeneration."

Don sighed. "How soon could we get some ads going?"

"At least a week," Bob said. "And we can only do that if we have the cash up front for the ads."

"Lawrence, get back to the companies that offered help. See what we can do without running into any campaign finance problems. Let's approach this as an issue outside our campaign. We can help in giving them pertinent information and coordinating their efforts, but let them address it. I'm sure they are capable of doing this as an independent, anonymous block of 'concerned businesses.' The race for the presidency doesn't have to be part of the issue here. How about it?"

"I'll see what I can do."

"Good," Don said to Lawrence. Then he looked at Bob Post. "My next speech to seniors is a week away. Can we get on the attack by then? Do we have enough statistical evidence as it stands?"

Bob shook his head. "It's a close call, Don. Both the facts and the ones who uncovered them are disappearing rapidly. You could be sticking your neck out."

Don thought a moment. "I say we go for it."

By the time they adjourned the meeting, they had decided to go on the offense regarding regeneration. Lawrence would contact the large corporations who had expressed an interest in seeing the legislation stopped. Trina would attempt to contact the remaining dissenters in the scientific and medical communities. Bob would have the writers working on a speech addressing the issue.

When Don traveled to Florida a week later, he was ready to begin the battle over regeneration. They had some factual information on their side, but for now they would focus most of their attention on an appeal for more research, which only made sense in the light of such a risky undertaking. As he sat on the platform in front of hundreds of senior lobbyists, he hoped his strategy would work.

" . . . and it is with these concerns in mind that we have begun to ask such questions."

Don Cole suddenly snapped to the present as he heard the words. He knew he would be introduced soon. His eyes swept out over the audience as the man at the podium droned on.

It was a meeting of the delegates of the Senior Voters Alliance of Florida. As the population of America aged, older voters had greater amounts of clout. Only a fool would ignore the concerns of those over sixty-five. As one who considered himself familiar with and sensitive to the issues that concerned them, he anticipated a friendly audience.

President Todd, who had made many promises to the elderly prior to his election, had done little to fulfill his commitments. Don, on the other hand, had a good record concerning the issues of aging, medical care, and long-term care—which stemmed from personal experience.

"So it is my distinct pleasure," the man at the podium said, "to introduce to you Donald Larson Cole."

As the audience applauded, Don rose and moved to the microphone.

"Good morning," he said and smiled. "It's a real pleasure to be here today. In fact, my mother is supposed to be here, but I guess she's running a little late. Anybody seen my mom?" He asked, shielding his eyes from the lights for a moment to look at the place where she should be sitting. The audience responded with laughter.

She waved and walked to the platform. He moved to the edge, bent down, and gave her a kiss. She spoke to him for a moment, then he returned to the microphone.

He took out his handkerchief and wiped the lipstick off his cheek. "She says she got stuck in traffic, but if I know my mom, she probably tried to play bridge till the last minute."

Another short round of laughter.

"It's a privilege to be in St. Petersburg and meet with you today. I can see why so many of you have chosen Florida as your home. But I know you have been wise in more ways than in retirement choices. Many of you have brought expertise from businesses you ran successfully before retirement into the arena where you serve now. You have created one of the most potent lobbies in the United States today . . . not simply by virtue of numbers, but because you are willing to think, to research, to organize, and to *act*.

"Today, I want you to listen to what I have to say and then apply all of those skills in selecting the man you will vote for in the next election. I challenge you to compare my past pledges with my record of service to 'Silver Americans.'

I have been true to my word. I have kept the promises I have made—something my opponent cannot say.

"Over the past year, I have spoken to tens of thousands of people in person, possibly millions by TV, but of all the groups I have addressed, your group would have to be the most well-informed, the most committed, and the most organized."

There was a round of applause before Don continued. "Why? Because you realize that, in a culture that worships youth, if you don't watch out for yourselves, things might not go so well."

He took a sip of water as the audience applauded again.

"I'm going to take advantage of all the work you have done and skip all the statistics and rehashing of what year this bill was passed or that increase was approved. What I would like to do this evening is take a bit of your time to discuss what's on the horizon.

"Actually, there are two horizons. One where I'd like to lead you; the other, where I believe my opponent is taking you. The only place where they meet is right here, in this room, with you. You will be given the facts concerning these two destinations, and you will have the opportunity to choose. The doorway to the horizon you choose is the voting booth.

"As you know, many new advances in medicine are being promoted as solutions in the care of our growing senior population. There is a great push to get them through Congress this very week. You will be told that they have been extensively tested in other countries— mostly China and Europe. I'm speaking of the so-called regeneration process."

He paused for a moment and looked out at his audience. "While most of you, I believe, would be willing to try something new in health care or lifestyle if it held the hope of increasing the length and quality of your life, how many of you are willing to trade the years you worked so hard to enjoy for the privilege of being guinea pigs? How many of you are willing to sign away all your entitlements and independence to receive what the government deems the best in the 'cutting edge' medical care and living facilities? In exchange for your 'courage' and willingness to participate in 'a great experiment,' what do you get? They'll show you impressive video footage of healthy men and women in their eighties—and older—jogging, skiing, and biking. You'll see videos of these same people enjoying an evening in attractive 'new quarters.' It all looks so *inviting* . . . especially when described by those who do not value you for who you are, but for what you can still contribute to them.

"I heard the reports earlier this year, just as you did, about these breakthroughs in 'regeneration.' But as tempting as this may sound, we must all realize that the side effects of these advancements may not be fully known for a decade or more. I have spent some time looking into *all* of the available data—not just the promotional propaganda—and, as much as I would like to join you in believing in the miracle of 'regeneration,' it's just *not* the wonderful phenomenon they want us to believe.

"While it would be of great financial benefit to the government, this treatment—and some of the others they propose—may cost a whole lot more than you'll want to pay. Remember who is making the promises.

"Let's look at the horizon that Todd promised before the last election. It seemed all bright and beautiful as he described it to you four years ago. The problem is that it was a sunset, not a sunrise. The things that looked so bright back then have faded, in most cases, to black.

"Four years ago, you were promised better health care, quicker response time in treatment, and less paperwork and hassle. What did you get? 'Orchestrated Medicine.' I don't have to tell most of you what this means. You know all too well. Are there less forms?"

"No!" the whole crowd responded.

Bob watched from the sidelines and smiled. No one could work a group like Don.

"'In-home care' is quickly going the way of 'in-home nursing'—as extinct as a doctor's 'house call.' A serious illness could land you in a 'Senior Specialty Facility' where, if you are diagnosed as chronic or terminal, you are quickly reduced to 'pain management' so you can die 'with dignity'—also known as going as quietly as possible. Scary but *true*.

"As this administration accelerates toward Alternative Health Care under the Assignment Program, let's look at what you get in exchange for signing over all your rights and benefits. Should you refuse a prescribed treatment, you forfeit all other benefits. Once you sign, it's the whole program or nothing. You will be given the *promise* of the latest in regeneration techniques. And *again*, I ask you to remember who's making the promise. The same people who promised 'better health care, quicker response time, less paperwork.' What you're envisioning and what they intend may be two entirely different things.

"I propose that we put the Alternative Health Care and Assignment Program on the back burner. Let's examine them more closely before we decide to serve them up to everyone. I understand that time is precious to you. It is precious to all of us. But before something becomes a law—a requirement—shouldn't we make sure it does what we want it to?"

Don could see many of the heads in the audience nodding in agreement.

"Now, before I'm accused of using terror tactics to win your vote and failing to offer any real solutions, let me show you what could be on the *other* horizon." He stopped for another sip of water. "When I was elected governor, my state ranked *forty-seventh* in quality of care for seniors. After three years, we were up to twenty-second, and with the legislation I signed before leaving office, my state now ranks *fifteenth*. If elected, I would propose many of the same reforms adopted by my state.

"All of you should have been given a packet containing the proposals I will make as president of the United States. I'd like to go on record as saying that I will sign similar proposals submitted to me by Congress regardless of who writes them or from what party they originate . . . and that while we are making these improvements for the short haul, we'll give a serious look at what's on the back burner."

Don spent another forty-five minutes describing what he thought could be done within the next four years and how those changes might affect their future. They were sensible, tangible plans, but as he prepared to watch the network news later that evening, he realized his plans would not be given a shred of "air time." Unfortunately, he had also provided the media with ammunition through a poor choice of words.

In the ten-second news "promo" that evening, the reporter looked up and said, "Cole uses terror tactics to get senior vote. Story at eleven."

The "story" contained almost none of Cole's actual speech and none of the positive things he presented during the course of the evening. Two other networks ended up using the "terror tactics" phrase the next day. The Universal Information Group—the largest news agency on the planet—not only picked up on the terror tactics line, but it also aired a report on the suspicious connection between the Cole camp and major corporations who would lose millions if the elderly suddenly became "more healthy."

Cole had, until now, always been unflappable. He was the kind of guy who could take almost any debate and turn it in his favor, but his patience was wearing as thin as his energy level. In the coming weeks, his growing frustration with the media's coverage of his campaign would hit boiling point.

CHAPTER SEVENTEEN

PRESIDENT SONNY TODD PULLED AT THE HAIR ON THE sides of his head as he paced around in the White House secure room. "How do they *do* it? In spite of every precaution, they keep up! It's not like a leak; one of us has to be *in* the Quick and Dead!"

Vice President Bartlett and Secretary of Defense Ernest Schollet listened to the tirade without comment. Todd wasn't saying anything they hadn't already thought themselves. Obviously, they had an information problem. Somebody in the upper levels of their organization was a spy.

Schollet had been given the bad news himself just hours before. He, in turn, was the one who got to share it with the president. The first piece of information was that Ross—the one who had blown their cover and done the "video" of them, the one they were going to have killed—had somehow gotten word of their plans once again and disappeared under their noses along with one of the intended plague "victims," Specialist 5 Joel Levine.

Their whereabouts were unknown. The second and more troubling bit of news was that two of the ERWs—thermonuclear devices—had disappeared on their way back to the United States from Africa.

"Tell me," Todd shouted at the two men, "*how* could this get any worse?" The phone on Todd's desk rang. He pointed to the phone. "Should I answer that, 'Office of the Quick and the Dead, how may I help you?'" The phone kept ringing. "I'm telling you both we are not leaving this room until we get a few things settled." He strode to his desk and picked up the receiver, after pausing a moment to collect himself. "Hello? No. I don't see any other options either . . . Yes. Face to face . . . just the three of us. If anything happens after that, it will be pretty simple to figure out where the problem lies. Yes. I know where you mean. Yes. Good-bye." He hung up the phone and ran his fingers through his hair.

"So what are we going to do?" Victor finally asked.

"You," the president said as he looked at Victor, "are going to stay here and look vice presidential. Ernie and I are going to go and meet with Yosef this afternoon, face to face. Whatever we decide to do, there are going to be no 'middle men' to mess it up or give it away."

Victor Bartlett sat and thought about this for a few moments before making a comment. "So why just the three of you? You think I'm the spy? Look, I have just as much to lose in all of this as you do!"

"That's not it at all, Vic. Someone has to stay here for appearances. You have a full schedule today. I had today cleared off for a rest day, anyway. I will brief you as soon as I get back."

Bartlett was not satisfied with the answer, but he didn't think he could say or do anything to change the situation. Obviously, he was a suspect. Fine. Hopefully they would soon realize he was not their problem . . . unless, of course, he was being framed. He tried to stay calm as they finished their meeting and went their separate ways. Todd and Schollet would meet with Yosef at an undisclosed location. If they failed to come up with a satisfactory plan, the results for all of them would be disastrous. If all went well, it might imply that he was the problem and they succeeded because they left him out of the loop. He didn't know which scenario would be worse, but he began to give some serious thought to protecting himself should he become a scapegoat.

Later, as Todd, Schollet, and Yosef met, they considered the possibility that the vice president might be helping the Quick and the Dead. Then again, it could be one of the two generals Schollet used who were the problem, or possibly someone in Yosef's group.

Finding and disposing of the spy was only one of several pressing problems. If the three of them were to ensure their own survival (in every sense of the word), they would have to get a handle on the situation. The Quick and the Dead, whose position seemed so tenuous only a few months ago, now apparently were within striking distance of the White House. Within days or weeks they could bring down Todd and associates. They must be dealt a blow so serious that they could not escape and survive.

Todd, Yosef, and Schollet all agreed drastic measures were called for. But when Yosef brought forth a plan, Todd was taken aback.

"You can't be serious," he said as he looked at Yosef, then Schollet. One glance told him that Schollet must have been aware of the plan before the evening's meeting. He looked neither shocked nor troubled at the things Yosef proposed. "Ernie," the president said, hoping he was mistaken, "you can't seriously think this is a viable solution."

Ernest Schollet said nothing.

Yosef finally spoke. "You have to see the position you are in now, Sonny. We went beyond being squeamish at details long ago."

"Details? *Details!* You call killing all those people—Americans—a '*detail?*'"

"Oh, I see," Yosef said, as he straightened in his chair. "Americans are so much more *valuable* than other people . . . You didn't seem to mind losing a few of them in Africa."

"That was different," Todd tried to rationalize. "Those were troops. They are set aside as expendable in any contest."

"And what of the Africans who would die . . . who did die?"

Todd was silent.

"It's too late to turn back, my friend," Schollet interjected. "This is war. The Quick and the Dead, and others like them, would do the same to us if they could. If they win, we're not just finished, we're in prison or dead . . . and think of all the progress you have made here. Think of the Global Plan. It will all go down the tubes if you turn back now. Are you willing to throw away everything you've committed to, everything you've worked so hard for, when it can all be your legacy to the future? It's a small trade-off. At most, several hundred lives for the world . . . not to mention how quickly you'll be able to move on the Zones projects after this. We'll be able to cut *years* off the schedule. None of us intended for it to go this way, but personally, I can see it's time for a strategic move such as this."

In less than an hour, they had convinced Todd he had only one option if he wished to continue on the course he had chosen so many years ago. The only thing needed was to select a target.

All of them knew that the major support and strength for the Quick and the Dead was out West where independent thinking was always more of a problem. This would have to be where they struck the blow. They would need to select a place that was well populated, yet somewhat remote; well recognized, but not essential in the production of food, fuel, or manufacturing. A place that could well be a base for fundamentalist operations, yet was where the government already had protected space within which to carry out such an operation. They reviewed their list of targeted cities and made their final selection: Denver.

Of course, Yosef knew that the president, vice president, and secretary of defense were in it so deep they would agree to almost anything, given the time to convince them of their "own good motives." Thinking that Yosef represented a small group of corporations that were looking to control certain technological advances and natural resources, Todd, Bartlett, and Schollet figured they were using Yosef as much as he was using them. They would hailed as heroes in the history books of future generations.

Only Yosef knew how well all of this would fit into the real agenda—dominion, peace, prosperity under the One who was coming, the One who would not be corrupted by their greed, the One who would rule without them.

CHAPTER EIGHTEEN

TONY BENSEN SIGHED. IT HAD BEEN A LONG DAY. CAMERA crews had just finished the last seminar of his new series, The Pilgrimage to Spiritual Excellence, for the Spiritual Oasis Network (SON).

As a young man he had been labeled a psychic, but he didn't really care for that title. He felt his gifts went far deeper than just "knowing" where to find lost objects or sensing people's thoughts. He worked at not being a mere amusement at parties or on talk shows. He avoided what he considered silly displays of his powers and encouraged a scientific approach to unlocking the mysteries of his giftings. University studies were conducted under strict standards. How he did what he did still remained a mystery, but many a skeptic became a believer in the process. Eventually, he was asked to host several series on the mind. The most recent, The Pilgrimage to Spiritual Excellence, consisted of seminars with live audiences journeying with him in exploration of the spiritual realm. The seminars had been a blend of videotapes from "masters" around the world, his own personal teachings, and practical demonstrations with the audience. They covered such topics as "finding God," "meditation," and "the journey to the center within."

Before the seminar tapings ended, Tony was forced to endure a personal crisis. His long-time companion, Sandra, left him. He had felt a rift in their relationship some time ago, but he did not feel led to pursue her. They had grown distant over the past year as his reputation and career had expanded to new heights. Sandra continually remarked on his absences from their Colorado home. In reality, Tony believed she was secretly jealous of his success.

Whenever he did manage to get back to their mountain home, he felt uncomfortable there. Although the area was considered a spiritual "mecca" for many, he began to have distinct negative feelings about the place and had made up his mind to sell the home just prior to Sandra's departure.

Now he had a dilemma. He needed to get away and meditate on his choices. For over a year, he had been increasingly dissatisfied with his life. At a time when he was achieving so much, he felt empty. Was it time to shed all of the outward trappings and go back to the simple? Did he just need to deal with some subconscious guilt over his good fortune? He would now take the time to find out. In two weeks, he would visit with friends in Washington, D.C. and even attend a dinner party at the White House. Earlier, he had been tempted to cancel the trip to D.C. and just head out to a wilderness to think, but his ego won out. He had to admit he liked the thought of being recognized even in political circles when so many with his talents were viewed as "screwballs." He knew Todd was not in his corner yet, but Todd's wife, Edith, was quite impressed by him—along with several people in Congress. He would speak to Edith on the phone in a few days, and he knew he would not be able to resist telling her what he had seen. The president might not believe what he said at first, but that was OK. Tony had met challenges before, and rarely did he lose.

After that he would go to a secluded place and sort out his life.

CHAPTER NINETEEN

SARA REISLING HAD TO BE AT HER SUBURBAN DENVER school early to make coffee for the teacher's meeting. She'd ironed her outfit for the day and then had trouble getting the cat outside. She barely made it to the school in time to find her new friend and fellow teacher, Joy, plugging in the large pot. Sara gave her a hand putting out the muffins and napkins.

"Sorry I'm late," Sara said, "I just wasn't very together this morning."

Joy had known Sara for a couple of months now and never recalled seeing her on time. It irritated her, but she had decided to say nothing.

Ms. Baxter, the principal, entered the room precisely on time and called the meeting to order. She had several things she wanted to discuss with the teachers and staff at Holmon Elementary School. Actually, she was going to tell them what she expected of them. Ms. Baxter's discussions seldom involved a response from the receiving party.

"May I have your attention?" she said, motioning for everyone to be seated.

"I would like to thank you for all coming in a little early. I have a couple of things I wanted to mention this morning, and then we'll open up the floor for discussion."

Sara and Joy exchanged glances.

Ms. Baxter continued, "First of all, your art displays for spring season will have to be ready in two weeks. There will be a contest this year before the spring break, and the school that wins first place will get a trophy, so let's do our best to meet the deadline, shall we?

"Also, I want to mention again, as I always do, that with the approaching time, there needs to be special attention given to holiday issues. As you know, soon it will be Easter, Passover, the Moon Festival . . . We need to be especially careful this year about religious comments and displays in our classrooms and in the school office that might be perceived by students as endorsements of certain beliefs or threats against another belief system. Most of you remember the unfortunate incident last year. I hope it will not be repeated."

Sara and Joy turned to each other again with puzzled expressions on their faces. What on earth was she talking about?

"Anything for discussion?" Ms. Baxter said. Her hawk-like gaze swept over the men and women assembled in the room.

Sara stood. "Excuse me. I want some clarification here. What would *you* consider a 'religious display or comment?'"

The older woman's eyes fixed on Sara. "Ms. Reisling, is it?"

"Yes, ma'am."

"Well, Ms. Reisling, as those of us with experience know, this is not an easy road to travel. We want each student to be free to embrace the lifestyle of one enlightened by mentors who will take them across a rich quilt of cultural heritage to a place of unity in the finished design." She moved her hand as if brushing it over the imaginary quilt.

Sara glanced around. Did *anyone* understand what this woman was saying? Not a soul moved. She tried to refocus on Ms. Baxter's continuing answer.

" . . . while holding this next to our hearts, we must be aware of the diversity of those placed in our care. It is only in *recognizing* our diversity that we can come into unity in the human experience. Did that answer your question?"

"Well, actually . . . no. I wanted to know what guidelines you could offer that define your perception of the rights and limitations of the teachers and staff."

Ms. Baxter looked vexed. "I will be happy to bring it into simpler terms for you, Ms. Reisling, but we are out of time. If you would care to come by my office any afternoon this week, we can discuss the matter. Any other quick questions?"

Sara sat down. No one else moved.

"Good. Well, that about does it. Remember to pick up your fund-raiser catalogs and forms for students at the office today!" she said and quickly departed from the room.

Joy looked at Sara and whispered, "Are you out of your mind?"

"No, but I think I know someone who lives in never-never land. Did you understand one word of what she said to me?"

People started getting up from their chairs. Most of them, who had not dared to look at Sara during the meeting, now turned and stared at her.

Edward Ulmer, the science teacher who sat on Sara's other side, leaned over. "Nice going, Sara."

She turned to look at him. He was an attractive man in his late twenties, with red hair but no freckles. His blue eyes matched the blue sweater he was wearing. He seemed very nice but rather effeminate. Sara wondered if he might be gay.

She smiled at him. "I fend off a flame-thrower after the evening show."

"Sara!" Joy and Edward said in unison.

"Stop being so flip about everything," Joy said. "You push her buttons too hard, and she'll get you fired."

"That's what she did last year," Edward offered.

"What happened?" Sara asked.

"A *new teacher,*" he said, looking at Sara, "let some kid give a report about Easter and then let him say a prayer in class. One of the other kids complained to his parents, and when the whole thing blew up, the kid who gave the report caved in and said the teacher made him do it. She got fired."

Sara fumed silently. *How come teachers can lead students into "guided imagery," find spirit guides for them, encourage them in martial arts, meditation, and yoga, but not dare mention Christianity?* "And the teacher didn't fight it?" she asked.

Edward shook his head. "She'll be lucky if she gets to teach again."

They each stood and collected their belongings. Edward departed first.

Joy started to leave, then turned and said, "You know, Sara, you need to be a little less militant. You offend people sometimes."

"Why is it no one has to worry about offending *me*? I am what I am, Joy. I can't just lie down and let people walk over me. Being a Christian isn't synonymous with being a carpet, you know."

"I don't think I said you needed to be a carpet. I'm a Christian, too, but I believe we should *be* sermons, not just preach them. Making Ms. Baxter mad at all of us won't help."

"Just because no one else has the guts to say something to her doesn't mean no one should," Sara blurted out. "Christians in this country have gotten so apathetic and passive."

"Well, I'm sorry I don't measure up to your standards!" Joy snapped as she started to walk away.

Sara caught up with her. "I'm sorry. I wasn't referring to you. I was just speaking in general terms."

"That's OK," Joy said, but the expression on her face said it wasn't.

Sara stopped walking. *Why do I do that?* she asked herself. *Now I've made her mad just so I could make a point.* She looked at her watch. *And I'm going to be late if I don't get moving.*

She walked quickly to her class, but she resolved to continue her conversation with Ms. Baxter at the first possible opportunity. It was time Christians had as many rights as everyone else.

Later, in the teacher's lounge, Sara saw Joy and tried to make amends.

"Listen. I know I have a big mouth sometimes, but I can't seem to help it. OK?"

Joy smiled. "If we could bottle that zeal and sell it, we'd be in good shape!"

"Forgiven?"

"Forgiven."

Sara breathed a sigh of relief. She really liked Joy and hoped they could become close friends.

"Change of subject." Joy said, finishing a bite of a cupcake. "Want to go with us to see that Don Cole guy give a speech tonight? He's going to be at the convention center, and some of us wanted to see him. Julie and Rhonda are coming."

"No thanks. I don't have any interest in him."

"I thought you of all people would like to see him in person."

"No. There's no one running this time that does anything for me," Sara said.

"Suit yourself. If you change your mind, give me a call before five."

CHAPTER TWENTY

AS THE DOOR OPENED, EDWINA GRANT QUICKLY CLOSED the desk drawer. Her husband, George, entered the room.

"I thought you were Ricky," she said. She opened the drawer again, removed a small package from a bag, and placed it in the drawer. "Everything else ready?"

"Yep," he said, "and the victim is packing up some blood samples. He's supposed to meet me in here when he's done. Everyone else is out front. Joan closed the hall door so he can't see the waiting room."

Edwina got up from the desk and hugged her husband. "Oh, George. Did I tell you I love you today?"

"No, I don't believe you did."

"I love you."

"Ditto."

She pulled back and looked at him. "You could sweet-talk a girl right off her feet like that."

"Oh yeah?" He wrapped his arms around her and picked her up off the floor.

Ricky started to come through the door and then backed out. "Sorry. Should have knocked."

They both laughed.

"No, it's OK. Really. Come on in!" George said. "Go ahead, sit, sit, sit." He pulled a chair out for Ricky. He pulled up another chair for Edwina, and then went around the desk and sat down. "Do you have any idea what today means to Edwina and me?"

Ricky looked at both of them and shrugged. "I guess not."

"It's a special day for us."

"Oh, congratulations. Anniversary?"

"No, birthday," George said.

"Really? Yours?" Ricky asked. He looked at George, who shook his head, and then to Edwina. "Yours, then?"

"No. It's *your* birthday, Ricky. Surprise!" she said.

His eyebrows came together. "Uh, I don't know what to say, Edwina."

"Happy birthday!" Edwina said as George pulled several small packages out of the desk and pushed them over to Ricky.

"No. Honestly, you guys, I don't know what to say," he said as he chuckled. "This is great and all, but . . . it's not my birthday. My birthday isn't till next week."

"We know. But if we waited until the actual day, it wouldn't be a surprise, now would it?"

Ricky laughed. "No, I guess not."

"So open your stuff," she said, handing him the first package.

It was a new wallet.

"I noticed you needed a new one last week," she said.

He opened the next one, a smaller package. It contained a pocket knife with all the gadgets in it. "That's from George," said Edwina.

"This is from both of us," George said as he pushed a flat, rectangular package over to his friend.

Ricky opened it and saw that it was an empty picture frame. He looked up at them. "You scheduled a glamour photo session for me?"

"No," George said as he chuckled again. "We wanted you to have this to frame your diploma."

Ricky's eyes moved back and forth between them.

"What he's trying to say," Edwina explained, "is that we see in you such qualities and intelligence that we feel you should seriously consider being a doctor."

He kept staring at them—as if he were not comprehending what they meant.

"What we're trying to tell you," George said, "is that we want to help you go to med school."

Ricky's mouth dropped open.

George clicked his fingers. "Hello? Hello? You OK?"

"I . . . I . . . " was all he could say.

"I think we really did surprise him, 'Wina. What do you think?"

"Yeah. I think *surprise* might be too mild a word, though. *Astonished* might work better. What do you think, Ricky?" she asked.

"I . . . I can't think of the words. I . . . I've never even considered . . . What can I say?"

"Say, 'Thanks. I'll give it some serious thought,'" George offered.

"Thanks . . . I'll give it some serious thought."

"And now, it's party time!" Edwina said as she stood and grabbed Ricky's hand.

They led the dumbfounded Ricky into the waiting room where there were friends, more presents, and a cake spiked with candles.

"Look who's here, Ricky. Mrs. De la Cruz! She made the cake!"

The wife of the police officer he saved came running up and gave him a big hug. "Oh, Ricky, we owe so much to you. Happy birthday! I thank God for you every day, and I pray He gives you your heart's desire."

Ricky had just raised a paper cup of punch for a toast when he looked up and saw Rosa entering the room. He stopped momentarily, then he continued speaking.

"To good friends," he said as he took a sip and looked across at her.

"Happy birthday!" Rosa said, producing a large package with a bow. "Sorry I'm late. I needed to finish something at my office."

"Thanks," he said, "Can I open it now?"

"Oh, please do."

All the chairs and flat surfaces in the room were filled with people or party debris, so he moved to the receptionist's office, and she followed. She watched him as he tore open the package and saw the leather, bomber-style jacket inside. He ran his hand over it. "This is so nice. But, I can't take something this expensive from . . ."

"Too late! Had it customized. Look on the back."

He carefully pulled it out of the box and turned it over. A large crown of thorns was appliqued on the back with "Isa. 53:5" in the middle.

"I thought it would give you that tough-guy-who-loves-Jesus kind of look. Know that Scripture?"

"It's one of my favorites . . . 'But he was wounded for our transgressions, he was bruised for our iniquities: the chastisement of our peace was upon him; and with his stripes we are healed.' How did you know?"

"I just saw it and thought it was you, that's all. And I already knew you needed a jacket."

He looked over the top of the jacket at her. For a moment, he saw her in a different place, saying, "Ricky, you're hurt . . . all over." The smile on his face faded.

"Well, go ahead, put it on," she said. "Let me see if it's big enough! I had to stop a man in the store who looked your size and ask him to try it on."

He put it on. It was a perfect fit. "Thank you," he said quietly.

"Happy birthday, Ricky." She came close to him and stood on her toes. "Well," she laughed, "I guess you'll have to work with me. Come down here." He leaned forward, and she gave him a peck on the cheek. "I wish you every happiness, my dear friend. Thank you for saving my life."

Edwina watched them from the doorway and smiled.

George came up to her. "I know that look. Stop it."

"Stop what? I didn't do a thing. I'm just enjoying the view."

In an hour, the party was over, and most of the people were gone. Rosa, Joan, Edwina, and Ricky still lingered. George was in his office using the phone.

Edwina looked around. "Boy, what a mess, eh?"

"No kidding," Joan chimed in.

"Why don't you and I get the big stuff thrown out before the cleaning lady comes?" Edwina said to Joan. They both stood and started picking up the plates, cups, and wrapping paper.

"I really should get going," Rosa said. "Oops. There goes my beeper." She pulled it off her belt and looked at it. "Can I use your phone, 'Wina?"

"Sure. Help yourself."

Ricky watched her as she went to the receptionist's desk and picked up the phone. She dialed a number and turned her back to him when someone answered. He could hear little bits of what she was saying.

" . . . No, I had to be somewhere . . . Oh . . . thought I'd have time to go home . . . suppose so . . . Yes . . . my friend's clinic . . . remember it? . . . OK . . . are you? Three blocks. OK . . . I'll watch." She came back out to the waiting room looking a little flushed. "Can I help you clean up before I go?"

"Oh no," Edwina said, "Joan and I will have all this up in no time."

Ricky stood and wadded up some paper as he spoke to Rosa. "How's the knot on your head?"

"See? It's almost gone." She showed him the top of her head.

He leaned over her. "Looks good . . . How do you feel about everything? I know they haven't found the guy, but I mean, are you doing OK with it?"

"Well, no. Not completely. I still about jump out of my skin anytime someone comes up behind me suddenly. But, I'm doing better . . . I hope I'm a little wiser. And I know now that if I'm going to be good at my job, I need to understand things better." She hesitated a moment. "I wanted to ask a favor of you."

"Name it."

"I know you and George usually go out with the clinic van on Saturdays into the neighborhoods. I'd like to go with you. I can be a volunteer or . . . ?"

"You know we leave out of here at 7 A.M."

"OK."

"If you're late, we'll leave without you. Wear casual clothes and good walking shoes."

"OK. It's settled then. Seven o'clock sharp, right here on Saturday," she said, looking out the front window. "Well, my ride's here. Bye, 'Wina! See you later. Bye, Joan; bye, Ricky. Happy birthday again!" She rushed out the door.

Ricky looked out and saw the black Mercedes Benz pulling up to the curb. He closed his eyes and rubbed his chest as she hopped in and rode away.

Edwina watched Ricky from behind but said nothing.

CHAPTER TWENTY-ONE

AFTER SHE GOT HOME TO HER SUBURBAN DENVER APART-
ment, Sara was tempted to call her friend and say that she
had changed her mind. It wasn't that she wanted so much
to hear Don Cole speak but that she wanted to go out
with friends. After giving it more consideration, however,
she finally decided she had better clean her apartment and
do some ironing. She had put her chores off for too long
as it was.

She started in the kitchen and took everything out of
the cupboards. She reorganized all her foods and utensils.
She looked in the refrigerator and made a face. Stuff was
growing in there. She cleaned out the refrigerator and
threw out all the garbage. Next, she tackled her closet.

As she sat on the floor of her room amid piles of shoes,
purses, blouses, and sundry items, Mr. Moo came in,
bumped up next to her, and sat down, whining. Then he
left her side to crawl into the closet she had just emptied.

"Sorry, Moo, that spot is taken. You can't use it as your
personal space."

That was the moment she first heard what she thought was a low rumble. Possibly a plane or someone's stereo, she thought. The rumble grew louder. She stopped working and looked around. She could see the mirror on her dresser vibrating. Before she had time to do anything, there was a sudden jolt, as if the whole house had been picked up, given one good shake, and then set back down.

Loud noises came from the kitchen as cans, jars, and dishes in her cupboards crashed from their places. She could hear the sound of breaking glass.

She had been knocked flat. She lay on the floor and waited to see if the shaking had ended. Nothing else happened. Had a car hit the house? She ran outside. Other people in the neighborhood streamed out of their houses, asking, "Did you feel that? Did you hear that?" She ran around to the front and knocked on the door.

"Mrs. Mueller! Mrs. Mueller! Are you all right?"

After a few moments the door opened, and Mrs. Mueller stood there, her eyes wide. "Did you feel that?" she asked.

"Yes! Are you OK?" Sara said as she looked at the old woman.

"Yes, I'm fine. I had just dozed off in front of the TV. But look at what's happened!" she said as she opened the door wider.

Inside, dozens of Mrs. Mueller's knickknacks had tumbled out of place. Some were in pieces on the floor. "I'm so sorry," Sara said, and suddenly she remembered the sound she had heard coming out of her own kitchen. "Oh! I'll be right back. I need to check on a few things."

She went back inside her apartment and surveyed the damage. Several glasses had shattered on the floor along with one bowl and a jar of jelly. Some of her canned goods were dented, but her losses weren't that great. She cleaned up the glass and looked for Peaches and Mr. Moo. Moo still cowered in the closet and wouldn't come out. She couldn't find Peaches anywhere, but figured he was hiding as well.

She went back around to Mrs. Mueller's to see if she could help with anything.

Just miles from Mrs. Mueller's home, Donald Larson Cole rested in a downtown Denver hotel. He had taken off his tie and slipped off his shoes. He was going to lie on the bed and read over his notes for the evening, but he gradually dozed off.

He didn't hear the low rumble, did not stir when the glasses next to the ice bucket began clinking together, or didn't awaken when the door chain rattled in its slot. He was still in a deep sleep when it seemed as if a giant foot gave his bed one swift kick.

Now he was awake. He jumped up and yelled, *"What?"* but no one was there.

Within moments, someone rapped on the door.

"Mr. Cole! Are you OK?"

For a few seconds he thought he dreamed the jolt. Maybe one of his aides had heard him yell and wanted to know what was the matter. Feeling a little foolish, he went to the door and opened it.

Jason, one of his faithful campaign troops, was at the door.

"Did you feel that, Mr. Cole? Are you all right?" Jason said, entering the room and closing the door.

"You mean my bed really did jump?"

"Oh, yeah," Jason answered. "There was a short rumbling before that, too."

"I must have been fast asleep. I felt the bed move and . . . " There was another knock on the door. Don motioned to Jason. "You want to get that?"

It was his running mate, Lawrence Cunningham, and Trina, his campaign manager's assistant.

Trina's dark hair was pulled into a ponytail, and she wore blue jeans with a knit shirt. Don knew he couldn't have slept too long, because if it were anywhere near the time to leave for the convention center, Trina would look as if she had just stepped out of a fashion magazine. Candidate Lawrence Cunningham, of course, looked immaculate. His hair was always combed, his nails were always buffed, and his shoes were always on. Sometimes Don wondered if Larry slept in his shoes.

"Hey, did you feel that?" Trina said, excitedly. "We thought it was a bomb at first. Check your TV." She turned on his set. "George is contacting our security to see if they can get a line on it."

Larry peeked out the window. "You suppose it's safe to stay here? We're on the twentieth floor."

What a sissy, Don thought, shooting a pained look at Trina. She ignored him. Larry was not exactly the guy Don would have picked for the vice presidential candidate, but, as often happens, theirs was an alliance made to bring differing sectors of "the Party" to a place of unity. If Cole wanted to be president, he needed Larry's Wall Street connections.

"Oh!" Trina said, "Here's a local news station . . . "

Within minutes the network reported that a quake of 3.5 had struck the Denver metro area. There were no reports of damage or injury. By the time the story came on more people had arrived, and Don's room looked like campaign headquarters.

As soon as the quake story was over, Trina snapped off the set. "Since we're all up and we're all together," she began, "let's hit a few last-minute details."

A collective moan went up.

Trina pretended not to hear and continued to give instructions to various personnel in the room regarding the evening's activities.

Local workers had already reported to the convention center. Trina and her group would go down there in about two hours. Don and Larry would be expected to arrive thirty minutes after the event started. After the speeches, the candidates would attend a dinner with the elite of Colorado's contributing society and the press.

Having covered all the details she could remember without her planner in hand, Trina dismissed everyone. " . . . and be sure to check in with me at the Center if there are any changes in your assigned format. OK?"

"Listen, Trina," Don said as she headed out the door with Jason. "Try to get one or two women at my table tonight, would you?"

She rolled her eyes.

"And I mean women who are single. And weren't old enough to vote for Kennedy. OK?"

She gave him a look he didn't like.

"It's OK, *Mother; I am* single, you know. I'm not necessarily looking for romance. I'd just like to have an interesting conversation with someone who doesn't use a cane or need to shave."

In fact, she was actually a little jealous. But they were in the middle of a campaign, and the last thing she needed to do was complicate her life further by giving Mr. Cole any sign that she liked him.

"Fine, I'll see what I can do."

After she left, Don went back to bed but found he couldn't sleep. He got up and showered, then worked on memorizing more of his speech. He called room service for a light snack. Dinner wouldn't be until late.

Sara Reisling and Mrs. Mueller picked up the mess left by the tremor.

"Well, I guess I've needed to throw some of this stuff away for quite some time anyway," Mrs. Mueller said as she swept up porcelain shards in the hall. "I guess I'd forgotten about the quakes. It's been so long since we had one."

"You've had earthquakes here before?"

"Oh, goodness, yes. Had the shakes continually for a while there."

"How come I never heard about this before?"

"Well, they weren't as bad as the ones in L.A. for one thing, and they happened long before you were born. When they figured out what was causing them, they quit doing it, and the quakes stopped."

Sara looked puzzled. "It's possible to cause an earthquake? What did they do? I've never heard anything like this in my life."

"Well, it was a case of putting two and two together eventually. They didn't intend to trigger earthquakes here. It was accidental."

"So what was it they were doing? And who was doing it?"

"Well, it was over at the arsenal there," Mrs. Mueller said, pointing toward the east. They wanted to get rid of this contaminated water back in the sixties and finally came up with the idea to pump it far underground."

"*You're kidding!*" Sara exclaimed. "They pumped contaminated water down into the ground . . . where all the other water is? What kind of contamination? What were they thinking?"

Mrs. Mueller shrugged. "I don't know. I just know it was contaminated. Anyway, they pumped it way down there under high pressure. Apparently, there's a fault line somewhere down there, and this set it off. We started having all these tremors all the time. Seemed like we were living on gelatin for a while there. Eventually, I guess they figured out what triggered it all, and they stopped doing it. The tremors stopped after that."

Sara didn't know whether or not to believe the story, but then, why would Mrs. Mueller make up such a tale?

"And no one ever worried about the contaminated water they put down there?"

"Listen, sweetie. There was worse than that to worry about. At the time Henry knew people who were working on all sorts of poisonous nerve gas and biological agents over there."

"*Really?* We go after people who do that now."

"It was a different time, Sara. We were all worried about the bomb and about the Russians getting us. It made us do all sorts of things that seemed to make sense at the time. Who'd have known it would have turned out like this? Henry's long gone, and the world is still spinning. We just keep living in spite of all the silly things we do. After they stopped using it for a military base, they spent billions of dollars cleaning it up, supposedly. But God only knows if they got all of it or what they did with all that stuff once they got it. Doesn't matter anymore, I guess. They just made it one of those new 'Zero Population Environmental Zones,' so nobody will be allowed in there anyway."

Sara finished helping Mrs. Mueller clean up all the broken debris and then returned to her apartment. Eventually, she found Peaches behind a dresser. Mr. Moo didn't come out until much later, and although it was against her policy, she let him sleep on the bed next to her that night.

Candidates Cole and Cunningham said little as they rode in the limo on their way to the convention center. Don turned on the small TV and scanned the channels for news of his appearance that evening.

As they neared the convention center, crowds of people, many with signs and large posters, lined the street. There were those in favor—"DC IS 4 DC" (the slogan adopted for the official bumper sticker, meaning that Don Cole belonged in Washington). The opposition carried signs that read "Of Don and Larry We Are Wary." There were all the "issue" people—"Save Mother Earth," "End Hate Speech," "Stop the Violence," "Abortion Is Murder," "Give Women Free Choice," "We have a right to 'keep and bear arms . . . '"

It was amazing to Don that someone would give over so much time to a single thought or idea. The signs along the road were visible evidence of a nation whose divisions were running beyond a healthy difference of opinion.

As the limo slowly approached the basement entrance to the Center, a woman broke through the barricades and threw herself on the hood of the car. Don and Lawrence sat in disgusted amazement as she began licking the windshield. The driver stopped the car, and policemen quickly removed her from the hood. She was shouting, but in their soundproof compartment they couldn't hear a word she said. As the woman struggled and started to break free, a policeman took out his club and raised it over her. The driver of the limo accelerated away from the scene.

"Driver, stop the car!" Don barked. "Avery!" he said to his personal security guard in the front seat, "Stop that man from hitting her! I won't have it!"

Avery leaped out of the vehicle. While he flashed his ID, he held up one hand to the officer and said something. Don wanted to hear and started to open the window a crack. One of the Secret Service guards put his hand on top of Don's.

"Don't do it, Sir. This is just the sort of distraction that an assassin could use. Driver, move on."

"Listen to him, go, *go!*" Larry commanded the driver.

As the limo began to move once again, Don looked out the back. He could see the woman was safely subdued and that Avery joined up with the security people in the car following theirs.

When they reached the basement elevators, the car stopped. The agent in the vehicle with the candidates waited for the doors of one of the elevators to open. Another agent emerged and gave a signal. They were then permitted to exit the vehicle and get into the elevator.

When the doors opened, they could already hear the sounds of the meeting down the hall. Congresswoman Ariel Ramos was preparing to introduce them. She would be getting the signal that they were approaching now.

" . . . and as the party moves forward, let us strive to remember this," she said. A round of applause broke out before she continued. "And now, it is my great pleasure to introduce to you, the representatives and voters of the great state of Colorado, the next president of the United States, Donald Larson Cole!"

Music began to play, people shouted and whistled, and pennants waved vigorously as Don and Larry entered the main hall of the convention center and moved across the stage to the podium. They both shook hands with Ariel, then stood and waved for a moment, permitting a good photo opportunity for the congresswoman as the media swarmed in front of the stage with cameras.

Ariel and Larry took their seats. The din in the room quieted. Don stood quietly at the podium, waiting for total silence. He had learned that silence created a certain electricity in an audience. It caused them to become alert, to want the void to be filled. So he waited, and the people became very still.

He had played a little with the beginning of his speech while he was in the hotel and had not been satisfied with it. The ride to the convention center had given him his opening lines.

Always say the name of the city you're in, he remembered.

"As I approached the Denver Convention Center, I noticed all the people who had gathered outside. Many of them carried signs. Some were for me, some were agin' me, as the saying goes.

"But there were many signs that were about issues. Issues so important to those holding the signs that they had been standing there in the cold weather—even through an earthquake—hoping to capture my attention, or the media's attention, or both. And for each view, expressed with intense emotion, there was an equal and opposite view expressed with equal emotion.

"America is a country of deep convictions. It is also becoming a country of deep divisions. People are becoming so possessed with one idea, one *passion*, that they eat, sleep, and breathe it. *Nothing* else matters. If it doesn't revolve around their issue, it doesn't concern them. These people have become the most vocal forces in America today.

"The old saying is, 'The squeaky wheel gets the grease,' and unfortunately, in this case it's true. These 'monoperceptive' people have gotten so good at pursuing their goals and punishing those who oppose them that the politician cloned from their midst actually has a chance at succeeding. When the final options are offered, you have a choice between two Cyclopes. This candidate has his one eye fixed on this issue; the other candidate has his one eye fixed on another issue. Ordinary people with two eyes and a good view stay home.

"Wouldn't it be nice to be able to step into a voting booth and know your vote wasn't a choice between the lesser of two evils? Wouldn't it be good to know you could elect a person who would take in a broader view and not just push a single agenda for the next four years?

"Tonight, America, I want to put an old-fashioned thing called common sense back into the arena . . . "
Applause and whistles filled the room.

"Tonight, America, let's covenant together to make some tough choices. Let's each decide to look at the whole picture and not just our personal slice . . . Our goal should not be to legislate, but to find solutions to the problems besetting this country.

"Toward the end of its existence, the Roman Empire became so concerned about its survival that it did several things: It tightened its grasp on the workers, taxing them beyond their ability to pay; and in the cities, where riots were likely to erupt, every effort was made to keep people distracted. There was free bread and all the entertainment you could watch. The coliseums, which held tens of thousands who cheered spectacles of incredible gore and violence, rarely stood empty.

"I find it interesting that the workers in this country are increasingly burdened with taxes that disappear into the coffers of a non-responsive government . . . "

Applause once again rose in the audience.

"At the same time, there are those who have had free bread so long that they expect it. And the entertainment industry, with the government as its happy accomplice, keeps us all hungering for the next installment of blood . . . "

Don stopped and listened to the silence for a moment.

As he spoke the next lines, he said them with all the conviction he possessed. "Are you saying 'ouch' yet? It's time to make some choices, America. It's time to sacrifice some of our pet issues and get back into the mainstream, *while we still have time.*"

The entire audience rose to its feet and applauded.

"Tonight, I propose we start making some of those choices . . . "

By the time he left the platform, Donald Larson Cole knew he had made some headway in his race for the presidency. He knew his speech would strike a chord in the American people, if enough of them heard what he said. He hoped that a sleeping giant—voters who had stayed home for years—could be awakened and would begin to move.

On their way to dinner, Trina noted that Don was unusually quiet. The speech had gone well, and she wondered why he was withdrawn. He was not himself lately.

Usually a good listener, now he was often distracted. Instead of his normal casual confidence, she saw an urgency and intensity in his manner that she hadn't seen before. When she mentioned this to Bob Post, she saw a glimmer of recognition in his eyes. He knew something, but he was not going to tell her what it was. The mystery gnawed at her, but she decided to leave it alone for the time being.

CHAPTER TWENTY-TWO

ANCHORWOMAN SHARON WEBB UPDATED THE TOP-OF-the-hour national news for the Universal Information Group—now the largest news network on the planet. This hour's reports of flooding in the Mississippi River delta had filtered in. Government sources stated that the *El Niño* effect was once again responsible as runoff from heavy snows continued to inundate the population on the river.

Pete Reisling watched the news as he drank his morning juice. His daughter, Sara, had called the night before about a small earthquake she felt just outside of Denver. He focused his attention as he heard the word "Denver."

" . . . while on the campaign trail in Denver yesterday, Donald Larson Cole and his entourage were present for an earth tremor measuring 3.5. No damage was reported from the quake that was felt as far away as Boulder. Mr. Cole, speaking before several thousand campaign workers and enthusiastic voters, mentioned the tremor in his speech. The main focus of the speech, however, was to encourage unity in the American people.

"In other news today," the anchorwoman continued, "President Todd signed into law a bill that set aside more federal lands for the Zero Population Environmental Zones. As he signed the bill, he said that this marked yet another stride his administration has made 'in the battle to save the spaceship we call Earth.' He says he hopes that this law will ensure the sanctity of wilderness in America. At a small reception after the signing, President Todd expressed his thanks to men of vision who have been willing to crusade, at great personal expense, for environmental security in this country and others. The honored guests included the general secretary of the United Nations, Dr. Damiano Polupapolis, and Mr. E. E. Kressman—CEO of our very own Universal Information Group. Both Dr. Polupapolis and Mr. Kressman stated that this was only the beginning of many joint-ventures between business and government worldwide that would benefit the environment."

Pete snapped off the TV. His wife, Naomi, had entered the room and was just sitting down to breakfast.

"So, was there any news on the quake?" she asked.

"Only a brief mention. They spoke more about that Cole guy than the tremor."

Naomi looked concerned. "Do you think we ought to call Sara tonight and make sure she's all right?

"No. We don't want her thinking we still consider her a little girl. If she needs something, she'll call."

CHAPTER TWENTY-THREE

DONALD LARSON COLE GOT INTO THE CAR THAT WOULD take him to the Denver airport. It was 8:00 A.M., and he was tired. He hadn't gotten to bed until 2:00 A.M. and hoped he could get some sleep once on board the plane. Running mate Lawrence Cunningham and Trina Watson rode with him in the vehicle, as well as his press secretary William Costa and his aide, Jason.

"Have you seen the news yet this morning?" Trina asked, looking at Cole.

Lawrence took it upon himself to answer. "Yes. We barely got a mention on Universal, and most of the other networks ignored us altogether."

"Have *you* seen the news yet this morning?" Trina repeated, looking at Cole.

"No. I'm tired. Frankly, if I don't get some uninterrupted sleep soon I think I could turn psychotic!"

Trina quickly looked around and put a hand on top of Cole's. "Don't even *joke* about stuff like that. You know what the tabloids could do to you?"

"It won't be a joke if you don't let me get some shut-eye on that plane today. I'm telling you, keep everyone off me until we get to . . . where are we going?"

"San Diego," Trina and Jason said in unison.

"Great. Wake me when we get there, OK?"

"Well, while you're sleeping, dream about a response to the environmental coup Todd had yesterday. He got two minutes of air time compared to your fifteen seconds. He's got Kressman in his pocket—or vice versa—and you'd better start making some friends in those kinds of places if you want to stay in the race, Don."

"While I'm sleeping, you and Jason here can decide what I think about the environment."

"My, aren't we cranky today?" Lawrence said in a chipper voice.

"May all your stocks crash and burn today, Larry," he said, knowing that Lawrence detested the name *Larry*. "May all your hair fall out, may someone spill Liquid Paper on your wingtips, may . . . "

"Boys! Boys! Do I have to call a mediator?" Trina said. "Gee! Where could we go to get a childproof gate to put between the two of you? Grow up, will ya?"

Cole closed his eyes, slumped down, and leaned his head back. "Yes, Mother."

"I am *not* your mother!"

Cole opened his eyes slightly. "Feeling a little cranky today, are we?"

She gave him the look that said she was close to turning him into ashes.

"Oops," he said and closed his eyes again. Trina's intuition was one of the things that made her so good at her job. Don knew he had to keep her at a distance, or she might figure out more than she should.

He napped on the way to San Diego and managed to smile his way through a luncheon and two quick stops at rallies in his honor. He and Lawrence avoided spending time in any sort of personal conversation and, when they got to the hotel, they went their separate ways for the evening. They would have to be up early the next morning for a full day of campaigning.

Don met with Trina and Jason for a while to work out a few new 'spins' on current speeches, then sat alone in his room and assessed his situation. He had been so sure last night that his speech was stirring enough to garner more air time on television than he got. Perhaps Trina was right and President Todd did have the media in his pocket. Perhaps the visitor on his balcony had been right as well. Maybe no one even considered his candidacy worthy of their attention. Short of the scandal the Quick and the Dead had promised, he couldn't think of anything else he could do or say that might get him out of this rut. It was as if a dark cloud had settled on him. The desire merely to serve his country in the office of president seemed almost childish as the revelation of America's true condition exposed a need greater than he could possibly fill. Even if he won, he now knew he could not single-handedly save the country. But did he even want to consider what might happen if he lost?

CHAPTER TWENTY-FOUR

SARA SAT IN FRONT OF HER SMALL TV EATING A BOWL OF popcorn. She had endured a miserable day at work and wanted to forget it all.

Being a fifth-grade teacher was not always fun, and there were times when she wondered why she wanted to be a teacher at all.

Most of the kids in her class were ten years old. Most were bright and endearing. Most of them. Then there were students like Mickey. She struggled not to think of him as an evil child. Often rebellious and hard to control, Mickey made her not want to touch him. Was it his clammy skin or something else that made him so repellent to her? And he made those weird noises all the time. Not the usual fifth-grade-boy kind of noises, but strange, guttural sounds. It gave her the creeps. She had met his parents on several occasions and found them stiff and unresponsive. Perhaps there was some sort of abuse going on in the home. Until she had definite clues, she could only watch the boy and try to work with him.

But Mickey had been particularly bad that day. The class was just finishing up its holiday decorations for the contest when Mickey decided to throw a whole bottle of poster paint on most of them. She took him to Ms. Baxter's office. Obviously the spring decoration project would not be on time, and she wanted Ms. Baxter to know why.

But when all was said and done, it was not Mickey who had gotten in trouble, but Sara. Ms. Baxter gave Mickey an obtuse little lecture and sent him outside to her secretary's office while she spoke to Sara.

"I suppose you know you have delayed the entire project," Ms. Baxter said.

"I didn't delay anything! That young man threw paint on my class's project! It's not the first time I've had a problem with him. He can be quite incorrigible."

Ms. Baxter busied herself with papers on her desk but kept talking. "Being a teacher means you must be able to control yourself and your students. It's something anyone who wants to stay in this profession learns, Ms. Reisling."

Sara felt the blood rush to her face. "Yes, ma'am."

"As you know, it's time to begin evaluations for next year's positions. In fact, I am looking at your file right now, Ms. Reisling . . . late five times this year . . . "

Sara cringed inwardly but remained silent. The principal continued.

"And I see that you have not committed to Service Affiliation for the Spring Drive. Was this an oversight on your part?"

This was one of Sara's pet peeves. "No, ma'am, it wasn't."

"I thought I made it clear to all my teachers that I require a minimum of a 5 percent pledge to Service Affiliation. This school has always met the 100 percent goal."

"I remember hearing you say that, but I do not believe it is within your authority to decide how I spend my salary or my spare time."

Ms. Baxter thought a moment before replying. "If it's some religious thing for you, there are many projects to which you can donate. Certainly you can't object to things like feeding people or teaching adults to read."

Sara's heart pounded. How dare this woman make it sound as if she were some kind of religious nut who didn't care about people. "That is not the point, Ms. Baxter. I work hard for my money. When I see a charity I would like to support, I give the amount I decide is appropriate."

"You can designate where you want your Service Affiliation to go. You must know that. Why wouldn't you want to help your school?"

"How did this turn into me helping the school? You know and I know that designations are not legally binding anymore, and although the program does do some good things, it also supports many things to which I am totally opposed. *Again*, I agree everyone should give to the poor and needy. But I can do that without the assistance of Service Affiliation and know that *all* of my donation is going where I want."

"So you would let the school miss its goal?"

Sara looked the principal in the eye. "I'm sure the school will get over it."

A few moments passed in silence.

"May I go now?" Sara finally asked.

Ms. Baxter looked up. "There is just one more thing."

"Yes?"

"I believe it was you who asked for clarification on religious displays, wasn't it?"

Sara straightened in her chair. She realized this was not the best time to have this discussion, but since it came up, she would speak her mind. "Yes, it was."

"I have noticed that you always wear that jewelry."

Sara didn't know where Ms. Baxter was heading with the conversation. "And?"

"And, if you would like to wear that necklace, I suggest you keep it inside your blouse."

Sara looked down at the cross around her neck and replied incredulously, "Are you saying I can't wear a *cross* to work?"

"I didn't say you couldn't wear it. I said you should consider not displaying it publicly. I realize it's unintentional on your part, but someone might get the wrong message."

"And what wrong message is *that*, pray tell?"

"Well, you know it has become such a symbol of hate."

"What?"

"You know. They burn them to threaten people."

"You're kidding! Just because somebody stole a symbol of my Lord and used it in such a way doesn't mean I have to relinquish it. This has been a symbol of love and hope for two thousand years. We already gave up the rainbow. God had it first, then New Agers stole it, and now gay people have it! I refuse to give anyone my cross."

"I see. And is this the same love and hope that was offered in the name of your cross during the Crusades?" Ms. Baxter finally said.

"Oh, like you don't know that Adolf Hitler was into eastern mysticism, so it's OK for every one around here to engage in meditation. Like the Chinese never killed anyone, so I could wear a yin/yang thing around my neck." Sara realized she might be going too far, but she was too angry to stop. "How come I could do almost any disgusting thing I wanted under the name of art or culture and that would be acceptable? But this," she said, pointing to her cross, "is offensive. Well, this cross is art to me and it's part of my culture, OK? And I won't take it off."

After a few seconds of silence Sara said, "May I be excused now?"

"By all means."

Sara had returned to her class and had taken her feelings out on the children. Now, as she sat in her living room, the thought of how she had behaved made her cringe. She realized she had let her anger lead her arguments, not the Lord.

The phone rang, jolting her out of her reverie, and she picked it up.

"Hello."

"Hi, Duchess!" It was her father. She was flooded with relief.

"Oh, Daddy, I'm so glad you called."

"What's wrong, Duchess? Another earthquake?"

"Oh, Daddy, I made such a fool out of myself at school today."

"Yeah? What'd you do?"

"It's so embarrassing. I sent a boy to the office and ended up getting in a fight with the principal over a donation to Service Affiliation. Then we got in another one over the cross I was wearing."

"Who won?" He was treating it lightly, but she knew he was trying to comfort her.

"That remains to be seen. I got all tangled up inside, and I said things she is going to use against me for sure."

"Like what?"

"Well, she said the cross was a symbol of hate, and I just lost it. I said that New Age people and gays stole the rainbow, but no one was taking the cross. I said stuff about Adolf Hitler . . . "

"Oh," he said. "And what you said isn't true?"

"Yes, it is, but I presented it all wrong. I let my temper get away with me, and I said everything in such an ugly and sarcastic way. Daddy, there's just something about that woman that really gets my goat. I don't know why I feel that I have to challenge her, but all she has to do is make some remark about my faith and my claws come out. Now she's going to tell everybody I hate New Age people and gays. I can hear it now. I'm sure she has this 'all-ways-lead-to-god' kind of philosophy, and I've rubbed her the wrong way. I stepped right into it."

"You think you should have said nothing?"

"It's not that, Daddy. The point is that I did it in such a snotty way. I tried to pick a fight with her in front of all the teachers last week. I was so proud of myself for standing up to her—like I was some big martyr. Then I went in her office today with an attitude, and she caught me. Now that I've had time to cool off, I realize it was more important to me to score points and express my opinion than to see that she heard about the Lord. I feel really bad about it." Sarah paused as she rested her forehead in her hand, "I thought I was going to go out and kick the devil. All I've done is make a fool of myself. And I'm really sorry I was such a crummy witness."

"You say that to the Lord yet?" her father asked.

"No."

"Don't you think it would be a good idea?"

"Yes."

"It sounds to me like there's a spiritual battle goin' on between you and this woman. You and I both know you won't win in the flesh. You'd better start prayin' God will change your attitude. Remember, you have to have truth *and* mercy around your neck. If you have one and not the other, you will never be effective. Figuring out the proper balance takes a lifetime, so don't quit trying. You know I love you, Duchess."

"I love you too, Daddy."

"Wanna talk to your mom?"

She spent another few minutes on the phone with her mother and felt better afterward. She was blessed to grow up with such nice parents. She didn't realize how blessed she was until she started doing summer youth camps during her college years. When she heard the unimaginable things that happened to some of those kids, she had trouble believing it at first.

That reminded her of Mickey. What was she going to do about him? And what was she going to do about Ms. Baxter? Should she apologize? The thought of having to say she was sorry to that woman made her grind her teeth. If she kept wearing her cross visibly, would it be in faith or in defiance? If she stopped wearing it, would it be a compromise? There were lawyers who specialized in such things. But did she want to make an issue of this?

"O Lord, I've been so foolish. I'm sorry . . . "

CHAPTER TWENTY-FIVE

LUIS KEMP LEANED DOWN AND HELD ON TO HIS BASEBALL cap as he watched the helicopter land on the grass. His denim shirt flapped around his thin torso like a flag in a gale. The skids of the helicopter touched down, and the door opened. A heavyset man in a suit emerged holding a satchel and walked toward Luis. The helicopter's engine began to wind down.

The big man shook his hand. "Nice to see you again, Mr. Kemp."

"Yes," Kemp said nervously. He'd proven he could actually do what they asked. And with the help of only two people. Now that he'd done it, he wasn't completely convinced he wanted to continue.

"How is your wife? And your children?" the man asked.

"I haven't talked to her this week; she thinks I'm working in Mexico. But they were fine the last time we spoke."

They walked a short distance to a small building, but the heavyset man refused to go inside. "We will walk over there in the trees," he said, pointing a fat finger at a small stand of evergreens just below them. They headed for the trees and did not speak again until they were safe within the shadows.

"You think you can actually do it this time?" the man asked.

Kemp's voice cracked a little as he spoke. "Yes, sir. We just need to increase the pressure. I studied all the previous data, and the test went exactly as planned; I don't foresee any problems whatsoever. I've done the math. We have the equipment."

"And you're sure it will work?"

"Absolutely."

The large man handed Kemp his satchel. "You know what to do then."

It was now or never. Luis Kemp had to decide. His two assistants were just young oil rig workers who had no idea what they were doing. They followed Luis's directions for a good hourly wage. Muscles with no brains. They thought they were involved with experiments for the Forestry Department and never connected what they were doing with the tremor in the area. Kemp, on the other hand, knew exactly what he was doing. That's why he was hired. He was a master with computers, mathematics, and drilling equipment who had unorthodox political views and wasn't afraid to bend laws for the right amount of money. With what was in this satchel, he and his family could retire to some remote island or to a spot on the Mediterranean. He'd be set for life. No more moving from place to place. No more taking orders. No more dirty jobs with oil companies. What did he care about all those "urban vermin" in Denver anyway?

"Yes," Kemp said, "we'll get right on it."

"Good."

The two men walked back up the small hill to the helicopter. Kemp held the satchel as he watched the visitor climb back into the chopper and take off.

After they were in the air, the large man got on a secure line and dialed a number. "Yes. This is Yosef. It's done," he said and hung up.

Yosef looked back out the window at the small patch of prairie. The Rocky Mountains rose majestically in the background. *It's a pity to risk losing access to such nice surroundings,* he thought. *But what can be done? If we don't move up the timetable, things might get out of our control. Sacrifices have to be made if the goals are to be achieved, and this might end up being one of the most effective things we have ever done. And at such a small price, really.* He sighed. *If only I could have gone hunting there a few more times. Oh well, maybe in a year or so, if there are no further outbreaks, I can return.* He knew the insidious nature of viruses. They could mutate and survive in unexpected ways. He'd let others go and walk about the place unprotected for quite some time before he returned.

Yosef watched the ground receding and was satisfied this was a good choice. It was as perfect as a man could plan it. He closed his eyes and visualized the scene. Mr. Kemp, who refused to accept an electronic transfer to a Swiss bank account, would have opened the satchel by now, triggering the release of the virus. Yes, his suspicious nature would compel him to go to his room and count all of the money. Soon after that, the illness would begin to explode in his system. Unaware that he'd been infected, he would go and turn on the equipment. Even as the first stages of the virus began working on him, he would be able to move, think, and give orders to his assistants. Then, Kemp would infect both of them by coughing on them for several hours. In about twelve hours, he would be unconscious. By morning, his assistants would feel ill but would be at the second location, unaware of Kemp's condition. By the time they realized how sick they were, they would be unable to flee the area. They might still be awake for the event, but Mr. Kemp would most likely be dead by the time it struck. The satchel, the money (most of which was counterfeit), and any other evidence left behind would be properly disposed of prior to the discovery of the bodies. There would be so much chaos after that, who would ever figure it all out?

CHAPTER TWENTY-SIX

DONALD LARSON COLE LEANED BACK IN THE VEHICLE. They were running late for his scheduled speech at an Oakland auditorium, and the driver pressed the gas pedal with a heavy foot to make up for lost time. The fact that they had a police escort, which could stop traffic for them, helped. He could get to like this.

Bob Post and Trina Watson followed in the car behind him. He and Lawrence Cunningham rode together with no other passengers. It was important they be seen together after rumors that they were on the verge of parting ways had circulated. Later, Don would dine with Lawrence and his wife, Diana, at an exclusive L.A. restaurant.

They did dislike each other; that part was true, but there were no serious considerations of a split by either Don or Lawrence. They knew that to split would be to lose the White House for the whole party, not just for themselves. Neither was foolish enough to think they would survive such a thing and stay in politics. Each would have to be more cautious about the way they spoke about (and to) one another. They couldn't afford to get derailed over such a petty issue as personality differences.

Lawrence looked out the window and waved.

"So," Cole said, trying to make idle conversation, "you ready for dinner tonight?"

Lawrence kept looking out the window. "Diana is looking forward to it. We haven't seen each other in two weeks. She could use an outing."

"Have you decided to meet her at the airport or at the hotel?"

"I told Avery and the Secret Service guys last night I'd like to go pick her up. They're making the arrangements for me to be able to get her on the ramp."

A Secret Service agent sat facing them in the vehicle, but he was trained to say nothing unless he was addressed.

"Great. Six o'clock then."

"Yes."

They finished the ride in silence. Occasionally, they leaned forward and waved to the crowds as they moved along.

When they arrived at the auditorium, instead of entering the room on the platform, they had decided to work the crowd. Although it would be a logistical nightmare for the agents assigned to them, Don and Lawrence knew it was a necessary move. They would enter the room together, split up and shake hands as they walked down two different isles, then meet at the platform. More personal contact was needed, so they decided the benefit outweighed the risks. Don was grateful that Lawrence hadn't opted for safety.

They entered the auditorium and split forces. Don started working his way down the left-hand aisle. Hundreds of people packed up close to get a handshake or an acknowledgment from him. He smiled his best smile and pumped as many hands as he could grab.

About midway down the isle, a small, middle-aged man grabbed his hand and squeezed it.

The man's expression was quite calm, and he leaned forward to speak. "You met my friend in Seattle one night, remember?" the man said, just loud enough to be heard over the din.

Don knew instantly the man meant his visitor on the balcony, and he stepped closer as he replied, "Yes, I remember."

"He asked me to give you an urgent message." The man eased his grip.

Don leaned forward and barely heard him say, "You need to read the Bible more often." Don pulled back and looked at him as if to say, *That's all?*

The man let go of his hand, and Don was pressed down the aisle in a wave of people.

Soon he stood on the platform and heard himself being introduced as "the next president of the United States." As he stood at the podium, he tried to locate the man who had spoken to him. It was impossible in the sea of faces out there. Though a little shaken, he managed to get through his speech without any mistakes.

Obviously the man who spoke to him was part of the Quick and the Dead, but what was he saying? Some cryptic religious message? Were they Christian extremists? Later, Don sat in his room later and wondered what to do about it. He had been unable to speak to Bob Post alone that afternoon. Bob had been trying to track down a source to check the weapons aspect of the information on the disk Don was given that night. So far, he'd encountered only dead-ends.

Don finally decided on a quick nap. He'd managed to get caught up on his rest and wanted to keep his energy level going. He lay down on the bed but couldn't sleep. *I ought to read the Bible more,* he thought.

He suddenly remembered that there was a Bible in every hotel room in America. He sat up and opened the nightstand drawer. There it was. A Bible. He flipped through the pages looking for a piece of paper or envelope. Nothing. He tried opening the book where the marker ribbon had been placed. It was in 2 Timothy at the end of chapter 3 and the beginning of chapter 4. He read without much interest until he came to the first verse of chapter 4 and the succeeding verses.

> I charge thee therefore before God, and the Lord Jesus Christ, who shall judge the quick and the dead at his appearing and his kingdom; preach the word; be instant in season, out of season; reprove, rebuke, exhort with all longsuffering and doctrine. For the time will come when they will not endure sound doctrine; but after their own lusts shall they heap to themselves teachers, having itching ears; and they shall turn away their ears from the truth, and shall be turned unto fables.

But what did that mean? He had no idea. He read it again, then noticed something about the ribbon marking the place in the book. A small arrow in the middle of the ribbon pointed toward the loose end. The arrow was visible on both sides of the ribbon, pointing in the same direction. Don flipped the ribbon up out of the pages. He picked up the end of the ribbon and pulled the way the arrow pointed. It was then that he realized the ribbon was not attached to the Bible, but to a piece of cardboard the size of a bookmark in the binding. He pulled the ribbon straight up, and the cardboard popped out with it. There was small writing on it. Don turned on the light and leaned forward to read.

"Sorry to contact you this way, but low-tech, long-distance is best. Remain quiet. Sound may be on, but there are no cameras. Disk is a no-go for now. Info leaked. Items in video on way back home. Retaliation imminent. Watch for news of Africa. Game not over, just delayed. Post OK. No one else! Your friend from Seattle."

Don folded the cardboard in half and stuck it in his pocket. He picked up his phone and rang Bob Post's room.

"Hello?"

"Bob, it's me, Don. Listen, something just occurred to me. Could you come right up?"

"Well, is it urgent? I was about to grab a bite."

"Just come up when you can, Bob." Don tried to sound casual. "I'm not leaving here until 5:30."

"All right."

Don hung up the phone and lay back down on the bed. It wasn't five minutes before he heard a knock at the door. Sure enough, when he opened the door, there was his campaign manager with a quizzical look on his face.

"Anything going on?" he asked after the door closed.

Don held a finger up to his mouth to signal Bob and said, "Well, I was just thinking, if we promised to look over some of the trade agreements once we were in office, wouldn't that help us with the Small Business Coalition?" While he was talking, he took the cardboard out of his pocket and handed it to Bob. "Just sit here a minute and listen before you say anything. Hear me out, OK?"

"OK," Bob said as he read and reread the note while Don rambled on about trade agreements for a minute. When he looked up, Don knew he was finished.

"So what do you think, Bob? Couldn't we do some brainstorming next week and come up with a better grip on these issues?"

"Gee, Don, I'd have to give it some thought, but yeah, I'm sure we could come up with something."

"I think you should still get your research together if you can, but come to the table prepared for some new thoughts."

"Fine," Bob said as he handed the marker back to Don. "Anything else?"

"No. I just wanted to speak to you while I was thinking about it. Maybe we'll talk again after dinner."

"Fine."

CHAPTER TWENTY-SEVEN

As Sara Reisling erased the chalkboard, the bell rang for recess. She turned and told the children they were dismissed. They bolted from their chairs, down the hall, and out to the playground. It was a crisp, bright day outside, and the students were anxious to enjoy it. The Denver nights were still cold this time of year, but as they worked their way toward summer, the days grew sporadically warmer.

She had gone home to visit during spring break and thoroughly enjoyed spending time with her parents and her younger sister, Noel. She didn't have the joy returning to school that she did when she first started. Now Sara was trying to get into the rhythm of things in her classroom, but her heart wasn't in it.

A few days after their argument, she had made an appointment with Ms. Baxter and apologized for her attitude. It was one of the hardest things she had ever done. She made up her mind that she would continue wearing her cross on the outside, and she would not make a donation to Service Affiliation, but she would tell the principal she was sorry for her poor attitude and sarcastic remarks. She vowed not to let herself be baited into another argument or to make any excuses. True, Ms. Baxter had been intimidating, threatening, and rude. But Sara was not responsible for the other woman's behavior. She was only responsible for her own. She prayed for the strength not to blow it and lose her temper. She felt sick the day of the appointment, but she pressed in and went anyway. When she apologized, Ms. Baxter seemed genuinely surprised, but remained cool. Sara was disappointed. She had hoped for better results.

"What'd you expect, Duchess?" her father said when she called and told him.

"I don't know. Some sort of breakthrough...that she wouldn't hate me."

"But that's not why you apologized, is it?"

"No."

"Well, I guess you'll just have to be satisfied with the fact you were obedient and thankful God changed *your* heart."

Even now, when she thought of it, she sighed. She wasn't certain the school would rehire her for next year. And if they offered, she didn't know if she wanted to come back. She had applied several other places, but she had not made up her mind yet about what she would do. Things were more difficult than she had planned.

The bell ending the recess period sounded, and she sighed again as she looked at the clock. Only one more hour, and she could go home for the day.

The children returned to the classroom and settled into their desks. In a few moments, they were quiet. Sara had earned their respect. She could speak to them quietly and they would listen, with the exception of Mickey, who, thankfully, was relatively calm today. *Maybe his mother gave him an extra dose of tranquilizer this morning,* Sara thought.

"This afternoon, we are going to begin our book reports, so I want the students in this row to my left to get out their papers."

The children started locating their papers, several others raised their hands, and two boys in the back whispered back and forth.

"Chet, Franklin, this is not the time to . . . " She stopped at the sound of a low rumble. She put up her hands for absolute silence and listened as it grew louder. "Everyone, listen to me! Quickly now! I want all of you to move your chairs and get under your desks! Now!"

The windows started rattling as she shouted commands to the children. "Stay under your desks no matter what! Robert! Get away from the windows! Get under that desk! Yes, now stay there!"

With the last words barely out of her mouth, she began to feel the ground under her move violently. Sara dove under her own desk. First the movement was a shuddering sensation, then it began to have an ocean-like feel, rising and falling in bigger and bigger waves as the windows shattered, the ceiling buckled, and the walls cracked and fell.

Sara waited for it to stop. She could hear children screaming but could no longer see them. Her desk was moving about like a ship in a heavy swell. The drawers flew out and one of them hit her on the leg. She pulled herself up tighter under the desk. The music room above collapsed into Sara's room, burying them in concrete, steel, and insulation. The ground continued to move with increasing violence, causing huge cracks to ripple through the floor as it undulated.

After an eternity of one minute and seventeen seconds, the quake stopped.

CHAPTER TWENTY-EIGHT

PRESIDENT SONNY TODD STOPPED AND LISTENED TO HIS favorite part of the music coming over the speakers. He loved classical music. Whenever he felt burdened, he could stop wherever he was—whether in the Oval Office, his private quarters, or this workshop—and listen to the music. It always relaxed and inspired him.

His favorite section passed, and he returned to the task at hand. He had been away from the project for so long that he needed to study it for a moment to reorient himself. He picked up the frame of the wing on the model plane he was building and inspected it. One of the wing spars hadn't been glued properly and would have to be fixed.

It was going to be a day that changed the history of the world, and the president was taking a vacation day at Camp David. Almost as soon as he'd arrived, Sonny headed for the workshop set up for him and began to work on the model airplane he had started when he'd only been in office for a month. Looking at the plane now, he wondered if he'd ever finish it. There were just too many other things to do these days.

The plans, which were intended for a much later time, would be put into action today. He realized now that Secretary of Defense Ernie Schollet was right. Hesitation on their part would certainly bring their demise. What they were about to do now, they did for the greater good and the long-term plan.

Sonny turned up the music. Soon they would be coming to tell him, and he didn't want to think of it just now. He wanted to work on his model and be filled with the beautiful sounds of the orchestra. He heard the sound of the door and jumped.

It was his daughter, Lorraine. Now, at twenty, she lived on her own, but she had come to Camp David with them at her mother's request. "I'm sorry, Dad. I didn't mean to startle you."

He smiled and turned down the music. "Hi! I was just lost in thought, that's all. What are you up to?"

"Mom is taking a nap, so I thought I'd come out and see what you were doing. I see you still haven't finished it," she said as she eyed the plane parts.

"Oh. No, I don't seem to get time to work on it anymore."

Lorraine sensed he wanted to be alone. "Well, you just go ahead and work on it then, and maybe we can all play a game or something later. OK?"

"Sure, sweetheart," he said, giving her a squeeze. He loved his daughter, but he couldn't bear to be in her presence just now. "We'll play a game later," he lied. He knew that within hours they would be on their way back to Washington after receiving the news.

His daughter left the workshop, and he let out a sigh. He turned back to the bench and placed both hands on it. *This is no time to fall apart,* he thought, and took some deep breaths. *In a few moments, this will pass.* He turned up the music again and put everything but its resonant sound out of his mind.

CHAPTER TWENTY-NINE

THE SHAKING FINALLY STOPPED, BUT SARA COULDN'T open her eyes yet. A choking dust clouded the air. Over the sound of her own coughing, she could hear the sounds of children coughing and crying. She also thought she could hear a woman shouting, but she wasn't sure. Everything seemed so distorted.

Finally she opened her eyes. It was dark, and she realized that they were under so much rubble that the light of the sun couldn't penetrate it.

"Can you guys hear me?" she asked. "This is Miss Reisling. Can anyone hear me?" Finally, she heard a small voice.

"Yes."

"Who's that?"

"Clois."

"Are you OK?"

"I'm scared," the little girl said and started to cry.

"You're going to be just fine, Clois. Can anyone else hear me? Hello?" Sara began to speak louder. "Can anyone hear me?"

Some of the sounds of crying and coughing stopped as a few children responded.

"OK now," Sara said as she groped around for any means of escape, "I want each of you to say your name, because I can't see you, OK?"

She heard from five children who were near enough to hear her. One by one she asked each child to call out and see if they could find anyone else who wasn't in the original group of five. They located four more children. Not even a third of her class. Three of the children thought they had something broken and were crying. All of them were trapped, and she repeatedly told them not to push or pull on anything or try to move around. She feared they might dislodge something and be killed by falling debris.

Sara knew the school was one of the first places rescue workers would come. Regardless of the situation, every able-bodied parent would be there digging and enlisting help in locating their children. But how much else was damaged out there? Could rescue crews and parents even get to the school? She couldn't allow herself to think of being trapped for an extended period of time. She had to believe that, somehow, help was on the way, and she prayed they got to the school before nightfall. The temperature would drop quickly once the sun set. How long could the children last in the cold?

"O Lord, Your Word says that we should give thanks in all things. I thank You, Lord, that we have survived this earthquake. I give You honor as the only God who helps the weak and the poor. More than that, You are my Father. Help us, Father. Send angels, if necessary, to provide for us. Be with these children and the others who have survived. Be our ever-present help in time of trouble. . . . "

CHAPTER THIRTY

MARTHA HINKLE TYPED UP THE DATA AS FAST AS HER FIN-gers could fly. A news flash had just come over the wire, and she worked frantically to get it into the teleprompter. A major earthquake had just struck the Denver metropolitan area, and early reports claimed there were going to be large numbers of casualties. Universal Information Group would be the first to get it on the air, and Martha's boss hoped to be the first with live, on-the-scene coverage. They had already chartered a jet and were working on several other options. While the news anchors sat calmly in front of the cameras, a storm of activity overtook the entire news center.

Jeff Lutz faced camera one and received his cue. "This is just in: UIG is receiving confirmed reports of a major earthquake that struck the Denver area about ten minutes ago. Accounts of widespread structural damage and possible heavy casualties are flooding into our news complex. We are going to break for a quick word from our sponsors, and then we will be back, waiting to go live as soon as possible. When we get an uplink with Denver, we will stay on the air without commercial interruption. This is Jeff Lutz for UIG."

Bob Post sat in Sacramento, waiting to catch the day's headlines. He had scheduled a roundtable discussion with campaign workers for later that evening and wanted to see if there were any developments in President Todd's campaign that they should take into account. A few days earlier, he and Don had noted with great interest a small blurb about the outbreak of a deadly virus in a small country in southern Africa. In order to prevent the virus from being carried throughout the region, a quarantine had been put into place there and in several surrounding countries where international troops were present to prevent rebel insurgencies. Travel into and out of the area was forbidden until the international community was sure all danger was past.

But today must have been a slow news day. There were stories about some horse trapped in a canyon and another story about a grocery store manager who found a Rolex and returned it. Bob had nearly dozed off in his chair when he heard something that caused him to wake up. An earthquake had struck Denver!

As UIG went to commercials, he flipped through the channels to see if anyone else was reporting it. After another minute, one other network was saying the same thing. He went back to UIG. Jeff Lutz and Sharon Webb were back. He turned up the volume, ran to the phone, and called Don's room.

"Yeah, Don. Put your TV on UIG! A major earthquake just hit Denver! I'm going to call Trina, and then I'll call you back."

Don went to the television and turned it on. He found the channel he was looking for after a few moments.

There were no pictures yet, but the reports of the quake were widespread. Don thought for a moment about the tremor he had felt when he was there just a few days ago. The network managed to get a call from a woman in an outlying area. She was on a cell phone. Don listened as she spoke.

"And you say, Mrs. Anderson, you're how far from Denver?"

"About fifty miles. About an hour's drive."

"And what does it look like where you are?" Lutz asked.

"Well, our house is a wreck, but it's still standing. Our stuff is thrown all over the floor. Our barn is tilting, too. Everything moved around and, uh . . . "

"I hate to interrupt you, Mrs. Anderson," Sharon Webb said, "but are you able to pick up any local reports about what Denver is like?"

"My husband is a ham radio operator, and he is already hearing from people that buildings everywhere have collapsed."

Don's phone rang again, and he picked it up. "Hello?"

It was Bob. "You watching it?"

"Yes. You get hold of Trina?"

"Yeah. And she's going to call Lawrence and the others."

"Think we'd better move the meeting up a little?"

"Definitely," Bob said. "The press will want any comments we have, so we'd better have one."

"How about three o'clock? Check and see if we can get the conference room in the hotel then. If not, we can meet up here in my suite."

"Done. I'll get back to you."

Don hung up the phone and turned up the TV.

Jeff Lutz was talking to someone at the National Earthquake Information Center.

"And you estimate this quake to be of what magnitude?"

"Unofficially, we are calling it a 7.9."

Don whistled. He was no expert, but even he knew anything above a 6.5 was bad.

Lutz continued the televised interview. "And what can be expected, Dr. Brenner, in a 7.9 quake?"

"You will see the total collapse of many structures. Most structures will have sustained damage. Massive destruction. The only bright spot is that Denver itself has many open areas, even downtown, so there will be places for people to get out from under buildings and stay safe in any aftershocks."

"Do you expect aftershocks?"

"Yes."

In Texas, Sara's father, Peter Reisling, had been at work when his wife, Naomi, called to tell him the news. He had rushed home, listening to the radio in the car the entire way. He couldn't believe what he was hearing.

Naomi had tried to call Sara's landlady and found (as everyone else had) that all the lines were down. All they could do was pray their daughter was safe somewhere. Even if Sara was safe, they had no way of knowing.

Within an hour, President Todd was holding a press conference to give a preliminary report on the quake and the government's response to it.

Within three hours, Peter Reisling and three other men were in a van full of equipment headed for Denver. He didn't know if they would be permitted into the area, but they would try. He and the others had been volunteer firemen for many years, so they had considerable rescue experience.

Sara's mother, Naomi, stayed home with their other daughter, Noel. She had gathered a group of women from church; they would pray around the clock until they had word.

Hours later in Sacramento, Don Cole sat in his suite while waiting to be taken to the airport. He would catch the next available flight to Colorado Springs, where he would then hop on a chartered helicopter to Denver. He felt a strange mixture of excitement and fear. He knew he must go to Denver, but by doing so he would be placing himself in peril. It could be the turning point in the race for the presidency, his only opportunity to win on his own merit and not by default.

He switched on the TV and surfed through the channels to see if there was anything new to report. Most of the channels continued to air the same video and repeated what was already known, showing clips of the news conference President Todd had given hours after the quake. As the different stations flipped past his view, he thought it remarkable there were still cartoons playing, and old movies and sitcoms. No matter what happened, the "idiot box" was still there to entertain. He wondered how long the signals would continue after all life had perished. Something on the screen caught his eye, and he switched back to it.

It was a Christian station—one he was sure nobody watched while anyone else was looking. One of those things you sneaked a look at when you couldn't sleep at 2:00 A.M. He had to admit to having done it himself. Sometimes it was interesting; other times it seemed just plain silly, but he'd seen the guy on the screen, Mark Rendell, a couple of times and liked him, so he decided to stop and listen. For a moment he wondered if his room was bugged and what they would think of him for watching the program. Then he thought, *Maybe Todd could use a good sermon about now.* He turned up the volume.

" . . . and in light of current events, what would you say, Rod? You think the Lord is coming back soon?"

A man sitting next to Mark in the studio answered, "He could come anytime. If you look at what is going on

in the Middle East, the signs and wonders, and now all
the natural disasters, you have to know the time is close,"
Rod Keach said, and then he looked right at the camera.
"I'm telling you, folks, you need to see what's happening
here. God is fixing to do something. He's going to send
His Son to rapture the church, the true believers from the
face of the earth, and you don't want to get left behind!
The Bible says that He's going to come like a thief in the
night and take us away. Trust me, you don't want to be
left here and suffer what's going to happen after that. I'm
telling you *tonight,* ladies and gentlemen, that you want
to go out of here on the *first* bus! And you can get that
guarantee tonight, you can get that ticket, if you simply
ask Jesus into your heart.

"Nothing else will qualify you for heaven. There's no
work you can do, no test you can take, no amount of
money you can pay that will get you on that bus. Only
belief in Jesus as your Lord. It's the promise to the
church—it's our blessed hope—to be on that first
bus. . . . And if you have any thoughts that you want to
wait and see, well, go take a look in the Book of
Revelation. There's not anything in there *I* want to be
around for . . . "

Could he be right? Don thought. *And most people have
no idea just how out of control things have gotten. Are all
these things signs that Jesus is returning? Haven't people
said this before?* The man said you needed only to have
accepted Jesus as your Lord, and Don had done that as a
kid. Was that all that was needed? Don certainly didn't
feel that he had a ticket on any bus.

A knock came at the door, and he snapped off the TV
before answering it. Avery and the others were waiting to
go with him to the airport. They picked up his bags and
left.

CHAPTER THIRTY-ONE

DURING HIS FIRST POST-QUAKE NEWS CONFERENCE, GIVEN within two hours of the quake, President Todd made general remarks about the earthquake: its size, the first reports of damage, what branches of the government would be involved in rescue and aid efforts, and so forth.

Then a second news conference was called. It had been eleven hours since the disaster, and President Todd had made no further comments since the initial news conference. As reporters from networks around the world gathered once again in the room where they would be briefed, officials informed them that the press conference would be delayed for one hour. But when he arrived, the president would be making an announcement of a serious nature regarding the *origins* of the quake. This tantalizing tidbit rated as top-story material to keep the world on the edge of its seat for another hour as the limited video footage of Denver was played over and over.

When Todd entered the room with a small entourage consisting of the vice president, Cabinet members, and others, all eyes were fixed on him. He looked like someone who had been making tough decisions all night. The strain showed around his eyes and mouth.

The press secretary announced that President Todd would make a statement, but no questions would be entertained at this time. Further news conferences would be held as more information could be released.

The president of the United States stepped to the microphone.

"Men and women of America, I come to you today with disturbing news. We all know of the tragic earthquake that struck the Denver area yesterday. Reports of casualties and damage continue to flood into our Disaster Office even as I speak.

"But I have not come today to discuss the damage done by the quake. I come to you today, fellow Americans, with news of a most alarming nature. It has been revealed that a small, insurgent group may be responsible for actually triggering the earthquake.

"Intelligence brought to me just hours ago has shown that technology—not tectonics—may have been behind the Denver earthquake. The reasons why this city was targeted will be given in the days to come. I want to stress that if this was done, it was a deliberate act of terrorism. We would have to look back as far as Pearl Harbor to find an act of infamy equal to this on American soil—an act that shall not go unpunished.

"For security reasons, I will not give all of the details now, but I make this announcement with a twofold purpose. First, by revealing this limited information, I hope to enlist the help of the American people in finding and bringing to justice this group and all of its participating members. A toll-free number will appear on your screen during this press conference and will be broadcast frequently in the days to come. This will be a hot line for any tips about the quake or militant groups that may have carried this out.

"The second purpose of this announcement is to inform the American people that as of midnight, I assumed authority under the Presidential Emergency Act. Under the provisions of this Act, I have powers, for a limited time, to act quickly and decisively against any threat to or enemy of the United States government, its agencies, or its people. Within thirty days, I hope to have a full report to give to you, the American people, and be close enough to solutions that an extension of the Presidential Emergency Act will not be needed.

"I have placed our military on full alert, and I will expect the cooperation of every citizen in this country. Anyone suspected of participating in the criminal activities of these groups will be arrested and detained pending a hearing to determine if such individual should be held over for trial. Charges may also be brought against any individual who fails to cooperate with any investigation into this matter.

"I have just left a meeting with the leaders of both houses of Congress and have been assured of their full support. I would ask now," the president said, looking directly into the cameras, "that you, the American people, would join with us in this, the darkest of hours, and work to see these criminals brought to justice. The blood of innocent men, women, and children is on the hands of all who let this pass without retribution. Swift action is needed if we are going to put an end to acts of cowardice such as this."

When news of the president's conference reached Don Cole, in midflight to Colorado Springs, he knew he and Bob Post were going to need a long talk. Could the Quick and the Dead have done this? Or was this a move by Todd to cut off all attacks against him? Given the paranoia his announcement would generate, he would probably get enough tips to shut down half of the paramilitary groups in America and have the rest running for cover. With his newly acquired powers, Todd could have virtually anyone who was suspicious slammed into jail. This mode of ridding oneself of opposition was a time-honored tradition in many other countries . . . but in America?

If he had not seen the contents of that disk, Don would be more willing to believe it was the Quick and the Dead or some such group. But he *did* see the disk, and it made him almost certain that Todd was lying. What could he do? Just by virtue of the fact he had that disk and the cardboard bookmark, could *he* be accused of being a co-conspirator? Could someone *really* have caused this quake? Was that even possible?

The visitor on his balcony had been right—this country was indeed in serious trouble. If Todd was that desperate to take control, that evil, and had that much power at his command, was there any hope that America could be pulled back from his grasp?

Another frightening prospect suddenly loomed in Don's mind. What if some of the militant groups saw this as a challenge to battle? Would they run to capture the red flag Todd was now waving?

God, he prayed silently, *I've never even thought to ask for this before, but if ever we needed Your help, it's now.*

CHAPTER THIRTY-TWO

TWENTY HOURS HAD PASSED SINCE THE EARTHQUAKE struck Denver. There had been two aftershocks. One had measured 5.3 on the Richter scale; the other, a 4.9. Some further damage to structures had been reported, but it was not known if there were any new casualties.

Peter Reisling, Curt Smith, Trever Hobbs, and Aaron Heflin slowly worked their way to the area where Sara's school stood. They had taken turns and driven around the clock until they arrived. Just before they reached the Denver area, Pete used a mobile phone to call home to Naomi. They weren't sure the phone would work once they got inside, if many antennae were down. They were hoping to hear that Sara had gotten out of the area and called home, but this was not the case. First they would try Sara's house, then her school.

Given the magnitude of the event and the news coverage, they were shocked at the lack of security they encountered. They drove, relatively unhindered, right into the area. A state trooper stopped them at one point, but he allowed them to continue once they showed their driver's licenses, badges, and equipment.

When Sara moved to Denver, Pete had helped bring her belongings and get her situated. Finding her house this time was much slower going. Several streets were impassable, so they had to do a lot of detouring and backtracking. When they finally arrived, they found Sara's home had collapsed. Most of the people in the neighborhood knew each other and had actively searched for one another. A neighbor said the old woman had been found in the rubble, slightly injured. She was down the street, staying with friends. It was believed Sara had been at school. None of them had seen her.

Pete and the others found Mrs. Mueller down the street and verified that Sara had been at school at the time of the quake.

By the time they managed to go the last mile to Holmon Elementary School, another precious hour had gone by. Pete was grateful that Naomi hadn't come. The school had been knocked flat. He would not leave until his daughter was found, but when he saw it, he had to admit his hopes of finding her alive were very small indeed.

One hundred fifteen adults and children had been pulled alive from the building thus far. Seventy-seven bodies had been found. Fortunately, most of the school was one story, so the victims were not buried too deeply. Only one part of the school had two stories. A combination meeting and music room had been added above three classrooms several years ago. This would be the most difficult area in which to work.

Pete decided to start digging wherever they told him. If they had already pulled Sara from the building—alive or dead—there was nothing more he could do for her. If she was still in there, he didn't want to waste precious time looking at bodies or finding where they took survivors.

He was glad to see someone had already organized a systematic search of the building. People had been everywhere inside when it fell, and time was of the essence. Those alive in the rubble had already endured one cold night. Minutes could make the difference. Once it got cold again, the ability of those under the rubble to stay alive would drop dramatically.

Since they had more experience than most of the people on the scene thus far, Pete and the men with him were put where the two-story part had been. His spirits rallied somewhat when a man whose daughter still had not been found showed up at the scene with equipment that would make a big difference in their efforts. The man owned a construction company and had generators, high-powered lights, heaters, blowers, and a small tractor they could use, in addition to a truck full of the fuel it would take to power them. It had taken him a full day to get them the three miles from where they were stored to the school. He also had flags they could use for signaling, helmets, gloves, rakes, shovels, pry bars—almost anything they would need. As they unloaded the equipment and began to form teams of workers, Pete introduced himself to the man.

"My name is Pete," he said as he shook the man's hand. "We're so grateful you've come with this equipment, I can't tell you."

"Carlos Hernandez," the man said in a shaky voice, and then nodded toward the building. "My daughter is in there." He pointed to a particular location and added, "Under the worst part. All the kids from two classes and their teachers are still in there. Let's go."

"My daughter is a teacher here," Pete said, "and she may be in there, too. I'll show you where we need to start, and you can decide where you want the equipment."

They worked out a system of two teams to start on either side of the mountain of rubble. If they needed to cut through any steel or move any large pieces, now they could do it. Once it got dark, they would use the generators on an alternating system. They would be on for a while, then shut off for a few minutes of silence to enable them to hear any one below. If quiet was needed at any time, people with flags could signal for it. Meanwhile, most of the rubble would be moved by hand, piece by piece, handed down a line of volunteers, thrown into wheelbarrows, and carted off.

Across the city, Donald Cole stood with the others as plans were made for digging out a nursing home. He had arrived in Denver earlier that day and had been taken to several locations. The first two, a shopping mall and an apartment complex, had many volunteers laboring to remove debris and locate victims. The nursing home, however, was short of laborers, and Don wanted to stay and help.

Against their recommendations, Cole released his Secret Service agents from responsibility for his protection before he got on the plane to Colorado. He tried to do the same with Avery, but his faithful bodyguard, who had no family and said he *wanted* to go to Denver, wouldn't hear of it.

Now Cole and Avery stood in front of the fallen building. There were only a few hours of daylight left, and it would get cold as soon as the sun set. Many of the frail, elderly people trapped inside needed medication, such as insulin, to stay alive. Workers had been moving rubble as fast as they could, but they were forced to stop when they ran into problems. Several unstable spots were located in what remained of the three-story structure. They would have to stabilize or dismantle those portions before they could dig much further. Equipment was minimal, so they were open to creative options. Don knew nothing about physics, engineering, or mechanical advantages, so he just listened.

When they had finished making plans, Don looked at the muscular man standing to his left. "You have any idea what they're talking about?"

"Nope. I just came to help."

"Same for us," Don said. "I'm Don. He's Avery."

"We all kind of figured out who you are," the man said as he stuck out his hand. "My name's Josh."

Ted Sorrenson, who appeared to be in charge of the rescue efforts, held up his hands for everyone's attention. "Listen up. We've got some ideas here, but there are no guarantees. If there are any more aftershocks—and maybe even without any—there could be further collapses in the building. I want everyone who goes inside to understand this. You *could* get buried in there. I know some of you are here to help, but maybe have no skills, *per se*. *Please,* don't move things without asking first or being told to do so. If you injure yourself or others, we're losing time and workers, so *be careful*. Watch where you step, look up, down, and around as you move about. If you are unsure about something, ask for advice. Stay with a partner. And one last thing. I hate to say this, but we're sure to find more dead people in there. Tomorrow, they'll probably start to smell. If you don't think you can handle it, nobody is going to call you a coward. You can still play an important role in this by being one of the workers that hauls rubble outside the building. If you still want to go in there, we'll take all the help we can get. Those who are willing to go inside, step over here," Ted said, pointing to his right.

Eleven volunteers stepped forward to join Ted. After more warnings and instructions, they divided into two groups of six. Avery, Don, and Josh were in Ted's group. Under his direction, they worked on supports and pulled one large, dangling piece down with chains, ropes, and a car. Once that was accomplished, the volunteers were split up into teams of two and given places to begin digging. If they found any victims, they were to call out and get more help. Two nurses among the volunteers would try to assess medical needs of victims prior to moving them.

Military personnel had come by to let them know a field hospital was being set up nearby and that a bulldozer would be clearing any debris from the roads leading to it. The injured could be transported to this location for treatment. The soldiers gave out some emergency rations and a few blankets. Within hours, they hoped to have more supplies available to the public. Their first priorities were to secure the area, deliver supplies, and clear the roadways. They would not be able to help with rescue efforts at this time, but when more troops arrived, they would assist with rescue efforts.

In the meantime, Don and Avery dug at a spot on the southwest corner of the building, which was twenty feet off the ground. They had been told to carefully remove any loose pieces they could lift and toss them down to the ground, where others would haul them away. They had only been at it for twenty minutes when an aftershock rocked the building.

"Everyone out, out, *out!*" Ted shouted. "Get out of the building!"

Don and Avery froze for a moment as the ground rumbled. "Let's go!" Avery said, and they made a run for the ladder they had climbed to get there.

Don got to the ladder first but stopped short as he saw it fall away from the building and bounce to the side. He turned to Avery. "I don't think we're going to get down from here."

The rubble under their feet began shifting, and they sat down to keep from falling down. Don felt as if he were on some sort of ride. Thoughts leaped through his brain. *Why did I come up here? What a stupid thing to do! I'm going to die up here!* The whole pile they were sitting on swayed. He looked at Avery and saw what was probably a reflection of his own expression—panic. The sensation of the fingers on his left hand being crushed between two bricks brought him to his senses. He yanked his hand up.

The shaking decreased, and the sound subsided. It grew quiet again.

Avery and Don sat stunned as dust rose in a cloud throughout the area and enveloped them.

"Anybody hurt?" someone below shouted.

"You OK?" Don finally asked Avery.

"Yeah. You?"

"Mostly," he said, shaking his left hand and then flexing it. "I sure thought we were goners there for a second, though."

"Me, too."

"Anybody hurt?" someone shouted again. "Everyone all right?"

Don leaned to look over the edge. "There are two of us up here. We're not hurt, but we lost our ladder." He looked back at Avery. "Want to leave? I'm shook up, but I think I'll be OK in a minute. I'll try to stay. What about you?"

"Same here. But ask me again in a minute."

"Look! Look!" a man below yelled.

Don and Avery both peeked over the edge. The man was pointing to the interior of the building, so they moved around and looked. A small woman in a nurse's uniform covered with dirt and dried blood staggered out of a dust cloud in the center of the building. The tremor had shaken the spot where she was trapped and set her free.

As the man approached her, she ran a hand through her matted hair, knocking off a dirty cap. She said, "You know, you really shouldn't be here. It's past visiting hours. . . . I have medications to deliver. Do you know where they are?" Her eyes had a glazed expression.

The man and several others reached her. "I'm sorry," he said. "I think the medicine is outside. Do you want to come with me to see where they put it?" He put an arm around her and helped her walk through the rubble.

Don and Avery looked at each other again. Obviously, there were still people buried alive here. They started moving rubble again. Within a few minutes, Don located someone. At first, all he saw was a wrinkled hand. When he felt the wrist, he got a pulse. Avery called down for a nurse and then returned to help dig out an elderly man who had been sitting in a chair next to his wife's bed when the earthquake struck. He was lying on the floor with the chair squashed flat under him.

The old man opened his eyes and looked at Don. "What happened? Where's Emma?" he asked.

"There's been an earthquake. The building collapsed, and you've been in here since yesterday," Don said, moving more debris. Soon he realized that one of the man's legs was trapped under a large piece of a cement column.

"Where's Emma?" the man asked again.

Don looked at Avery and then shrugged. "We don't know where Emma is. Do you know where she was the last time you saw her?"

"She was right here. She was sleeping on the bed."

The nurse arrived, and Avery moved back so she could tend to the old man.

"Hi. My name is Connie. What's yours?" she said.

"Charles Shelby. Where's my Emma? Have you seen her?"

Connie glanced over at the two men who shook their heads. "How are you feeling, Mr. Shelby? Where do you hurt? Do you have diabetes or anything else I should know about?"

"I'm fine. I want to know where my wife is."

Don called down for more help to get the column off the old man's leg. While they waited, he and Avery moved away more debris to see if there was a bed next to where Charles Shelby was lying. Two men came up with pry bars.

"Your leg is trapped, Charles," Don said. "But we'll have you out in no time."

"I'm not leaving here without Emma."

"We're looking for her right now, Charles," Connie said, pulling his face toward hers to shine a small light in his eyes. "We'll find her. Look into this light, Charles."

He pulled his face away from the nurse. "I'm not . . . " he said, his voice starting to quaver. "I'm not leaving here without her. We've been together for sixty-one years." He grabbed Don's hand and with an imploring look said, "Please find my Emma."

Connie looked away from him for a moment to compose herself, then she patted him on the arm. "We're looking, Charles. But I need you to cooperate. OK?"

The four men carefully but quickly moved bricks from the pile beside Charles. Avery found the corner of a bed sticking out at an odd angle. He looked at Don but said nothing. Soon, they could see that the entire head of the bed was crushed under another large chunk of the column.

They moved back to the old man. "Listen, Charles. We need to move you out of here so we have room to dig out Emma," Don said, trying to sound positive. "The sooner we get you out of here, the sooner we can start."

"OK. But you'll bring her right to me, won't you?"

Don's jaw clenched tightly, and he had to force himself to relax it. "I promise. As soon as we get her out, we'll bring her down and let you know."

The four men got the concrete off Charles' leg, then tied him onto a stretcher and lowered him down to workers below. As soon as he was gone, they set about the grisly task of finding Emma. Just as they feared, the old woman was dead. The only comfort they would be able to give Charles was that she had probably died instantly.

They tenderly placed her body on another stretcher and lowered her down. Don went to tell Charles.

As Cole made his way back into the building, the press, who had heard he was in Denver, managed to track him down. President Todd had just finished a third news release from the Oval Office. He had stressed the need for calm, but once again spoke of the insurgent group that may have committed this act of terrorism. Once again, Americans were urged to report any suspicious activity. Don was apprised of this and asked for his response. The cameras were rolling, and the lights were on. He looked ashen as he agreed to the interview.

"Is this the first location you have visited?" he heard a reporter say.

"No. We've been taken to several locations since we arrived."

"What is your assessment of the situation?"

"We need more help. People have no idea how bad this is. I am personally overwhelmed by the sights I've seen. Your viewers just cannot imagine what has happened here."

"What do you suggest, Mr. Cole?"

"We need to get more emergency and military personnel and more equipment here as quickly as possible. In addition, the people need tents, generators, blankets, and heaters . . ."

The reporter did not let him finish his sentence. "Do you agree that this is the work of some insurgent or militia-type group? Is enough being done to hunt down the people who did this?"

Don exhaled slowly. "To begin with," he said angrily, "I am not completely satisfied that this was an act by some insurgent or militia-type group. Even so, for now, our primary efforts must go to the victims of this disaster. People are perishing here, and Todd is sending federal agents looking for the bogeyman while he sits in the comfort of the White House. He has spent more time soliciting anonymous tips than aid for the people of Denver. There is enough paranoia to go around already. Let's get our priorities straight."

President Todd and several aides watched the interview with Cole on television. Todd swore and pounded the arm of his chair with a fist. "Just who does he think he is anyway?" the president seethed. He took comfort in the thought that soon those who had been infected by the virus would be found, and this would bring the second wave of fear to the situation. Once the news of the virus was out, a greater degree of control would be his. And maybe he would get lucky and something would fall on Cole.

His interview over, Cole slowly climbed back up to the southwest corner of the building. He was grim, but he kept digging with the others until dark. While he worked, he came to a decision. Unless he felt a compelling need to say something, he would give no more interviews—at least not for a while. He would help dig people out first. As far as Don was concerned, this was a time for action, not discussion.

In the remaining minutes of daylight, they found another old woman, barely alive, and a man in a wheelchair—dead. The teams found a total of seventeen people—five were still alive when they were pulled from the building.

Don said few words as he worked. He tried desperately to make sense of what had happened. If someone had intentionally caused this, what was their purpose? He still could not imagine how the Quick and the Dead—or anyone—could do such a thing. What would they have to gain? Thoughts of the visit on the balcony in Seattle came back to Don. The intruder did say that the other side thrived on chaos and that the plan of Todd and the others was to create such upheaval that people would be happy to trade their freedom for the peace and security that would be offered. This certainly fit that scenario.

As he helped to lift crushed victims from the debris, Don became certain of one thing: He wanted to know if someone did this and, if so, who they were. *If people have indeed managed to trigger an earthquake here,* Don thought, *death is too good for them.*

All work had to stop at dark. With no way to generate power, it was too dangerous to keep working. Flashlights couldn't give enough light to be of value. Even though it was dangerous, and they both were exhausted, Don and Avery both hated to come down and stop for the night. They wondered how many they were leaving to die in the cold.

Don brought two changes of clothes with him to Denver and ended up putting them both on over his other clothes to stay warm. Avery did the same.

Tonight there would be a fire to help keep them warm. The night before, broken pipes had been leaking so much natural gas that it had been too dangerous to have open flames. They were grateful to huddle around a large bonfire, and they slept as well as they could on the ground.

Don looked up at a dark sky filled with stars. It was amazing how bright the tiny specks of light were when viewed from a dark place. He had forgotten how awesome the sight was. The fleeting nature of life suddenly overwhelmed him, and he wondered if God were up there looking down from a distance, or if He was right there with them, sharing their sorrows, giving them the courage to go on. *Could all of this be a sign that Jesus is coming back?* Don wondered before he fell into a fitful sleep.

While the press played up the growing war of words between the two presidential candidates in the nightly news, the rescuers at Holmon Elementary School kept feverishly digging. There was no time to listen to the news. Every minute was precious. Because they had generators and lights, Pete and the others continued to work into the night. Just before midnight, they found the first child under the music room area, a little girl, who was barely alive. The mere sight of her brought strength and hope to the workers. With renewed fervor, they picked up the pace as much as they dared, still stopping occasionally to call out to those below and listen for any response. Had this been the only building affected, dramatic video footage of it would have been seen around the world, but in fact, it was one of hundreds of places where people were working feverishly and praying to God for those who were trapped underneath. There was no way to capture the magnitude of the events unfolding with a camera. News crews throughout the region could only give the world bits and pieces of the disaster and use words like "incredible," "unbelievable," and "indescribable," until those words lost their meaning.

Sara woke up because of the noise. She could hear workers somewhere above or beside her. She couldn't make up her mind as to where the sound was coming from. It was dark, and she was so cold. Then it got quiet. *They haven't given up, have they?* She remembered she had a chunk of cement in her hand and banged it against the metal part of the desk.

"Clois? Clois? Can you hear me? It's Miss Reisling. Jody? . . . Can anyone hear me?"

Only silence. Maybe she had fallen asleep again and was dreaming. She remembered singing with the children. She had wanted to keep them occupied. She had heard a man singing with them. Did she imagine it? She tried to speak louder, but her throat was so dry, she could barely manage a sound.

God, please keep us warm. . . . Don't let them give up looking for us, she thought.

Pete had begun feeling ill earlier in the day, but he had continued on. At first he told himself he was just tired and ignored the symptoms. As his temperature started to rise, he figured he had caught a chill and was coming down with a cold. But there was no time to feel sick. He had to keep digging. He took some aspirin, drank plenty of water, and continued working. Even when several of the other workers collapsed, it was assumed they were exhausted and that a little rest would make them better.

It wasn't until eleven that night that they realized just about everyone was feeling ill. The symptoms varied, but most had fever, chills, and a bad cough. Had they all caught the same cold? They had no time to compare notes with thousands of others in the Denver area and see that this was no ordinary cold. By 2:00 A.M., however, they would realize they had more problems than just digging out quake victims.

President Sonny Todd originally had planned to make the White House a command post for the duration of the disaster, giving out bits and pieces of the insurgent's plot while looking presidential to the American people. But when Cole implied that he was a coward looking to instill paranoia in people, he began to rethink his strategy. Maybe he needed to actually go to Denver and at least land a few places in a helicopter. He was preparing to do that very thing at midnight eastern standard time when word of the widespread illness there reached the White House. He called an emergency meeting.

When everyone arrived for the meeting, they got right to business. A report was given that some sort of unknown illness had manifested in a majority of the people in the Denver area. Its source was unknown.

Todd panicked. The virus Yosef used was supposed to be so fast-acting that the spread would be limited. The victims would die too quickly to allow them to take it anywhere. The infected workers were intentionally isolated from outside contact. Could something have gone wrong? Had one of them escaped the protected area and loosed the virus on the general populace? They intended to find the victims and *imply* that the virus might spread, but secretly know it was contained. They would be able to control media coverage and travel into and out of the area. There would be increased public feelings of hatred toward the insurgent group who had done this. The plan was perfect. Todd could have it all wrapped up in thirty days and come out a major hero.

Descriptions of the disease's symptoms did not completely coincide with what he had been told of Yosef's virus. Could the virus they planted have mutated already? Or could this be something else altogether? He would need to consult with Yosef immediately. He asked for a recess of the meeting for one hour. During that time, a team from the Office of Disease Control would be dispatched to Denver, the military would completely cordon off the area, and Todd would consider his options.

In one hour, the full cabinet was assembled, along with several aides and a representative from the Office of Disease Control. The president had consulted with Yosef, using a code on a secure line. While it was possible that somehow the virus had not been contained and had mutated, it was also possible that something that had been pumped underground all those years ago had actually resurfaced in the water or been loosed into the air through cracks in the earth. But they decided not to panic. As long as they could keep the disease contained, this too could work to their advantage. It would make the American people even more anxious to have the situation solved, more accepting of tighter security. No one could question any action that Todd would take concerning this now. And perhaps Cole, who had gone there to grandstand, would even contract the disease!

By the time he entered the room for the second meeting regarding the illness, the president felt energized and in control. Within another hour Vice President Bartlett would give the press an update on the situation and say that Todd was in a closed meeting with members of Congress.

By 4:00 A.M. mountain time, Pete was burning up with fever, as were most of the workers, but they kept digging. Fifteen more children had been found, six of them still alive. They had finally gotten to the level where the victims were. It was no time to stop. A signal came. Two more children, both alive! The workers kept moving rubble, finding little chairs and desks.

Sara heard sounds nearby. Although exhausted, she took the piece of concrete in her hand and hit the desk a few times. A few small shafts of light penetrated an area by her feet, and she heard voices.

"We're in here. Please keep digging," she said in a barely audible voice. She knew they probably couldn't hear her, so she banged on the desk again.

Someone above thought they heard a tapping sound.

"Stop! Stop! Be quiet!" he cried.

Signals went around the area.

Sara heard someone tapping above the area where she could see the small dots of light. There were three taps. She tapped three times. There were five taps. She tapped five times.

"Over here! Someone is signaling over here!" More workers moved into the area and gingerly helped remove rubble.

The area of light that Sara could see grew to the size of a grapefruit. She saw a hand, which felt around the rubble, and then heard a man's voice say, "Can you hear me?"

She tried to swallow and clear her throat. "Yes," she managed to squeak out.

"Are you pinned down?"

"No. I'm under my desk."

The light got bigger as the sounds of rubble being removed increased.

She heard the man's voice again. "Are we on a side where you can crawl out?"

"Yes," she said.

"Are you hurt? Can you crawl out, or can we pull you out?"

"My leg hurts, but I can move. I can crawl out."

"OK now. Stay under your desk. Don't try to crawl out until I say so. We have to move a really big piece of concrete here, so stay there until it's gone. Can you see my hand?"

"Yes."

"Where are you in relation to my hand?"

"I am facing the back of your hand, and I am closest to the thumb."

"You see the back of my hand, and you are close to my thumb?"

"Yes."

"Can you touch my hand?"

With trembling fingers, Sara reached out and touched the hand. It felt so warm. She began to cry. "Yes. This is me."

"Do you know if anyone is in the area facing the palm of my hand?"

"I don't think so. Unless they came down from the room above."

"OK. We're going to pry this piece of concrete in the direction my palm was facing. Stay under your desk. It will take a few minutes."

After what seemed like a very long time, the area under her desk suddenly filled with a splash of light and the noise of the outside world. A man covered with dirt leaned into the hole and said, "C'mon. It's time to get out of here." He grabbed her hands and then put his arms around her and pulled her out. The man carried her through a mass of rubble before setting her down on the ground outside. Someone put a blanket around her.

"Sara! Sara! It's me, Duchess! Daddy!" she heard another man say. She looked up and couldn't believe her eyes. There was her father, covered with dirt, leaning over her. Streaks of tears ran down through the dust on his face.

It didn't occur to her to wonder how he had gotten there. She wanted to stand up and throw her arms around him, but she couldn't muster the strength. "Daddy!" was all she could say, and she held out her arms.

"I don't want to touch you, honey. I'm sick. So is almost everyone else here. Just lie there and get warm. We've boiled some water and have hot coffee to drink. They'll be right here with it. Your mama is home praying for us. . . . They'll have somethin' to celebrate now, won't they?"

Sara nodded her head. "Children. How about the children? How many?"

"I can't tell you, Duchess. Some of them are going to make it, but we're not done yet. I have to get back to work now. Drink something hot. A doctor will be over here soon, OK?"

In Texas, Sara's mother, Naomi, and the others remained in prayer during the night, occasionally checking the television for news. Pete had not called again since they first reached the city. Groups of people came and went at the house. The wives of all the men who had gone with Pete were there. Everyone tried to remain hopeful in spite of what they saw in the news.

When the story of the mysterious illness was televised in the early morning hours, Naomi's heart felt like melting wax. She knew Pete was in trouble. She left the living room and went to her own bedroom to be alone. She lay face down on the floor and prayed.

"Most high God, I gave You Pete when I married him. I gave You Sara before she was born. I have trusted You with them every day since then, and I've never been sorry. I will not take them back from Your hand. You know how scared I am and how much I want to hear they are fine and that they will come back to me, but God, I know You are wiser than I am. I say Your kingdom come, Your will be done, in all of our lives today as it is in heaven. I know Your plan is for our greatest good. With my own eyes I have seen this again and again. I know I can trust You, Lord, even if everything else should fail. As an act of my will, I surrender . . . "

Naomi remained on the floor for an hour before someone knocked on the door and then entered.

"Naomi!" a woman said as she rushed in. "Someone's on the phone! They've heard from the men!"

Naomi got up instantly and ran out of the room to the small crowd huddled around the phone. Curt Smith's wife was speaking on it.

"Yes . . . yes, she's right here."

She handed Naomi the phone and said, "They found Sara! She's all right!" to the others in the room.

"Mrs. Reisling?" a man's voice said.

"Yes," Naomi answered.

"This is Paul Deering. I am a ham radio operator. I'm sorry to call you so early in the morning, but I have received a message from someone in the Denver area asking me to contact you about your family. I assumed you would want to know as soon as possible."

"Oh, yes! Thank you!"

"Peter Reisling sends the message that your daughter has been found. She is bruised and dehydrated. She lost three of the students in her class and is taking it hard, but she will be OK."

"Praise God," Naomi said as tears came to her eyes.

"He also says that all of the men have gotten ill with some sort of virus. So far, they are OK, but he asks for prayer for the situation. . . . He told me to tell all the wives that they love them. That's all."

As they slept by the fire that night, Avery and several other workers at the Denver nursing home started coughing. By morning, he and two others alternated between burning fevers and chills and were taken to the field hospital. Many more of the volunteers began to feel sick as well, although most were still able to work.

CHAPTER THIRTY-THREE

OF ALL THE WORKERS AT THE DENVER NURSING HOME, Don Cole and Josh Thornton were the only two who remained symptom free. Avery was ill, and Josh's partner—although he was still getting around—had the bug as well. It soon became apparent that the sickness might incapacitate many of the volunteers. Since Don and Josh were the fittest at this point, it was decided that they were less likely to fall or hurt themselves than those who were dizzy with fever. The two men agreed to work together on the southwest corner of the building, the highest level of the nursing home still standing. They referred to it as "the pile" and spent long hours looking for survivors in the maze of twisted metal and concrete.

Josh, Don soon learned, was a co-pastor in a church in New York. He had come to Denver the week before and was attending seminars when the quake hit. He and six other pastors came to the site of the nursing home and offered to help.

Once he found out what Josh did for a living, Don was a little nervous working with him. *What if I hurt myself and start swearing?* Don thought. *What if he starts cramming Bible verses down my throat all day?*

But as he got to know Josh and several of the other pastors, he began to genuinely like them. In fact, the tougher things got, the more Don appreciated their inner strength and their ability to encourage one another. A bond of friendship existed between these men that Don envied. He couldn't remember ever having friends as close as these men were.

Although he was not a very spiritual person, Don felt drawn to spend time with the pastors, even when they prayed or did other things that would normally make him uncomfortable. He rarely spoke during these times, but he was grateful for the companionship they gave him. On the third and fourth days after the quake, when much of what they found was too horrible for words, Don began to seek refuge in their presence.

As the physical strength of others ebbed with illness, Josh and Don were forced to work to their absolute limits. Although height and general size were their only similarities, within a day they were both so dirty that their differences became hard to discern, even when they were standing right next to one another. Rarely seen singly once they began work together, they became known as "the twins."

At noon on the third day, someone brought hot food for lunch. They got down off the pile and went to the place where tables were set up. The twin joke had started, but they were not yet aware of it.

"How do you tell each other apart?" one of Josh's friends said.

Josh looked at Don and said, "He's the dirty one."

They both laughed. Don was grateful for a little humor. It had been a hard morning for them. They had found only one man early in the day, and he was dead.

Don knew he and Josh had become desperate when they were both ecstatic about Spam and eggs. He was never so grateful for food in his life, and Josh ate as if the food meant the same to him. After a quick meal, they went back up on their pile to dig. Soon, Don had to run back down. He threw up his lunch.

Josh came down after him. "You OK, buddy?"

Don wiped off his mouth and tried to catch his breath. "I don't know . . . I don't think I can take much more of this." He walked over and leaned against a nearby truck. After a few moments he looked at Josh and asked, "Do *you* think someone could have done this? Or do you think this is some sort of sign from God?"

"One thing I can tell you, Don, is that people are capable of anything. I've been a pastor for fifteen years, and I don't think there is *anything* that would shock me anymore. There was a time when I thought I would have to quit. I got to the point where I'd seen too much, I'd heard too much, and I didn't want to see or hear any more."

"So, what happened?"

"I had to get a hold of God again, Don. I'd taken my eyes off of the Lord and gotten off track. If I kept looking at all that evil, I wasn't going to make it. I was getting cynical, all dried up, and bitter. I took some time off and really tried to figure out what made me want to be a pastor in the first place. Did I do it for me, for men, or for God? Eventually, I came back to the answer. God had called me. And if I wanted to be able to go on, I had to keep my eyes on *Him*. God isn't evil, and He doesn't do evil things, but He will allow us to be overtaken with the result of our own sin, whether that's through the hands of our enemies or through nature. So—yes, I think that, one way or another, people caused this."

Don frowned. "People caused this, but God allowed it? And we deserve it? What happened to peace and mercy?"

"The Bible says that when God's judgments are in the land, people will learn righteousness. He's not looking at this the same way we do. He has eternity in mind. God is not willing that any of us perish, but when *He* says 'perish,' He doesn't mean physical death. He means spending eternity in that place no one likes to talk about anymore—hell. He wants us to turn around and live— forever, in glory. When all else fails, yes, He sends judgment—not with the intent of destroying mankind, but to get us to turn around."

"But what about you? You're a preacher. Isn't God supposed to come and take all the Christians away from this?"

"Obviously we're still here, aren't we? Maybe God is waiting for those He called to start being faithful to speak the words—and yes, warnings of the judgments—of God to the people of this country. Not with a superior atti- tude, but with *His broken heart.* Maybe we should stop worrying about being politically correct and say the words we were created to say. This country used to be a Christian nation. It has been the most blessed nation in the history of the world. If you look, you'll see that we have departed from God. We have left the standard of His Word, and in the process, we have seen the blessing of the Lord depart from us. Yet men still reach for the darkness and don't care whom it hurts. They continue to pursue the grossest evil and call it freedom. If you were God, what would *you* do to get our attention?"

Don looked down at the ground.

Josh put a hand on his shoulder. "Sorry, but you asked. Come on. We'll get through this. Landis and Bobby were down with the bug this morning. Let's take a break and find them."

Landis and Bobby sat and listened when Josh asked if he and Don could talk about what they were finding up on the pile. The two pastors let them unload, then prayed for them before they returned to digging.

When Don and Josh returned to work, they found a man who was alive and in surprisingly good shape. Workers rushed him to the hospital to be treated for exposure and to receive fluids. Somehow, Don managed to make it through the rest of the day and stay on the pile.

That night, "the twins" began the nightly ritual of visiting the field hospital to check on Avery, other co-workers who had gotten sick, and victims they had rescued. While at the hospital, they received the news that the illness most people had contracted was from bacteria in the water. Medicine was being distributed, which should cure most of them. Don and Josh were given some as a preventative.

They returned to the nursing home for the evening feeling cold, tired, and dirty.

The following morning, they were informed that donated clothes would be made available to anyone who wanted them. Both Don and Josh were desperate. After days of heavy labor while wearing the same clothes, they could no longer stand their own smell. During their first break, they quickly made their way to the tent that held donated supplies. Piles of clothing filled the tent. Unfortunately, almost all of the regular sizes were already taken, and the majority of what remained was either very small or incredibly large. Soon, they realized this wasn't the only problem.

Josh finally located a pair of kelly-green polyester pants in his size. "Gee," he said, "I wonder who was thoughtful enough to part with *these?*"

"Beggars can't be choosers," Don said before he actually looked at the pants Josh was holding up.

Soon, however, Don realized that the only pants in *his* size were a blue plaid pair. "I suppose you'll say I deserve these," Don said, waving them in the air for Josh to see.

Josh let out a laugh that was more of a panicked cackle. Everyone in the tent turned to see what the noise was all about. "And are they by any chance bell bottoms?" he asked. "Please say yes. It'll make my day."

Most of the shoppers in the tent could sympathize. It seemed that all the clothing in the tent had come from a time warp. Of one thing they could be certain: The attics of America were now clean.

CHAPTER THIRTY-FOUR

THE FOURTH DAY HAD DAWNED SINCE THE DENVER earthquake. Again President Todd had not slept well, but he didn't mind so much. He wanted to *look* the part of a concerned commander in chief. As he readied for another news conference, he was torn. Should he wear a black suit or a navy blue one? Black looked so much like death. He looked better in the navy, but maybe it would appear he was not taking the situation seriously. He decided on the black suit.

He had issued bulletins through his press secretary at regular intervals over the past two days. Now it was time to make a personal appearance. He had a well-crafted speech and was going to deliver it in two hours.

His wife, Edith, entered the room, and frowned. "Don't wear the black. You look embalmed. Blue is a power color for you. Wear it."

"You think I should? I don't want to appear flippant about all this."

"Wear the navy."

"How about this tie?"

"No. Wear something with contrast," she said as she ran her finger past several candidates. She poked her finger at one. "This one. Wear this one."

He picked up the tie and put it around his collar. "Will you tie it? You do it so much better than I do."

She began to work with the tie. "You know, I talked to Tony Bensen this morning."

He rolled his eyes. "Edith. I wish you wouldn't do that. The tabloids will eat me for breakfast if they think I'm getting advice from a psychic!" He and his wife shared many common views politically, but spiritually they were worlds apart. He felt he had a practical, simple view that embraced nature and the physical world around them. She, on the other hand, was always delving into the invisible to find answers in the physical. It made no sense to him.

"I'm not so sure about that, Sonny. Tony isn't some looney who goes around making predictions about movie-star divorces. He has an excellent record. Isn't he on public TV and the SON channel all the time? Did you know the All Science Network did a special on him two weeks ago? He's gotten quite a bit of positive attention lately. Anyway, he says you need to be careful about alliances. He says there is a realignment in negative and positive forces right now, and you just need to wait it out. I know you don't want to admit it, but didn't he tell me last week that a shaking would come to your office?"

It gave him a little jolt as he remembered it, but he rolled his eyes again. "What a bunch of dreck! And did he also predict the sun would rise this morning? Ooooo, I feel chill bumps! What a guy!"

She pushed the knot of his tie very hard and made him choke. "That's not funny, Sonny. I don't make fun of your friends."

He put a finger under his collar and pulled outward. "I'm sorry, dear, but I just don't buy that stuff." The truth was, it kind of scared him.

"Well, he's coming to our dinner next week. If you embarrass me about this, you'll need to send an ambassador to get me to sign a treaty! Get my drift?"

"Fine. Fine. I'll be nice. But now, I have bigger things to work on," he said, trying to change the subject. "Is Victor here yet? How about my secretary?"

"They're both here and ready when you are."

Good. She was going to let it drop. That sort of thing made him feel all weird on the inside. What if this guy really could see what was happening? What if Bensen already knew what Sonny was doing? It made him shudder to think. He was relatively certain this stuff was all just stupid parlor tricks and lucky guesses, but if that guy showed up at the party, Sonny Todd wasn't going to get anywhere near him. He made a mental note to be busy at introduction time and to have Mr. Bensen placed at a table far away from his own.

He went down to his office and met with the vice president and his secretary before letting the makeup people come in.

"Victor," he said, "do you have the report from the Office of Disease Control?"

"Here it is. Hot off the press. ODC says it's in the water. They say it's actually bacterial in nature, that it shouldn't be deadly to most people, and that the teams of doctors they sent in are making good progress in getting treatment centers organized all over the city."

"Great! What about the transports with extra food and the mobile units with kitchens?"

"All in place."

"Wonderful," he said. "Have you heard from anyone else?" He meant Yosef or Schollet, but he didn't want to say the names in front of his secretary.

"Yes. But there is nothing new to report."

The vice president left the office so Sonny could cinch up a few last-minute details with his secretary. Soon it was time to have makeup put on and get before the cameras.

A prompter screen with a copy of his speech lay on the surface of his desk. He hoped he wouldn't have to look at it often, but he wanted it there, just in case. His remarks would be carried live on TV and radio.

The countdown started. "OK, Mr. President. Three, two, one," the man said as he pointed to Todd.

"Good morning. I come to you today with an update on our progress in the Denver earthquake.

"Four days ago, there was a 7.9 earthquake near the Denver metropolitan area, centered in the Rocky Mountain Reserve Zone. Shortly after the quake, evidence came to light revealing that this was not just a random earthquake, but an orchestrated event. As we have investigated this incident, we have concluded that the persons who organized and carried out this attack selected this sight for several reasons. Denver is a large, metropolitan area. It is also near what was once the Rocky Mountain Arsenal. The land formerly used as an arsenal has been the focal point of a massive cleanup effort for many years now. It had become a jewel in our Restoration of Natural Areas Project and one of the first established Zero Population Zones.

"In the 1960s, contaminated wastewater was pumped at high pressure down into the earth at this location. Earthquakes began shaking the entire region, and eventually, they realized it was the pumping of the water that caused the quakes. Doing such a thing with contaminated water would be inconceivable with today's enlightened thinking, but all we can do now is hope to learn from the mistakes of the past. Millions of tax and corporate dollars have already been spent in an attempt to clean up the results of these misguided experiments in the Reserve. Now, due to an act of terrorism, we will pay not just in dollars, but in public health.

"I have here a report from the Office of Disease Control stating that the probable cause of the mysterious illness that has stricken the inhabitants of the Denver area is contamination of the water table there. Biological contaminants, pumped deep into the earth four decades ago, have risen into the aquifer that supplies water to Denver and the surrounding area. This is a consequence of gross environmental ignorance. But we're told, at this time, there is little cause for alarm. Denver has been temporarily quarantined. The Office of Disease Control has already begun to distribute the necessary medications to those affected, and I have been assured that most of those who are suffering from this illness will recover.

"Tragically, the death toll already stands at one thousand two hundred eleven. We know now that this number will rise as more victims are discovered in the rubble and as others die from the bacterial infection. Truly, this is the worst disaster in the history of our country.

"As I address you, military and public aid of all kinds continue to pour into the Denver area. Tents, heaters, food, blankets, and medicine are all being widely distributed from dozens of disaster centers set up in the region. Several large field hospitals have also been established in the city and suburbs to handle the medical needs of victims.

"The Corps of Engineers has arrived to survey the damage to the city's infrastructure. The National Guard is maintaining order and preventing looting. The National

Emergency Assistance Agency is preparing to help victims begin the long process of rebuilding their homes and lives. Nothing can repay the cost of losing a loved one, but we are doing everything in our power to make the road to recovery as smooth as possible.

"I am confident that every measure has been taken to meet the needs of disaster victims. In addition to meeting the physical needs of survivors, we will continue to seek justice for those who were casualties in this evil plot. As I speak, the largest federal task force in the history of this country is at work to uncover, pursue, arrest, and convict those who are responsible for this outrage. We have several very promising leads and will continue to investigate them. Those who are indicted will be tried for treason, murder, and crimes against the environment. We will no longer tolerate those with sick fundamentalist views who think they can dominate our politics, our government, and now our very lives. They have used the battle cry of freedom while they have defied our laws, poisoned our land, and killed our children. They have done this for no other reason than that we do not share their narrow, sectarian view. But now the thing they hold the most dear, their freedom, will be taken from them, and they will be prosecuted to the fullest extent of the law.

"It is tragic to note that Mr. Cole and others in his party have decided to play a game of partisan politics during a time of national disaster. They have criticized me for the strong stance I have taken, yet they have offered no solutions. They would like to think we live in a world where things like this do not happen, but *obviously* they *do*. I believe, now more than ever, that this country needs strong, clear leadership. If you, the American people, will unite under our leadership, we *will* win America back. For us and for the sake of our children and their children.

"It is my earnest prayer that this incident be remembered as our *last* great national tragedy. May the blood that has been shed serve as a catalyst that will cause us to rise up as one and turn back the tide of evil that has sought to engulf us. . . . "

Don Cole sat in the tent with a cup of coffee in his hand watching the small, battery-operated TV. He hadn't shaved, and he still wore the ridiculous clothing he had gotten the day before. In spite of his clown-like appearance, he was not happy. He could not believe what he was hearing. Todd probably engineered this whole thing, and now he was accusing his enemies of being the perpetrators. And he would probably get away with it! The media seemed a more-than-willing participant in this as far as Cole was concerned.

He finished his coffee as President Todd concluded his speech, then listened to another ten minutes of news commentary about the speech. When he got up and went outside, he found about twenty reporters waiting to get his take on the speech. They rushed at him.

"What did you think of the president's speech, Mr. Cole? Is it true that you still feel he is not handling the situation as he should?"

That was it. He'd had enough. "Is anyone in America still capable of thinking? Are things such as reason and logic still in use out there someplace? To listen to the press, one wouldn't think so. I don't even know why you bother to call it 'news' anymore. For every fifteen-second bite of actual news there are five minutes of opinion. This morning I heard one network saying their poll had 'found' that a radical group had started this earthquake.

Excuse me? Since when do polls find facts? But apparently—for the media—polls *do* determine facts.

"Wake up, America! Stop letting others do your thinking for you. Don't decide the issues based on the one-sided 'infobites' you get from the networks. There is no doubt that what has happened here is a tragedy of the highest degree, but I refuse to let the truth of the matter be decided by innuendo, paranoia, and polls! I agree—let's investigate, but let's *not* become a police state in the process! What has happened is indeed scary. I'd be lying if I said I haven't been truly shaken by these events. But we *cannot* let ourselves be so overwhelmed by fear and lose our freedom in process. If we yield to it, we become silent partners in this madness."

Most of the cameras were still taping, but many of the networks stopped their live coverage of Cole's remarks after his second sentence. Why give him free time to criticize them? Later, only a small segment of video showing his mismatched clothing and dirty appearance—but missing the audio—would be aired. A commentator would do a voice-over saying merely that Cole was angry at Todd.

Only the Banner Network and several radio stations carried Cole's remarks in their entirety. The Banner Network, labeled "conservative" and "right-wing" by the other networks, was garnering a greater and greater share of the viewing market. Their no-frills sets and reporting were a joke in the industry at first, but the laughter died down as some Americans began to turn off the "talk show journalism" and listen to Banner's simple reporting. The public was allowed to view uncut interviews and unedited reports and draw their own conclusions. In an age where sensationalism had gone to new heights, Banner Network's simple statement of the facts was a refreshing change.

Cole didn't care if any of the networks aired his remarks. He was so angry that he didn't know what to do. Finally he decided he'd better go back to volunteer work and just keep his mouth shut.

The army had shown up at the nursing home that morning and planned to take over all the digging and rescue efforts. Volunteers could stay and help with other recovery tasks. Don and Josh, along with everyone else in the region, were still under quarantine. They agreed to work in the kitchen plopping globs of food on paper plates with big spoons and to help keep the tables clean.

Don walked over to the food distribution tent and found Josh Thornton. "OK, I'm back from my break. You can go."

Thornton took off his apron. "You look like you're ready to punch somebody. You sure you don't want to walk around some more?"

"The press is out there. I might commit murder if I were out there walking around."

"OK," Josh said.

"Thanks."

"Don't mention it, bro."

Don put on his apron and stood on the side of the counters where the food was distributed. He had been serving for about ten minutes when a man in an army officer's uniform approached him.

"Are you Donald Cole?" the man asked.

"Guilty," Don said as he scooped a white gravy and meat mixture on people's plates.

"I'm Major Marsh, and I need to speak with you for a few minutes."

"Sure. What do you want?"

"I need to speak with you alone," the officer said.

"Oh." Don wondered if he was in trouble somehow. Had Todd sent this man to tell him to stop speaking to the press? Or worse, did they want to question him about his contacts with the Quick and the Dead? He tried to keep a relaxed look on his face. "Well, in that case, hold on a second." Don spoke to the woman who had oversight of the tent volunteers. He soon returned with a man who would take his place, gave the guy his apron, and then turned to the officer. "I'm all yours."

As they left the tent, Cole saw Josh, who gave him a puzzled look and asked him where he was going.

"Major Marsh here wants to speak with me," Don said. He hoped Josh was paying attention and could identify Marsh. If they were planning to incarcerate him, Cole hoped that someone would know he was missing and would make inquiries.

Josh looked back and forth between Marsh and Don a few times. "OK. I'll catch up with you later."

Don just nodded and then walked away with the officer. Josh watched the major escort Don to the passenger seat of a jeep and then go around and climb into the driver's seat. He remembered that Avery, who was still in the hospital, begged him to keep an eye on Don. Cole had refused his guardian's pleas to send for another bodyguard or a Secret Service man. Avery almost had to be tied to his bed until he became too sick to get up.

Josh ran to the jeep. "Excuse me, Major; what exactly do you need Mr. Cole for? Where are you taking him?"

The officer started the jeep. "We just need to question Mr. Cole. I'll bring him back in time for dinner." Marsh put the jeep in gear and popped the clutch. The vehicle sped away before Josh could respond. Don looked back at him but made no attempt to communicate.

At first Don had wanted Josh's help, but now he thought better of it. *What if I really am in trouble? No sense in dragging poor Thornton into it. It's a good thing Avery's not here, or there'd really be trouble.*

Josh went to find some of the other men. He didn't know what was going on, but he had a feeling it wasn't good. If Don wasn't back soon, they were going to find out why.

CHAPTER THIRTY-FIVE

SARA REISLING SAT ON THE CURB. SHE HAD BEEN VISITING her father in the large medical tent and suddenly had been overcome with a need for fresh air. She didn't know what had triggered the panic attack. There had not been an aftershock. She hadn't received any additional bad news. In fact, only three of her students still remained in the hospital. The others had already been claimed by their family members and taken home—wherever that was going to be. But for some reason, as she sat with her father and he began to cough, it sent a panic through her. Although he had been very ill, he was recovering. She had been reassured of this several times, but she just couldn't seem to get a grip on everything. She had a constant feeling that things were out of control, and she longed to get away to a place where things were normal again.

She had been able to see every one of the surviving children from her class and talk with them about the experience. Most of them had two common recollections.

One of them was that someone had come and covered them with a blanket. The other was that Sara and a man had sung with them when they were afraid. Even though there were no men found in the rubble anywhere near Sara and her students, she distinctly remembered a man's voice singing with them, but Sara didn't recall getting a blanket. She knew that God had visited them.

Now all she could think of were those who had perished . . . three of her precious children, her friend Joy, Edward Ulmer, and the principal, Ms. Baxter. At least, in the case of the children, she felt she'd given them the love that Jesus would have. Edward and Ms. Baxter were another story, though. Sara had wondered if Edward were gay but had never tried to befriend him or share her faith with him. She had only been arrogant and proud about her public challenge of Ms. Baxter . . . a woman who was also now dead. Sara had wasted so much time arguing and spent almost no time praying or trying to live the witness she so loudly professed.

She realized how foolish she was, how fleeting life was, and how futile her efforts at witnessing had been. She never felt so worthless in all her life.

The words Joy said to her the day of the teachers' meeting came back to her: "You know, Sara, you need to be a little less militant. You offend people sometimes."

And now, Joy was gone, too. What a faithful witness Joy had been. *God, why didn't You take me and spare her?* she thought. *You'd have been better off.*

Words suddenly came to her mind, and she knew they were not her own. *Joy finished her race. Yours is just beginning, Sara. I had a purpose for you before you were born. Don't despair, I am with you. Repent and learn.*

Those words would change Sara's life. She asked the Lord to make her a woman of faith—not just words. She prayed that nothing would stop her from being the person Jesus created her to be, regardless of the cost.

CHAPTER THIRTY-SIX

MAJOR MARSH DROVE THE JEEP FOR SEVERAL MILES WITHOUT speaking to his passenger. Although Don Cole's mind leaped to all sorts of conclusions about why Marsh might want to question him, he also remained quiet.

As they bumped along Don noted that most of the roads had been cleared by the military. Much rubble remained alongside the roads, but it was evident from the man-made mounds of bricks and other debris that many of the structures had been explored for survivors.

Marsh drove in a direction that would take them out of the city; eventually they reached open road. The only other evidence of civilization was railroad tracks. Marsh suddenly turned onto a gravel road, traveled until they were perched atop a small knoll, and then stopped.

Don looked at him. "You're not taking me in for questioning, are you?"

Marsh turned off the engine and looked at Don. "You don't remember my voice, do you? I see you haven't taken the advice I gave you on the balcony in Seattle about the bulletproof vest. In fact, lately you don't seem to care much about your safety at all. You've run two of our guys totally ragged watching over you."

Recognition settled over Don's face.

"You have Quick and Dead people watching me?" he asked.

"Nobody else seems to be doing the job. But we watch you even when the others are on duty. . . . Hope you don't mind me taking you like this. It was an opportunity we couldn't resist. Nobody, other than your preacher friend, knows you're gone right now or whom you're with. I'll take you back before he gets too upset and creates a stir."

"So, what is it you wanted to say to me?"

"Actually," Marsh said, "we wanted to show you something."

"Another video?"

"No. It's on the reserve over here. If you agree to go, I'll take you. We can talk on the way."

"The reserve. You mean the one where there aren't supposed to be any people?"

"That's the one. If we get caught, you can say I brought you here against your will. Your friend can corroborate the fact that you thought I was taking you some place for questioning. But I don't think anyone will see us. We've been watching them for quite some time and haven't been caught. . . . "

"Watching whom?"

"Todd's people. You up for it?"

"Why do you keep dragging me into all this? I can't help you, even if I wanted to—and I'm not sure I want to."

"Listen. They saw we were getting close to bringing them down and decided it was war. They set that virus loose in Africa to get some of our guys and create a distraction. They didn't care how many people it killed. While it *did* cover their tracks in the African escapade, they still had *us* to deal with. They don't know exactly who we are or what else we might know. So they decided to step up the war another notch, this time on home turf—and they did *that*," Marsh said, pointing back to Denver.

"They're arresting people right and left," the major continued, "and they're getting away with it so far. Some of our people and many others who have absolutely nothing to do with anything have been jailed. We're hoping the American people will see what's going on and they'll turn on Todd. At first, we let you in on things because we wanted you to know we were on your side before anyone else was. Now it's a question of needing your help as well."

"What is it you think I can do?"

Marsh's eyes focused on some distant spot as he spoke. "We want to prove to you here and now that we are not responsible for the quake here. You could still make it into office. As president you will have the power to pardon anyone you choose. Right now, we have upwards of three hundred men and women who are facing the death penalty or are stranded outside the United States because of false charges against them." He turned to look at Don. "We are guilty of fighting against a corrupt system, but not of plotting to harm the American people. If we have to die for that, we will, but we are hoping for your help in turning back the tide."

Don shook his head. "Even if I were to make it into office, I'm only one man. Pardoning your friends might help them personally, but it won't do much to change the situation. In fact, it could stir up even more trouble."

"I already told you," Marsh said, "that we have people occupying positions within the military and the infrastructure of the government. As president, you would be in the position to promote, demote, transfer, or remove many people who were not elected to the positions they now hold. We could help you make those choices."

For the first time in his life, Don had no answers. When he started the race for the presidency, he knew he would face life-and-death issues if he won. Certainly, every president had faced many such things often without the knowledge of the public. He thought he was prepared to make tough decisions, to send men and women to their deaths . . . to do whatever it took. But all of those things were predicated on the belief that he would have access to all the facts. Now he was beginning to see that "the facts" could be tailored to fit the situations and the affected parties.

Even if he won, would Todd's people just roll over? Unless they were stopped, they would keep all their secret alliances and government workers and keep moving toward their own goals. And what of the Quick and the Dead? What kind of people were *they*? What did he really know about them anyway?

Cole shook his head. "Are there any decisions you guys make that don't involve death or charges of treason as options?"

"For now? No sir. You want to come with me or not?"

The night this man gave him the video disk, Don made a choice. He still didn't know if the choice was motivated by ambition, curiosity, or intuition, but the same force caused him to make the same choice again. "OK. Take me to what you wanted to show me."

Marsh started up the jeep, and they traveled two miles until they came to a large, double fence strung with barbed wire across the top. The officer drove the jeep parallel to the fence for another mile. Don noted large signs on the fence that said "WARNING: Reserve Zone. No Entry."

A gate came into view, and Cole could see two armed soldiers on guard. Marsh brought the vehicle to a halt just outside the gate. One of the soldiers approached. Marsh pulled a large ID badge from his pocket and flashed it at the soldier, who returned to the gate and opened it. Without a word being spoken, Cole and the officer drove through the gate and into the reserve.

Don looked at Marsh, who answered his question before he asked it. "Our guys. If asked, they'll say no one has passed through that gate."

They drove down a dirt road, crossed a small creek, and went into a stand of trees. Marsh shut off the engine, pulled the brake, and reached behind the seats for something. He handed a pair of binoculars to Don and got another pair for himself. "Let's go."

Before they reached the top of the hill, the major put the strap to the binoculars around his neck and got on his hands and knees. He told Don to do the same. They crawled to the crest, then got on their stomachs.

"I don't think there's anyone nearby," Marsh whispered, "but it wouldn't hurt to keep your voice down."

Don nodded.

The officer put the binoculars up to his face and located something. "Look over there," he said pointing to their left.

Don held up the binoculars and looked in the same direction. He saw movement, but everything was out of focus. "Wait," he whispered. "I have to focus these things." As he did so, he saw people moving around a small building. They were all wearing biohazard suits, and most of them were spraying down the building using small, hand-held tanks. "What are they doing?"

"They're trying to decontaminate the area. You see, their original plan was to infect a few people with a really nasty virus, let them die here, and then find them. They would pretend it had to do with the contamination pumped underground and then have a heyday with the panic. Only thing was, they didn't count on a *real* outbreak making people sick. Sudden change of plan. They just never mention the dead people here, and let the real sickness run its course. They accomplished what they were looking for all the same. Only problem now is disposing of their virus victims and sanitizing the site."

Don put the glasses down. "Wait. You're telling me that they intentionally let a deadly virus loose here?"

"Yes sir."

"They would risk killing off half the country?"

"Well, yes and no. They put the people out here so it wouldn't spread, but there's always a risk."

"How do I know what you're saying is true? This could be a legitimate operation. These people could be cleaning up some chemical spill. Or maybe this has something to do with the bacteria in the water."

"Did you see anyone in Denver wearing those suits once they found out what it was?"

"No."

"Now, look over there," Marsh said, pointing once again.

Don looked through the binoculars and focused them. More men in the biohazard suits were standing near what appeared to be three bodies in separate plastic bags. A small, domed metal structure stood nearby, and two suited men waited near a hatch in the side of the structure. "What's that domed thing?" Cole asked.

"Portable biohazard incinerator. It will vaporize just about anything and then clean the vapor. They'll crank that baby up now, and by tonight there won't be any evidence left to tell the story."

Don felt a chill run down his spine. "So why didn't you bring some hot-shot reporter out here to have him film all this?"

"Trying to tell this story will only get a hot-shot reporter killed. Right now we just want to make sure that somebody other than us knows about this. Besides, if someone—anyone—had videotaped this and given it to you, wouldn't you suspect it was fake? The only thing we had going for us in the Africa video was the fact that the soldiers' records would verify they were sent there, and we had the numbers on the ERWs. In this case, we don't even know the identities of those dead guys down there. And soon, even their bodies will be gone. All we can hope for here is an eyewitness who might get into a position to help."

Don suddenly remembered looking down into the face of a young reporter who thought she was going to change the world with her story. His words came echoing back: *"Listen, little one,"* he'd said, *"it's not about truth; it's about power, and you haven't got any."* How ironic that he was now in a position to experience the full reality of that statement. Truth without power is meaningless; at the moment, he wasn't sure he had the power to tell this story.

"Well," Don said, "as a matter of fact, how do I know you're not staging this whole thing for my benefit? This could be a play—complete with costumes."

"If you think you've got the guts, I'll take you down there."

"Are you serious?" Cole was incredulous.

"One hundred percent. I have two biohazard suits and a set of orders ready. If you come with me, you can at least satisfy yourself that those are real bodies down there.

I can't prove how they died, unless we take samples, but
the means of disposal itself says something about how
they died. And of course, you realize that if we are caught
down there, the 'taking-you-in-for-questioning' story
won't work for you, and we'll both be nothing more than
clean vapor by sunset."

Don could hear his pulse pounding in his ears. He had
challenged a man who was willing to call any bluff. Now
it was time to put up or shut up. "How do we know the
suits are safe?"

"Fresh out of the bag. That's about as good a guarantee as you can get in the field. If it has a leak, it won't
be long before you know," the major said.

"Thanks. That's a real comfort."

"Well? What do you say?"

Don was scared. Probably more scared than he'd ever
been before. But he suddenly remembered all the bodies
he'd dug out of that building. Especially Charles' wife,
Emma. He wanted to know who did this. His anger won
over his fear.

"Where are the suits?" he said before he lost his nerve.

"In the back of the jeep. Let's go."

The two men crawled a few feet from the top of the hill
and then walked to the jeep. Marsh unzipped a large,
black bag in the back of the jeep. The suits were inside
the bag, each in its own wrapping.

"They're the same size. You pick first," Marsh said.

Don selected a suit.

"I'll show you how to put it on."

It took them thirty minutes to get suited up. Don was
grateful it was a cool day. Marsh checked Don's suit,
asked Don to check his, then they both removed their
hoods.

"Oh," Marsh said, reaching into the bag again. "Put
these on." He produced a fake mustache, a goatee, and

glasses with slightly tinted lenses. "Don't speak once we get down there. Someone might recognize your voice." He helped Don with the disguise and then stood back to look at him before speaking again. "Remember," the officer said, "once you put that hood back on, you are stuck in the suit till I say so. Do *not*, under *any* circumstances, break the seal on the suit without my permission. If you need to scratch your nose, forget it. If you throw up in there, live with it. You understand me?"

"Yes," Don said and swallowed.

"These suits are made to be pretty sturdy, but move slowly and avoid any sharp edges. Got it?"

"Yes."

"If at any point you don't know what is expected of you or what to do, make some sort of weird hand signal to me, like it's a secret sign language you and I know. I'll say something like 'Good idea, Joe, we'll make a note of that,' or 'Yeah, let's go,' or whatever and try to let you know what to do. OK?"

"Got it."

They got back into the jeep and drove to the little road that ran by the trees. Within five minutes, they pulled up outside the area they had been watching through binoculars. A uniformed man with a rifle stopped them. Marsh reached behind Don's seat and produced a clipboard with papers.

"I'm Captain Willard and this is the observer, Mr. Pendham. I'm his escort. We've been sent by Colonel Tobin to ensure the clean-up and disposal are all within the parameters given."

The man called for another soldier to verify the orders. Soon, the other man appeared and checked the papers. "Were you hoping for a sunny day?" he asked.

Don thought that a rather odd question, then realized it was probably some sort of password.

"No. I'm from Oregon, and I like rain," Marsh responded.

"How come you have suits on already?" The man was suspicious.

"Oh. Well, we suited up at the other sight. Then Tobin got on the horn and told them to send us here instead. You know how it is. Didn't see any point in going through all of it again. Stupid brass. Can't make up their minds. Who's going to argue? Especially in the mood the old man's in today!"

"Yeah," the man with the clipboard said. "If Tobin is in one of his moods, I'm not going to be the one who questions his reasoning. Tobin eats people like me for breakfast," he said, returning the papers. "OK, Captain, you know the procedure."

Marsh took the clipboard and placed it back in the jeep. He got out, and Don followed his lead. They went to the area where people suited up and put on their hoods. After they had rechecked the seals on their suits, they walked the short distance to the building where they had observed the men spraying. Two of the men took turns standing in something that looked like a round kiddie pool with a small ring of pipe suspended about seven feet above it. Liquid shot out through nozzles in the pipe, and the men were showering with their suits on. The major had already told Don they would have to do this, then remove their suits before they would be allowed to leave the area. Prior to putting their suits on, Marsh had taken all pins and bars off his uniform.

As they got close to the building, Marsh spoke loudly to Don. "You want to inspect this one first?"

Don nodded.

The men had nearly finished spraying down the entire area. It was unlikely any virus lingered there, but no chances were being taken. Cole and Marsh walked around inside and looked. At one point Don stopped and pointed to a refrigerator then made a sign by patting the front of his left shoulder with his left hand.

"Good idea." Marsh said, then looked at one of the men in the building. "You. Yes, you. This refrigerator and everything in it should be deconned or destroyed."

"Yes sir," the young man replied.

They went outside and walked over to where they had seen the bodies and the incinerator. When he looked closely, Don could see that the lifeless forms inside the bags on the ground were indeed bodies of people who'd been dead for several days. The things he had seen in the previous days had prepared him for this. *At least these bodies are neatly trussed up in bags.* He was surprised at how something that would have been revolting just days before now had so little effect on him.

Don saw Marsh was looking at him with concern. *He probably thinks I'm going to get sick.* He shook his head no and moved his fingers like he was pinching something in the air then pointed to the bodies.

"I'll make a note of that," Marsh said.

Cole noted the men working around them were getting nervous.

The decontamination process was almost complete. It was time to throw the bodies and some of the other materials from the site into the incinerator. After it was lit, four guards would remain until the process was complete. In a few days others would come and dismantle the incinerator.

There were two handles on either side of each body bag. Cole and Marsh looked on as soldiers hoisted them up and threw them into the hatch of the incinerator. Don watched as they picked up the first, then the second body and sent them through the hatch without a problem. When they lifted the third bag, however, there was a complication. The body inside the bag was much larger than the others, and when they lifted it, a handle tore loose.

As the bag tore and slipped from the hands of the soldier whose handle broke, a set of keys in the clothing of the body caught his leg. The weight of the body crashed against him and the keys not only tore his suit, but gashed his leg as well.

For a moment, no one moved. They all looked at one another in disbelief. The young man holding the torn handle stared at his leg then started to scream.

Marsh grabbed Don's arm and pulled him away from the circle of men that now closed in on the young man.

"Wait! Wait!" he cried in vain. "There must be an antidote! I'll stay right here until you get it. I swear, I won't go anywhere!"

The men drew closer still.

The young man reached down to the ground and snatched up the keys that had torn his suit. "Stay back!" he yelled. "I'll do the same thing to the first man who gets near me."

Another man in a suit came up behind the circle with a revolver, put it to the back of the young man's head, and shot him.

Don almost jumped out of his skin. Marsh's hand rested on Don's arm, and he squeezed tightly. The look on his face said, *"Don't move; don't speak. Stay out of it!"*

The man with the gun, who must have been an officer, started swearing, then barked orders to the men in the circle. "On the double! Hansen, Blake. Pick both of them up and put them through the hatch. Now! Porter, Rice, Gantillet, go for shovels!"

The men scrambled while Don and Marsh just stood and watched. As soon as the soldiers returned, they were ordered to shovel all the grass, dirt, and rocks in the area of the bodies into the incinerator. The two men who hoisted the last two bodies were sent to the showers first, next would be the ones who were digging.

Don stood frozen to the ground. Dead bodies he had learned to deal with. Killing was something altogether different.

Marsh squeezed his arm on and off again to get his attention. Don looked at him.

"What do you think, sir? Have adequate precautions been taken?"

Cole drew a few deep breaths, then held his hand out, palm down, and made several sweeping motions.

"Do you really think it's necessary?"

Don repeated the motion and held up three fingers.

"OK," Marsh said. He turned to the man who fired the revolver. "He says you have to go three inches deeper in this whole area."

The officer nodded, then looked at Don. "Look. You know the orders we had. I did what I did because of orders. We were to allow *nothing* contaminated out of the perimeter. You of all people should know what this virus can do."

Don looked back at him and said nothing.

The men finished shoveling the dirt into the incinerator, threw the shovels in, and closed the hatch. Soon it was lit. Even at a distance of ten feet, Don could feel the heat of it within minutes.

Marsh got Cole's attention again and raised his eyebrows as if to ask a question. Don put a hand on his mask and then pointed west.

"Yes sir. Right away," Marsh said, then addressed the other officer again. "We have to leave now. We realize what happened was not your fault. Actually, you're lucky we're here. We can back up your account of what happened."

The look of relief on the other officer's face was obvious. "Yes. Thank you, sir. Is there anything else you need?"

"Yes," Marsh said. "We'd like to take a look at your directive to make sure it's in order—just for your protection, mind you. If there were errors that went through and got caught later, you know your neck would be the one on the line."

The young man nodded grimly. "Yeah. I'll tell Sergeant Jenkins to show them to you after you decon. And thanks again, Captain. You too, sir." He directed the last remark to Don.

Marsh and Don went to the kiddie pool and started the decontamination process. When they finished, they found Sergeant Jenkins, who handed them a folder. Marsh looked over the papers first and then, with a sober look, handed them to Don.

The documentation was all there. These men were on orders from the highest authority. Don recognized several of the names authorizing the actions. This was, indeed, being carried out from the highest levels of government.

"Satisfied?" Marsh asked.

"For now? Yes. Now get me out of here."

They returned to the jeep and quickly exited the reserve. It was late afternoon.

Don felt numb. No fear, anger, or horror. Just numb.

"So . . . will you join us?" Marsh finally said.

Don looked at him. These were people who played life-and-death games against others who were willing to do the same.

Is this what it takes to lead the country? Life can mean nothing to you. They kill some of ours; we kill some of theirs. Casualties among bystanders are expected, and by the way, what's for lunch?

"I can't give you an answer right now." he said. "I've seen what you wanted me to see. I believe you, but I haven't decided what I'm going to do about it. Suffice to say, you've given me a lot to think about."

"Just one more thing," Marsh said as he slowed the jeep to a halt. "You need to be aware of something. Remember the ERWs in the metal cases in Africa?"

"I got the message your people gave me," Don said, putting a hand up. "They brought them back to the United States to cover their tracks."

"Not exactly, Mr. Cole . . . two of the cases have disappeared. We have no idea who's got them at the moment, and apparently, neither does Todd. They're in hyperpanic mode trying to find them. No one knows for sure if they disappeared over there, on the plane, or after touchdown here. Our sources say the Russians took 'em and then sold them on the black market." He shook his head. "It's perfect for the Russians. Even if the bombs are found, they're United States bombs . . . and we can't help but think they're on their way back to this country . . . or to the Middle East. Can you imagine . . . ," he didn't need to finish the sentence.

Don looked out over the fields of dried grass. The majestic Rockies rose sharply in front of them. He could hear birds singing. *This can't be real.*

"I know this is a lot to absorb, but we are running out of time, Mr. Cole. *America* is running out of time."

Cole could not bring himself to speak.

"Well, if you decide to contact us, send a birthday card to John Smith at this address." He pulled out a card and handed it to Don. Don took the card and stuck it in his wallet.

Marsh was silent the rest of the ride. When they pulled up to the tents in front of the nursing home, he left the engine running. "Stay safe, sir."

"Yeah," he said, exiting the jeep.

Marsh pulled away and drove out of sight. Don wanted only to be alone, but figured he'd better find his twin first and let him know he hadn't been abducted.

Josh showed relief when he saw Don. "Are you OK? What did that guy want?"

Don just shook his head. "I can't talk now, Josh."

"Are you in any sort of trouble?"

"With the government? No, I don't think so."

"Can I help you with something, Don? You look awful."

"I know. But you can't help me, Josh. This is something I have to work out," he said and walked away.

For the rest of his stay in Denver, Don was strangely silent. Even the media could not badger a response out of him. It was a drastic change. Don Cole had been the man with a clever answer for any question, the man who could rise to the level of any debate. Now he was a man with nothing to say.

During the darkest hours of the nation's history, something had kept it from destruction. Something greater than patriotism, or cleverness, or strength. Was it God? Now that the shield was slipping away, what could anyone do to draw it back?

Josh could see that his new friend was in a deep depression, and the others agreed. Something terrible had happened to Don. They didn't push him to talk; they let him go with them whenever he wanted to, and they treated him as one of their own.

CHAPTER THIRTY-SEVEN

Tony Bensen got himself another juice from the large bowl of chipped ice. He had only been at the White House dinner party for thirty minutes, and already he wanted to leave. He had wanted to meet with President Todd and his wife, Edith, but so far neither had appeared. At least dinner would be served soon. He hoped he wouldn't be stuck at a table with Washington socialites. He hated stupid conversation about redecorating and stock market tips. The only thing worse than getting stuck with them at a dinner table was getting trapped on an airplane with them. At least he could leave the dinner if it got bad.

As his eyes scanned the crowd, he did spot several interesting looking people and a few good-looking women. Hopefully, one or two of them would end up nearby. He sipped his juice and went to find a chair to relax in until it was time to eat.

At the other end of the room, Daniel Ingram and Ricky Ruiz stood uncomfortably. Neither of them cared for social events. Daniel had been invited to the White House along with people representing twenty other inner-city agencies who had outreaches to the needy. They were to have met with the president in the afternoon to discuss the state of the inner cities and receive certificates of appreciation. The only reason Daniel had come all the way from New York for this was that he wanted to look the president of the United States in the eye and tell him something. The co-pastor of the church, Josh Thornton, was still quarantined in Denver and could not attend. Daniel was happy to invite Ricky to come in Josh's place, because he considered Ricky to be one of his best front-line workers. But after all the schedule juggling and the traveling, the meeting with the president was canceled at the last minute. They were invited to the dinner instead and told that President Todd would address them at that time.

Ricky looked as if he were suffocating. He hated wearing ties, and the collar of his shirt was too tight. He leaned over to Daniel and said, "I'm about this close to ripping this tie off and running from the room. You think he's ever going to show up?"

Daniel looked up at Ricky and had to smile. The man looked as if he were on death row. "Really enjoying yourself, eh?"

"And *you* are?"

"Got me there . . . I guess we just should have stayed home. I was so sure I was going to get to say . . . "

The room grew silent as the president and his wife were announced. They entered the room arm in arm. He stood about six feet tall, and with her heels on, so did she. They made a stunning couple. They walked past the assembled guests and directly to the dining room.

Soon everyone was seated, and a three-piece ensemble played while dinner was served. Ricky and Daniel sat at a table quite a distance from the president, but they could see him. There were three women at their table, four other men, and an empty chair. One of the men looked vaguely familiar to Ricky, but he couldn't place him.

Tony Bensen was irritated. He had come to this dinner to visit with Edith and other friends, and here he was stuck at a table far from everyone he knew. As soon as the dinner was over, he planned to leave. There were three women at the table with their husbands and two other men besides himself. The two men appeared to be friends. One of the men was quite large and dark skinned, and Tony noticed he was missing half a finger on his left hand. Not the kind of guy you would want to run into on a dark night in an alley, but interesting looking, none the less. There was a strange intensity about him, and he looked people directly in the eyes. What was even more intriguing was that Tony could read almost nothing about this man or the older man seated next to him. Maybe the evening wouldn't be a total bust. He liked a challenge.

After a few minutes, Edith got up from her place and mingled around the room for a while. Eventually, she worked her way over to Tony. He could tell she was anxious about many things. He offered her the empty seat next to him, and she sat down. Everyone at the table was interested in what was going on, but because they were trying to be polite, most of them looked away occasionally or spoke to each other. Ricky and Daniel made no pretenses and watched as Tony put a hand on top of hers and then turned it over. He pinched some pressure points on her hand, and she closed her eyes.

"You really need to relax," he said softly.

"I know. It's been a dreadful day. There's still Denver stuff to think about and several other things that really backed up on us today. And I'm sorry you got stuck out here in the back forty. It wasn't my doing. Honest. The whole day has gone like this."

"Let's count down," Tony said calmly. "Ten, nine . . . "

She began to count down with him, " . . . eight, seven . . . "

"Mrs. Todd," Ricky said, interrupting them. "Are you and your husband still planning on visiting New York next month?"

She opened her eyes and looked at Ricky. She was amazed that she hadn't noticed him until just that moment. "Why, yes. As long as the Denver problems get cleared up, we should be able to come. And of course, I am scheduled to speak at the global warming conference there anyway. I wouldn't miss that for the world. Even if my husband can't come, I'll still be there."

"Global warming. And you would rate that as a problem greater or lesser than poverty?" Ricky looked directly into her eyes.

Everyone at the table turned to look at the First Lady.

Wow, Tony thought, *this guy is more than interesting; he's like a human bomb.*

She stared back directly at Ricky. How dare this man pick a fight with her at her own dinner party! "Well, you might not agree with me, but I feel that the two problems are inextricably intertwined with several others. Over-population, global warming, and reduced crop capacity all add to human suffering."

Another woman came to the table and spoke to Mrs. Todd quietly. Edith looked around the table and said, "Excuse me, I'm needed elsewhere." She looked at Tony and said in a softer voice, "I'll try to get back to you later."

"Sure," he said, smiling. "Bravo, dear."

She smiled back and left.

Tony turned and looked right at Ricky. "So. What do you do?"

"I'm an emergency medical technician in New York, but that's not why I'm here."

Very interesting, Tony thought. *Answered the question before I asked it.*

"I'm Ricky Ruiz, and this is Daniel Ingram. He's the pastor of an inner-city church in New York. I work with him in ministry to youth, addicts, and the homeless. And you are?"

"Tony Bensen," he said as he reached over and shook Ricky's hand, then Daniel's.

When Ricky heard the name, he vaguely remembered seeing Tony on TV once. "Television?"

"Well, yes, occasionally."

"Oh," Ricky said, cutting off a piece of his chicken.

Fascinating. Most people will go out of their way to flatter anyone who might be considered a celebrity. But this guy is truly unimpressed. Tony smiled and ate his vegetables. *Well if nothing else,* he thought, *I'll get some humility out of the evening.*

The rest of the dinner passed in relative quiet. Tony was about to excuse himself when Daniel Ingram and about ten others were asked to come to the head table. Tony decided to stay for at least a few more minutes and watch. Ricky sat at the table and prayed silently.

Men and women with cameras gathered on one side of the table and snapped photos as the president stood and made a few brief remarks in appreciation of what "these brave men and women" were doing in the inner cities of America. He said he wished there were more like them and that he hoped the spirit of volunteerism would grow in this country. He handed each one a certificate and shook their hand. When he got to Daniel, he paused after the handshake. Tony could hear that Daniel was saying something, but he couldn't make out the words. From the president's countenance, Tony could tell it was not being well received. There was an awkward moment when Daniel finished saying whatever it was and Todd just stood there waiting for him to move away. Eventually, he made a small reply and Daniel walked to the table.

As he approached, he looked at Ricky. "Well, I think that about does it. What do you say, ready to go?"

Ricky looked at Tony as if he were considering something for a moment, then he looked back at Daniel, "Yeah."

Fascinating, Tony thought as he watched them leave. *I would love to know what the smaller one said to Todd. I guess that won't be hard to find out. But what I'd really like to know is what the big guy was thinking.*

After they got outside, Ricky spoke first. "So. Did you get to say everything you wanted to?"

"I told him that God was going to hold him responsible for the blood of millions of people. That if he did not repent of the things he was doing secretly, he had no hope of escaping God's wrath. I told him that in spite of the fact that things looked under control right now, his problems were going to return to him, and that by the end of the year, there would be an end to his service in this country. I wanted to say more, but I felt that's all the Lord gave me permission to say. I'm satisfied."

"The guy across the table from us. He has something to do with this. Sad to think the White House uses a medium to get by."

"Think so?"

"With her, it's already happening. With him? Wait till he gets in more trouble. It's only a matter of time."

"God help us."

"I was kind of torn about leaving. I really wanted to talk to that guy. But I felt that this wasn't the time or the place. Maybe we'll get another opportunity."

Ricky and Daniel took a cab to their hotel for the night. The next day, they left for an early flight back to New York.

When they got to the airline ticket counter, they were told the back of the plane was full; they would be bumped up to first class.

The clerk reassigned them to their new seats, and they went to wait on the flight. After a few minutes, Ricky looked up. "This is so great. Praise God."

"What?" Daniel, who was distracted with sermon notes, asked.

"Look who just walked up."

Daniel had to chuckle. It was the man who had sat across from them at dinner, Tony Bensen. "Well, you wanted another chance."

"And if he's in first class, he's mine. OK?"

"Gotcha," Daniel said. "I think I ought to bring you wherever I go. The Lord really lets you have your way."

Soon the flight was boarding. When they got on the plane, Ricky entered first, then turned around and gave Daniel a huge grin.

Daniel stuck a hand up in the air. "Don't tell me. I know already."

"Yeah. Great, huh? You'll pray for me, right?"

Tony Bensen had just settled into a window seat when he looked up and saw Ricky Ruiz standing over the seat beside him. He instantly recognized the large man who had been at his table the night before. The man took off a leather jacket and folded it in half. Tony saw a large crown of thorns embroidered on the back with "Isa. 53:5" in the middle of it.

"Nice coat," he offered.

Ricky smiled. "Yeah. Thanks."

"Someone you like gave it to you?"

Ricky just smiled.

Tony spoke again. "Remember me? From last night."

"Sure I do. In fact I saw you before you got on the plane, but you didn't see me."

"So, you're going back to New York?" Tony asked as Ricky eased into his seat. *No wonder he rides first class. How would he get those legs in coach?*

"Yeah. You going there to visit? You live there?"

"Neither. Just passing through. Actually, I'm on my way to Europe, and then parts unknown."

"Oh."

They were quiet for a while. As soon as they were off the ground the stewardess asked them what they wanted to drink, and it was silent once again.

"So what did your friend say to the president last night?" Tony finally asked.

"She didn't tell you?"

"Who? Oh, Edith. No. I didn't talk to her again last night. I decided about the time you left that it was time for me to go, too. Those things really bore me."

Ricky was silent for a while before Tony realized he hadn't answered the question. This guy was intriguing— not rude—just a mystery.

"So, you're not going to tell me, are you?"

"No."

"OK. I can respect that. You live in New York long?"

"All my life."

"And you're an EMT?"

"Yes."

"I bet you must see a lot of things that make you think about life."

"Yes, I do."

"And if I remember it right, you work with teens and homeless people or something like that, right?"

Ricky nodded his head.

Tony decided to give up. It was too much work to get something out of this guy.

They sat in silence again for a while, and then Ricky spoke. "You do that meditation stuff for a living?"

Tony didn't know if he should be insulted or not. He smiled slightly. "Yes, I guess you could say that."

"Must pay well."

"Yes, it does. But I work hard at what I do."

"And what do you think is the source of your power?"

Tony remembered the Scripture reference on the back of the coat, so he wanted to be careful not to get cornered by this guy if he was a Bible thumper. "God."

"And what is your God's name?"

"You first."

Ricky pointed to himself and smiled. "You want to know about my God? His name is Jesus."

"I believe in Jesus."

In spite of what Bensen was saying, Ricky knew they were coming from different places spiritually. "Jesus as what?"

"I believe Jesus is God."

"Yeah. But is He *your* God?"

Tony knew they were wrestling, yet he kind of enjoyed it. The man seemed different from others he'd known. He seemed more curious than threatening. Tony also sensed intelligence and kindness, and it made him want to know what Ricky thought. "I don't know. I suppose so, in the grand scheme of things."

"Oh . . . so you believe in Jesus in a prophet and teacher light, but not as your personal Lord?"

"Well, it's not easy to put into words. I believe that Jesus came and that He died, but I believe there's more to God's plan than that. I can believe in Jesus and still hold other beliefs as well."

"Your belief in Him is not exclusive then?" Ricky asked. He knew it wasn't a question of just quoting a few Bible verses to straighten out the path between them. This man had already heard it all. He wouldn't be won in a debate. If he didn't want to know, he never would.

"Exactly."

Ricky grew quiet again for a while.

"And *your* view?" Tony finally said.

"Exclusive," he smiled.

"And you are not open to a greater truth?" Tony smiled back. They weren't saying many words, but he was savoring this. He could like this man. It was like meeting an equal.

"Are you interested in the truth? Do you believe there is such a thing as truth? Ultimate truth?" Ricky asked.

"Yes. Maybe man will never know it, but yes, I believe there is."

"And you seek this truth?" Ricky's eyes danced with light.

For a moment, Tony almost envied him. "Yes, I do. It's why I'm traveling now. I want to spend some time just seeking."

The seatbelt sign came on. They were almost at their destination.

"Then we can agree on something before we land," Ricky said.

"Yes?" Tony felt they were connecting on some level.

"Yes. May I pray for you? May I ask that, in God's time, you find the ultimate truth?"

"Yes, you can."

Ricky put a large hand on Tony's shoulder, and it was as if something warm shot through him. "Father," he began, "this man is seeking the truth. We're in agreement asking that he find it. That his soul find ultimate rest, ultimate peace, ultimate truth. I pray You would show him the way Lord, in Your time. I know I can trust You to do this, because You still hear and You still answer the call of any heart that seeks You. Thank You. In Jesus' name, amen."

The plane landed, and they went their separate ways. Ricky knew God had touched Tony's life and was satisfied that if Tony really wanted it, he would eventually find the ultimate truth.

CHAPTER THIRTY-EIGHT

PASTOR DANIEL INGRAM WOKE UP. HE TRIED LYING QUIETLY for a while and then sat up. *I must get up.*

Anne rolled toward him. "Are you OK?"

He reached over and put a hand on her arm. "I'm fine. Go back to sleep."

"Did you have the dream again?"

"No. I think I'll just go and sit in my study for a while."

"You want me to get up with you?"

"Thanks. But I've had so much excitement today with Josh making it back and hearing what he had to say about Denver, I'm just all stirred up inside. I think I'd like to be alone."

"You sure?"

He patted her shoulder. "I'm sure," he said, and left the room. He went in his study and closed the door. He started to turn on the light and then decided not to. Instead, he sat in the darkness and prayed for a while. What he'd said to Anne was true. He felt very stirred.

The co-pastor of the church, Josh Thornton, had been in Denver when the earthquake struck. The whole church had prayed for the people of Denver, Josh, and the other visiting pastors. While others questioned why God would permit a disaster in a city where so many pastors were visiting, Daniel considered the fact that the pastors had been there by a divine appointment. Who needed pastors more than people in dire straits? Several hundred pastors, who would not have to worry about digging out their own family members or churches, were on the scene and ready.

Most amazing of all was the fact that while he was in Washington, D.C., speaking to President Todd, Josh was in Denver speaking to Donald Cole! When Josh returned, he and Daniel met in his office and compared notes. They were astounded at what God had done. Especially interesting to Daniel was the news of Donald Cole. He was deeply moved by Josh's description of the man. As Josh continued to speak of Cole, something even greater began to stir in Daniel's heart.

" . . . and you know," Josh had said, "I really believe God's hand is on Cole. He was *this close* to surrendering it all—more than once—but then something happened. I don't know what transpired that afternoon, but a soldier came and took him away in a jeep. When Cole came back, it was as if he'd visited hell. I've never seen anyone so devastated."

. . . he will not be of your choosing, but of Mine. A man who has no wife, no child, who will be set apart by Me . . . Pray for this man, for his enemies are great in strength and number, echoed in Ingram's mind. "Wait a moment, Josh. You say Cole is not married? Has no children?"

Josh was puzzled by the sudden shift in conversation. "Yes, that's right."

Daniel had only recently told Josh and a few others that the Lord had spoken regarding a Gatekeeper. He had not shared any of the details God had given him concerning the man, but he had asked the men to pray for whomever God was raising up. Now he felt he could share just a bit more. He brought his chair back to an upright position. "Cole's the one, Josh. The Gatekeeper . . . It's beginning to make sense to me now. The Lord said it was someone I wouldn't choose, a man without wife or children. . . . I was thinking of a pastor or a prophet, but I could never see whom God would pick to represent us as a nation. God means to put someone in a national seat of authority all right. In the office of president."

Josh felt a sudden weight of responsibility. He tried to recall all of his conversations with Don. Then, as he remembered their final moments together, he felt like a failure. Maybe he should have offered to pray with him or done something more meaningful than just hand him a business card and shake his hand. After some thought, Josh concluded two things: He *had* sought the Lord on Don's behalf, and he *hadn't* felt the urge to do more than he'd done. Although this wasn't very satisfying at the moment, it would have to do. He finally shook his head and said, "Well, it will definitely take God's help, because he's in deep trouble—political *and* personal. And right now, I don't think he has the heart to go on."

As Daniel sat and thought of it, he felt moved to pray for Don Cole. He prayed God would draw him to a place of safety and give him the courage and strength to go on. "And, Lord," he said, "I believe You're saying he is the one. . . . You said that You would bring the Gatekeeper to me. . . . I will not go out to him, but if You bring this man to me, I will anoint him."

CHAPTER THIRTY-NINE

DON COLE LEANED BACK IN HIS AIRPLANE SEAT. A FRIEND had offered a vacant penthouse apartment in New York if he ever really needed to get away and rest. If ever he needed to get away, it was now. He would hole up there for a couple of days and get his thoughts together. No one from the campaign was to contact him; he wasn't even going to watch the news. He needed to think.

Don had been shaken to the core by all he had seen and heard in the last few weeks. For the first time that he could remember, he wasn't even sure he *wanted* to be president of the United States.

He looked out the window and saw the plane careening through a layer of clouds. That was how he felt, too—as if he were lurching forward at five hundred miles an hour to an unknown fate. Just that morning, he'd had sobering words from Bob Post. Bob told him he needed to get a grip on himself and that he'd better make some friends in the press if he wanted to rejoin the race for the presidency.

He shook his head at the irony. Here he was, probably one of a handful who knew the truth, and he would be institutionalized or jailed if he dared tell anyone. And a man capable of Hitleresque evil was well on his way to staying in the White House.

But that was not all. During what Bob described as Don's "absence from sanity," Congress had been busy. While the country's eyes were fixed on the Rockies, legislation regarding regeneration managed to work its way through both houses. Only two scientists and one doctor dared to appear before the Senate to protest the legislation. (The doctor was now in the process of being investigated for fraud and unprofessional practices by the National Medical Board, facing the possibility of losing his right to practice medicine.)

But due in part to Don's efforts with lobbyists for seniors, approval of the total program was waylayed. Instead, a three-tiered process would begin for instituting the Alternative Health Care program, during which the regeneration process could be scrutinized more carefully before being put into the permanent health-care system. The bill needed only the president's signature to become law.

As the clouds whisked by the window, he reflected on what Josh had said to him. America used to be a Christian nation and knew the benefit of God's blessing. As the country moved away from its heritage—ironically, in the name of freedom—God was withdrawing His blessing.

How far have we gone? How much farther can we go and still exist as a free nation? he thought. *Are we now going to be trapped between Todd's people and the Quick and the Dead, who for the sake of freedom would go to who-knows-what lengths? And if the Quick and the Dead were in power, how would they rule? By force? How can anyone govern a man who has lost the ability to restrain himself?*

Don shut his eyes. He realized he had become much too cynical and thought once again of Josh, who said he had "seen too much and heard too much." Like his friend who had been in the same situation, Don needed to get his direction straight. He felt cold all over and shivered.

"Need a blanket?" the flight steward said.

He turned and looked at the man offering the blanket. "Thanks," he said as he took it and turned to face the window again.

"How about a pillow?"

Why won't he just leave me alone? Don thought. "No thanks," he replied without looking back.

Soon he heard the voice of the steward asking Avery, his personal bodyguard, about dinner. Good old Avery. His faithful protector had fully recovered from his illness and was back on duty.

"Does he want anything to eat?"

"I think he just wants to rest for now," Avery said. "But go ahead and heat up something. He may be awake and hungry by the time you serve it."

"Beef or chicken?"

"He's a beef kinda guy. In fact, make mine chicken, and I'll switch with him if he'd rather have mine . . . OK?"

"Great. Thanks."

Don kept his eyes closed. As a matter of fact, he *was* hungry, and it would be a long flight. He decided he'd probably take the meal when it came around. He dozed for a while after he got warm, but he woke up when they hit a slight bump and the seat belt light dinged on again.

The steward had arrived with the food. Don sat up and looked over.

"Beef or chicken, Mr. Cole?" the steward asked.

"Beef, please," Don said and tried to let his face relax into a smile. He put down his tray and inspected the dinner. It looked pretty good, actually. He'd been eating out of an Army tent for two weeks, and this definitely looked better than anything he'd seen in a while.

After he'd had a couple of bites, he felt a little guilty about the mood he'd been in the past few days.

"Thanks for ordering my dinner. I guess I'm not very good company," Don said to Avery, who had moved next to him.

"Who can blame you? You've been through a lot, Mr. Cole. I know you feel discouraged right now, but you'll see; it'll turn around. You're a man of honesty and sincerity, and people will see that."

"Yeah, right," Cole said before he realized how sarcastic it sounded. He shook his head. "Sorry. Told you I wasn't good company." *All I know right now is that being honest in a world of thieves is not enough. Being sincere in a world of liars is not enough . . . it's just not enough,* he thought.

As he ate he marveled at how quickly things could turn around. Just a few months ago, he thought he was on a roll. He was making stirring speeches, getting along with news people, staying out of no-win arguments—even getting along with Larry.

"What are you planning on doing when you get to New York?" Avery interrupted his thoughts.

"Rest mostly," Don said, but that wasn't entirely true. He had sent his Secret Service people packing before he went to Denver. Avery was the only man who had come with him, and the poor guy ended up in the hospital for a week. Don and his "twin," Josh, had nearly worked themselves to the bone. Not only was Don tired, he was more depressed than he had ever been. Looking back over the past days, he realized it was Josh and the others who had kept him from giving up altogether. They left Denver the day before Don. Two went back to Texas, one to Philadelphia, and three—Josh, Landis, and Bobby—returned to New York.

On the day he left Denver, Josh gave Don his card. "Hey, if you're ever in the Big Apple, look me up. . . . Or if for any reason you decide you want to talk to somebody, my number's on the card. Home number's on the back."

"Thanks. I just might do that," Don said. He shook Josh's hand and watched him leave.

After thinking about it for a day, Don decided to go to New York. He knew that by the time he left the city he would either be running for president or back to being an ordinary man.

After dinner he excused himself and turned back to the window. He slept the remainder of the flight. In a matter of minutes, it seemed, they were landing in New York. Within two hours, they were safely ensconced in his friend's apartment.

When he was alone, Don ventured over to one of the large windows and looked out at the city lights. There are millions of people down there, he told himself. All blissfully unaware of what's going on.

He sighed and moved away from the window. He wondered what the Quick and the Dead were going to do now. Would they attempt some kind of coup? He decided it was best not to consider the possibilities.

He got out his wallet, found the card he was looking for, and read the large print. "Joshua Thornton, Co-Pastor." Apparently, Thornton had missed receiving some sort of presidential recognition for the church's work in the inner city while he was quarantined in Denver.

Don picked up the phone and dialed the number on the back of the card. After two rings a woman answered.

"Hello?"

"Hello. Could I please speak with Josh Thornton?"

"Sure. May I ask who's calling?"

"It's Don Cole."

There was a short silence before he got a response. "Oh! OK. He's here. Can you hang on a moment?"

"Sure."

"Hello?" Josh said.

"Hello. It's your twin. You're probably surprised that I'm calling so soon, but you did say that if I was ever in town, to look you up."

"You're here? Great!" Josh looked at his watch. It was eight o'clock. "When did you get in?"

"Just now, actually."

"Have you had dinner? Are you hungry?"

"I ate on the plane," Cole said.

"Tasted OK after the army food, huh?"

"Yeah, it did."

"What can I do for you, Don?"

Don was silent for a moment. Why did he call Josh anyway? "I had an offer to stay in a friend's place here to recuperate, and I remembered I had your card."

"How about if I come to where you are?" Thornton offered.

"Is it too late for you?

"No. I'm rested up now. Too late for you?"

"Here's the address," Cole said, and he read it off another card from his wallet.

Before he left his house, Josh called Daniel Ingram.

"You'll never guess who just called me."

"Don Cole just called you? Where is he?"

"He's here in New York," Josh said. "He wants to see me right now. I wanted to call you and let you know so you could be praying."

Daniel had almost fallen into a chair when Josh told him where Cole was. "Definitely. I'll tell Anne and some of the others. . . . Would you call me when you get back home?"

In an hour and a half, Josh was sitting in the penthouse with Don.

"So, did you come to New York for any particular reason?" Josh asked.

"A buddy of mine owns this, and he told me I could use it to rest whenever I wanted to. I was exhausted, the apartment was empty, and you had invited me, so I got on a plane. . . . I'll need to get back on the trail in a couple of days."

Josh looked at him. "Still really ticked off at the press?"

"Yes."

"But I see the Secret Service guys are back . . . and you just came here to rest."

"Well, that's not entirely true. . . . I guess you already know that. The truth is that I wanted to talk to you. I wanted to spend time with somebody who isn't angry at me or doesn't want something from me." Don had intended to work his way up to the subject, but before he realized it, he blurted out, "I'm so confused right now that I'm not entirely sure that I want to be president anymore. I've seen and heard things. . . . " He looked directly at Josh, hoping his friend would understand the magnitude of what he was trying to communicate. "Things I can't tell you. Really terrible things, Josh. If people had any idea how much trouble we're in . . . " Don didn't finish the sentence.

Josh thought of the day Don was taken away by the man in uniform. Whatever he had seen or heard had brought him to this point. Josh guessed it had to do with the quake or those who caused it.

Don went on, "Remember telling me that you almost quit because you saw too much? That's where I am right now. I don't know why I'm running for president . . . even if I am elected, I don't know if I could do anything to change the course of this country."

Josh turned to look out the window. "But you came here hoping to find answers, didn't you? You must have some hope that things could change, or you wouldn't have come."

Don thought for a moment. "In the middle of the worst of it—finding those dead people, digging up others to have them die later—I watched you and the other guys. I saw a certainty, or . . . like a fixed purpose, that seemed to keep you going."

Josh looked directly at him. "Well, you kept going, too. What kept you going?"

Don looked down and shook his head. "Boy, this sounds stupid. . . . It was watching you guys that kept me going. I mean, I'm a Christian. I go to church when I can. I believe in having a moral standard. But it's not enough. At least, for me it's not enough."

"Define what you mean when you say you are a Christian. Lots of people use that term, so it's kinda lost its meaning these days," Josh said.

"I prayed a sinner's prayer at an altar when I was eleven or twelve. I got water baptized . . . I believe in Jesus . . . what else is there?"

"Do you spend any time with God anymore? Do you read the Bible? Do you ask God for His advice?"

Don gave him a look.

"I'm not trying to be critical of you, Don; I'm just trying to figure out where you are."

"Well, I pray . . . sometimes. I guess I'm just not that kind of guy. Seeking a spiritual answer isn't the first thing that pops into my head, OK?"

"Define *spiritual* for me. That term has lost its meaning, too."

"Like on my knees. Holy. Choosing the right words . . . "

"Did the others and I insist on getting on our knees? Did we get real religious on you? Did it seem we were just saying words we were quoting out of a book? Tell the truth, Don."

"Well, no. But I didn't feel I could begin to measure up to the way you guys prayed."

"Why is that, Don? Is that because we're pastors and you're not? I don't think so," Josh smiled. "Real prayer is having a running conversation with God. Open-ended, never completely done. Knowing He hears everything I say or think—and even things about me that I won't admit to myself. It's letting Him speak back to me," Josh said, and then quickly added, "Please understand me. I'm a man—just like you; I make mistakes—just like you. But I had to come to a place where I realized I couldn't fix myself, much less all the people I saw and all the problems they had. It was too much for me. I had to realize that the only one who had the power to fix anything was God. And if I was His and in fellowship with Him—if I was in His care, if I allowed myself to be His friend—then I was no longer the center of things; He was. It does give me a fixed purpose, a certainty—not in myself, but in God. Boy, does that take the heat off!"

Josh smiled at his friend before continuing. "Think of it this way: You're a soldier during a war. You're alone, behind enemy lines. The commander in chief is the one with the reinforcements, the reconnaissance, the big weapons. Do you try to get back to where he and his other troops are? Or do you just keep going without any contact or instruction, thinking you can win the war alone? You still have a uniform on, so whenever the enemy soldiers see you they'll shoot at you. You can do one of three things: You can take off the uniform and try to blend in with the enemy till the war's over. You can try to be a hero and go it alone, without orders—possibly messing up your own army's plans. Or you can find your way back to your troops and get the plan from the commander."

Josh was quiet for a moment before adding. "Even God wants something back, Don. He wants His people to have a relationship with Him and with each other. Not a one-time acknowledgment or a minimum of well-chosen words on special occasions, not superficial junk. A relationship . . . you know? Being part of your everyday life. You came here to talk to me. Why? Because we've spent time together, developed a relationship—even in the middle of really terrible things—and you know you can be honest with me. . . . Maybe you feel that you can't talk to God because you've never spent time with Him."

"So let's say I buy that. What should I do now?" Cole asked.

"Just start. Tonight, just start talking to Him. Tell Him how discouraged you are. If you're scared, tell Him you are. Tell Him how mad you are at the press. Tell Him how bad things are. . . . Tell Him you don't know why you're running for president. It's not as if He doesn't know all this already, but when you tell Him, you're rolling it over on Him. Tell Him you're giving Him permission to set it—or you—straight. Then give Him space to tell you something back. You'd be surprised how clear it gets when you've been honest and are willing to hear an honest answer."

The two men spoke for another hour and agreed to meet again the next day. Don asked Josh if he could take him to meet the other pastor at the church, Daniel

Ingram. Don had heard of Ingram and his work in the inner city. He was interested in meeting the man.

That night, Don stayed up and talked to God. He felt stupid at first. What if someone were listening? Did he care anymore? What if God was listening? Once he got over his initial apprehension, it felt good to unload. No actual words or thoughts came to him in response, but he did feel at peace—something he had not experienced in a long time.

Don went to bed and slept better than he had in six months. When he woke up, he felt as if a burden had left him. Things seemed clearer.

He had Avery get him a large breakfast, and he just sat for a while looking out the window.

Josh knocked on the door at ten. The look on his face said he had great news.

Don studied at him for a moment. "What's going on?"

"Well, Banner Network has done pretty good by you today . . . and I was listening to the results of one of those polls you love so much, and well, you probably know what they are saying now."

"Actually, I haven't seen any news for two days," Don said.

"Really? Well, it seems public opinion against Todd is really starting to swell. They think he's gone too far with the investigations. Apparently, over a thousand people were rounded up at first, and now all their families are creating an uproar. There have been several stand-offs with small militia groups across the country . . . and Todd's toll-free number is being dubbed the 'national turn-in-your-neighbor hot line.'"

"When did you hear this?" Cole couldn't believe his ears.

"This morning on Banner and then later on one of the other networks. I'm surprised no one else told you."

Don blinked and looked around the room. "Two days ago, I was just about handed my hat and shown the door by these guys," he chuckled. "My campaign manager is probably having the world's largest fit by now. I didn't give him this number, and I haven't called him."

"You want to call him now?"

"No. Let him suffer a while. I'll call him later."

They drove to the church and went into Daniel Ingram's office. Josh could sense Cole was nervous after the introductions, so he spoke first. "Don and I are old digging buddies now. We got to be known as 'the twins' because we were covered with so much dirt no one could tell us apart. We were about the only ones who didn't get sick, so they almost worked us to death instead. This guy probably knows more about me than my wife!"

"That's true," Don said, smiling. "And the way he smelled after a couple of days, I'm not sure his wife would have stayed as close to him, either!"

Josh and Don took turns telling stories about the things they had seen and done. Eventually, Josh and Ingram could see Cole had relaxed enough to talk easily.

"So tell me," Ingram said in a casual tone, "why do you want to be president?"

"Actually," Don laughed, "last night I wasn't so sure. . . . But today, I feel that I'm back on track. Even as a young man, I felt my call was to public office. I know most people consider it a really dirty job, but I ran for public office because I always thought I could make a difference. The only thing that shook my resolve is the realization I might not be able to make a difference."

"You've seen what's happening haven't you?" Ingram said.

Don knew Ingram wasn't just talking about some invisible, mystical thing, but what was actually happening in the country. What could be seen if someone dared to look, what might be intruding on the lives of everyone soon, whether they wanted to see it or not.

"Yes. And far worse things may happen soon," he said.

"Who do you think is behind all of this?" Ingram asked.

"You mean, do I think there's some huge conspiracy with one person who's directing it? I don't think so. All I see is chaos. I don't know if one person, or even a group of people, would be capable of orchestrating all of it. Josh told me he thought we were all somewhat to blame. I'm beginning to believe he's right. Last night I was going to quit because I knew I couldn't possibly fix the horrible things that are going wrong. Now I realize that was part of the problem. Our whole generation has been taught to look within for answers, that truth is relevant, and that each person can find his own way. It dawned on me that we are now reaping the results of this mind-set."

"And what do you intend to do now?" Daniel asked. Even before Cole's answer came, the Lord began speaking to him, "This is the one I choose."

Cole shrugged. "I may win, I may lose, but I realize that unless somebody in authority is willing to stand in the face of what is coming and seek God's help, we will not survive. If He allows me, I will stand in that place and I will seek His help."

Daniel inhaled slowly, then exhaled before he spoke. "In essence, Mr. Cole, what you have asked is to be the gatekeeper of this country . . . the one who will be responsible before God for this country. The one who will stand in the way of the judgment coming. I need to tell you that you've asked to be in a hard place. It may cost all that you have. Are you sure you want to go there?"

"Yes."

Daniel Ingram sat in silence for a moment. Josh knew that look. He knew that the Lord was saying something to Daniel.

Ingram looked over at Josh and said, "He's the one." He came from behind the desk and stood in front of Don. "Mr. Cole, not only have you selected that place, but I believe God has selected you for it. If you would permit me, I would like to pray for you."

"Great."

"Can we go into the sanctuary? No one is in there right now."

"Sure."

The three men walked into the back of the large sanctuary. Ingram flipped on the lights for the altar area, then led the way. As they approached, Don's heart pounded with expectation. It was as if something warmer than his own blood was pumping through his veins.

Don and Josh stopped at the altar, Ingram went up to the podium and returned with a small bottle of oil. "You see this oil, Don?"

"Yes."

"I've had it here in the sanctuary for months. I've been waiting for someone that God would bring to me. The one He is calling to be a gatekeeper. I believe it's you. If you'll allow me, I will put some of this oil on you."

"Just like in the Bible?" Don asked.

He smiled and nodded. "Yes. Just like in the Bible. This isn't magic oil or anything. It isn't the oil that accomplishes the work—it's just a confirmation of what God is doing; that OK?"

Don needed no convincing. He got on his knees.

Daniel broke the seal on the bottle, poured some oil on his hand, then asked Josh to hold the bottle.

Don looked up at them. "Can I make a request?"

"What is it?" Ingram asked.

"Could you pour that whole bottle on me? I know this sounds crazy, but it's a symbol of God's selection and His help, isn't it?"

The two men nodded.

"I want to do this in His strength, not mine. I want all of God that I can get . . . so could we use the whole thing?"

Ingram looked at Josh. They both grinned. "We'd like nothing better."

Don closed his eyes, his arms lifted up. "Go ahead."

Daniel Ingram poured the whole bottle of oil on him, then put his hands on Don's head. Don could feel oil dripping down on his clothing. He didn't care.

"Lord," Ingram prayed, "You have said You resist the proud, but that You will exalt the humble. This man has humbled himself, Father. He has admitted to You, to himself, and to us that he can do nothing in his own strength. He has asked for Your help, has knelt at Your altar, and even allowed me to pour this whole bottle of oil on him—something that would seem foolish in the natural—all because he wants as much of You as he can get. . . . As I place my hands upon him, Lord, I ask for Your unction, Your power, wisdom, strength, grace, peace, and mercy to fill him to overflowing."

Silence came upon them like a thick blanket. No one moved or spoke.

When Daniel Ingram broke the silence, his words seemed to pierce right through Don's chest. "The Lord would say to you, that before you knew Him, He chose you. He says that, yes, He has called you to be the gatekeeper, and by His grace to stand in a place of power. He calls you to stand in the gate to resist the flood of evil and stave off the judgment of this country, whose sin has reached to the heavens and whose fate still hangs in the balance.

"The Lord says that your enemies are great in strength and number, but to remind yourself—daily—that greater is He who is in you than he who is in the world. You have said that you do not believe that one person or even a group of people is capable of doing the terrible things you have witnessed. The Lord says that this is the truth, but there is one, Satan, the ultimate enemy of your soul, who guides many. Some of them are guided subtly through desires and appetites; others are guided openly. They are not all aware of one another, or even that they move in concert at times. The Lord says the enemy will fight against God's people, but not prevail.

"God is saying no matter how it looks, He will be with you. No matter what you see with your eyes, God is with you. And no matter what, the Lord wants you to know He is able to finish what He starts."

Somehow, Don knew Ingram had spoken the truth. Every word had gone to the depths of his soul. He knew he would become the president of the United States. He knew this was what he was created to do.

CHAPTER FORTY

YOSEF PUSHED A CARD INTO THE SLOT AND PLACED HIS right hand on the screen. The doors to the elevator closed, and he waited in silence as it sped him to his appointment. Soon the doors opened, and he stepped into the small white waiting room. A single chair was in the room, but he did not sit in it. Filled with anticipation, he preferred to stand. Soon, he could be "In Proximity." He had been called to the meeting suddenly and wasn't quite sure of the purpose, but he knew it must be of the utmost importance.

Yosef had recently been called to another such meeting to receive the Denver plan, but he had not seen the One he longed to see. Perhaps he would this time. Possibly he was called to be rewarded for a job well done. Just standing In Proximity would be reward enough for Yosef. How many could say they had done this? He had already experienced it twice and could not wait to be there again. It was a strange mixture of terror, adrenaline, and ecstacy.

It was like the thrill of coming within a hair's breadth of death.

After several minutes, the door at the opposite end of the room opened. He hesitated for a moment before moving forward, feeling the warm, humid air coming from the room beyond. This could mean the One was actually there. His master hated air conditioning, preferring warmer surroundings.

His heart rate quickened as he stepped into a dimly lit room full of tropical plants. There was a wooden chair just inside the door, and Yosef knew he should sit on it. He did. When the door behind him closed, the room was almost dark. A figure approached and sat in a chair facing him. Was it him?

Yosef was glad the light was so dim, so that his disappointment wouldn't show. The man who sat in front of him was John Klost, one who worked In Proximity continually. Yosef envied him.

"You are disappointed that it's me, aren't you?" Klost said.

Yosef searched for words to express himself without giving offense. "You must understand that for people like me who have only had a few fleeting experiences, it is very hard not to look forward to every possible meeting. Is that wrong?"

"No . . . I understand. I felt that way once too, before I was brought closer to the center of things. . . . Even so, you may get your wish today, after we address a few things."

Yosef could barely contain himself. "Whatever is necessary, I will do it. You know that."

"Yes. He knows that. You have been a most faithful servant."

Yosef would keep those words as a treasure and play them over and over in his mind.

"But," Klost said, "there are many tasks at hand." He got up and brought back a cup. "Drink this first, and then we will talk."

Yosef took the cup and drank the bitter, yet salty, mixture. He knew many things had been mingled in the drink. Weren't chemicals and other mixtures his own specialty? He drank the whole thing without hesitation.

"Good," Klost said. "You know it will open your thoughts and help seal your mind on what we must do."

"Yes," Yosef said, beginning to feel the effects of the drink already. He was being prepared to be In Proximity, and in spite of the drugs, he already felt the terror he had looked forward to.

Several hours would pass before he left the room and exited the building. He would have lost all track of time. His mind would be numb for a few days, but this was to be expected. He would remember but be incapable of acting until he had recovered from the effects of the meeting.

Soon, he might need to visit the president again to carry out his master's wishes. President Todd had almost completed his useful time. He had held the gate open for many portions of the plan to be brought in and set in their proper places. In fact, for a few brief days, there was a glimmer of hope that the time had finally come. But it was not to be. While the master was pleased with the progress, he noted that Todd had aroused too much resistance. The plan would have to be put on hold once again.

America was a difficult place. One had to be aware of just when to draw back and allow a feeling of freedom to relax the people again. The enemy was on the rise—it was something that increased daily. Things would be hindered for a much longer time if this particular enemy became aware of its full strength and used it. They had to be allowed to *think* they were winning for a while. That would quench their desire to press in, and then all could finally be fulfilled.

If President Todd would not surrender his office, he would have to be forced to do so.

The vice president, Victor Bartlett, would take Todd's place in the Oval Office. Mr. Bartlett's poor leadership skills would soon be exposed to the American people, and he would be unable to win the election.

It was regrettable that Don Cole was the one who was running against Todd. Recent reports of him created great concern to those in the organization, but Yosef felt no need to worry. He had seen men of greater strength than Cole's succumb when precise pressure was applied.

Yes, there had been a few glitches in Africa and Denver, but nothing insurmountable. In spite of the problems, the pieces were falling into place. Destiny was being fulfilled, and Yosef could not believe he was actually such an integral part of it. It was more than anything for which he had hoped.

CHAPTER FORTY-ONE

WHEN DON RETURNED TO THE APARTMENT SEVERAL HOURS later, he knew it was time to get to business. He showered, then checked his computer mail. One message was from his mother—a gentle rebuke for not calling since he'd been to New York. There were also several messages marked urgent from Bob Post. Don smiled and shook his head.

Next, he called Bob.

"Hello." Bob sounded grouchy.

"Hey, Bob. It's me. The bad boy."

"Where have you been? What on earth are you doing? Haven't you seen the news? My phone is ringing off the hook. Everyone and his sister want an interview with you!"

"Does Banner Network want to talk to me?"

"As a matter of fact, they do! They want an exclusive one-on-one interview with Paul Gable," Bob said. "His studio is in New York, you know."

"Call and say tomorrow is fine if he wants."

"Great! We'll need to get our thoughts together, though," Bob said.

Don could tell all was forgiven. He could already hear the gears in Bob's head flying at lightning speed. "Sure, Bob. Want to fly up?"

"I'm already booked on the three o'clock."

"I should have figured that," Don chuckled.

"The race is about to go in the dumper if we don't do something soon. We've gotten a break, and we really need to milk this for all it's worth, Don."

"Don't worry. We're going to pull this out yet."

"Don?"

"Yeah?"

"You sound different."

"I know. I feel different." Don closed his eyes. Yes, it was still there. That sense of knowing. "We'll talk when you get here."

"How about if we bring Trina and some of the others in tomorrow? We might be able to get quite a bit done."

For the first time in months, being on the campaign trail sounded good. "Great. Where's Lawrence?"

"He went home for a few days. We ran out of things to say to reporters, so he's laying low."

"Sorry," Don said. "I'll call him right now. He can come up tomorrow or the next day, and we'll all regroup."

"Great! What's happened to you?"

"We'll talk tonight."

That night, over a late supper, Don and Bob brought each other up to date.

"Regarding your research," Don said, looking intently at Bob, "there have been new developments. I've spoken to an old friend from Seattle." He watched Bob's eyes. *Yes. He knows what I'm saying.*

Don spent several moments trying to formulate the words that could communicate that even more terrible things had happened. Then he thought better of it.

"There's no more need for research. We'll just plod ahead knowing what we know and hope everything surrounding those issues comes out all right."

"You're different, Don. What's happened to you?"

"Some of it I can't put into words, Bob. I know you thought I was crazy for staying in Denver and all. And actually, I think I almost lost it there. Maybe I had to get knocked flat so I could see where I'd gone wrong."

"So where'd you go wrong?"

"I was trying to fight something evil with my own strength," Don said, and watched his friend's eyebrows go together. "In the past, I could debate my way into office. It was merely a case of my solutions as opposed to the solutions of someone else. I could convince people I had better ideas and would follow through on them. This is not the same thing. What Todd is doing is not just different—this isn't just an 'our-party-versus-his-party' thing—the man is putting programs into place that could destroy us as a nation. I'm going to give him the fight of his life, and I am going to win."

"That's the spirit!" Bob said, slapping him on the shoulder.

"I'm going to win because God is on my side."

His campaign manager's grin disappeared instantly. A look of fear replaced it. "Oh, Don, you're not going to say that on television, are you?"

"Why? You scared of what it would do to me?"

"Are you *kidding*? We could kiss the race good-bye! 'I think God is on my side,'" he said, making quotation marks in the air. "They'll eat us alive! I can see the headlines now! 'Candidate Becomes Fundamentalist Pawn in the Conspiracy to Capture Presidency—Says That GOD Is on His Side!' Don! What's happened to you? You might as well go home now if you're going to say things like that! Your mom and I will be the only ones voting for you!"

Don laughed. "Slow down, Bob . . . I didn't say I was going to make some big proclamation about this. I just told you why I thought I was going to win."

"Oh," Post said, putting a hand over his heart. "Don't *do* things like that to me. So what makes you think *God* will help you win all of a sudden? I know this sounds cynical, but evil guys have been getting into power for at least as long as history has been recorded. Look who's in office right now!"

"Funny you should mention history. Someone proposed this theory to me, and I've really been thinking about it. There is a pattern here. Evil men come to power when people have demonstrated a total lack of restraint for a long period of time. If people will not be restrained by their own consciences, then the result of their own bad choices catches up with them."

"So . . . if that's true, what's going to make the difference here? What's going to take Todd out of office?"

"I can't describe it to you completely. I believe something has been set into place that has caused people in this country to at least stop and consider what they are doing to themselves. People are scared. And they're starting to seek God again. . . . I know *I* have prayed. I mean, I have *really* prayed, Bob, and I feel that God answered me."

Bob clapped his hand over his eyes. "We're doomed. . . . Now he's hearing voices. . . . O God, what will become of us?"

"Are you praying now, too?" Don teased. "Or was that just a rhetorical question?"

Bob opened a space between his fingers and looked at his friend. "Maybe you should take a few more days off. You know—kind of rest up."

"I've never been saner in my life. I have never been more certain of anything. I *am* going to win."

"OK, great. But promise me that you won't say God talks to you or anything like that in interviews."

By the next morning, Don had convinced Bob that he had not lost his mind and that he had no intention of blurting out verses from the Book of Revelation in front of the press. The interview with Paul Gable was scheduled for taping at 10:00 A.M. The one-hour show would be aired during prime time that evening.

When the show was about to air, Lawrence, Trina, Jason, and several other campaign workers gathered in Don's temporary New York apartment. Most of them had arrived on the same flight and had taken the same cab to the apartment. Lawrence and Jason showed up an hour later. Bob ordered pizza so they could all spend the time together before the show. The room fell quiet as Don told them about what had happened in Denver. He omitted the part about being taken to the Reserve, but spoke at length about the other things—about finding the old man, Charles, and then his Emma, about Avery, the aftershock they had experienced while sitting on the pile, and many of the things that had touched him personally. After that, Don gave everyone a rough draft of changes he would like to see in disaster response when he was elected; then he asked for more input from Lawrence and the others.

At last all of the pizza boxes were empty, and it was almost time to watch the interview. Jason went around taking drink orders. Trina went to the living room and looked out the window. Don gazed at her as she sat at the same window he'd enjoyed so much. She was wearing a soft yellow shirt with slacks, her brown hair pulled back in the usual ponytail. As his assistant campaign manager, Don had often seen her brainstorming, giving orders, and relentlessly reorganizing things. He'd rarely seen her at rest. He studied her for a moment with the intent of starting a conversation.

Bob Post entered the room and spoke to Don, breaking his train of thought. The two of them left briefly and then returned with all the others. Chairs were brought from the dining room and placed around the room, facing the TV.

Paul Gable appeared on the screen. Bob Post put his hands up for silence. "This is it! Everyone be quiet," he said, turning up the sound on the set.

"Good evening. I'm Paul Gable. Tonight, we have an exclusive interview with presidential candidate Donald Larson Cole. We won't be taking any calls because the show was taped earlier in the day. However, I do hope you'll stick around to hear what Mr. Cole has to say about his days digging out victims of the Denver quake, his views on insurgent groups, and his plans for the race now. We're going to a commercial, but stay tuned."

"OK, everybody," Trina said, "when he comes back on, let's pay attention. Let's listen for good points we can expand on or any weak areas the other side might use against us. Don't rely on memory; take notes."

Soon the commercials were over, and all eyes and ears in the room were riveted on the set. The host introduced Don and gave a brief review for the audience.

"So," Paul said, looking through his trademark reading glasses at a paper in front of him, "you are forty-two? Unmarried? Running for president of the United States . . . " The camera shot included both men. Don nodded to each question. Paul went on. "Let's see if I have this straight. You were actually campaigning in Denver a few days before the quake, and there was a tremor?"

"Yes. Lawrence Cunningham and I were both there. I was taking a nap when it happened."

"Did it wake you up?"

"I thought someone had kicked my bed! Yes, I was wide awake after that."

"But everyone thought it was no big deal, and you even went ahead with your speech that night, is that right?"

"Yes. Ironically, I spoke about the deep divisions that have developed between people in this country."

"Interesting . . . all the while not knowing that a radical group was about to set off a devastating earthquake in that very city."

"Exactly," Don said. "In fact, we packed up the next day and went on to California. That's where we were when the quake hit Denver."

"What went through your mind when you heard the news?"

"Well, even though we had been there for the tremor, we were all shocked. It was hard to imagine something like that happening, especially when we'd been there only a few days before. I couldn't help thinking about the people we'd met and the places we'd been. It was possible that some of those people were dead, and some of those buildings were leveled. . . . It's an eerie feeling."

Paul nodded. "Do you really think someone could have caused this earthquake?"

"Initially I doubted it on two levels: First of all, it was hard to believe that such a thing was *possible*. Second, I couldn't imagine that anyone would do such a thing. . . . But apparently, the technology is there, and this was the case."

"Who do you think it was? What possible motive could they have had?"

Don looked at Paul. "You know, I spent days asking myself those same questions. I still can't speculate about who it might have been." His jaw tightened and his eyes flashed. "But no motive could justify an act this contemptible."

"What made you go back, Mr. Cole?"

Don's face softened, and he sighed. "I had to see it with my own eyes. I didn't go with the intention of staying, but after I got there, I just couldn't leave. I felt I should help. I mean, if I were buried under a building, I'd like to think that people who came along would feel compelled to help dig me out, not just sightsee or give interviews and move on."

"And you did help dig people out, didn't you?"

"Yes, along with hundreds of other men and women. Everyone there began to pull together, to support one another. I'd work alongside those people any time. It was very inspiring to me personally."

"We'll speak more about that later. Then there were the—shall I say it—ugly interviews. Although Banner was the only TV network to air all of your interviews from the quake site, most of the other networks didn't air much of what you said. You were really railing against Todd and the media. What sparked all the anger?"

Don thought a moment before answering. He wanted to convey some of the frustration he had felt during that time. "We were digging human beings out of rubble. We needed a lot more help than we were getting at first. Who knows how many more people would have survived if we could have gotten to them quicker. The things I saw will be with me the rest of my life. Paul, there's nothing like looking out on a cold night in the middle of a huge city and realizing none of the lights are on. That none of them are going to be coming on soon. That if you fell down and broke your neck, there would be no one to call, no place they could take you. Far worse than that is the knowledge that hundreds of people are buried alive nearby, and you have to leave them—possibly to die—in the dark and the cold, because you have no way to find them. . . . *That's* what really got to me. The thought that the government and many of the networks were focusing the bulk of their efforts on chasing the possible culprits while the victims were dying under tons of debris—that was unacceptable to me."

Paul took a sip of coffee, then spoke. "So you don't think they should have announced that an insurgent group did it? You don't think they should have arrested anyone? You think the government should have only sent as much as it could as quickly as it could to the Denver area?"

Don put his hands up. "I didn't say that. What bothered me was the amount of time and resources that were so quickly devoted to the search for the insurgents and the paranoia—which I felt was being intentionally stirred up. Fear is one of the most powerful weapons one can use against someone else. In its extreme, fear can make a person almost incapable of rational thought. . . . I agree that whoever triggered the quake should be pursued and punished to the highest degree. I do *not* agree with detaining over a thousand people simply because some of their neighbors might think they're weird! There should be strict criteria for determining who qualifies as a suspect. If there is evidence to support charges being filed, then arrest the suspects and let them know specifically what the charges are. Then try them in full public view."

Paul studied Don's face. "Would you be in favor of the death penalty?"

Don looked into the camera and imagined he could see Todd's face. "To tell you the truth, I wish there was something worse we could do to these criminals, but I can't think of what it would be. If we do not catch the culprits, we will have to settle for the knowledge that they will eventually answer to a higher authority for what they have done."

"That brings us to a good question. I'm told you spent most of your time in Denver hanging out with a bunch of pastors. Several of them are from right here in New York. In fact, you've been seen with one of them in the last day or so. Did you have some kind of conversion experience?"

This was exactly the kind of question that Bob had dreaded. He feared it would be followed by some sloppy confession that the press would hop on and ride until it was all over.

Don smiled. "Actually, Paul, I have been a Christian since I was a young man. What happened to me was that I was given several gifts. I was given the gift of seeing just how small we humans really are. I was given the gift of seeing how short life is and how little I appreciated it. I was given the gift of great friendship at a time when I needed it most. And I was given the gift of realizing, once again, that God should get more of my life than an occasional word or visit to church. . . . It's sad to say that it takes something so terrible to make us appreciate what we have," Don said, looking directly into the camera again. "I suppose most of the people watching can identify with what I am saying. Eventually, everyone is confronted with darkness and finds that he or she, as a single entity, cannot make it through that darkness alone. . . . "

As Trina sat and listened to the interview, her eyes flitted back and forth between the screen and Don, who sat across the room from her. In spite of the fact he was talking about spiritual matters (which could be disastrous politically), she didn't think this would harm him. Something about what he said, and even the way he said it, made contact with her. She knew it would do the same with others. As long as the rest of the interview didn't get preachy, she thought it might do wonders for Don, who needed to connect with the hearts of voters.

At a commercial break, everyone started talking at once. Bob held up his hand for silence. "One at a time. So far, what do you think?"

"You don't go on and on with the God stuff, do you?" Jason asked.

"No," Bob said. "Actually, while I was sitting off-camera during the interview, I was holding my breath. But I won't make all of you sit on pins and needles the way I had to. He did great. Really great."

Trina watched Don. He seemed calm. He'd been so jumpy and angry before he went to Denver. Now he seemed confident, rested, strong. Once again she realized how much she liked him and forced herself to think of something besides his attributes. They were still in the middle of a campaign, and she needed to keep her energies focused on seeing where the opposition might attack.

Yes. That would be better, she thought. *Try to find his flaws. That's a much better idea.*

When the interview was over, the group spent two hours in discussion and agreed to break and meet again the following day. They all felt the campaign had been given a big boost by the interview. All they needed to do was to keep the momentum going.

CHAPTER FORTY-TWO

SARA REISLING SAT ON THE EDGE OF HER BED. IT WAS ELEVEN in the morning, and she still felt like sleeping. An open bag of cookies lay on her nightstand, and she got one out to nibble on. A knock came at the door.

"Come in," she said as she chewed.

The door opened. It was her mother. "Hi. Just thought I'd see if everything is all right."

Sara shrugged.

"I see you're having breakfast in bed again."

Sara ignored the implied meaning and offered her the bag. "Want one?"

"If you keep this up, you're going to look as if you fell into a cookie factory and ate your way out."

She shrugged again.

Naomi sat on the bed next to Sara and put an arm around her. "I know you're trying to understand all this, but you have to go on."

Sara leaned her head over and put it on her mother's shoulder but said nothing. Naomi decided to change the subject.

"You know your daddy got up and went to work today."

"Really?" Sara seemed to perk up for a moment. "I should have gotten up to say good-bye to him."

"Oh well. You can get up with him tomorrow. If you want, I'll let the two of you have the morning to yourselves. You can make him his juice and get his breakfast for him if you'd like."

Sara thought about it for a moment. "OK."

"Want to come out and have some coffee with me?"

Sara shrugged again. "OK."

Naomi smiled. "Good. I'll go make some." She gave her daughter a slight squeeze and left the room.

Despite the visible apathy, Naomi was hoping this signaled that Sara was actually going to come out of her room. She had been home for five days and only came out to use the bathroom or to find food that she could take and eat in bed. Her father, mother, and sister tried to look in on her occasionally and see if she felt like talking, but so far, no one had managed to get much out of her.

She had been buried under rubble for two days, then lived in a tent keeping constant watch on Pete who became ill while looking for her. After two weeks her father recovered, and the quarantine around the Denver area was lifted. Sara collected what little remained of her things at her apartment and returned home with Pete. Peaches, her cat, had disappeared. Mr. Moo had survived the quake, and Sara had wanted to take him home with her, but she changed her mind. Mrs. Mueller had been caring for him and had become very attached to him. Sara decided the dog would be both protection and company for the elderly woman, who had purchased a small trailer and planned to put it on her lot when it was cleared of rubble. Eventually, Mrs. Mueller's insurance would more than pay for a newer, nicer home to be built where the old one once stood.

So far, however, Sara had not wanted to talk about what had happened to her. At first, she hoped she could just go on as her mother said. But each day dawned, and she felt paralyzed—somehow unable to find her way out of the mental rubble that still seemed to trap her. She had made a commitment to herself and to God in her heart . . . it was the rest of her that did not seem able to follow.

She was home again, yet Sara had no idea what to do with herself. She had lost confidence in her ability to do anything. She didn't know if she could teach anymore. She didn't know if she could ever get over how she felt, or if she could let herself care about anything or anyone.

She remembered what the Lord had said to her that day outside the medical tent: *I had a purpose for you before you were born. Don't despair; I am with you. Repent and learn.*

"How can I start?" she said softly.

Later, Naomi saw Sara leave her room, get a towel, and enter the bathroom. After thirty minutes, she appeared, showered and dressed, in the living room. "I'm sorry I've spent so much time in my room, Mama. I guess I've just been feeling sorry for myself. Can I help you do anything today?"

Sara and her mother spent the remainder of the day together. After several hours, Sara was able to share with Naomi some of the things that had happened to her. She cried, but Naomi knew it was a healing thing for Sara, so she just listened. Over the next few weeks, they would have several talks like this about different things; each time, she could see Sara getting stronger, more able to deal with what had happened. As she did so, they were brought closer together than they had ever been before. A bond of understanding and respect formed between them that would never be broken.

One Friday night, after a month at home, Sara received a call from Angela, a friend in Oklahoma, regarding a teaching position. The opening was at a very small school with mostly Native American students. A teacher at the school quit unexpectedly, with few weeks left in the school year. Would Sara consider coming up for those weeks? She could stay with Angela while she was there. If she liked the teaching position, she could probably stay and work the summer session and on into the next school year. It was a difficult job in a poor area, but it would be very rewarding, according to Angela, who had been there for two years.

Instantly, Sara knew she was supposed to do it, but she presented the idea to her parents for their opinion. Only a year before, she had been so sure of herself, so positive, so eager. Now she felt a little unsteady, a little intimidated. Her parents thought the job was a good idea (even if it turned out to be only for a few weeks), but they told her they knew it was her decision. She called Angela back, accepted the offer, and packed her bags. She would travel to Oklahoma by plane on Sunday afternoon and be at the school on Monday morning.

CHAPTER FORTY-THREE

ROSALINDA SANCHEZ SAT WATCHING RICKY AS HE AND Edwina entertained a small group of children seated outside the mobile clinic they all called "the van." Edwina held a puppet and was making funny noises. Ricky had two children on his lap and was enjoying the show as much as the kids.

"OK," he whispered to one of the youngsters on his lap, "here's your part."

The boy jumped up and said, "My partner and I will save you!"

Ricky led the cheers for the hero, then leaned down and whispered to the other child, who promptly jumped up and said, "I will save you! With my partner also!"

All the adults laughed, and Ricky initiated another round of cheers for the second hero. The puppet show was nearly over, and they would be packing up to leave.

George and Edwina had always wanted to do more than just dispense medicines. They wanted to spend time with people, to be part of their lives. This had inspired the idea of the mobile clinic, which they operated with two other doctors who shared their vision for the inner city.

The van could provide medical exams, immunizations, and even minor surgery if required. But soon they realized they needed to have something for the children while the parents were being examined. There was no waiting room, so they had learned to do impromptu sidewalk shows for the kids while George saw patients. Often either Ricky or Edwina would be in the van with him, but today had been a slow day. There was another large Vital Union rally being held nearby, and they supposed many people had gone there for the day.

Rosa had volunteered to work with them in the van almost every Saturday throughout the summer months, and she had proven to be very helpful. She could talk to parents and children about concerns, fill out government forms, and was skilled at helping patients network with the proper agencies or organizations. She had even made up a skit about safety for the children. Ricky watched her with people. She wasn't at ease in the beginning, but each time they went out, she seemed to be more discerning and more able to respond to their real needs.

They had spent a couple of hours at this location, and the patients had all been seen, but as they prepared to leave, Ricky kept looking around.

"Something wrong?" Rosa asked.

Ricky shrugged. "I don't know. There's a girl I was seeing near here the last few weeks."

"Really?"

Ricky saw an odd expression on her face. "Oh, not like that," he said, trying to clarify things. "I mean, some friends and I come down here a couple of times a week at night to witness to gang kids. I've been talking to this girl. She couldn't be more than fifteen. She's been prostituting herself."

"How sad," Rosa said.

"I've really tried to reach her. I was hoping I could get her to come here and let George see her. She doesn't look well . . . and I was kind of hoping once she was here she would meet you . . . so that you could talk her into a shelter or find a safe place for her."

Although she said nothing, his words meant a lot to Rosa. It was the first time she felt that he valued something she could do.

Ricky continued, "I haven't seen her all week. I hope she's OK."

George came around the van. "Let's head 'em up and move 'em out." He opened the side door for Ricky and Rosa.

Ricky hesitated and looked around again.

"You're really concerned, aren't you?" Rosa said.

"I guess I am."

"You're going to stay here and look for her, aren't you?"

"Yeah, I guess I am."

"May I come along?"

His coal-dark eyes looked into hers for a moment. "I'd like that very much, but I don't think you should come with me today."

"Why?"

"Please don't take this personally, but I'm afraid if you come with me, no one will help me find her. You're a stranger to the people I need to see. That makes you suspicious. If they knew you worked with HCW, that would really do it. I'm grateful for your offer, and I may yet need your help if I find her, but I don't think you should come today."

"So what's the girl's name?"

He was glad Rosa was not offended. He smiled faintly. "Dana. Her name is Dana." Then he jumped through the door of the van, turned around, and said, "Let me tell George and get my bag."

She followed him into the van and watched him retrieve a backpack.

"What's in the bag?" she asked.

"It's my 'just-in-case' bag."

"Just in case what?"

"Just in case I see someone who needs a little first aid or something. People respond better when you demonstrate that you care for them." He rooted around in it for a moment and then looked up at her.

Her expression became serious. "I'd be lying if I said I wasn't scared for you. You sure you should go alone?"

"No, but . . . I have a real sense of urgency about this."

"That sure doesn't make me feel any better."

"Want to pray with me? It will help both of us."

She didn't know what to say. It had never occurred to her, until that moment, that prayer was really an intimate sort of thing. She couldn't ever remember praying one on one with a man (other than her papa when she was little). Sure, she had prayed in groups of people, reciting things like the Lord's Prayer, but this was . . . kind of intimidating. She managed to say, "OK," but her heart was pounding.

Ricky grabbed her hands. "O Father, thanks for helping Rosa. I know what joy You have in the way she is growing every day. I'm so glad we can talk to You. Thanks for the blood of Jesus that makes it possible. Please keep me safe and give Rosa peace while I look for Dana. Show me where to find her if she needs help. I love You, Father. Give us wisdom. In Jesus' name . . . " Ricky looked at Rosa. He squeezed her hands and she opened her eyes. "Anything else?" She shook her head. "Amen," he said.

"Amen," she added.

He said good-bye to George and Edwina, then stepped out onto the sidewalk.

"That was nice, Ricky," Rosa said from the doorway of the van. "You always pray like that?"

"How?"

"As if you're just talking to God."

"Oh, yeah. Best way. You can keep it up while I'm out here," he said with a big smile. "See ya' later."

"Will you call and let someone know what happened?"

They could hear the sound of the engine starting on the motor home. He looked at her but said nothing.

"Call me," she said. "Or George and Edwina . . . just let us know you're all right . . . and if you found the girl . . . you know." She felt silly now. She waved and shut the door.

Ricky watched the van drive off, then turned and walked rapidly. Now that it was late afternoon, many more teenagers milled around. People stood in small groups.

They're getting ready for their day to begin, Ricky thought.

"Hey, Remo," Ricky said to a homeless man sitting on a curb. "You seen Raul or any of the guys around yet?"

"No. Go down to the avenue and see if they're out."

"Hi, Ricky," a large woman on the corner called after him as he crossed the street.

"Hey, Colleen," he said, and kept walking.

He walked two more blocks and turned the corner. Along the way, many people knew Ricky and greeted him by name. He stopped and spoke with one man briefly. Ricky asked him if he was staying clean. He said, "So far," and they both praised God.

Eventually he found Raul hanging out on a corner with three women. "Raul, how you doing?" Ricky said, shaking the man's hand.

"Not so good. I cut my foot last night, and it really hurts."

"Want me to look at it?"

"Would you?"

"Sure. Here, just sit on the steps and take your shoe off."

The man sat down, gingerly took off his shoe, and held his foot up.

Ricky held it between his hands and examined it. "Yeah, it's a pretty good cut, Raul. How'd you do it?"

"Broken bottle."

"Had a tetanus shot in the last few years?"

"You kiddin'?" Raul chuckled.

"Really," Ricky said as he fished some things out of the bag. "You need to take better care of yourself, Raul." He finished cleansing the cut and dressed it. "Come down to the van next Saturday, and we'll give you a tetanus shot. OK?"

"Yeah. Thanks."

Ricky pulled out some bandages and handed them to Raul. "Keep it clean and change the bandage at least once a day. If it starts getting infected, you'll need to see a doctor," he said. He picked up the bag, started to walk away, and turned. "By the way, have you seen that Dana girl around?"

"Why? What you want?"

"C'mon, you know me, Raul. What do you think?"

"She's under the bridge up there," Raul said, pointing to his right. "If anybody asks, I didn't tell you."

Ricky began to walk in the direction Raul indicated. When he got to the bridge he couldn't see anyone under or around it. There were lots of bottles, some syringes, and other evidence of human presence, but for now, the area appeared uninhabited.

Just one more place, he thought as he walked up the embankment under the bridge. *She could be up there behind one of the support beams.* He climbed up the steep slope to where the columns went from the bottom of the bridge into the concrete embankment below until he reached the first support beam.

Ricky looked on the uphill side. *Nothing.* His eyes went to the next beam, about twelve feet away.

"Dana? Is that you?"

A young black woman was sitting, with her back against the uphill side of the column. Ricky approached her slowly.

"Dana? Is that you? It's me. Ricky Ruiz. Remember me? I just wanted to make sure you're OK . . . "

By now, he had reached her. There was no response. No movement. He noticed a terrible stench in the air. The girl was covered with bruises and dried blood. He squatted down. "Dana? Dana? I just want to take your pulse. OK? Nobody wants to hurt you." He did not take his eyes off the girl. Homeless people, he had learned over the years, could get spooked or provoked at the slightest touch and suddenly attack. The girl had been beaten badly, and she didn't move even when he gingerly took her wrist. There was a very weak pulse.

He scooped her up and started down the embankment. When he got to level ground, he gently set her down. She remained unconscious.

Ricky held out his hands and spoke, but not to her. "Thank You for letting me find her, Lord. Only You know what has happened and what all is wrong with her, but I know You called me here because You want her to live. And right now, in the name of Jesus," he said as he squatted down again and placed hands on the girl's shoulders, "Dana, I say you shall live and not die. You shall live to declare the works of the Lord."

The girl's eyes slowly opened. Ricky found a bottle of water in his bag and opened it. She smelled so bad that he had to breathe through his mouth. He lifted her head and shoulders with one arm and put the bottle to her lips. "Try to drink this."

She took several swallows and choked a little.

"Dana, do you know who did this?"

"Yes," she whispered.

"Who?"

"Stepfather."

"Can you drink some more water?"

"Yes."

He gave her another sip, then put some on a wad of gauze and gently mopped her face.

Within minutes, Ricky had carried Dana to a place where he could call for an ambulance. Soon she was being transported to a hospital.

Later, Rosa received a call from Ricky. He briefly told her what had happened and asked her if she would come to the hospital. He also wanted to know if she could personally handle the case. She said she would come down to the hospital and help with the preliminary report, but didn't know if she could be permanently assigned to the case.

When she arrived, Ricky seemed in a hurry.

"Thanks for coming, Rosa. Dana is in room 416, in bed A. She's very dehydrated, has internal injuries, and some broken bones, but she'll be OK. . . . I need to go, but I didn't want to leave before you got here." He retrieved a paper from his pocket and handed it to her. "I wrote down a brief account, and I'll be willing to make any other official statements you might need later."

"Where are you going?"

Ricky ignored her question. "Her parents should be here soon. What will you do to them?"

"She told you her stepfather did this to her?"

"Yes. I suspected he was abusing Dana from my previous conversations with her. This time she flat out said he did it. What will you do?"

"Well, for now, I can place her in protective custody. The police have been called, and I want to be allowed to sit in on the interview with the parents. If Dana makes the same statement to me or to the police, he will be arrested and charged. If Dana refuses to accuse him now that she's safe—something I'm sure you know frequently happens—then we can only investigate him on the basis of your accusation. But either way, Dana will be in custody until it's settled, and her parents will not be allowed to have unsupervised visits with her."

"Good enough . . . If you don't need me for anything else, I'd really like to go," he said, then added, "If you hadn't come, I would have stayed."

"But now that I'm here, you're going to take off?"

He looked at her. "Yeah, I know I can trust her to you."

He had complimented her twice in the same day.

"I'll watch over her," she said, smiling.

He just stood there a second as though he were trying to think of something else to say. "Call me if you need me. Thanks."

She didn't know if she would ever figure him out. "OK," she said.

He turned and walked away.

A half hour later, she received word that Dana's mother and stepfather had arrived at the hospital. They were given a choice: They could submit to a less formal interview at the hospital, or be taken to the police station for a statement. They chose to stay at the hospital. Rosa was allowed to sit in on the interview.

The stepfather was very well dressed. Dana's mother wore the familiar black head wrap, and Rosa realized they belonged to the Vital Union. She remembered the day she and Ricky had walked through a Vital Union "oasis" in that slum.

Before the interview, Dana's stepfather took Rosa's hand and shook it. "I want to thank you. We've been worried sick about Dana."

"That so?"

"Yes," Mr. Haynes continued. "We called missing persons about her some time ago. We've done our best, but she is rebellious and keeps running away. We have been praying that she'd come home and that, somehow, we could all work this out together."

"And you have no idea what happened to Dana?"

"None whatsoever."

During the remainder of the interview, Mr. Haynes maintained he knew nothing of his daughter's whereabouts, much less what might have befallen her. His wife substantiated his story. At the end of the interview, Dana's father shook Rosa's hand again.

"Now, we'd like to go see our daughter."

"I'm afraid you can't do that right now, Mr. Haynes."

"Why not?"

"Well, first of all, the doctor tells me she is not conscious right now."

Mrs. Haynes started to cry when she heard this and grabbed hold of her husband's arm. But she said nothing.

Rosa continued, "Secondly—I'll be honest—you're suspected of beating her, Mr. Haynes."

"She's just mad at me and trying to get even. I'm sure she'll retract her statement. Isn't a man innocent until proven guilty?"

Rosa nodded her head and looked him in the eye. "Yes, Mr. Haynes, you are innocent until proven guilty, but you may yet be arrested and charged. Even if Dana should decide not to accuse you formally, the fact remains she did tell someone that you beat her—so you will still be investigated. If my office is not satisfied by the time Dana is released from the hospital, she will be placed in a safe home pending the outcome of the investigation. Meanwhile, you will not be allowed unsupervised contact with her. You may contact my office tomorrow for an appointment," she said, handing him a card.

"You are persecuting us because of our faith."

"Well, Mr. Haynes, you can think that if you want to, but I have found that abuse is an equal opportunity kind of thing. It happens in all races, all religions, all incomes. And if you have injured this girl, I don't care who you are; I will make sure you are dealt with accordingly. Clear?"

"You'll be hearing from my lawyer," he said in a measured voice.

"You and your lawyer will be hearing from my office," she said in the same tone.

CHAPTER FORTY-FOUR

RICKY AND THE OTHERS IN THE PRAYER GROUP STOOD around the assembly hall, one of the meeting places for the Vital Union. Rallies of growing size were being held there every night. This evening's rally had been over for hours, and the participants were gone. Ricky had left Rosa at the hospital with Dana more than an hour ago.

When Ricky met Dana, he worked hard to obtain her trust. He knew she was a runaway and found out she had not gone far from her family's home in New York City. The sheer size of the city allowed her to hide just miles from where her parents lived. Ricky purposed to look into it.

At the same time, he and several men from his church were attending Vital Union rallies in various places around the city. They were told that this was a cult and thought some reconnaissance was in order. They did not want to make a judgment without knowing more facts, and this would enable them to pray with wisdom.

Of the many meetings Ricky had attended, he noted the founder, Melvin Woodsworth, was present and spoke at only the largest one. As Mr. Woodsworth carried his "gospel" across the nation, other men kept the message going at the local rallies.

Reuben Haynes was one of the more prominent speakers at several of the meetings Ricky attended. It was only after Ricky had spoken with Dana several times that he realized Reuben Haynes was Dana's stepfather.

Ricky would do whatever was necessary to see that Dana was protected, but for now, he hoped to continue to attend the rallies in anonymity. Being such a large man, it was hard to blend in the way others could. Once he'd seen his accuser, Mr. Haynes would certainly be able to spot Ricky in a crowd, and that would be the end of any reconnaissance. Although a confrontation was inevitable, he wanted to delay it as long as possible.

He decided not to tell Rosa about this, so she could honestly claim ignorance if it ever came up. Meanwhile, he prayed for Dana's salvation, for the souls trapped in the Vital Union, and especially for Mr. Haynes.

As he stood outside the assembly hall that night and prayed with the others, Ricky felt a deepened sense of sorrow. A spiritual shackle remained on millions of people. The enslavement passed from generation to generation, and it seemed that whatever people chose to do, each means of escape became the same bondage in a different package. Many messiahs had come into these ghettos. Each had a new plan, with its own look, its own hairdo, its own uniform. As each savior departed (usually by assassination), his icon was placed beside the others with the knowledge that, had this one lived, things would have turned out differently.

Christianity, as far as Ricky was concerned, had made little impact on the lives of people here. While various groups who claimed to represent Christ debated what to

do, the endless cycle of sin and death continued un-
abated.

Some charitable groups opted to become a second
form of welfare—"just love them and supply their needs
and they will respond appropriately." Some went with the
"if he will not work, neither shall he eat" philosophy and
figured anyone who *really* wanted to get out, could "by
golly, get a job and get out." Neither of these schools of
thought seemed to make a measurable dent in the
avalanche of death and poverty engulfing the inner cities
of America. The task for the few who were looking for
real, lasting solutions was overwhelming. There were no
easy answers.

Even if the spiritual bondages that held a man were
broken, he had to learn to maintain freedom. Choices
bring a test of strength and will. For someone who has
never had to make choices, the strain can become unbearable. Often, it was easier to stop being accountable and
let others make the decisions. It was easier to fall back on
the familiar, to do things under compulsion rather than
choice.

There were only a handful of ministries in each large
city willing to tackle the task of leading people to Christ
and holding them accountable while helping to sort out
the tangles in their lives. At the same time, these ministries had to resist the strong temptation to exploit and
enslave those who were struggling with their newfound
freedom.

It was just such a ministry that had reached out to
Ricky ten years ago while he was awaiting trial for murder.
Fear and desperation had made him open to any possible
solution. Daniel Ingram, pastor of the church, visited the
jail and spoke to the prisoners about God's plan for
man—how the Lord Jesus had come to open the prison
doors in people's lives and set them free. Ricky wanted to
be free in his mind even more than he wanted to be free
from the jail cell he occupied. He gave his life to Jesus

that night and continued to go to Bible studies the church held in the jail. Later that year, he was acquitted and released from prison.

He joined Daniel Ingram's church and let his whole life get turned around—one thing at a time. It wasn't just the church or the pastor that changed his life; it was Jesus. The pastor and the people of the congregation had a clear mission: to bring him to a place of having a relationship with Jesus Christ that would stand on its own wherever he went. They knew if they only brought Ricky into submission to their authority, his resolve could crumble once he was outside their sphere of influence.

Since then, Ricky had seen hundreds of people set free through the ministry of Ingram's church. Some struggled to maintain, some fell away entirely, but the majority of them continued to grow in their faith.

But Ricky knew that unless more of God's people prayed and were moved to action, terrible things would soon happen in this country. The Lord weighs a people by how they treat their poor and helpless, by whether or not godliness and justice are found in their midst. The country was filled with violence, bloodshed, and filth. The love of many believers had "waxed cold" as they viewed great sin with increasing passivity. How soon would God be at the door with His judgment? And judgment would begin in the household of faith. What would all those who claimed to know Him do when they were shaken from their pleasant little existences? Would they be grateful for the chance to repent and make a difference while they could . . . or would they shake their fists at heaven and curse Him?

Meanwhile, cults in America continued to grow while most of the church stayed in the comfort of their living rooms.

Ricky had learned that the founder of the Vital Union, Melvin Woodsworth, had grown up in a Detroit ghetto. As a young African American, he was immersed in a culture that struggled for identity and recognition by mixing pagan religions with pop culture. Eventually, Melvin came up with an idea. Through "divine revelation" he said he was given a "Seven-Year Plan" to "overturn the paradigm of wealth" in this country. Put simply, he wanted to redistribute the riches of America. He said that corrupt politicians had conspired to lock the rich in and the poor out. He convinced multitudes that it was possible to force the hand of their oppressors to let go of what was rightfully theirs: decent neighborhoods, food, medicine, and education. They needed only to unite and then work to overturn a system that had been stacked against them. If they were unified, no one—not the gangs, not the rich, not even the government—could stop them from achieving their goals. His Seven-Year Plan would give the money and property of America back to the people from whom it was "stolen."

On the surface, the plan seemed ludicrous to politicians. But Woodsworth did his homework in every city he visited. He knew how many people lived in that city, how many of them were rich, and how many of them were on the lower end of the scale. He railed against the tax system that was taking nearly half the income of middle-class families. He lashed out against the government, which took away welfare but hadn't found jobs for the people of the inner cities. He hammered on the rich who strove only to get richer. He pounded on health care, education, crime, and many other sore points with an ever-increasing number of those who could not afford to be sick or to send their children to decent schools—people who were afraid to leave their homes at night.

As middle-America grew poorer and government support systems deteriorated, more and more people of all walks of life were affected. In spite of all the talk about sharing and caring, *no one* seemed to care unless it was for their own profit. The frustration of many Americans had reached a boiling point.

It was here that Woodsworth played his best card. Although he did have specific spiritual beliefs, it was not necessary to commit to those beliefs prior to receiving help from the Vital Union. *Anyone* who needed a haven could shelter with them—as long as they would be participants in the Seven-Year Plan.

The Vital Union's Seven-Year Plan called for people to unite and then to build a place of safety and provision. As space became available, any who desired a haven could shelter with them—as long as they, in turn, worked to enlarge the place of safety and provision. Specific spiritual plans were offered for widows, single mothers, young men, and families on a regular basis at neighborhood rallies. But they were told that as long as they worked to bring about the Seven-Year Plan, they would be welcome to stay in the community regardless of faith.

However, those who did not embrace the faith of the Vital Union after a prolonged period might be seen as "not working toward the Seven-Year Plan," and they would be asked to leave the community. When faced with such a choice, many opted to become part of the faithful.

The Vital Union held open rallies for nonbelievers who they hoped would be joined. You did not join the Union; the Union "joined" you. An offer would be made at the end of each rally. The wealth, the power, and the fellowship of believers belonged to those in the Union. And those in the Vital Union were waiting to join *you*, to empower you, to fellowship with you. All that was needed was to accept their gracious offer and be brought "out of the famine of life into the wealth of the Union."

Ricky felt Woodsworth used desperation to make God seem distant, then substituted an institution to fulfill people's immediate needs. Who needed a personal relationship with God when others could just tell them what He said? And the works they did gave people such a sense of goodness and purpose, who needed to think about judgment?

Those who became joined at rallies attended closed meetings that taught the Code of doctrine, and adherents were brought to maturity of faith. As with most cults, no one in the beginning phases was ever told what the ultimate beliefs were, but as people submitted to and mastered each level, they could choose to step up to the next. Secret induction ceremonies preceded each level, and vows were made concerning restrictions on diet, dress, and lifestyle. Adherents took oaths stating they would willingly receive the punishments prescribed by Vital Union leadership if the Code was broken. At the highest echelons, the vows would include provisions for the ultimate punishment—death. Those ambitious for status and power could rise quickly in exchange for total submission.

As Ricky stood outside the assembly hall with the other men and women, he felt a great weight on him. They had walked around the building and prayed separately; now they would gather and pray as a group.

When they were all together, Ricky spoke. "O Father, we have not been the salt and light that You asked us to be in this present age. I see what this sin has brought about, and I am so grieved. Forgive us, Lord. . . . As I look at this place, I see a stronghold for the enemy being built brick by brick. A stronghold built to hold people in bondage. We make war tonight, Lord, for the souls of these people who were created in Your image. Your Word says that our weapons are not physical weapons, but they are mighty to the pulling down of strongholds. You have said that we win not by might nor by power but by Your Spirit. We realize that we do not war against people, but against principalities and powers, the rulers of this present darkness. We war against the hosts of wickedness in heavenly realms who are building this stronghold . . . Father, Your Word says that the gates of hell itself cannot prevail against the church. You have also said that Your Word is as a fire and as a hammer that will break in pieces every

stubborn rock of resistance. Tonight I set Your Word
against this stronghold in the spirit realm, and I say it
shall be broken in pieces. In the name of Jesus, I say to
this stronghold that your walls shall split and the captives
within you shall spill out, and you shall not again overtake
them. . . . "

CHAPTER FORTY-FIVE

THE DAYS OF AUGUST SPED BY. FOUR MONTHS HAD PASSED since the Denver earthquake, and President Sonny Todd sat at his desk considering his next move. He had another appointment with the Federal Disaster Assistance people, but he sat alone, motionless, staring out the window. The realization had finally struck him. Soon, if he didn't take some risks, he would no longer be the president, and he would have to find something else to do.

He went through the motions of making campaign speeches and sending memos to party headquarters on new ideas for strategies . . . but he knew his days at this desk were numbered unless he found a way to change the minds of the people—especially the ones Yosef represented. He'd had only one conversation with Yosef since the Denver thing, and that had been weeks ago. He'd been told that support of his campaign was being withdrawn. When he demanded a reason, they said that he and Secretary of Defense Schollet had not consulted them in the investigations of militant groups. He'd gone too far and aroused too much ill will with the public. In response to this, they feared the press would be obligated to turn on him.

Corporate entities could not afford to be associated with unpopular people or causes. Yosef's people wouldn't take such a risk for someone who obviously was "given to acts of impetuousness." As far as they were concerned, he had run amok in thinking that he could do what he pleased simply because he was the president of the United States. He had failed to look at the big picture. That failure would cost him the office.

The fact that the nation had been wracked with the weirdest weather in decades hadn't helped either. The federal government had run out of money to keep paying for what Todd considered the stupidity of disaster victims. They lived on flood planes and in places where mud and rocks would slide on them. Laws were passed. As each disaster came, the people in its path were being told they must move to be paid, but each disaster took in a larger and larger area. Eventually, there was just no more money. Of course, who was getting blamed for this? He was. Yosef's people were right about the press. Todd couldn't control the water, the wind, or the waves, but who was being cursed each time someone's house slid down a hill and they didn't get paid for it? He was.

Then there was Cole. Todd frowned. Cole's interview on the Banner Network after the Denver earthquake was only the beginning of a slide in public opinion. National magazines were featuring Cole on the cover and writing about him "waking up the soul of America." Even nightly news shows devoted time to questions about God, truth, and morality.

Todd shook his head. *Haven't I always made public references to God and prayer? Don't I have religious leaders here for public functions? He makes one sappy speech about "being alone in the dark," and now he's some sort of Moses. And those horrible Christian television stations going on and on about how they like him better than me all the time. They can't endorse him, but they make it plain they like him!* Todd frowned thinking about it, then comforted himself. . . . *But this Moses has no idea with whom he's dealing or with what he is getting involved.*

Todd, on the other hand, knew *exactly* with whom he was dealing and what was important to them. It wasn't just a case of withdrawing their support. Yosef's people knew they had enough dirt to bury Todd if necessary—and they were virtually *telling* him to get out of the race. They'd been careful over the years, so if it got ugly, the only people he could drag down with him were Bartlett, Schollet, and Yosef. And Todd had no doubts as to whether they'd be willing to sacrifice Yosef if it came to that. Game over. Or was it?

Sonny Todd had a card he hadn't played yet. He and Ernie Schollet had suspected they were being undermined when things went sour with the plan in Africa. They began working on something with which to bargain. It was so secret that even the vice president knew nothing of it. They didn't trust Victor anymore.

Todd stared out the window. If he couldn't effect a turnaround soon, he was out of a job. It was now or never. *Once Ernie and I play our card, we'll see who needs whom,* he thought, leaning back in his chair.

Even though Cole had become a serious contender, he was only one man. Yosef's people would have a change of heart soon. *And then we'll see what they do with Moses.*

CHAPTER FORTY-SIX

THE DAY HAD NOT STARTED WELL. RICKY HADN'T BEEN able to get to sleep until three in the morning. Sometime after that, the power flickered and the battery, which was supposed to sustain his clock through such things, died. He woke up at a quarter to eight in the morning and realized he had overslept.

An offer of a job he had applied for ages ago came in the mail the day before. When he applied for the job, his life was a lot simpler. He wasn't employed by George and Edwina at the clinic, and he hadn't been offered help with med school . . . and then there was Rosa. How had all these complications crept up on him?

What would he do? He would pray. And that is what he did until 3:00 A.M. It was then that he finally finished wrestling. The peace of God came, and he knew what he needed to do.

Now that he was late, the peace he felt at 3:00 A.M. seemed distant. He would have to skip a shower, forget

breakfast, and really move to get to work—and he'd still
be late. He hated being late.

When he got to the clinic, one minor emergency followed another. A man with a sliver in his eye, a woman
with a fractured finger, a trip to the hospital with a
woman about to deliver a baby, two people who required
stitches . . . and the day wasn't over yet.

Ricky planned to tell George and Edwina at lunch
time. He would sit down with them, thank them for their
offer, and then say no. But patients crowded the waiting
room through lunch time, and there seemed to be no end
in sight.

Around three o'clock the pace settled down. Then two
men in gray suits entered the clinic and asked to speak to
George. Ricky knew they were from the Vital Union as
soon as he laid eyes on them. He wondered what they
were doing there since they would normally transact business with a fellow cult member. In New York they
probably had at least a dozen doctors within their grasp.
Why would they come to the clinic?

George had them shown to his office and spent about
twenty minutes with them before they left. Then he asked
to speak to Ricky.

When Ricky entered the office, he could see that
George was concerned.

"What's going on, George?"

"What do you know about those Vital Union people?"

"Well, I would consider them a cult, but I don't know
if you would."

"A cult. Like what kind?"

"Like non-Christian, closed-society, secret-ceremony,
follow-the-leader-or-get-the-stuffings-beat-out-of-you
kind of cult."

"You think they are capable of violence then?"

"Why? Did they threaten you?"

"Well, not in so many words," George said. "It was
more implied than direct."

"What do they want from you?"

"Well, they want to 'join' us," he said as he made quotation marks in the air with his fingers, "with our work in the van. They have been watching us as we have visited various communities, and they feel they can help us to be more effective. They said they didn't see any need for duplication of efforts, and since we go most of the places they are or want to be, we should avail ourselves of the 'opportunity to be of greater service to people' by letting the Union join us."

"They say anything else?" Ricky asked.

"Well, just that it would be a pity if something we've worked so hard for would be 'irretrievably damaged' in the neighborhoods where 'things are so unpredictable.' They felt they could get us more doctors, volunteers, and young men to 'watch over' us to be sure we were safe."

Ricky was not surprised that behind all their caring rhetoric lay strong-arm tactics that mimicked the gangs from which they claimed to be helping people escape. "What are you going to do, George?"

"I don't even know if I should tell Edwina. I don't want her to worry, but then I guess I want her to be more careful. Frankly, I'm really angry about it. How dare they come in here and threaten me?"

"What did you say to them?"

"I'm not foolish. I told them we already had all the help we needed right now, but that we would take their offer into consideration."

"What offer?" Edwina asked as she came into the room.

"Oh," George sounded casual, "some guys from that Vital Union thing came by and wanted us to consider being part of what they are doing in the neighborhoods."

"You're kidding," she said.

"No. Didn't you see those two guys in suits?"

"Yes, but I figured they wanted a donation or something."

"Well, they did want a donation. They wanted us to donate ourselves and the van to them."

"*Ha!*" she said loudly.

"Well, we'll just keep that opinion to ourselves, won't we?" George looked seriously at her.

"Why can't we just be regular people doing what we do? Why does everything have to be associated with something else?"

"I don't know, honey."

There was a lull in the conversation, and Ricky decided to take advantage of the fact that he had them both in the same room. He cleared his throat.

"Uh, George. While I have you both here, I have something to tell you."

"Yes?"

"Edwina," Ricky said, "why don't you have a seat for a moment?"

"Why do I get the impression you are going to give me a piece of bad news?"

Ricky smiled. "Well, I don't know if it's necessarily bad news, but it is . . . well, let me just get to it. I have considered the offer you and George made to help me with med school. I want you to know how overwhelmed I was by it. I don't think anyone has ever made me such a generous offer."

"But . . . ," George said.

"But I cannot accept your offer."

"Why? Is it because you don't want to feel obligated to us?" Edwina asked.

"No. It's because I don't feel that's what I'm called to do."

"What do you mean? I don't know anyone who would make a better physician, Ricky," George said.

"Thank you. But I believe God has another plan for me. And that brings me to the next thing I want to tell you. Before I came to work here, I had applied for a staff position at a youth ranch in Oklahoma. I really believed I would go there. When it didn't happen, I applied here, and you hired me. Well, yesterday, I got a letter from them. A position different from the one I applied for—actually a better one—has opened up, and they offered it to me. I have prayed about it, and I am going to take the position. It doesn't start for three months, so you have plenty of time to find my replacement."

George and Edwina looked at each other and then back at Ricky.

"And you're sure? We couldn't offer you anything that would make you stay?"

"I don't think so, George," Ricky said as he looked at the floor. "I want you to know that working with you has been a wonderful experience, and I will always be grateful to you for all you have done for me."

Edwina got misty-eyed. Ricky became embarrassed and smiled nervously.

"Goodness, Edwina," George said, "he's not gone yet."

"I know," she said as she stood up and went over to hug Ricky, "but I just hoped . . . never mind. We'll really miss you, Ricky."

"I'll miss you guys, too."

Joan, the receptionist, appeared in the open doorway and knocked on the frame.

"Excuse me. Edwina, do you know where Rosa Sanchez is?"

"Who wants to know?" she asked as she straightened up and walked toward the door.

"That handsome guy, Bertrand, is here looking for her."

"I'll be right there," Edwina said and then turned to look at the men again. "You guys need to discuss this some more." She left the room.

George and Ricky looked at each other and shrugged. What else was there to say? Ricky got up and headed out of the room. "I'm going to go catch up on some of the work from earlier today." He walked down the hall to Joan's desk.

"Hey, Joan," he said, "if I get that supply list together, do you think we can still get it out today?"

"Sure."

He lingered for a moment. He wanted to see why Bertrand was there. He watched through the window to the waiting room. Edwina's back was to him.

Suddenly, Bertrand looked up and saw Ricky. "You're a friend of Rosa's, too; let me get your honest opinion," he said as he motioned to Ricky to come out into the waiting room. By then, George had made his way down the hall. Bertrand motioned to him also. "Oh, and you too, George; come on out here."

George and Ricky exchanged glances and then went out to the waiting room. As they came through the door, they could see that Bertrand was showing something to Edwina. It was in a small jewelry box.

When they got closer, Ricky could see it was an engagement ring—probably the biggest solitaire he'd ever seen.

"What do you think? Think she'll like it?"

Edwina's eyes grew large. She looked at the ring, at Ricky, at Bertrand, and then back to the ring. "Goodness. What's not to like? Does she know about this?" Edwina looked puzzled.

"No. It's a surprise. I figured I'd just catch her off guard, you know? Roses, dinner, then show her the ring. What do you think?" he said to George and Ricky.

George exhaled loudly. "Sounds like a plan to me."

Ricky just nodded.

"So, do you know where she went? She left work for the day."

"Haven't got a clue, Bertrand," Edwina said. "Why don't you beep her?"

"Yeah, guess I'll have to settle for that. Thanks. Wish me luck," he said as he left.

Edwina, George, and Ricky just stood there for a moment.

"Well," Ricky said, a little loudly, "I guess I'd better get back to work."

As soon as he was out of earshot, Edwina grabbed George by the sleeve. "Your office. *Now.*"

When they got there. She closed the door and spoke to him in a hushed voice.

"Listen to me, George. This is not right."

"What's not right?"

"None of it. I know for a fact that Ricky and Rosa belong together. We can't let this happen."

George laughed. "In case you didn't notice, they are adults now—you know, they live in apartments, pay rent, take themselves to the dentist. What exactly do you think we could do?"

"Has Ricky ever talked to you about Rosa?"

"Well . . . "

"C'mon."

"You know how I feel about interfering in other people's love lives, 'Wina."

"If we don't do something, she might marry Bertrand, and Ricky will move away for sure."

"Maybe we should interfere."

Edwina had a momentary look of triumph on her face. "Yes!" she whispered. "OK, spill it, George."

Fifteen minutes later Edwina emerged from George's office humming a little tune. She had beeped Rosa with their secret emergency code. Rosa immediately called her back.

"Rosa, where are you?"

"Shopping. What's wrong?"

"I need to see you ASAP! It can't wait. Where can we meet?"

Rosa agreed to meet her in thirty minutes at their favorite coffee shop. She left explicit instructions for George: He was not to let Ricky escape from the clinic under any circumstances until her return. George had saluted in military fashion. Now, she was ready to go.

"Oh, Ricky," she said cheerfully, "I have to go out for a while; can you and George hold down the fort?"

"Sure."

He looked terrible. *Good,* she thought.

Edwina made her way to the coffee shop and got a table in the back corner. Rosa was a few minutes late and looked worried.

"Sorry. I got here as fast as I could. What's happened? What's wrong?"

"Everything. Bertrand was just at the clinic. He has a rock the size of a baseball on a ring to give to you as soon as he finds you."

"No."

"Yes. And Ricky is moving away to Oklahoma." Edwina watched with satisfaction as the color drained from Rosa's face.

"Oklahoma?"

Several people in the restaurant turned and looked at them for a moment.

"Yes. And Bertrand showed him the ring just now— implying that it was a done deal."

Rosa remained silent.

Edwina finally spoke. "You're not going to marry Slick, are you? If ever there was a time to get totally honest with yourself, Rosa, this is it."

Ricky finished inventorying the medical supplies in the clinic. It took longer than he expected. He couldn't keep his concentration. He didn't feel well. What was he going to do?

He found George out front.

"I finished the inventory; anything else you want to add to the list?"

George slowly read it. "Nope. Not that I can see."

"Good."

"You're not leaving, are you?" George asked suddenly.

Ricky laughed a little. "Well, I wasn't planning to. Why?"

"Oh, no reason. I just . . . well, no reason."

"Actually, I have someplace to go at seven, and it's not far from here. I was thinking I would hang around after you closed up. There's not enough time to go home and get anything done. I was going to eat out, but I'm not hungry now," Ricky said as he rubbed his chest.

"Great. I mean fine. That's fine with me."

Ricky felt worse by the minute. "Could I lie down in your office a while? I didn't get much sleep last night, and I'm not feeling so good. You can get me up if you need me."

"Help yourself."

"Thanks."

Ricky went down to the office. He felt lousy, but he knew it wasn't because he was sick. He closed the door in the office, went to the sofa, and knelt down.

"O God, I don't know if I can take it. . . . help me. I don't know exactly what I had hoped for, but I know this wasn't it. I realize my own interests are blinding me, but I have no peace about her marrying that guy. If he's not the one, please guard her from him. Help her settle for nothing less than Your best. . . . As for me, You know how I feel; I'm way past being able to deny it. Nevertheless, Father, help me to go after those things You place in front of me."

CHAPTER FORTY-SEVEN

SARA RETURNED TO HER CLASSROOM TO FIND A SMALL bouquet of wild flowers wrapped in a paper towel lying on her desk. It was recess, and the children should all be outside playing. She thought she saw a movement in the rear door of the classroom. She slowly turned and sat at her desk so she might be able to catch a better view of the child peeking at her from the doorway. She wasn't sure, but she thought it might be Jack.

It had been four months since she left Denver. She had taken a temporary position teaching at a grade school in a small Oklahoma town. Most of the children in her class were Native Americans. Almost all of the children came from poor families who barely managed to get by. Sara had taken the job with the knowledge that she might be asked to stay on for the summer session and even into the next year. When she arrived, she had no preconceived ideas. She only wanted to start over.

The first day she met her fourth-grade class, she was very nervous. All of them seemed tentative as well. They wondered if she would expect them to know more than they had learned, if she would give lots of tests, and—most importantly—if she would be mean. She had each child write his or her name, age, and address on a piece of paper and then hand it in. As she called out each name, the child was to stand and tell her their favorite hobby or the name of their favorite animal. She carefully noted each child on a seating chart so that she could study it later. One of the papers had only the word *Jack* on it, and even that was barely legible. The "k" was backwards. She looked at it for a moment and then called out the name.

"Jack."

A small boy in the back stood up.

"You're Jack?"

"Yes," a girl in the front row said. "And he's not in his right seat! He belongs right here!" she said, pointing to an empty desk next to her.

"He's too ugly! Let him sit in the back!" another girl said, and they all laughed as Jack plopped back down and looked out the window as if he didn't care.

"Tell you what, Jack," Sara said, after quieting the class. "You and I can have a conference at recess, and you can help decide where you get to sit."

The children looked at each other. No one else got to decide where they were going to sit. Several hands went up. She called on a boy she'd already identified as Billy. "Yes, Billy?"

"I want to sit over by the window!"

Sara tried not to smile. "Well, I only have one seating conference a week, so you'll have to wait until next week, Billy." The rest of the hands went down.

When the morning recess came, Jack tried to escape out the back door.

"Ooooh, Jack!" she called out sweetly. The boy froze in the doorway a moment and then returned without speaking or looking directly at her.

"Here, Jack, grab a chair and come sit around here with me," she said, motioning for him to bring a chair behind her desk. He dutifully complied. "I have a snack here," she continued. "I really brought too much today. Could you help me eat it?"

Jack looked over the orange slices, the banana, and a couple of pieces of hard candy on top of the desk. He glanced at her and then grabbed one of the candies and sat down. She tried to look at him in short bursts so he wouldn't feel that she was staring. He had a large, dark birthmark on his neck and the lower left side of his face. He had straight, jet black hair and shining black eyes. Were it not for the birthmark, he would be a nice-looking boy. However, his problems went deeper than the birthmark. He was the class scapegoat. Just as obvious was the fact that he couldn't, or wouldn't, write very well. She had yet to find out if he could talk.

"Would you like half of my drink?" She said, opening a can. "I can pour out my half in my cup here."

"OK," he said, looking out the window behind her.

During the remaining minutes of morning recess she managed to get several sentences out of him. She told him he could remain in his selected seat if he paid attention and did his class work. She knew she had to be careful. Once a child was the class scapegoat, well-intentioned help by others could make matters worse. The change would have to come from inside Jack first. There would have to be a difference in the way he thought of himself before there would be any lasting change in the way the other students treated him.

After their first encounter, Sara had made up her mind. She was going seek a way to make a difference in this boy's life.

In the coming weeks, she found out that Jack's father, a Native American, had run off with another woman. The boy's mother, a white woman, seemed to have no real concern for him. Sara tried to speak to her on three occasions.

The first two times she was rebuffed. The last encounter was when she had asked Jack's mother to meet her in the classroom after school. The woman arrived late with a cigarette in her hand and a man in tow. Sara marveled at her creamy complexion, green eyes, and chestnut hair. The woman put a hand up and said, "Skip the Mrs.; just call me Rita."

Sara had hoped to speak candidly to both Jack and his mother. Jack was in desperate need of remedial classes if he had any hope of passing in the next year. But Rita and her boyfriend were apparently in a hurry.

"I had hoped for a private conference," Sara said.

Rita looked at her escort. "Could you wait in the car, honey? I'll just be one more minute, I promise." The man got a sullen look on his face and left the room. Rita looked back at Sara. "So, what do you want? Jack been bad again?"

"No, Jack has not been a behavior problem. As you know, I'm a replacement teacher. I've only been here a short while."

"So what is it?" Rita said, looking down at her watch.

"I think Jack may actually be a very bright boy, but it seems he may have some learning challenges."

"What do you mean?"

"I'd like to see Jack get some tutoring."

"Oh, sure." Rita said. "Like I have money for that."

"There's no money needed. One of the other teachers and I are going to do this with several students. Every day for about thirty minutes after school. He doesn't ride the bus, so you could just pick him up later."

Her eyebrows shot up. "You want to keep him? Extra time?" She looked as if the thought was incredible to her. "OK. Sure."

"We have permission from the school to do this, but you'll have to sign papers," Sara said, handing the permission forms to Rita.

"Sure. Have a pen?" Sara gave her a pen, and she signed the papers without reading them. "Can I go now?" Rita left with Jack.

Tutoring began on the following day and continued for the next two weeks.

When regular school was out for the summer, Jack, who would not be allowed to complete the fourth grade if he did not master reading and writing skills, was enrolled for the summer session. Sara was asked to continue teaching at the school, and she accepted a position through the summer and the next school year. For the fall session, she would be a fifth-grade teacher. She and her friend, Angela, continued tutoring Jack and several other students. During that time, Sara discovered he loved to draw. As Jack accomplished reading and writing assignments, she rewarded him by giving him art paper, drawing pencils, and lending him books on drawing.

Jack passed the fourth grade by the skin of his teeth. He still frowned most of the time, but occasionally, when he was drawing, his face relaxed, and she would see a hint of a smile. This was a greater reward for Sara than money could buy.

Now the summer session was nearly over. This was the last day of school before a small break, and then the regular school year would start. She sat at her desk and smelled the small bouquet. The figure in the door had disappeared. The bell rang, ending recess, and the children returned to the room.

Several of the girls noticed the flowers. "Where did you get the flowers?" one of them asked.

Sara smiled. Jack was staring out the window, but she knew he was straining every cell to see and hear her. "Someone gave them to me. Aren't they the most beautiful flowers you've ever seen? I'll have to take them home and put them in water."

Actually, by the time she got home, they were wilted. She took three of the flowers and carefully pressed them in a book. To Sara, they would always be a symbol of grace—a chance to start over.

CHAPTER FORTY-EIGHT

RICKY HAD FALLEN INTO A DEEP SLEEP LYING ON THE couch. He was so tall that his legs and feet stuck out about six inches past the armrest. His left arm had slipped off the side of the sofa, and his hand rested on the floor.

Rosa watched him for a moment, then quietly knelt down beside him. She gently picked up his arm and, bending his elbow, placed it across his waist. His sleep was so peaceful that she didn't want to wake him. She placed a hand on his shoulder and leaned forward to rest her head upon his chest. She smiled and closed her eyes as she listened to his great heart beating steadily.

Ricky awoke gradually. He was thinking of Rosa. Even the air around him seemed to smell of her perfume. *O God, help me. What can I do?* he thought. And just as he crossed over from sleep to consciousness, he heard the Lord's voice say, "Go ahead; tell her."

He suddenly realized something was on his chest and opened his eyes. There was . . . Rosa?

She felt him stir and opened her eyes to see him looking at her. The expression on his face said he was totally confused. She smiled at him and said, "Hi."

"Rosa?" he said, blinking several times. "What? . . . Where are we? What time is it?" He started to sit up and look around as if he had overslept and was late getting somewhere.

She moved back and smiled at him. "We're in George's office and it's . . ." She looked at her watch, " . . . six o'clock."

He still looked confused, so she said, "At night."

This didn't seem to help. "You've only been asleep an hour," she added.

He exhaled, lay back down, and covered his eyes with the back of his hand. "Oh," he said and then moved it away to look at her again. "And did you tell me what you were doing here?"

She giggled. "You don't wake up very with it, do you?"

His eyebrows came together in a frown.

"Oh, I'm sorry," she said, placing her hand on his chest. "I wasn't trying to make fun of you. It's kind of cute, actually."

The frown remained. "Yeah. Cute."

"Don't be mad at me."

He closed his eyes, and sighed. "I'm not mad at you, Rosa . . . I'm sorry . . . so did you say why you were here?"

"Something wonderful happened today, and I wanted you to be one of the first ones I told."

He felt a pang of sorrow. "I hope you are very blessed, Rosa."

"So you know already then?"

"Well, yeah."

"You are being very disingenuous about this."

He looked at the ceiling. "Oh, I'm the 'D' word again."

"And what does the 'D' word mean?" she asked.

"I think we discussed this before, didn't we? Uh . . . not forthright? Dishonest?"

"Exactly."

He fixed his gaze on her. "In what way do you think I have been dishonest with you?"

"What did you think I was about to tell you?"

"That Bertrand proposed to you."

"And you have nothing else to say?"

"What else is there to say? I want God's very best for you, Rosa. That's the truth."

"And you've always told me the truth."

"Yes."

"And you always will?"

"Yes."

"The truth, the whole truth, and nothing but the truth?"

He was starting to get irritated again. "So what are you driving at?"

"Why haven't you told me how you feel about me?"

His pulse quickened. "Like, exactly what is it you want me to say?"

"Do you love me, Ricky? Not like a friend or a sister. I mean, do you love me?"

He blew air between his lips and turned his face to the sofa back. "Why are you doing this to me?"

"You said you'd tell the truth. Do you love me?"

He kept looking away from her. He felt as if he were on the edge of a cliff as he remembered the words, *Go ahead; tell her.* He took a deep breath. "Rosa, I love you more than you can possibly imagine." Now he was in a free fall.

"When did this happen?"

He closed his eyes and remembered. Her small hand still rested on his chest, and he covered it with his own. "The first time I saw you, I thought my heart would stop beating. And even now, it might pop out of my chest." The sensation of falling continued, but he could feel the ground rapidly approaching. "Happy now?"

"And you would have moved away and never told me?"

"Who said I was moving?"

"Edwina."

"Oh. Well, I just got the job. I would've told you I was moving."

"Let's not get sidetracked here, shall we? Our topic was you not telling me that you love me."

"Well, you know *now*. . . . " *Splat,* he thought.

She leaned close to his ear and said softly, "Yes. *That's* what I found out today. You know when I first began to love you? I think it was when I woke up in that dumpster and saw you smile at me with those beautiful white teeth."

His eyes snapped open, and his head suddenly turned to her. The confused look had returned. "What did you just say?"

"I said I love you, Enrique Ruiz. And I don't know how I could live if you moved away without me."

A few moments later, George went into the office under the pretext of needing a prescription pad and then quickly returned.

"Well?" Edwina almost couldn't stand it.

"Well, what?"

"You are so exasperating! Were they talking? Were they fighting? What?"

"They're not speaking at the moment."

"George, what are we going to do to make them stop fighting and see they need each other?"

"I didn't say they were fighting."

"Well, you said they weren't speaking; isn't that about the same thing?"

"Let's see . . . would this qualify under your definition of fighting?" He suddenly grabbed her, leaned her backward, and kissed her.

When he stopped, Edwina fanned herself with her hand and laughed. "Goodness, George! Is it just me, or is it hot in here?"

Back in the office, Ricky was gazing at Rosa and studying her face as her head rested on his chest.

"Tell me again," he said.

"I first began to love you when I looked up in that dumpster and saw you standing over me with that beautiful smile," she said as she ran a finger over his lips.

He closed his eyes for a moment. "That's so funny. You know, when I hopped into that garbage bin it was as if my whole life was over until I knew you were alive. But it was the same day I lost all hope of ever loving me."

She sat up. "Whatever made you do that?"

"Because," he said, "you saw how ugly I really am. If you could have seen the look on your face when you touched me . . . "

"Oh, Ricky, how could you even think that? I was going into shock. Later I thought I had imagined it, but when I told Edwina about it, she said it was probably true. She told me how all of you went to the beach once, and you kept your shirt on all day . . . and I realized what it cost you to let me see. It broke my heart at first, and I really wanted to talk to you about it, but I couldn't find a way to bring it up. *That's* why I bought you the jacket. I wanted to say something to you . . . but when I mentioned why I was giving it to you, you should have seen the look on *your* face. Your eyes were filled with such sadness, I didn't know what to do."

"Yeah," Ricky said. "Then there was Bertrand. I will never forget seeing him lean over you in the hospital. The way he looked at you. The way he touched your hair." Ricky now stroked her hair. "I thought I might die. . . . Rosa, tell me again. Tell me I'm not dreaming this."

"You're wide awake, and I love you with all my heart."

"You don't love him?"

"Never did."

"Then why did you keep going out with him?"

"Well, at first, it was nice to be pampered like that. You know? But more than a month ago I told him the relationship was finished."

"You did?"

"Yes. That's why he came by here looking for me. He didn't know where I was, because I don't return his calls anymore. I realized I wasn't being fair to him or to myself by seeing him. I decided that I wanted to do something I'd seen *you* do. I wanted to talk to God about things and then let Him guide me . . . but the more I prayed, the closer I got to the Lord. And the closer I got, the more I loved the Lord. And the more I loved the Lord, the more I loved you. Does this make any sense at all to you?" she asked, looking directly into his eyes. "Because nothing like this has ever happened to me before."

He beamed at her, and she kissed him.

"You were saying how you love me and not him," Ricky reminded her.

"Oh, yeah. Poor, charming Bertrand," she said. "The more I avoided him, the more he pursued. He isn't used to people turning him down. I'm sure the whole reason he bought me that ring was because I'd already said no. Even now, he probably thinks I'm using some sort of ploy to entrap him." She smiled.

"So why didn't you let me know how much you cared for me?" Ricky said.

"What could I have done? Oh . . . if you only knew," she said. "The first night we met, you asked me about my faith and cornered me about being a spoiled child. And you were right. I've been given exactly what I wanted most of my life, yet there were so many people I hated for hurting me or standing in my way when I wanted something . . . and then I saw all your scars. I realized you must have lived a life I never could have endured. Yet, you have never shown any evidence of bitterness or anger about these things. Instead, I have watched you pour out the most tender love on people. Even when they aren't lovable."

Her eyes filled with tears. "I can't tell you how this has broken me, Ricky. To see how selfish and petty I am. I remember telling you I was raised in the church and being so ticked off because you weren't impressed. Now, I'm so ashamed of myself. I walked around for all that time thinking I was a Christian, and until I met you, I had almost no concept of what that means."

She leaned down again and squeezed him tightly. "I know you want to be like Jesus with every cell of your body, Ricky. If more people lived as you do, I can't see what would stop the whole world from wanting to know Jesus. As I watched you, I came to think so much of you that I couldn't see how *you* could want *me*. The very thing you find so ugly about yourself has stirred a love in me that is so great . . . " She stopped for a moment and searched his eyes. "Now, all I know is that I want to know the Lord the way you do. . . . and I want to be with you, serving Him, all the days of my life." She nuzzled up under his chin. "Please, tell *me* again."

"I love you more than you can possibly imagine," he murmured.

"And yet you would have let me go? Just like that?"

Ricky smiled. "There was no 'just like that' to it, *mi corazón.* I never planned on loving anyone the way I love you. I always thought, 'There is so little time. . . . Is there time for love, a wife, a family?' I figured not. And I know what my call is, Rosa; I know what God created me to do . . . so I've tried to press toward it with all my heart, thinking there wasn't room for anything else. And then I came down the hall that night and saw you standing there.

"Rosa, I think I can safely say there's not much that can scare me anymore . . . but you scared me whenever I got close to you. I remember riding on the subway with you that first time, sitting next to you, smelling your perfume . . . the sensation for five whole minutes of putting my arm around you when we walked, as if you were mine. It was like being intoxicated." He squeezed her tightly and inhaled her fragrance. "Then . . . being near you after that, thinking you only considered me a friend . . . knowing I had *nothing* in the natural that would tempt you to love me, struggling every day not to go out there and fight for you. I got so pathetic over it that I hated myself."

He stopped and thought a moment before continuing. "These scars are what Ricky and the devil did to me when I thought I should take anything I wanted. . . . But I have learned the truest joy is in trusting the Lord with all that I want, all that I am, all that I will be . . . and where He opens the way, to run with all my heart. . . . Rosalinda, will you marry me?"

Later, when Ricky and Rosa tried to leave the office, they couldn't get the door open. They didn't realize that, while they were talking, Edwina had crept up and locked the office door on the outside. All the doors in the hall had small hook-and-eye locks at shoulder level to keep small children out of empty rooms in the clinic.

Ricky knocked on the door and called out, "Hey, out there . . . Hello? The door is locked. Can you let us out?"

Edwina and George went to the door, and George started to unlock it. Edwina smacked his hand back and said through the door, "I'm not unlocking the door until there's a promise of marriage. You guys have been stupid long enough. I've known you belong together all this time, and I can't take it anymore. When you're ready to make a commitment, just say so, and I'll unlock the door."

"OK," Ricky said, smiling at Rosa. "We surrender . . . we agree to your terms."

CHAPTER FORTY-NINE

IT HAD BEEN FIVE DAYS SINCE RICKY HAD PROPOSED TO Rosa. She called her stepfather and mother in Miami. They would fly up in two weeks to meet him. Ricky's mother had been dead for two years, and getting acquainted with his four half-brothers and his half-sister could wait. But Ricky was most anxious for her to meet his pastor, Daniel Ingram, who was the closest thing Ricky had to a father.

It was Sunday, and today she would go to church with Ricky for the first time. She was already nervous when he picked her up. The closer they got, the more nervous she became.

"You OK?" he said as they neared the building.

"Well, I'm a little jittery. This is like meeting your family."

He put his arm around her and smiled. "Trust me. To know you is to love you. Of this I am certain. I only hope to do as well with your parents."

"And I've never been to a church like this."

"It's a piece of cake, *mi corazón*. There's nothing you have to know how to do. If you want to stand during the worship, you do. If you want to sit, you do. If you want to raise your hands, you do. If you don't want to raise your hands, you don't. If you want to cry, go ahead. "

Now why would I want to do that? she thought briefly.

"Nobody's keeping score, OK? The only one whose opinion counts here is Jesus. Just allow yourself to enjoy it, that's all." He squeezed her shoulder. "OK?"

"OK."

When they got to the doors, they were inundated with hugs and best wishes. Rosa had to give them one thing— they were affectionate. As the couple made their way down the aisle of the church, they saw Kendrick, the young man she and Ricky had clashed over almost a year ago. He reminded Ricky of their usual basketball game. Then they met Dana, the girl Ricky had found under the bridge. She was still under state care because charges against her stepfather were pending. Rosa had helped to place her with a foster family Ricky knew that specialized in battered kids, and Dana appeared to be glowing with health.

As they walked to their seats, they met and spoke to many young people. As each one hugged them, Ricky asked them questions about what was going on in their lives. Eventually, they arrived at the front row. Her eyes widened.

He saw her expression. "What's wrong, sweetheart?"

"You sit in the front row?"

"Well, yeah. I guess I do. I'm sorry, I wasn't thinking. Does it make you nervous? We can sit someplace else if you'd like. There's no set seating or anything."

She swallowed. *Oh well,* she thought, *might as well dive right in. If this is what your life will be like, you might as well try it out.* "No. That's OK. I . . . I guess I just never sat in the front row before."

"You sure you want to?"

"Yes."

"We have a special guest praise and worship leader on the piano today. He's supposed to be very good. You'll enjoy the music. I promise."

They were seated for just a few minutes before the music started. Rosa was surprised. It really was good. Some songs were soft and slow, some lively, and everyone clapped. Ricky was right. Some people sat, some stood, some lifted their hands.

After a few songs, Rosa stopped thinking about whether or not anyone was watching her and allowed herself to enjoy it. She gradually became aware of a sweetness—a tenderness that was almost tangible, and it made her want to cry, so she did.

I'm ruining my makeup, she thought. *But how wonderful this is! I can't help myself.*

Ricky made it a point *not* to look at her directly, but he did risk a side glance. When he saw she was crying, he gave her his handkerchief and put his arm around her for a moment. The man at the piano played and sang so beautifully about drawing near to God that it was as if he were pouring warm oil into Rosa's soul. She could not stop crying.

As the music came to a close, the man at the piano, Thomas, turned to Pastor Ingram, and said, "Pastor, if I may, I have words for a couple of people, and I believe the Lord wants me to say them in front of everyone. That OK with you?"

Daniel smiled. "Go ahead."

Thomas stood up and took the microphone with him. "Miss?" he said as he walked to the front of the platform. "Miss?" he said again. He was looking at Rosa.

Rosa's eyes opened, and she realized the man on the platform was addressing her.

"Yes, you," he said. "Could you come closer? I feel the Lord is speaking to me about you. May I tell you what He is saying?"

She stepped forward and nodded slowly.

Ricky leaned to the woman on his left and asked her to write down whatever was said.

Thomas continued. "What's your name, dear?"

"Rosa."

"Rosa, I see you have many unresolved questions in you, but you are pressing into the Lord in the midst of them. This is why He is speaking to you now."

Rosa felt as if she had been enveloped in a warm cloud. She was no longer aware the others in the church, just the words she was hearing and the warmth.

"And the Lord would say to you, 'Daughter, I have seen your struggles, and I'm pleased that you have been seeking Me. I have such joy in the way you have talked to Me lately, in your hunger and thirst to know Me and My will in your life. . . . When confusion or conflict come, continue to seek Me. Read My Word. . . . Soon, you will endure a testing of your faith, but don't be afraid. I hear every word that is on your lips and in your heart. Know your prayers are important, that they make a difference. Invite Me to act on your behalf and on behalf of those you love. Do not fear. I am with you, I will never leave you or forsake you. Believe on Me, and I will bring you out of every trial.'"

As he spoke to her, she felt the strength melting out of her body. At his last words, she fell on the floor. Then the speaker on the platform turned to Ricky and spoke.

"You, sir, come forward."

Ricky moved up next to Rosa, who was still lying on the floor.

"What is your name?"

"Ricky."

Thomas turned to the pastor and asked, "You know this man well?"

"Yes, I do. In the Lord, he's my son."

"Would you stand here with me as I speak to him?"

Daniel got up and stood beside Thomas on the platform.

"Daniel, you have borne good fruit in the Lord and I believe that the reason God had me ask you to stand here is because what I am about to say is something in which you will share. This man," he said, pointing to Ricky, "is part of the crop the Lord has given you, and you have faithfully planted and watered in his life, so you will share in his reward.

"Ricky, the Lord wants you to know tonight—in front of all these people—how much He delights in you."

Now Ricky started weeping. Rosa could hear what was being said and knew it was being said to Ricky, but she could not muster the strength to move.

"The Lord would say to you, 'My son, My son, how much I love you! Even though you felt rejected by your earthly father, you were never an accident. You have always been a delight to Me. I have watched your faithfulness; I have seen your sacrifices. There is nothing you have withheld from Me, and I tell you, truly, I withhold no good thing from you. I saw how you suffered as a child, and I want you to look back on every sorrow and know that, yes, I was there, and yes, it hurt to watch you; but it was for such a time as this, so that you might be able to enter the pits of darkness and save others with My love and compassion for them. I knew you would make it to this very day, and I will use everything in your experience for My purpose.'"

Ricky was sobbing.

"'I brought this man, Daniel, into your life to pour into you the love of a father that I have for you. Through his example you have learned the love of a father and the love of a good shepherd. From him you have learned that you can run to your heavenly Father when you are hurt or have any need. And now I say to you that *you* have become a good shepherd. You have been willing to lay down your life for the sheep. You would leave the ninety-nine and search for the one. You have suffered great loss in your life, but you have allowed that emptiness to be filled with Me. And I say to you this night, I have pre-pared much for you because you have been faithful with the little you were given. You will be a shepherd in the wilderness. You will tend to My flock in the wilderness. You will not be like other shepherds, nor will you have a flock as other shepherds have. I will bring it about. You will see. I will lead you and your flock to places of safety, of food, of water in the midst of the wilderness. . . . '"

By this time, Rosa sat up and looked at Ricky.

Thomas looked down at Rosa and then at Ricky. "Help her up. She should stand next to you for this. Are you married yet?"

Ricky wiped his face with one hand and offered the other to Rosa. "No, but we are to be married in a couple of months."

Rosa had never seen Ricky cry before. She put an arm around his waist and they leaned together.

Thomas began to laugh, then went on speaking, "And the Lord says, 'It is My delight to heal every wounded place in you, Ricky. You have given everything to Me; now it is My delight to raise you up. You, whom the world would despise, I will raise up. I delight to give you the desires of your heart, Ricky. I do not do this as a pay-ment for works—for you have a reward waiting for you in heaven. I do this simply because I delight in loving you. I have sent this woman as oil and wine. This woman is a vessel of My oil and wine. She will pour like oil and wine into the scars of your life. . . . She will be the wife of your bosom, your companion. I give you to one another as a gift because I delight in you both. You will be a type of My Son and of His bride, the church . . . Ricky, I say you have begun to know how much I love you. Now, through her, I will show you the passion, the consuming love my Son has for His church, and you will understand it as you never have before.'"

Both Ricky and Rosa fell to the floor.

Thomas went back to the piano and played another song. Before the song was over Rosa opened her eyes. She couldn't believe it. She was on the floor again! She looked to her left. Ricky was on the floor too, and he opened his eyes to look at her.

"I think I fainted," she said to him.

A huge smile came to his lips. "No, you didn't. We'll talk about it later. Can you get up yet?"

"Yes."

They got up and went to their seats. Rosa still felt warm all over—almost as if she'd had a little too much to drink. The rest of the service seemed to flash by, and before she knew it, it was over.

Afterward Ricky and Rosa walked to a small restaurant that had very private booths with candles and lace tablecloths.

Rosa got close to Ricky as soon as the waitress was gone and said quietly, "So tell me, what happened to me? I've never experienced anything like that before. I didn't faint?"

"No, not exactly," he said as he pushed some of her hair behind her left ear. "If you look in the Bible, it happened when men became aware of God's presence . . . although He's everywhere all the time, we're just not aware of Him all the time. But as we draw near to Him in our hearts, we become more able to experience Him. When His presence becomes manifested to us, often our strength just . . . melts. It happened to Abraham, Daniel, Elijah, John the Apostle, even to the men who came to arrest Jesus."

"The soldiers? Really?"

"Says so in Scripture. You were just never looking for it. They came to arrest Him, and they said they were looking for Jesus. When He said 'I AM,' they all fell down. He waited for them to get up again so they could arrest Him."

"Where does it say that?"

"Gospel of John," he said, "chapter eighteen or nine-teen. Somewhere in there."

"Has this happened to you before?"

"Oh, yeah. What do you think?"

"I'm so overwhelmed by all this, Ricky. This sounds really selfish, but I'm so full, so happy, I can't think of anything else."

He hugged her for a moment. "I've been saved for ten years, and I'm still so full. Now to think I have the Lord and I have you, too. I think I might burst!"

"The man who spoke to us—he could actually hear God speaking to him?"

"Yes," Ricky answered, "but probably not in an audible voice. God gives the truth to *anyone* who is willing to hear it, and He can speak it to them in a way that *they* will understand, whether that's in reading the Bible, speaking to their minds, dreams, visions . . . any number of things."

"How do you know it's the Lord and not yourself . . . or the devil?"

"The best way to know is to make sure you are seeking *God*. His Word says if we seek *Him,* He will answer us. Most people have no idea how we humans try to manipu-late things all the time. We want a job or a wife, or whatever, and we focus on that. Now, if we keep asking, God may let us have it, but that doesn't mean it was His best for us. He withholds no good thing from His chil-dren. If I look to Him every day and don't have something, it's either not good, or it's not good for me!

"And when a word from the Lord comes through another person, it usually will be something you've already heard from God yourself. Their word should be like a confirmation, an encouragement. Otherwise, it's like trusting a person to control your life and not the Lord. The night you found me in George's office, I had gotten on my knees and asked for God's very best for you, and then I believe He spoke to me and told me to tell you how I felt. The next thing I knew, there you were, and you wanted to know how I felt."

Ricky squeezed her close and continued, "In my natural thinking, I had always thought I would never marry. A dark time is coming. I figured it was best not to marry. Then you came along, and I was so confused it wasn't funny. I sought the Lord. Not to have you, not to stay unmarried, but to have His will. I just kept seeking Him, and He answered me. Did my passion for you overwhelm God's voice? . . . Today, when we stood there, the Lord spoke through that man and said you were His gift to me; we would be husband and wife . . . It's like your father saying, 'Yes, that's right; go ahead.' Does that make sense?"

She nodded.

Ricky continued, "But even if you like what you're hearing in your own mind or through someone else, you should test it. Ask yourself who is being glorified by what is being said. Does it make you want to seek God more? Will what you're hearing give you an opening to share Jesus with others? Does it conflict with Scripture? For instance, if I told you God said He wanted us to just live together before we married, what would you say?"

"Absolutely not."

"Why?"

"I went to parochial school for thirteen years. I know that 'fornicators shall not inherit the kingdom of God.'"

He laughed. "That's my girl. You see? God's Word about this is already in you, and you know He's not going to contradict Himself. This is why it's good to have a working knowledge of the Bible—not just bits and pieces of verses, but a knowledge of what is consistent with God's nature. Even the devil can quote Scripture, but someone who knows God will know if something is being taken out of context. . . . And if the word you're getting is saying something will come to pass, as long as you're faithful to Him, it will come to pass. You don't need to make it happen; *He* will."

"What about what He said to me today? I think I already forgot some of it!"

Ricky smiled and took some folded papers out of his pocket. "That's why it's good to have someone write things down. God has always had people write things down because it's hard for us to hold spiritual things in our minds. It's also very easy to twist stuff around to our own thinking if there's no record of what was actually said. Here you go," he said as he handed her the papers. "Keep this for us. Look to see if the Lord is requiring anything of you, be faithful, and trust that He will do the rest."

CHAPTER FIFTY

MELVIN WOODSWORTH TIGHTENED HIS SEATBELT AS THE
aircraft made its final approach to Kennedy International
Airport. He had been away for two weeks and was glad to
be returning to New York.

His wife, Tomika, and their two daughters, Shandra
and Tamara, would be waiting at the airport with the
usual throng of Vital Union members and occasional representatives of the press. He had missed Tomika during
this trip. Usually, he thought of her as a distraction amidst
his busy schedule, but this had been a long, stressful trip.
Unexpected antagonism and hostility from the crowds
left him feeling alienated and alone. Maybe next time he
would take her along.

It was October, and the chill of fall pierced the air. The
captain of the plane informed them that the temperature
in New York that evening was forty-seven degrees.

He turned to his aide. "Did you order the flowers for
Tomika?"

"Yes, they should have them at the door to the ramp," Roy said.

"And the traffic. How's the traffic? I don't want to be late."

"Gerrard checked just fifteen minutes ago. The traffic is fine. We should make the meeting with thirty minutes to spare."

Woodsworth would head directly from the airport to a large gathering where he was scheduled as the guest speaker. After that, he'd do an interview on a late-night news show. Then he'd go home and rest for a few hours.

Saturday was their day of worship, so he would have to be up early. After the service, he would attend one of the largest rallies in the history of the Vital Union (which they called simply *VU*). They had gotten permits for a large public park, and he hoped the weather would cooperate. So far, it looked as if he'd get his wish. Although he was enjoying considerable success, he was somewhat disheartened.

While the Vital Union was growing at an unbelievable rate, so was the opposition. Threats against his life were becoming more numerous. Why did people hate him so much? He had worked hard to change the lives of so many people living in poverty. Why was this such an offense?

He had grown up in one of the worst slums in Detroit. He'd gone to church with his mother as a boy, but finding no leadership there, he drifted into a gang, then into Islam. None of these things had satisfied his soul. None gave him the sense of purpose he longed for—the realization of his destiny. His fruitless journey led him to search within. Eventually, he received the vision that would bring it all together. The vision of the Vital Union. He had started with a small group in New York and now had satellite groups all over America, with the number of inquiries from around the world growing daily.

But something had gone wrong, and now he was trying, rather unsuccessfully, to correct it. Having experienced racism firsthand, he wanted to devise a way to end it. At first he thought the Vital Union could bring this about, but as they branched out and embraced members from almost every people-group, a solid core of resistance developed in the inner-city gangs—especially those comprised of non-black minorities. When VU began to have large numbers of converts in cities and got people off the streets, the "cottage industries" of the gangs (drug-dealing, stealing, prostitution) suffered dramatically. This made them belligerent. Naturally, they could not acknowledge the real reason for their animosity, so they claimed he was "a racist looking to make a profit off other minorities." This really galled him. How dare they make such an accusation? Now they were organizing pickets and protests at his rallies. And worse, there had been sporadic violence between the groups.

A much smaller corner of opposition came from Christians and Muslims who said they objected to the way he had borrowed ideas from both camps. In the beginning they didn't take him seriously, but when he suddenly had thousands of followers in all the major cities, they took notice. The real problem, he figured, was that they hated the competition. The Christians took verbal potshots at him from pulpits, but they were content to leave it at that. The truth was, most of them lacked the commitment it took to do any more than that.

The next group of detractors was made up of white (and black) supremists and others of that ilk, who objected to mixing the races the way Woodsworth advocated.

Last, but not least, were those in the government, who, in the beginning, seemed to appreciate his efforts with the poor. But now they were uneasy about the large numbers of voters over whom he had sway.

Nobody wanted those people or their problems, so he took them. Yes, the VU was strict on certain issues, but the disciplines worked to the benefit of those who conformed. After all, couldn't anyone be "joined" by VU? Didn't they permit anyone to shelter in their care?

Woodsworth was aware of the accusations that some had made regarding high-handed methods of recruitment and violence against disobedient followers. He realized that *some* of them were probably true, but that was because VU had grown so fast. Out of sheer necessity, people were raised up quickly and given places of authority when perhaps they were not quite ready for the responsibilities that came with those positions.

The Code of the Vital Union was simple; it governed body, soul, and spirit. Each level of attainment required greater commitment, more knowledge. Certainly a Novice would not be expected to know what a Disciple knew, any more than a Disciple would be expected to live to the standard of an Elder. Each level required study and proof of mastery. At the initiation to every level, people were informed of what was expected of them, and they agreed to it. The ceremonies for initiation and discipline were secret, but this was to make sure that such sacred rites did not become a spectacle for nonbelievers.

As the organization matured, Woodsworth was sure the problem with public perception could be solved. He was still convinced that no action had been taken by the Vital Union that would not bring about the eventual good of the majority.

During this last trip, he met with the leadership to stress kinder, gentler relations with those under their care. He told them that, although their tactics for outreach should be aggressive, they needed to learn how to market themselves better. A series of teachings on this subject was now being packaged and would be ready to be sold by next week.

He looked out the window of the plane as the ground rushed up to meet them. He was so tired. But there would be no time for rest. When things became more organized and efficient, maybe he could take some time off.

The plane landed and taxied to the gate. Woodsworth covered last-minute details with Roy. They picked up their belongings and walked into the terminal. Roy collected the flowers and handed them to Woodsworth. As they cleared the gate, he saw Tomika and the girls. The girls ran to him and hugged him. Tomika joined the throng and hugged and kissed him, too.

Soon they were in the car headed for the rally. Even though he wanted to look over his speech again, he decided to forego that and spend a few minutes enjoying his wife and daughters.

Shandra had lost a front tooth in his absence, and Tamara had gotten a blue ribbon in gymnastics. Tomika was wearing a new dress and looked positively lovely. How could he be depressed when he had such a family?

He looked at his wife a moment, rested his hand on hers, and said, "I'm going to have to go out to L.A. in two weeks. Why don't you come with me?"

She would have been thrilled at the prospect six months ago, but now the idea was not appealing. She was tired of the life they were living. Tired of the threats on their lives. Tired of being an ornament with no real voice, no right to an opinion, no life of her own.

"Why don't we discuss it later tonight?" she said.

His brow furrowed with concern, but he decided not to pursue it until later. "All right."

An urgent phone call came through, and he decided to take it. Tomika was grateful for the interruption. It would give her time to think of an excuse she could make not to go.

At the convention center they entered through a special gate in the garage and took an elevator up to the

meeting room level. Tomika saw police posted everywhere. There had been more threats. She knew even
though she had not been told. Officers with dogs strolled
the hall as they walked in. She hated this. The constant
stream of threats against them was almost more than she
could bear. The thought that anyone could kill someone
else over an idea was unthinkable. Yet, obviously it was
possible. What kind of person would do that? She
despised having to expose her children to this.

They waited in a small room for a few minutes before
he made his official entrance. While he covered details
with aides, she took the girls for one last trip to the ladies'
room and fixed Shandra's hair. Soon it would be over for
the night. Soon she and the girls could go home. Later,
after an interview, Melvin would be home. By then she
could be asleep.

It was time. She and Melvin stood at the doorway. Roy
looked at both of them for a second and brushed the
shoulders of Melvin's jacket. The girls would walk behind
them. The doors opened, and they entered the hall
looking radiant. The people applauded. They smiled and
waved.

Soon I can go home, Tomika reminded herself.

And actually, the evening did pass quickly. She had
heard the speech before, but Melvin seemed to be in his
stride tonight. It was one of those times when all the
threads seemed to come together, the right message with
the right people in the right place. Soon, Roy packed her
and the girls into a car with two bodyguards and sent
them home.

She tucked the girls in and retired to her room. She
turned on the TV and listened to it as she changed her
clothes and took off her makeup.

Ron Darnell was the interviewer. At least, he wasn't
hostile to Melvin.

"So," Ron said at one point, "here you are with thousands of followers. What's next?"

Melvin smiled. "Well, Ron, it seems to me that we're just getting started. We have a Seven-Year Plan to fulfill. Harder times are coming. If we're going to make it, we have to find a better way to live."

Ron held up a hand and looked at Woodsworth. "Wait just a moment here. Let me focus in on something you said. 'Harder times are coming.' Everyone keeps saying that. Everyone thought the world would end in the year 2000! We're tired of the gloom-and-doom stuff. Do you really see it all that dark ahead?"

Woodsworth looked into the camera. "Poverty is everywhere in America. It used to be that the urban poor were pretty much just African Americans, Hispanic Americans, and the more recent immigrants. But now the poor are everywhere. The elderly and those who have chronic or terminal illnesses, regardless of race, can tell you that. The gap between the have's and the have-not's has grown to massive proportions. Millions of people who gave money into this nation's retirement system are now reduced to poverty! Our kids have to join the military just to get the promise of college. Our government is in a state of decay. It wouldn't take much more to send us over the edge. We don't want any more government promises. We are going to take control of our own destinies. It's time we made provision for ourselves."

The camera rolled back to Ron. "We have some callers on live this evening. You want to answer some questions?"

"Sure."

Ron pushed a button and said, "Doris from Seattle, you have a question for Mr. Woodsworth?"

"Yes."

"Go ahead."

"Is it true that you're a wealthy man?"

Ron pushed the button again and looked at Melvin. "Well? What do you have to say to Doris?"

"Well, Doris," Melvin began, "I'm certainly no longer a *poor* man. And for anyone who is interested, I make my tax return a matter of public record every year. I am willing to put my money where my mouth is. I live well beneath my means and I give 50 percent of my income to the outreaches of Vital Union. My money makes a difference in the lives of others. Not many of the rich in this country can say that."

"Next caller," Ron said, as he pushed another button. "This is Dave. What's your question, Dave?"

Tomika stared at the TV screen, but there didn't seem to be any sound. She saw Ron's and Melvin's eyebrows shoot up, then the sound suddenly returned.

"Well," Ron said, "for those of you who are wondering what happened to the sound on your set, Dave's remarks were blocked, and we don't care to repeat them, so next caller, please. This is Eddie from Indianapolis. Eddie, what's your question?"

"Yeah. Mr. Woodsworth?"

"Yes, Eddie, what's your question."

"Well, I am a Christian, and I want to know what your views on hell are."

Ron pushed the button and looked a little amused. "So? What do you say to that, Mel?"

Melvin cleared his throat. "Well, what about it? Heaven, hell, Nirvana, Purgatory, Paradise, who cares?"

Ron laughed. "You've just hacked off a bunch of people out there, Melvin. In another few seconds our switchboard is going to explode! What do you mean by that?"

"I mean, who cares? For most, the hereafter is irrelevant. There are people out there who couldn't buy decent food for their kids *today*. There are people who couldn't afford their insurance *last week*, who don't know how they're going to pay their bills or care for their parents. Who has time for hell? Some of your viewers probably feel they live there already. We have to get back to simple things. Simple lives. Simple rules. We are going to seize the day. The Great One expects us to live life and to respond to the needs of our brothers now. That's what the Vital Union is all about. *Vital* means 'alive, active, dynamic, essential, fundamental, healthy, integral, spirited, strategic, useful.' *Union* means 'accord, alliance, bond, concert, fusion, integration, and unification.' We are going to work together to bring vitality back to the human race. Let the rich sit on their fat rear ends and ponder the esoteric stuff. . . . "

Tomika had to smile. That man did have a way with words. In fact, she knew he would probably talk her into traveling to L.A. with him. It wouldn't be so bad.

CHAPTER FIFTY-ONE

THE MAN IN THE TORN KHAKI-COLORED RAINCOAT WATCHED the ship as it docked on Saturday morning. The ship's name, *Empress,* was barely visible on the starboard side of her rusted blue hull. He had waited for the ship for several days. A storm at sea had delayed her arrival.

Now that the *Empress* was in New York harbor, Harold Ross must consider his options. He needed, first of all, to ascertain if the items he had seen taken aboard the ship in France were still there. He would wait for his contact to disembark and question him about the exact location of the items. If they were still aboard, all would be well.

Ross, a member of the Quick and the Dead, had originally been sent to Africa with a false military ID. As Major Ross, his purpose was to prove that the United States government had illegally stationed small nuclear devices (Enhanced Radiation Weapons) in southern Africa with the intent of taking over many of the valuable resources there while fighting a staged war. When the Quick and the Dead discovered the plan and prepared to go public with the information, President Todd and those he represented decided to move the weapons and start a mini-epidemic instead. They could then quarantine the same area while they figured out their next move. Unfortunately, two of the weapons—in large metal suitcases—disappeared before shipment back to America. The Quick and the Dead had tracked them to France, where they were sold to a group who wanted to use them in America and was willing to pay any price.

Ross saw a familiar man walking down the gangway. He waited until the man had gotten a distance from the ship before approaching him. When they talked, Ross was informed that the weapons had made the entire crossing. They were still in the aft portion of the cargo hold in a shipment of many similar cases.

The American compulsion for the latest in security had created a new fashion statement in luggage. Metal suitcases were now the rage, and the cases from France were the top of the line. The two cases Ross was looking for would be among hundreds of metal suitcases. The weapons' cases would look enough like the others to pass through customs—as long as the agent was given the proper "incentive" to be nearsighted.

Now Ross would have to make a judgment call. If he let Todd's people know where the bombs were, and they recovered them, all incriminating evidence would be gone. No one would be able to prove what they had done. The other, more appealing choice was to track whoever picked them up and then call in the local police and the media for a *very* public bust of what Ross would tell them was a massive shipment of drugs. The desire to keep any confiscated money or other salable goods for their own department, and the rabid competition between agencies, would discourage the local police from calling in the federal cops. Once the *real* contraband was discovered and caught on video by a local station, the executives at the local news network wouldn't hesitate a second to put the evidence on the air. The competition between the networks in New York was as fierce as the competition between government agencies. Once it had been seen by such a wide audience, there would be no way Todd could keep a lid on it. The only problem with the last scenario was the fact that these were indeed nuclear weapons. If the people who bought them got away from him, the consequences could be disastrous.

Haven't I been able to track them this far? he thought. *Within twenty-four hours, Todd could be history.*

Although the temptation was great, the risk was even greater. He decided he would phone in an anonymous tip to the National Security Agency. Meanwhile he and his contact would track the cases and whoever picked them up.

CHAPTER FIFTY-TWO

ONLY THREE WEEKS REMAINED UNTIL RICKY AND ROSA were to be married. Edwina had purchased a weekend at a spa for Rosa and herself. The two women would take a train there on Friday night and return on Monday morning.

Rosa had agreed to go, but as the time drew near, she had second thoughts. She didn't think she could bear to be away from Ricky that long.

Edwina laughed at her. "Oh, girl, you are so gone on this guy. But trust me, there's no chance that he'll forget you or find another woman while you're away. George will probably have to keep him going until we get back. *Meanwhile,* you should spend some time with your *dearest* friend before you move away to Oklahoma, of all places. I can't believe you are doing this to me. Besides, isn't there a Queen Esther in the Bible? Didn't she go and get all spiffed up for several months before she got married? A spa is just what you need. And when you get back, you'll be all the more irresistible."

"Well," Rosa said, "OK."

"Goodness, Rosa, you act as if I'm dragging you to the chamber of horrors! This is a spa! Hot tubs, gourmet food, massages!"

Rosa laughed at herself. "Oh, you're right! Let's do it!"

On Friday afternoon, Rosa came to the clinic. George and Ricky planned to eat a light dinner with them and drive them to the train.

As soon as Rosa arrived at the clinic, they closed and drove to a restaurant. She and Ricky sat quietly huddled together. George and Edwina did most of the laughing and talking.

When dinner was almost over, Edwina noticed how the lovebirds were looking at one another. "Oh *pleeeease,* this is too much. George, were we ever this gooey? You guys are incredible. Maybe you ought to just elope."

They smiled at each other.

"I don't know about you, George, but I think we'd better get out of here before Rosa gets hysterical and decides to stay home and stare at him some more."

They smiled at Edwina.

"You're right, 'Wina," George said. "They don't even need dessert. Let's go."

When they got to the station, there seemed to be a large number of well-dressed people coming out. Once inside, they realized the Vital Union was holding a large rally at the convention center.

After about fifteen minutes more together, it was time to go. Rosa's eyes filled up with tears, and she fiddled with the collar of the leather jacket she had given Ricky. "Beep me. Remember I have the beeper you can put messages on."

Ricky kissed Rosa and said good-bye, while George did the same to Edwina.

"Come on, girl," Edwina said as she grabbed Rosa's hand. "You'll make it. Let's go."

Soon they were on a train, speeding down the tracks. It wasn't long before Rosa got beeped. She looked at the little screen on the beeper and read the message: *MISS YOU ALREADY. COME HOME SOON. LOVE, R.*

Rosa held the beeper next to her heart. "Isn't he wonderful?"

"Oh *pleeeease,* give me a break," Edwina said as she rolled her eyes. "To think I worked so hard for this."

When they arrived at the spa, a huge bouquet was waiting in Rosa's room. A single white rose swam in an ocean of red ones.

"Now, I wonder who could have sent those?" Edwina said.

Rosa grabbed the card and read it. "Oh, Edwina . . . "

"That's it. Maximum sugar overload. I'm going to my room."

When Edwina got to her room, another large bouquet was there as well. She smiled and opened the card. It read: "Ricky isn't the only one who can romance a lady. I still love you, my dearest. For life. George."

She pressed the card to her lips before she heard Rosa in the doorway.

"Oh, *pleeease!"* Rosa said sarcastically.

Edwina looked up. "Nice guys, huh?"

On Saturday morning George and Ricky met at the clinic early and loaded up the van with the supplies they would need for the day. They were going to Ricky's old neighborhood. He had been lobbying George to do this for some time, and today would be their first venture into that area with the van. He had not mentioned this to Rosa. Although her injuries had long since healed, she still had nightmares about what happened there. Officer De la Cruz had recovered from his wounds and was back at work. The man who attacked them was still missing. The Vital Union had increased their presence in the neighborhood and now owned five entire blocks there. Tensions ran high.

Ricky's replacement, Bobby Plantis, was going with them. A nurse practitioner with two years experience, he came to them highly recommended. He was twenty-seven, white, and unmarried. He had been raised in the city, so he was aware of the possible problems involved with a street clinic in the neighborhoods. He seemed to have no problem relating to the diverse clientele they saw at the clinic and had already begun to fit in.

After some discussion they decided to place the van on a lot only two blocks from Greenie's house. Ricky felt that Greenie's people were less likely to vandalize the van and would probably come to their rescue if there was any sort of trouble.

Many gangs in large cities were uniting against the Vital Union, and New York was no exception. For the most part the division fell along racial lines. The trouble had been brewing for quite some time, but so far only minor skirmishes had erupted. For people like Greenie, who were both black and Hispanic, the choice was decided by loyalties. Being a gang leader who would lose both turf and members, Greenie's choice was obvious. Because he had the largest gang in the area, his territory was the most secure for the moment.

By ten o'clock that morning the van was ready. George, Bobby, and Ricky were seeing patients, and a line of people waited for treatment. Ricky "sorted" the patients. He sent ones who needed immunizations or had small injuries to Bobby. He sent the ones who might require diagnosis or exams to George. Some just needed to ask a question or talk, and Ricky tried to field as many of those as possible. When the afternoon rolled around without incident, Ricky felt pleased that everything had gone so smoothly. They had done it. They had succeeded in their first expedition into his old neighborhood.

It was about time to pack up and leave when Ricky noticed someone running. Within a few minutes, he saw several more people running. This was not good. No joggers lived here. There was only one reason people ran in this neighborhood. Trouble. They either ran to it, or they ran away from it. All but one, a woman, ran in the same direction. She appeared to be running toward him.

As the she drew closer, Ricky recognized her. It was Greenie's aunt, Tina. He got up from where he was sitting and ran to meet her.

"You gotta help us, Ricky."

"What's wrong? What's happened?"

"They got Damian and Akim. They beat 'em bad, Ricky, and they won't let 'em go."

"Who did?"

"Vital Union. Greenie said to come and get you."

"Hold on," Ricky said and headed back to the van. He went inside and told George and Bobby what had happened.

"They call the cops?" George asked.

"Not likely."

"Ambulance?"

"I guess not yet. Greenie sent his aunt to get me, so they're probably in trouble with the police . . . and I have to tell you, George, this could get ugly real quick. If there's violence, we'll lose the van for sure. Why don't you and Bobby get out of here. Give me my backpack. I'll have a look. If they need an ambulance, I'll call one. If I can't get to them, I'll leave."

"Tell you what, Ricky . . . "

There was a knock on the door and Ricky opened it. Three young men stood outside. Ricky knew two of them. They were part of Greenie's gang, and he assumed the third was, too.

"Greenie says come right now. He sent us with a car for you," one of them said.

George looked at Ricky and spoke in a low voice. "I'm not letting you go out there alone."

"Yeah?" Ricky said. "What about Bobby? I'm safer alone around here than he is."

"Can we get Bobby some sort of escort out of here?" George asked.

Ricky looked at the young men outside. "Ramon, Devo. You go with this guy, Bobby. He needs to get out of here safely. Take the subway back home; here's some money. If anything happens to him or to this van, you'll answer to Greenie. Got it?" They stepped into the van.

George turned to Bobby. "You know how to drive this thing. Get it out of here."

George and Ricky threw some supplies together and exited the van. As Ricky got out, he said a prayer for Bobby's safety and put his hand on the doorpost, asking for the van to be kept intact. They got in Greenie's gold convertible with the third young man, José, as the van pulled out onto the street.

José drove like a maniac, and soon they were at the border of Vital Union territory. A crowd had gathered, and more were arriving. Greenie stood on the corner waiting for them. It was getting cold, and Ricky zipped up his jacket as he and George got out of the car.

"What's going on, Greenie?" Ricky asked.

"They caught Damian and Akim walking around in there," he said as he pointed to a building across the street, "and they beat them with those sticks."

"What were they doing in there?"

"Nothing, man, nothing."

"It's me, Raton. Don't give me that. What were they doing in there?"

"Well, the Union people said they were boosting the sound system."

"Where are they now?" George asked.

"Still in there," Greenie said as he nodded toward the building.

It was a Vital Union Meeting Hall, freshly renovated and painted.

"George and I will go over there and see what we can do," Ricky said. "Just don't let things get all stirred up out here, Greenie. We can still all walk away; let's leave it that way." He was anxious to get in and out of the building. It would be dark in about forty-five minutes.

George followed Ricky, who wove his way through the crowd in the street. As they approached the front doors of the meeting hall, several men in gray suits came out and blocked their way. The crowd was watching.

Ricky set down the backpack. "We have no weapons. This man is a doctor; I am an EMT. You can search the backpack if you want. We just came to get a look at the two boys you have here."

One of the men leaned down and picked up the backpack. Ricky saw a gun in a holster inside the man's coat.

Must be a bodyguard for someone, Ricky thought. He sized up the other men. They were probably all bodyguards. All big and muscular, all wearing suits, no sticks, probably all had guns.

The man searched through the backpack and then motioned at Ricky and George. Two men approached and frisked them.

"OK," the first man said, "you can go in."

They entered the building with bodyguards in front of and behind them. They went through a lobby, then a large meeting room filled with people, and then to a small classroom on one side. The two young men lay on a blood-soaked blanket on the floor. As soon as Ricky and George entered in the room, the door was shut and locked behind them.

George took Akim. Ricky went to work on Damian.

"Mine's dead," George said, feeling the boy's neck and then looking in his eyes. "He's been dead a while."

"Oh, Lord," Ricky said, "how will we tell his mother?" He stopped a moment, then looked again at Damian. "Mine's alive, but he's unconscious."

George and Ricky carefully rolled him over. His face was badly swollen. They felt down his arms and legs. "Arm's busted," Ricky said.

"Legs are OK," George said.

"Damian. Damian," Ricky said as he hovered close to the boy's face, "can you hear me?"

The boy's eyelids fluttered.

George leaned close to the boy's face. "Damian? My name is George. I'm a doctor. Ricky and I are here to help you. Can you hear me? Can you open your eyes, Damian?"

One eye opened slightly.

"Can you talk at all?"

The boy made a sound.

"Let us look in your mouth, OK?" Ricky said as they pulled their hands into disposable gloves.

"Broken teeth, lots of torn tissue," George said. "Damian. We know your arm hurts. Anyplace else?"

The young man pointed to his side, and they opened his shirt to look.

The door to the room swung open, and the man with the concealed weapon leaned in.

"You," he said, pointing to Ricky. "Come with me."

Ricky looked at George. "I'll be right back. If I'm not back, and you have a chance to get out of here with him, do it," he said as he walked to the door.

The man leaned back to let him out of the door, then closed and locked it again.

He led Ricky to a room on the far side of the building, where the bodyguards and more men in gray suits stood around a seated figure. They parted as Ricky came into the room. Soon he could see the man in the chair. It was Reuben Haynes, the stepfather of the girl Ricky had found under the bridge.

This was not good. The reason Ricky hoped to be able to get in and out of the building alive was that he and George were neutral parties, uninvolved with the struggles between the Vital Union and the gangs in this neighborhood. But he hadn't planned on Mr. Haynes being here.

Unfortunately, Ricky and Mr. Haynes had met in court just two weeks ago when the case regarding his stepdaughter, Dana, convened. Ricky testified against Mr. Haynes and had made it possible for Dana to stay in a safe environment. Dana hadn't testified yet. Mr. Haynes' lawyers had gotten a continuance on a technicality.

Now here they were, face to face under much different circumstances.

"Let's see, your name is . . . Ruiz, isn't it?"

"Yes."

"I thought I recognized you when you came across the street. Have you seen to the men whom we caught stealing?"

"One of them is already dead, Mr. Haynes," Ricky said.

Mr. Haynes appeared shocked by this news and looked at several of the men near him.

Ricky continued, " . . . .and the other one is in pretty bad shape. If you're smart, you'll let us call the police and the rescue squad. Surrender the men who beat the boys, and you may get out of this neighborhood alive if you leave along with the cops."

"You think we couldn't get out of here?"

"I *know* you can't get out of here. And it's only a matter of time before they come in and get you. Are you aware of the firepower in this neighborhood? Why do you think even the cops are afraid to come in here?"

"We have firepower of our own you know. And we have the Great One on our side," a bodyguard said.

Ricky blew air between his lips. "Right. Well, you'd better do whatever it is you do to get your Great One to save your carcasses now, 'cause you don't have enough guns in here to save yourselves once they find out one of those boys is dead. And, trust me, those sticks may work on defenseless children," he said as he looked right into Haynes' eyes, "but they won't work on several hundred people with guns."

Almost on cue, there was a loud noise outside the building.

"The Great One will deliver us," Mr. Haynes said, trying to rally the men—who were beginning to catch on to the real situation.

"I don't think I'd trust the kindness of a god that demanded I beat people on a regular basis," Ricky said.

"Strike him!" Haynes shouted.

Ricky turned his head as one of the men in the room struck him with a wooden rod, grazing his face.

"Now repent," Haynes said to Ricky.

"I don't see a need. I think you have proven my point quite well," he said as he rubbed the blood off his cheek.

Another loud noise made everyone in the room jump. Haynes was seething, but he realized he had bigger problems at the moment than Ricky's disrespect. He got control of himself and told the bodyguards to put Ricky back in the room with the others. When the door opened and George saw Ricky, his face flooded with relief.

"Boy, am I glad to see you," George said, then noticed Ricky's swollen cheek. "Oh, I see you decided to hit something with your face. . . . How bad does it hurt?"

"Not much. How's Damian?"

"He may have some internal injuries, but I don't think there's anything life-threatening at this point. We should try to get a splint on his arm."

Ricky helped George set and splint the arm as best they could. They had several doses of pain killer, and they gave one to the boy.

Outside the building, the crowd had grown larger. The police had arrived and were trying to find out what was causing the disturbance. A message came over the police radio to all units. They were to pull back to another area and wait for instructions. They all left.

After Ricky and George set Damian's arm, Ricky became aware that something was very wrong. It was dark, the loud noises had stopped, and now there was an eerie quiet. Next, came sirens, but instead of coming toward them, they were receding.

The door to their room opened again. Haynes and three bodyguards entered. Haynes looked scared. "Something's happened," he said. "We'd better try to get out of here."

"Then leave us here and go," Ricky said. "They're not mad at us."

"Exactly," Haynes replied. "You will have to stay with us till we're safe."

Ricky hated to leave Akim's body in the room, but thought it might be worse if they went outside with it. He picked up Damian and moved out of the room with George, who brought the backpack. As they all entered the main hall, the power went out. Through the darkness, they could see an exit at the far side of the room. The door opened and closed several times. Each time the door opened, a dim light from outside came into the room silhouetting those exiting through it. Then it was dark again.

"Quick," Haynes said, "we must catch them before they get away with the cars!"

He was referring to the limousine and another car that he and his entourage brought to the neighborhood just after the trouble started. They moved toward the door and heard the racing of engines and the squeal of tires as everyone who could possibly squeeze into the vehicles attempted to escape. Those who failed to get one of the choice spots in the cars ran for their lives into the sanctuary of Vital Union territory. They hoped to take refuge behind locked doors before their pursuers could overtake them. To their advantage, the attention of the angry mob was drawn to the moving vehicles, giving them time to scurry like roaches into hiding places. Ricky and the others reached the door of the meeting hall just in time to see the mob chasing the vehicles around the corner.

"What will we do now?" one of the bodyguards asked.

"We take hostages," another one said, and began to draw his weapon. But before he could get the gun out of his coat, there was the sound of the pump action on the barrel of a shotgun.

"I wouldn't do that if I were you," Greenie said, as he and several others came up behind them. They had broken into the building and crept up quietly.

Everyone's eyes had adjusted to the darkness now, and they could barely make each other out in the dim light that came streaming in through windows near the ceiling.

"I'd just as well shoot you right here, so you'd better be *real* cooperative," Greenie added.

Haynes and the bodyguards carefully put their hands up. Some of the men with Greenie frisked the bodyguards and Haynes. They tucked all "found" items into their own belts.

"Where's Akim?" Greenie asked.

Ricky stepped closer to his friend. "He's dead. But think now. There's nothing you can do to bring him back, Greenie. If you do anything to these guys, you know you'll end up in jail. Do you want to pay for this with them? Are they worth it?"

Greenie hit Haynes with the butt of the shotgun. "I ought to kill you right now."

The sound of gunfire rang outside, and the air smelled of smoke. Ricky realized things had escalated beyond the incident stage, and now all of them would be in peril. Violence was about to take full control of the neighborhood.

"We'd better get out of here while we still can," Ricky said. "Everyone will be fair game."

"Leave them here," one of the men with Greenie said. "Something might happen to them once we're gone."

"Yeah. But they might be more useful to us alive, if it gets really bad," Ricky added. "How do we know who will be in power even an hour from now?"

"Yeah," Greenie said. "Hostages."

This wasn't what Ricky had intended, but it might keep them alive for a while longer, so he didn't correct Greenie's line of thinking.

Haynes and the bodyguards were relieved to hear they were not being left behind, regardless of their status.

Greenie decided they had better run for his house. Ricky was carrying Damian, but the young man was large, so they agreed to take turns carrying him. This slowed their speed considerably. When they got to Greenie's, they would see if they could call an ambulance or get a car from the neighborhood.

As they ran down an alley, Ricky could smell more smoke, and he knew things were about to get entirely out of control. They heard shots behind them but didn't know who was shooting or the intended target. Was it Greenie's people shooting at Haynes? Vital Union people trying to save him? The police? He heard George cry out and saw him fall.

"I've been shot! I've been shot!" George yelled.

The others stopped. Ricky handed Damian to one of them and ran to George.

"Where?" Ricky asked as he put George's arm around his shoulders to pick him up. He could hear people running toward them and started to drag George along.

"In the leg."

The sound of people approaching grew louder. They needed to run faster. Ricky stopped to hoist George up over his shoulder. "Hold on, George!" he said as he started to run.

They barely made it up the steps into Greenie's house before the sound of gunfire increased dramatically.

CHAPTER FIFTY-THREE

AT ABOUT THE SAME TIME RICKY, GEORGE, AND BOBBY were preparing to take the van into Ricky's old neighborhood, Melvin Woodsworth was just waking up. His eyes opened before the alarm went off, and he lay there for a while thinking about his day. Tomika moved, and he scooted over and nuzzled her ear.

"Your face is all scratchy," she mumbled.

"Good morning to you, too," he said.

" . . . morning."

The alarm sounded, and he shut it off.

"Time to rise and shine, my princess."

You shine. I feel a little dull this morning, she thought.

"I got a lot less sleep than you. Come on. You can do it."

The phone rang, and she moaned.

He leaned back to his nightstand and picked up the receiver.

"Hello?"

While he was on the phone, she got up and went in to wake the girls. When she came back in the room, he was still on the phone. She made a face, but he didn't see her.

"Yes. I understand that," Melvin said. " . . . yes. I know what I said, Roy. But this is one of those times I think discipline is needed. Yes. He stole the money. He should be punished. Yes. We should announce it to the disciples at worship. It should be demotion, at least one year on watch, and punishment by ten men. . . . Well, wouldn't everyone know if it was someone else who stole it? Wouldn't someone else be punished? There you have it. . . . I don't see how we can let this go. Silence would send the wrong message. . . . Look, I have to get ready. I'll be there early, and we'll discuss this. Bye."

"Problems?" she said as she walked to the closet.

"Yes. One of the elders was caught embezzling money. They don't think we should have him punished. I don't see how we can avoid disciplining him. He would do the same to someone else under him."

"But *ten* men to discipline him?"

"It was a lot of money. He can opt to leave, but then we'll have to go to the police. If he wants the world's way of doing it, that's what he'll get. He can go to prison instead," he said as he walked to the bathroom.

She stepped inside the closet. Ten men. They were going to beat the daylights out of that guy. He had signed permission to be punished in this manner when he was inducted as an elder. Now, if he refused the punishment, they would put him in prison for who knows how long. She understood the need for order, but this seemed so . . . barbaric.

"Something wrong?" he asked as he peered in at her.

"No. Just looking for a dress to wear."

"Keep it simple, baby. Keep it simple."

Even though it was tradition to wear a head wrap, this was where she drew the line. Melvin did not like it, but in view of her recent coolness toward him, he tolerated this little rebellion. She selected a plain dress and went back into the bedroom. Maybe she wouldn't go to L.A. She needed to think.

They finished getting ready and went to the meeting hall. The elder who had embezzled the money confessed in front of everyone and publicly repented. He was demoted and put on watch for one year. The fact that he would receive strikes from ten men was announced only to the disciples, but their mood made the service very somber. They knew that they also had agreed to be punished if they broke the law.

After a prepared lunch, they were to head to the rally. Tomika said she was not feeling well.

"What did you eat yesterday?" Melvin asked her.

"I didn't eat anything I shouldn't have," she snapped. "I just don't feel well. Can the girls and I go home? Maybe we will come later."

He frowned. He wanted her there, and he wanted the girls there, but he knew he was going to lose this round. She was upset by the punishment they announced today. Women were more tender about such things.

"You think it's better to let this embezzlement thing get dragged out in court for a year and have a scandal, not to mention this guy rotting in jail for who knows how long? Isn't it better to get it all over with and let the healing begin?"

"I suppose so." She had no intention of arguing with him.

He went back to the original topic. "If I let you go home for a while, do you think you could make it to the rally by five? I really wanted you up there with me for the closing. It's important to me."

"OK," she said with a faint smile. "Five o'clock."

He kissed her and sent her home with the girls and two bodyguards. He would go to the park and mingle with some of the leadership for a while before the meeting.

When they arrived at the park, he was upset to see protesters lining the street outside the entrance. Their signs said things like "Reject Racist Religions" and "We Came to America to *Escape* Communism!"

He sighed as they drove past the signs and into the park. A large contingent of police had been dispatched for the event, and when it was determined that the protesters on the streets did not have a permit, the police started clearing them out.

As his car pulled to a stop where the main event was to take place, Woodsworth could see his personal security force around the platform already. The police did the original sweep of the stage. Then, as agreed, they let the VU guards assume responsibility for the platform area. The police would handle crowd control. Woodsworth, his aide, Roy, and the other leaders made their way through the guards and up onto the stage.

Soon after arriving, he was informed of an incident in one of the newer VU housing developments. Some gang members who were caught stealing the sound system from the meeting hall had been punished—perhaps a little too zealously. Woodsworth called Roy and several other leaders for a small conference on the matter. They decided to send one of the more popular local leaders, Reuben Haynes, to the site to determine what had happened. He would call Roy on a mobile phone and update them as soon as he had interviewed the people at the hall.

The rally finally started. A large crowd had gathered in the park, and the meeting went well. Several local leaders had praised the movement.

The late-afternoon weather had turned chilly by the time Melvin Woodsworth was to address the rally. He realized he needed the notes from his briefcase and almost panicked when he thought he had left it at home. Roy left the platform, found it in the trunk of the car, and quickly returned. Woodsworth motioned to his guards to let Roy back onto the platform.

Woodsworth placed the case on his lap, unlocked it, and opened it. There was a small click and then a violent explosion. The force of the blast knocked people in the front of the audience flat. Within seconds, hundreds of screaming people streamed out of the park and onto the streets, trampling everything and everyone in their path.

CHAPTER FIFTY-FOUR

OUTSIDE THE NEW YORK PARK, A MAN NAMED ADOLPHO sat in his rented vehicle with two other men. Traffic had come to a standstill because of some rally. He swore and smacked his hand on the steering wheel. He had a terrible headache, and he wanted to get to his sister's apartment to take something for it. He had hated New York when he lived here, and he hated it even more now. *All this protesting and talking, that's all Americans ever do,* he thought. *At home, this would not be tolerated.* He wouldn't have come if he hadn't received special orders.

Adolpho had picked up two metal suitcases and stored them in a warehouse in Manhattan. Once there was a delay, they had been told to rent a temperature-controlled space much larger than they needed, saying they had "good furniture and books" they wanted to store. They had paid six months' rent in advance for the space—despite the fact that they would be going back to retrieve the cases tomorrow. The important thing was not to attract attention to themselves.

He and Paulo placed the cases in the rented space and locked the door. Adolpho would keep the key. No one was to move or even touch the cases except he and Paulo. Although he hadn't been told what they contained, their value was so great for their size and they were to be handled with such care that he figured they must be stolen microchips for government weapons systems. He would make the exchange with the purchaser tomorrow and leave this terrible place.

If the ship had not been delayed, they could have done it all in one day. Adolpho beeped the horn of the car to vent his anger.

Eventually, police on horseback arrived and began moving the traffic again.

Good, Adolpho thought, *maybe I will at least make it in time for dinner.*

Soon enough, he was on his sister's street, but Paulo thought perhaps they were being followed. Adolpho drove past the building once and then went around the block, letting Paulo off at the corner. When he came back around, Paulo was not in front of the apartment building. This meant he had seen something suspicious. Adolpho slowly drove around a four-block area and cruised by the apartment again. Paulo was out front this time, but he quickly got in and told Adolpho to keep going.

"What happened?" Adolpho asked.

"The same man I saw when we got to the warehouse. He was following us."

Sirens screamed in the distance.

"Do you think he's going to have us picked up?" Mo said from the back seat.

"No. He's dead now. Get going, Adolpho!"

Because of street construction, Adolpho was forced once again to drive by the park where the rally was being held. Just as their car rounded the corner, the sound of a blast filled the air. Trapped in traffic, they could not move the car, and they dared not leave it. The crowd, now in a total panic, was pouring out of the park toward them.

Isn't this why I hate New York? Adolpho thought. *Always something bad is happening here.*

CHAPTER FIFTY-FIVE

LATE IN THE AFTERNOON, ROSA CAME BACK TO HER ROOM at the spa. She was not feeling well and wanted to lie down. She got into bed but couldn't rest. Edwina came back to the room to find out how she was doing and ask if she wanted to go to dinner.

"No. I might order a little something to eat here if that's OK with you. I think I'd just rather stay in the room."

They heard the sound of Rosa's beeper, and she jumped up and ran to the other room to retrieve it. She pushed the buttons and read the message:

"WE ARE SAFE. STAY PUT! REMEMBER WORD GIVEN. GOD FAITHFUL. NO WORRY—PRAY. WILL CONTACT ASAP. LOVE, RICKY

Edwina watched as the look of elation on Rosa's face faded.

"Something bad has happened, 'Wina."

"*What?*" Now Edwina was upset. "What has happened?"

"I don't know. Look," Rosa said, showing Edwina the message.

They hadn't watched TV since they arrived, but now they went to the set and turned it on. At first only the news channels were carrying a headline story about a bomb blast in New York. Soon, however, every station carried the story. Rosa and Edwina watched in horror as each minute passed and the magnitude of the story grew.

"We now have confirmation," one newscaster said, "that Melvin Woodsworth, leader of the Vital Union, was killed by a bomb at a rally in New York late this afternoon. City officials are asking for calm as rumors of extreme nature are beginning to circulate. A rumor control hotline has been established by the mayor, and concerned citizens are asked to call the number on your screen with *any* concerns. . . . "

The two women watched, unable to speak for about twenty minutes. In that time, accounts of rioting throughout the city and surrounding boroughs were reported.

Video footage showing columns of smoke rising over New York appeared on the screen. Names of the neighborhoods where rioting was the worst included the area where Ricky had taken Rosa the day she was attacked and thrown in the garbage bin.

Edwina suddenly remembered something.

"They keep a *phone* in the van!" she exclaimed. She jumped up and ran to the phone. With trembling fingers she dialed the number and waited what seemed an eternity for an answer. Finally, a man's voice came on the line. It was the man they hired to replace Ricky.

"Hello?"

"Bobby? Is that you? Oh," she said, exhaling loudly, "I'm so glad to hear your voice. Is everything OK? Can I speak to George?"

Rosa watched with increasing alarm as Edwina stretched out her hand to steady herself on the table. She looked as if she were going to faint as she listened to Bobby's account of the last time he saw George and Ricky and his escape from the area. "How long ago?" she said, gripping the edge of the table. "Let me give you the number here. Please let me know where you go and if you hear any-thing, *anything* . . . please." Edwina gave Bobby their location and the phone number before she hung up.

She stood there for a moment and looked at Rosa.

"Where did they go today, 'Wina?"

Edwina could barely say the words. "Ricky's old neigh-borhood."

"O God!" Rosa cried out, nearly hysterical. "What did Bobby say? Where are they now?"

Edwina wobbled to a chair and sat down. "One of Ricky's friends sent some guys to come and get them. There was a problem with the Vital Union people, and somebody was hurt. They realized there was danger, so they sent Bobby out of the neighborhood with the van. They were going to see what they could do to help who-ever was injured. . . . That was about two hours ago."

Rosa remembered the message on her beeper. She looked at it again and read it several times.

"WE ARE SAFE. STAY PUT! REMEMBER WORD GIVEN. GOD FAITHFUL. NO WORRY—PRAY. WILL CONTACT ASAP. LOVE, RICKY"

Ricky was alive just minutes ago when he sent the mes-sage. She squeezed the beeper in her hand. "O Lord, thank You," she said, looking at it again. The words "REMEMBER WORD GIVEN" suddenly seemed to jump out at her. She got up and ran to the bedroom.

Edwina was numb. She sat staring at the television set.

Rosa quickly found the Bible in her suitcase and opened it to where she had placed the pages Ricky had given her after her first visit to his church. She opened them and read them again with new understanding.

"Rosa, I see you have many unresolved questions in you, but that you are pressing into the Lord in the midst of them. This is why He is speaking to you now. And the Lord would say to you, 'Daughter, I have seen your struggles, and I'm pleased that you are seeking Me. I have such joy in the way you have talked to Me lately, in your hunger and thirst to know Me and My will for your life. When confusion or conflict comes, continue to seek Me. Read My Word.'"

She felt a chill as she read the next words.

"'Soon, you will endure testing of your faith, but don't be afraid. I hear every word on your lips and in your heart. Know your prayers are important, that they make a difference. Invite Me to act on your behalf and on behalf of those you love. Do not fear. I will never leave you or forsake you. Believe on Me, and I will bring you out of every trial.'"

She read the words several times and wiped away tears as she continued.

"Ricky, the Lord wants you to know tonight—in front of all these people—how much He delights in you. The Lord would say to you, 'My son, my son, how much I love you! . . .'"

The words poured into Rosa's heart as she thought of how much she loved Ricky. She continued reading until she got to the part about Ricky being a shepherd. This she read slowly.

"' . . . you have learned that you can run to your heavenly Father when you are hurt or have any need. And now I say to you that *you* have become a good shepherd. You have been willing to lay down your life for the sheep. You would leave the ninety-nine and search for the one. You have suffered great loss in your life, but you have allowed that emptiness from loss to be filled with Me. And I say to you this night, I have prepared much for you because you have been faithful with the little you were given. You will be a shepherd in the wilderness. You will tend to My flock in the wilderness. You will not be like other shepherds, nor will you have a flock as other shepherds have. I will do this. You will see, I will lead you and your flock to places of safety, of food, of water in the midst of the wilderness.'"

"I will lead you to places of safety," Rosa repeated before continuing.

"'... This woman is a vessel of My oil and wine. She will pour like wine and oil into the scars of your life. She will be the wife of your bosom, your companion.'"

"I *will* be your wife ... ," Rosa said. A small ray of hope began to shine into her soul as she looked again at the message on the beeper.

"WE ARE SAFE. STAY PUT! REMEMBER WORD GIVEN. GOD FAITHFUL. NO WORRY—PRAY. WILL CONTACT ASAP. LOVE, RICKY"

Rosa walked back into the living room of the suite with her Bible and the letter in one hand and the beeper in the other. She spoke quietly. "Edwina, we need to stay calm. Ricky and George are still alive." She set the beeper on the table.

It was true. That message was probably only minutes old. Edwina tried to force the panic out of her mind.

"But we both know that could change. We need to pray," Rosa said.

Edwina didn't know how to respond.

"I don't have time to explain it all now, 'Wina, but God spoke to me about this the first Sunday I went to church with Ricky. The Lord promised me He would help if I prayed. That's what Ricky was saying on the beeper. To pray."

Edwina was frightened. *Will God even listen to me? Isn't it a little late? He'll know the only reason I'm talking to Him is George. What right do I have to ask God for anything? And what about George? Does he really know God?* Thoughts of the few, meaningless hours they had spent in church on special occasions flashed through her mind. She had always intended to get to know God better ... someday. *But Rosa has been seeking Him. He might do it for her.* At this point, she was so desperate she would try anything. "How do we start?" Edwina said. "What should we say?"

"It's not so much saying exact words—it's talking to God. Ricky showed me how the people in the Bible would 'reason' with God. They would talk to Him and be honest with Him. They would remind Him of His promises . . . and they would praise Him."

Edwina closed her eyes, and a tear rolled down her cheek. "I don't know what to say . . . I don't know why God would even listen to me. It's a little late. . . . "

Rosa put her hand on Edwina's shoulder. "Ricky says it's never too late to talk to the Lord, and I think he's right. As long as we're alive, the Lord is hoping to hear from us." She set her Bible and the letter on the coffee table and knelt down. Edwina knelt next to her.

"Lord, it's me, Rosa. And Edwina. We're not real good at this, but I know You understand. You gave me this message here, and I'm so grateful You did it. You really are the God of all hope. You sent Your Son, Jesus, to die for us and said that if we believed in Him, we could come right into Your presence and get help at any time."

Edwina nodded her head and covered her face with her hands.

Rosa continued. "We put our hope in You right now, because we know You are the only one who can keep Ricky and George safe. Even now, I'm thinking of what I read last week about Daniel in the lions' den. He was thrown in with all those hungry lions, and men closed up the exit, but the king prayed for You to save him. That king didn't know You very well, but You honored his prayers for Daniel. You sent angels to hold the lions' mouths shut and keep Daniel alive. . . . I'm asking You to send angels if Ricky and George need help. Keep them safe from any harm, please, Lord. . . . "

CHAPTER FIFTY-SIX

THE ELECTION WAS ONLY WEEKS AWAY. ON THIS PARTICULAR Saturday, President Sonny Todd would spend a few short minutes in the Oval Office and then travel to Chicago to campaign. After lunching there, he would return home. He was certain word would have reached Yosef's people by then.

Within minutes of his return from Chicago, Todd met with Secretary of Defense Ernie Schollet and Yosef in the Oval Office. A situation had come up, and Yosef demanded an audience.

Todd knew why. Just that morning, he announced his intention to line-item veto a bill for defense funding that amounted to billions of dollars. The changes he planned would have a profound effect on several companies.

"Just what do you think you are doing?" Yosef demanded.

Todd put a leatherbound book in the bookcase and then turned. He appeared perfectly calm. "This may come as a shock to you, but I was elected to the office of president. I represent the American people. I am paid to act in their best interest. It's a sacred trust," he said, putting a hand to his heart with a melodramatic flair.

The phone rang. Todd walked to the desk and answered it. He sat down as the information was relayed to him. "So why are you telling me all of this? Seems like the mayor's problem to me. I'm in an important meeting, so don't disturb me again unless it's urgent . . . " He looked exasperated. "Well, just keep track of what goes on and let me know later." He placed the receiver back on its cradle.

"What happened?" Ernie asked.

"You know that crazy guy Woodsworth? The one who is building up the slums?"

They nodded.

"Somebody just blew him up in New York. The mayor wanted to know if I would send troops. Why is it everyone thinks they can put the bite on the federal government?" He looked at Yosef. "Some people are positively shameless. . . . Well, I guess the mayor of New York is going to have to cry on someone else's shoulder . . . and you know what really galls me?" he asked, more thinking aloud than expecting an answer. "If I helped him, I'd be accused of setting up a police state again! Let him rot for all I care!"

"Back to matters at hand," Yosef said in a serious tone. "I want to know what you thought you were doing this morning. I don't know what you're trying to pull here, but it won't work. You won't win; you must know that."

"Is that so?" Todd asked. "Well, let's see here. The bill can sit on my desk for *how* long? Well past the election. If I choose to carry out the vetoes, your friends could be forced to save money and share the same bankruptcy lawyer! It's positively *amazing* how I'm suddenly important in the scheme of things! If I'd called you last week, you probably wouldn't even have returned the call!" Todd looked at Schollet.

Yosef placed a pudgy hand on Todd's desk. "You know as well as I do that those contracts are for more important things than toys. They are for strategic mechanisms that could very well affect the balance of power."

"Yes. But whose power?"

The phone on Todd's desk rang again. He snatched it up. *"What?* The governor? So the mayor is getting him to call and twist my arm, huh? Well, tell him I'm in an urgent meeting and cannot be disturbed . . . and Russell, if you ring this phone again before I'm done in here and a war isn't in progress or something, you'll be working the phones in North Dakota by tomorrow. Got that?" Todd slammed the phone back down.

Yosef leaned across the desk. "What do you mean, 'whose power?'"

"Oh. Did I imply something by that? I'm so sorry. Of *course,* Ernie and I will do whatever we can to find useful contracts for your people. Ernie, didn't you tell me just yesterday that someone needed to develop a better mosquito net for jungle troops? And pocket protectors. How many uniforms do you think are ruined in an average year by leaky ink pens? Yet not one company has offered to make olive-green pocket protectors for us. . . . Yes, the possibilities for honest enterprise are endless."

It was the first time Todd had ever seen a look of shock on Yosef's face. "Are *you* threatening *us?* How stupid you are!"

"Let's see," Todd said, leaning back in his chair and folding his hands. "Ernie and I have been checking into a few things. It seems that a number of your companies have gone way over their margins. *Someone* led them to believe that the president himself was on their side, that he'd just sign the bill and give them the contracts. I wonder who did such an impetuous thing? If obtaining those contracts should be delayed much more than a month . . . my, my, my. Wouldn't that be scary?"

"You will never get away with this," Yosef said, his face red with anger.

"Really? You wanted to play hardball with *me*, Yosef. You forgot one thing: I still have a few shreds of power that you can't maneuver around. Even if you were to expose me tomorrow, the investigations would take forever. I may lose this office, but not before I've used my pen on this bill. And if anything happens to me, my secret journals, several copies of which have been put in safe keeping, *will* be released to the public. The evidence I have against some of these guys may only be circumstantial, but we'll let the *public* weigh it *all*. The evidence I have against *you*, on the other hand, is substantial. . . . Have I covered all the bases here?"

Yosef sat down. "What do you want?"

"To remain president of the United States for another term. By the end of that, hopefully all of us will have kissed and made up, and I can launch a successful career in the business world—with a little help from friends. Oh, and Ernie has a few ideas for contracts that could be negotiated now."

CHAPTER FIFTY-SEVEN

DONALD LARSON COLE WAS EATING DINNER WHEN BOB Post called.

"Have you been told yet?"

"Told what?"

"That Vital Union guy, Woodsworth, was just splattered off the face of the earth. Bomb blast. He was at some sort of rally in New York. At least five people are dead, and twenty-three are seriously injured."

"Wow. Do they know who did it?"

"Not yet . . . but I'm sure there'll be plenty of accusations flying around. This is going to go up like a powder keg, Don. Half of New York has already been set on fire! The press is going to be at you any minute now, so we'd better conference."

"How soon can you be here?"

"Thirty minutes."

"Anybody tell Larry yet?"

"No, but he might have seen it on TV"

"OK. I'll call Larry; you gather up everyone else."

"I'm on it," Post said, and hung up.

Don set down the phone. Had the whole world gone insane?

He walked back over to the table to retrieve his glass of water before the phone rang again. He tossed his napkin in his plate and went back to the phone.

"Hello?"

"It's Jenny," his new night-shift secretary said. It was only two weeks until the election, and he needed staff around the clock.

"Yes?"

"I'm sorry to disturb you, sir, but I have a call I think you'll want. It's E. E. Kressman."

"Kressman?"

"Yes. He wants to speak to you about the Woodsworth thing."

Cole thought for a moment before responding. "Ask for a number. Tell him I'll call him back in two hours, or that he can call me."

"OK. I'll ring you back in a minute."

"Thanks."

He hung up the phone and sat down. Why was Kressman calling him? Did he want an exclusive interview on one of his networks? Don wondered if Kressman had called the White House as well.

The phone rang again.

"Hello?"

"It's me again," Jenny said. "He says he'll call you back in a couple of hours."

"Excellent."

Bob, Lawrence, Trina, and six other staffers assembled in Don's room within the hour. They sat together and watched television for the latest developments before proceeding.

Less than five hours had elapsed since Woodsworth's death, and rioting was already reported in Miami, Tampa, Chicago, Detroit, New Orleans, Dallas, Houston, Los

Angeles, and other major cities. Hundreds of fires burned out of control. In New York and several other cities, the violence had gotten so bad the police and fire departments were told to withdraw to a safe distance and wait for the National Guard.

Rumors concerning Woodsworth's death spread faster than the fires. The most-reported rumor held that Latin gangs were behind the assassination. Others said it was white supremists, the government, or an Islamic group. In actuality, it didn't matter who was responsible. The frustration Woodsworth stirred and directed toward gangs and the government now overflowed its carefully constructed boundaries and flooded out in all directions, engulfing everything in its path with boiling fury. One of the targets of this rage— the gangs—saw it as a golden opportunity to rid themselves of the Vital Union once and for all, and they struck back with incredible ferocity. Within hours, however, most of the rioters realized it was possible that *none* of them would survive to savor a victory.

Reporters in cities across the nation gave anxious narratives to pictures of masses of people running and smashing everything in their path while whole city blocks went up in flames.

"President Todd has declared a state of emergency," UIG's Sharon Webb reported. "National Guard troops are already surrounding most of the affected cities and are making preparations to quell the riots. *All* military personnel have been placed on alert. In New York, quick-response troops are attempting to secure the areas surrounding the United Nations and the World Trade Center. In fact, our sources inform us that the entire southern tip of Manhattan has been cordoned off. In addition, all trains and traffic between the Bronx, Queens, Brooklyn, and Manhattan have been stopped. The Lincoln and Holland tunnels remain open to military traffic and evacuees only. The Coast Guard has secured the South Ferry area and will hold all ships for use in evacuation if necessary."

If Don Cole hadn't seen such destruction in Denver, it would have been hard for him to believe what he was seeing. But he *had* been to Denver, and visions of rubble and crushed bodies flashed into his mind. *O God, I'm asking you to protect Josh and the others out there. Please keep them safe,* Don prayed silently as he watched.

"In Washington, D.C.," Ms. Webb continued, "an incredible display of military presence has served to keep relative calm. Several small pockets of violence have erupted in the past hour, but the military has made strides to restore order. Elsewhere . . . "

Don switched off the TV. "OK. We have the picture here. How are we going to respond?"

"This is even more serious than Denver," Bob Post said. "I think we should appeal for calm. As long as Todd's trying to restore order I think we should back him."

"I agree," Don said, and the others nodded. "What if Kressman wants an interview? Should we give him an exclusive?"

Post threw up his hands. "God only knows what angle *he's* trying to get on this, but if he's willing to go for an *uncut* interview, I'd say go for it. If he wants to tape and edit, no way. It's only two weeks until D-day, and we might not have time to do damage control if he decides to trash us."

Everyone nodded again.

The phone rang, and Don answered it.

"Hello?"

It was his secretary. "Kressman's on the line. You want to take it now?"

"Go ahead," Don said, waving his hand for silence in the room.

Everyone watched Don's face and listened with interest to his half of the conversation.

"Hello . . . No, Mr. Kressman. Fine, thank you . . .
Yes . . . " A brief look of shock crossed Don's face. "To
New York? For what purpose? . . . They have? . . . Well, as
long as he is moving to restore order, I think you and I
both should be supportive of Todd. . . . "

There was a long pause as Don listened to the phone.
Bob quickly jotted down a question on a note pad and
handed it to him: "He wants you to go to New York?"

Don nodded to Bob, then spoke into the receiver,
"Yes, I realize that, but you need to understand my caution here, Mr. Kressman. You want me to stick my neck
out. How do I know you're not going to cut my head off
once I do? Pardon my distrust, but what proof can you
give me that they asked for this? . . . What assurance do I
have that UIG isn't going to twist this around somehow?
These cities are in a meltdown situation, and I have no
desire to participate in something that might make matters worse."

Bob wrote on the pad again. "To negotiate?"

Don nodded, then spoke into the phone again. "How
about Todd? Is he aware of this? . . . When? . . . OK.
Then here are my terms: I will go provided that I can
speak to Todd and that I have some proof that the people
I'll speak to in New York have the power to stop the violence there . . . Yes, I'll be near the phone all
evening . . . OK, Mr. Kressman. 'Bye."

Don returned the receiver to its cradle and looked at
the others in the room. "Todd is going to call me in a few
minutes. The leaders of a coalition of gangs in New York
have called UIG. Everything they own is already up in
smoke. They are aware that troops are moving in, and
they figure it's going to be a case of 'kill first and ask
questions later.' They're willing to surrender the quad-
rants under their control and help in other areas *if* they
have media coverage—UIG—and a neutral party—me—
to ensure they aren't ambushed by troops. Apparently,
Todd is desperate enough to go for it. He hopes that if

they can squelch this in New York, the others will be easier to deal with."

Lawrence whistled. "You sure you want to get into this?"

Don shook his head. "No, but I don't think it's a question of what I *want* to do anymore. Every hour that this goes on is adding to the cost we're going to pay. We may never know who killed Woodsworth for sure, but I can't think of anything that could have made this country more vulnerable. This could be the beginning of a civil war if things don't get calmed down. It could even invite an attack from forces outside the country. . . . "

Everyone sat in silence for a moment. How had things been allowed to come to this?

Lawrence finally spoke. "You're right, Don. Want me to go with you?"

Don was impressed. The little guy had *some* guts after all. "Thanks, Lawrence. It means a lot to me that we're united on this, but I think you should stay here and be available for interviews if things start to go awry. Would you do that?"

"Sure. But I'm willing to go."

Don looked at Bob Post. "What do you think?"

Trina bit her lip. She wanted to say neither of them should go, but she knew that no one would listen.

Bob exhaled heavily. "Let's not put all our eggs in one basket. There won't be much time for damage control, but if Lawrence is in a safe place we'll be able to get at it sooner."

"It's settled then," Cole said. The phone rang and he picked it up.

"Hello? Yes, put him on . . . Yes, Mr. President . . . "

"Yes sir, I want to cooperate. This is more than a political thing; we have to hang together on this one," he said. "As long as you are using reasonable means to restore order, you have my full support. . . . OK. What time? . . . I'll be ready. . . . One other thing, sir. I plan to make full disclosures to you; I want you to make the same commitment to me. No surprises. Do I have your word on it? . . . I'll go and pack now. Yes. Good-bye."

Don hung up the phone and started giving orders. "Bob, I want you to contact party headquarters and give them a heads-up on this. Trina, get with Bill and the others and start working on statements for me and for Lawrence. Jason, notify the Secret Service guys that we're about to be on the move. I'm going to go shave and pack my bags. . . . Any questions?" Don waited for a moment for a response. "OK then. Let's get moving."

When he got to his room, Don closed the door. He looked up. "I don't know what You are doing, but I know You're not surprised by any of this. And I know You are the one who made them pick me. Please help me to have Your wisdom. . . . We're all in a lot of trouble, and I know it's our fault. But I'm asking You to forgive us and give us a chance to turn around."

He decided to try to call his "twin," Josh Thornton. He sure hoped Josh was safe. There was no answer at the church, so he tried the home number. Josh picked it up after the first ring.

"Hello." He sounded a little breathless.

"Hello, Josh. This is Don. You OK?"

"Yeah. We're asking for God's protection here. Of course, we could lose all our buildings, but lives are what count right now."

"I agree. . . . Listen, Josh. I've just spoken to Todd. The man really needs our prayers. He needs wisdom most of all . . . and so do I. I'm headed your way to help with negotiations. I'm asking for your prayers, too."

"Wow. I'll continue once we hang up and call others if I can, but let's pray now."

CHAPTER FIFTY-EIGHT

FORTY-FIVE MINUTES AFTER PRESIDENT TODD'S MEETING with Yosef began, it was over. Shortly after the others left, Todd was again informed about the situation in New York. By this time, he had calls from eleven mayors and nine state governors. While he delayed, the situation had mushroomed to gigantic proportions.

He went back to his office and called Schollet. He also called the vice president. He needed to think quickly.

By the time Schollet returned to the Oval Office, he'd received reports of the riots as well. Several major cities in America teetered on the brink of total destruction. And there were additional problems that required immediate attention. The United Nations building in New York was in danger, with dignitaries and ambassadors from around the world stranded there. The World Trade Center and the Exchange were in jeopardy as well. Then there was the problem with aviation. Due to the density of the population in the Northeast and the location of so many airports within urban areas, the safety of air traffic in most of this corridor was seriously compromised. All commercial and private aviation in the area might have to be shut down.

Todd realized he'd picked a bad day to play his card. But this was not the time to panic. As other countries realized the severity of the situation, things could get complicated. If he withheld military help, the violence would escalate until there was nothing left of New York and many other metropolitan areas. And who would get the blame? He would. On the other hand, if he intervened and there was the slightest hint of an excessive use of force, it wouldn't matter what Yosef's people did for him. As long as there was an election, he'd lose.

To add to his humiliation, he'd received a call from E. E. Kressman. The man had a plan for a possible settlement in New York. All Sonny would have to do is call Cole and ask him to go and negotiate for it. If he refused to play along with Kressman, he knew he was history— lots and lots of televised *bad* history. Of course, if Cole succeeded, who would get the credit?

Something in Sonny snapped. For the first time in a year he'd actually been in control. He'd been in control for what, a whole hour?

Oh, yes. By all means, he would call Mr. Cole—a man he hated. By all means, he would ask Mr. Cole to negotiate. *Curse that man! If only he'd died in Denver.*

As soon as he'd spoken to Cole, he went upstairs to speak to his wife, Edith. On his way up he muttered to himself. "'We have to hang together on this one . . . As long as you're using reasonable means . . . you have my full support,'" Todd said to himself, in a voice that mimicked Cole's. "That liar." An agent in the hall looked at him. Todd ignored him and went through a doorway to his quarters.

He had never been open to Edith's spiritual ideas before, but perhaps it was time to call on a higher power. He'd certainly had enough of *men* jerking him around like a dog on a leash. Maybe Edith's religion *was* the answer. As long as it wasn't Christianity. The fact that he'd just had to crawl to Cole was the final stroke. He hated Christians and everything they stood for. He'd had to fight them tooth and nail to get this far. He would never yield to their God. Never.

Edith said that Christians had a distorted, limited view of spiritual matters, that they had fallen into error and negative thinking. Because they continued to insist that theirs was the only way, they could not be seriously considered on the same spiritual plane. She said that if someone became open, he could be enlightened with deeper truths and tap into great powers. Sonny realized he had nothing to lose.

Edith would call an advisor, and Sonny could listen to what she had to say. Her favorite advisor, Tony Bensen, was spending time in the Himalayas, so she would have to call upon another one—a woman named Raiza. Edith liked Tony better, but this was probably because they had such sympathetic vibrations. Raiza, however, came highly recommended and would do.

That evening, as the three of them met in the private quarters, Raiza, an attractive woman in her fifties, spoke boldly to Todd.

"My spirit guide says that you are an unbeliever."

He shrugged. "Let's say skeptic."

"He says that when you were twelve, you and your uncle Chester got drunk in a boat."

Sonny got a chill. No one living, except himself, knew what had actually happened. Certainly, it was an accident, but he still felt responsible to this day.

Raiza continued, "The two of you anchored out in the middle of the lake. You stumbled and pushed him into the lake. . . . " She looked from Sonny to his wife and then back at him. A look of sympathy crossed her face, and she put a hand on his shoulder and spoke softly. "He knows you didn't mean it. . . . Would you like other proof my master knows who you are and cares about your life? He knows what you are seeking now. You want to stay in public service here, but you are troubled. You have little hope of remaining."

Todd looked directly at her. "Yes."

"And you want my master's help."

"Yes."

Edith clasped her hands and put them to her heart. She had waited so long for this day. They had endured so much trouble, but if Sonny's eyes were opened, it would all be worth it.

Raiza looked at Edith. "You must leave. Go and meditate in the next room. Pray against negative energies. Even now, I feel the Christians bombarding this place. Efforts are being made to influence his thinking." She turned back to Todd. "You poor dear. No wonder things have been so hard for you. Don't worry; if you believe, the god of forces will be with you."

Todd nodded in agreement. He had no doubts about his situation. He was sure that even now Christians were calling curses on him. But perhaps all he'd ever needed to do was to fight them with a god of his own.

CHAPTER FIFTY-NINE

GREENIE WAS REACHING NEW HEIGHTS IN THE REALM OF swearing when Ricky interrupted him.

"Would you stop that?"

"Since when do you tell me what to do, Raton?"

"I didn't *tell* you anything," Ricky said. "I asked if you would stop that. It isn't helping. We need to think."

When they got inside Greenie's house, his sister, Carla, told them what had happened to Melvin Woodsworth. They would not be able to leave the house. And until things calmed down outside, no ambulances, police, or any other helpers were going to arrive. Now, with even the semblance of law enforcement gone, all restraint would go out the window. No one knew how long the mayhem would last. Ricky had managed to call Rosa's beeper before the phone lines were cut. The power had been shut off, and as the National Guard and other branches of the military attempted to bring about a surrender, they would soon turn off the water as well. Ricky advised Greenie to have his guys fill up the bathtub, pots, jars—any vessel they could find—with water. It was just a matter of time.

They had several things working against them. They didn't know if anyone else knew they had Haynes and company. If the Vital Union people found out and survived the initial onslaught, they might attempt a rescue. If the other factions in the neighborhood knew, they might mob the house and try to take Haynes by force. Then there were those who might decide they could take advantage of the free-for-all and attempt to loot whatever inventory Greenie might have on hand.

However, they also had several things in their favor. They were with Greenie, so at least maybe some of the people outside would not bother them. And they were in Greenie's house. Being the sort of man he was—a gang leader and a drug dealer—his home was a virtual fortress. The doors were made of steel with reinforced hinges and locks. The windows were treated and had shutters on the inside that could be swung into place. So as long as they were locked inside, Ricky and the others felt safe from all but a heavily armed assault or a fire.

Greenie's men were already stationed on the roof and near windows and doors to watch and listen for any signs of activity directed against them. They could hear bursts of gunfire and occasional screams outside. The smell of smoke grew stronger by the minute.

Ricky had to push all other thoughts aside and prepare to remove the bullet from George's leg. It was lodged in the thigh, but it had not hit the bone or the artery. It had almost gone right through the leg, and they did not have an instrument long and slender enough to reach down the pathway and still grab it. After some consideration, he and George agreed Ricky should make an incision near where the bullet would have exited to retrieve it. The next problem was sterilization. There was no way to boil water.

"Got any rubbing alcohol?" Ricky asked Greenie.

"Nope."

"How about bleach?"

"Nope."

Ricky got a frustrated look on his face.

"What'd you expect? This ain't a hospital or a laundry, you know."

Ricky walked down the hall to the cupboard where Greenie kept the liquor.

"Hey! You keep out of there."

"Sorry. Have to have it," Ricky said, shining a flashlight around in the cupboard. He saw a bottle of one hundred twenty-one proof rum. "This'll do."

"Not that, man. My sister got that for me in Puerto Rico!"

"I'll save the bottle. You can put flowers in it," Ricky said as he headed to the kitchen. His friend started swearing again as he walked behind him. Ricky turned and said, "You really need to get yourself a vocabulary, Greenie."

The response was a barrage of profanity—in Spanish.

Ricky shook his head and walked to the kitchen. He found a loaf pan with water in it and poured it out. Some of the instruments Ricky needed were in his backpack, still in sterile wraps. Everything else he needed he'd have to find in Greenie's kitchen. He set the pan on the counter, began rummaging through drawers, and put any of the utensils he thought he might be able to use in it. Next he poured the rum into the pan.

"You got any hydrogen peroxide?"

Greenie just looked at him. "What do *you* think?"

"I'm thinking George is going to hate this." Ricky shook his head again. "You know, for someone with such a high risk of getting shot or stabbed, you sure aren't very prepared."

While he waited for the instruments to soak, Ricky went to the dining room, their makeshift operating room.

Haynes's men were told to sit on the floor where they could be watched. Not that any of them had a desire to escape at this point. It would be suicide to set foot out the door.

Two of Greenie's men, Robert and Lazaro, would hold the flashlights. Several old oil lamps were found and lit. Originally, they planned to lay George on the table but decided against it. Ricky was concerned the legs might give way during the operation.

They took the table out of the room and put a twin mattress on the floor with a shower curtain over it. Finally, they were ready to have George brought in. He tried to make a joke.

"Boy, I'm really wishing I had sent you to med school now!" he said to Ricky.

Ricky smiled. "Yeah? Maybe I'll make a praying man out of you yet!"

George winced as they set him on the mattress, but he managed to reply, "You just might at that."

Ricky had collected all his instruments on a tray and pulled on gloves. He asked Greenie to help him and made him wash and put on gloves as well. When George saw Greenie come into the room with gloves on, he said, "What kind of prayers would you suggest?" and they all had a little laugh.

Before they started, Ricky bowed his head. "Father, You know where we are and You see what we're working with here. I humbly submit all of this to You and ask for Your hand to guide us. Hover over us, Lord. Help George and Damian to fully recover. I ask it in Jesus' name, amen.

Ricky was sure he heard a very quiet "amen" from George.

Before he started, he asked once again, "You're sure you want to be a tough guy about this, George? No painkiller?"

"Yes. Save it for the kid. Besides, if things turn sour with him, you might need my help. I'd need to be able to think."

"All right," Ricky said as he turned to Robert and Lazaro. "You stand over here. You stand right over there. Try to hold the lights steady. Come down closer. Yeah. Like that." Next he looked at one of Haynes's men. "You," he said as he pointed at him. "What's your name?"

"Tyrell."

"You're the biggest. Get up here by George's chest. Be ready to lay across him and hold him down when I say so. You, next to Tyrell, what's your name?"

"Richard."

"Richard. Get down here by George's feet. Hold them down. Don't let him move this leg, and don't let him kick me with the other one. Got it?"

Richard and Tyrell moved into position.

Greenie stood there a moment with his arms bent at the elbows, holding his hands up in his best television-doctor pose. "What about me, Raton?"

"Oh, yeah. Come around to the other side over there. You hold stuff when I tell you. And make sure the guys keep their lights on what I'm doing. OK?"

"Got it."

Ricky looked at his light holders one more time. "Neither one of you is going to faint or anything, are you? If you hate the sight of blood, just say so, and we'll get someone else to do it."

They both shook their heads.

"OK then," Ricky said, swallowing. "Tyrell, do your thing."

The large man stretched himself over George, who had started to protest.

"You too, Richard. No time for small talk, George. Here goes."

Gerrardo, another of Greenie's men, came into the dining room.

"We got a group of about twenty workin' their way down the street," he said, pointing east.

Greenie looked at Haynes's men and then asked Gerrardo something in Spanish.

Gerrardo shook his head no.

"OK. Keep watching them. Don't shoot at them unless they shoot first."

Ricky removed the bullet. "OK!" he said as he pulled the large object from George's leg.

"See?" George said shakily, "I knew I could do it."

Tyrell started to get up. Ricky bumped him with his elbow to get his attention and said, "Not yet!"

Tyrell got back down, and Ricky looked at Richard as if to say, *Are you ready?*

Richard nodded and leaned forward holding George's ankles.

"Just another minute, George. This isn't going to be fun, but you know we have to clean the wound out. I'm sorry, but we only have one thing we can use. Now, Greenie. Do it."

Greenie produced a small glass full of rum and poured it into George's leg.

George started yelling and resisting with all of his might, then suddenly turned completely still.

Ricky went up to look at him and got close to his face to be sure he was breathing. He moved back to the leg. "Passed out. Just as well."

They were nearly finished by the time George awoke. They moved him out of the way while Ricky sterilized the instruments again. They would have to work on Damian's mouth and face while they still had working flashlights.

CHAPTER SIXTY

DAWN FINALLY ARRIVED ON SUNDAY. NOT THAT THEY could tell in Greenie's house—with all of the windows covered, it was dark inside. They opted to partially open the shutters on a few small windows just so they could see to get around.

The smell of smoke hung heavy in the air, and intermittent bursts of gunfire still sounded nearby. Everyone in the house hoped that, now it was daylight, the government could move in and restore order.

It may have been what Ricky hoped for, but he knew it was not going to be so. He had the distinct impression that this was going to last for a while longer. To conserve the batteries, they listened to the radio only periodically. At last report, the National Guard had its hands full just containing the areas affected by riots. The situation was still so volatile that no attempt had been made to restore order.

George had weathered the night as well as could be expected. He had a fever, but Ricky prayed it would break. Damian's mouth injuries needed more care than could be provided, and the young man moaned with pain. They only had two doses of painkiller left, and Ricky decided to keep the vial in his pocket for fear Greenie's men might decide to take it when no one was looking.

Ricky had finally drifted off to sleep on the floor between George and Damian, who were on twin beds in a back bedroom. He woke up praying. He hoped Rosa got his message and that she was praying as well. He knew the danger was still very real.

As he prayed he heard words in his mind. *Keep everyone in the house. Anyone who leaves will die. Men will come to the house. Do not open the door or let them in. My host encamps about you. There are more for you than against you. Stay inside until I tell you it is safe.*

He got up and went to a window. He took the pocket-sized Bible out of his jacket and found a slip of paper in it. He wrote down the words and put them back in the Bible. He remembered how God's army had encamped about Elisha's house and kept him safe.

"What are you doing?" Greenie asked.

Ricky turned and looked at him. "The Lord has spoken to me."

"Yeah?" Greenie looked a little scared.

"Yeah. He says we can't leave right now. Anyone who leaves the house will die. And we can't let anyone in. Even if it seems safe, we need to wait, OK?"

His friend seemed to be weighing his words.

Ricky yanked on the gold zodiac sign around Greenie's neck. "Why is it that people can look at stars in the sky or talk to psychics, ghosts, saints, and angels to get advice and assume a higher power has communicated with them, yet they can't believe they could just ask Jesus something and He could tell them the answer?" He shook his head. "Greenie, it's important that you listen. I know the others will take orders from you."

"OK . . . for now."

They could hear the sound of Damian moaning. Ricky went to his bed and leaned over him. "Damian. It's me, Ricky. How you doin'?"

"Hurts," the boy mumbled.

"I know. But we're almost out of painkiller. Do you think you can hold on for a while so that we can make it last longer?"

Again Ricky barely made out the words. "Yeah . . . thirsty."

He went to get water for Damian and propped him up while he drank. The young man looked with a squinted eye around the room. "Dark here."

"Yeah, there's a riot going on outside, and we're all hiding out at Greenie's house."

Greenie's sister Carla appeared in the doorway.

"Can I help?"

"Well, if you think it won't bother you, it would be good if you got water and a clean cloth and carefully cleaned his eyes and face. Get a bowl and some more water in this glass. Let him try to swish some water around in his mouth and spit it out."

She returned with the bowl of water and the news that the water was now officially off. Ricky knew they would have to plan all water usage from now on.

He heard George stir and moved to kneel near the head of his bed.

"Hey, George, how's it goin'?"

"Please tell me I'm having a nightmare and then pinch me."

"Going that well, eh?"

"Where on earth are we?" George said, rubbing his eyes.

"Don't you remember?"

"Greenie's house?"

"Yeah."

"When can we get out of here?"

"Not soon. There's still the small problem of a riot going on outside."

"Well, how long do they usually take?"

"Oh, yeah. Like we ghetto folk have a timetable. Were you looking for the economy-plan riot or the full-scale-total-meltdown model?"

"Sorry. That was stupid. . . . Edwina's probably having a cow by now. Do they know where we are?"

"I managed to beep Rosa before the lines went down. I'm hoping they got the message that we were safe so far. I told them to stay put. You know, this isn't just a little neighborhood thing. Somebody killed Woodsworth, the Vital Union guy yesterday."

"No."

"Yeah. There's a radio in the other room. Apparently, a good-sized hunk of New York's on fire. And it's happening in big cities everywhere. The president is calling in the military."

George was trying to absorb all of this when there was a commotion in the front of the house. "I'll be back," Ricky said and left the room.

He followed the noise to the kitchen.

Two of the men who had helped with George the night before were about to fight. One was the Union guy, Richard; the other was one of Greenie's guys, Robert.

Greenie and another one of the Union men, Tyrell, held them apart. Greenie looked at Ricky. "You want to pound some sense in them? They want to fight over who can tell whom what to do."

"Why don't we just throw him outside?" Robert said as he struggled against Greenie's restraint.

Richard spat on Robert. "You're nothing but a low-life."

"Just hold on," Greenie interrupted. Lazaro and Haynes entered the kitchen. "You guys, take them out of here. Keep them apart till they cool off."

The two men were taken to separate rooms, leaving Ricky, Greenie, and Haynes to talk it out.

Greenie looked at Haynes. "Why don't you go in the room with the others?"

"Actually, since he's their leader, he might be able to help keep them in line," Ricky said.

"Before we go any further," Haynes said, "I want you to know that neither I nor my bodyguards took part in beating those men. We arrived shortly before you did. If you ask Damian, he could tell you we didn't do it."

Greenie grabbed the front of Haynes's shirt and pulled him forward. Ricky got ready to intervene if necessary. *"Men?"* Greenie shouted. "Does it make it sound better when you call them *men?* The boy you killed was fifteen, and my nephew is only fourteen."

"I didn't kill anyone," Haynes said, looking at both of them.

Ricky stepped closer to both men and spoke in a confidential tone. "This isn't solving anything. We've got more pressing problems to settle at the moment. One of them is water. It's been shut off. It's possible we could run out before the riot stops. Besides drinking and sanitation, we have to consider what we will do if there's a fire."

Greenie let go of Haynes' shirt. All three men stood in silence for a few moments.

"How much water do you think each of us would need?" Greenie said.

"We'll need at least a couple of pints per person per day. Damian will need more. We can use the water in the tub for flushing—only when absolutely necessary. I think you should call a meeting of everyone in the house and lay out the rules. Maybe you could appoint someone to keep track of the water. Also, let's keep the tap on with a pan or something under it in case we get even a trickle; it's better than nothing," Ricky said.

"And there's food to think about," Haynes said.

"Oh, yeah," Ricky interrupted, "we're going to have to throw out all the perishable stuff in the fridge before it really starts to stink, Greenie."

"What are we going to eat?" Haynes asked.

"I have a few things stored away. We'll do OK," Greenie said with an amused smile.

Later, they had a meeting of the entire household, except Damian, and discussed what they would do. Greenie assigned jobs to everyone except George and Damian. Watchmen would guard the house around the clock to be sure no one came up on them by surprise. Each watch would last eight hours. Greenie and his men would take turns. Carla would run the kitchen during the daytime. Robert would watch over the kitchen at night.

After the meeting, Greenie took Ricky aside. "Come with me." They went to Greenie's bedroom, and he locked the door. He went to the closet and opened the door. He slid the clothes on the rack to the right and turned to face the inside left wall of the closet. He knelt down and pushed on the bottom of the wall, and it swung away from him like an awning on a window, exposing a narrow shaft that ran along the side of the closet down to an area below. Greenie got a stick from the far corner of the closet and used it to prop open the wall. "Here," he said, tossing Ricky a flashlight. "Shine it down there."

Ricky shined the light down the hole while his friend went down a ladder on the far side of the shaft.

"OK, now toss me the light and come down."

When Ricky got down the ladder he looked around. They were in a room that was about six feet wide and ten feet long. The walls were lined with shelves. Some of the shelves were empty. Some held guns and ammo. Others held canned food.

"You keep food down here?"

"Well, I figured I could hide in here if I had to. There's a little water over here too, but not much. And this is the best part," he said as he started to laugh. "Look what food I have."

Ricky went to the shelves and saw canned goods. The vast majority of the cans were of one thing. Ham.

"I can hardly wait to hear Haynes begging for their share of the food!" Greenie said, laughing.

Ricky had to chuckle. "This all you have down here? Ham?"

"Hey, when you get your own little hiding place, you put what you want in it. I happen to like ham. And there's at least a dozen cans of other stuff."

They passed most of the food up through the hole and left the water where it was for now. After they had replaced the panel and the stick, Greenie went to his bed and put two cans of ham under it.

"This way, if anyone comes in here looking for more, they'll think that's where I had it all."

They made several trips to the kitchen and stocked the cupboards with all the cans.

Ricky calculated that the twelve of them had enough water for five or six more days. After that, it wouldn't much matter if they had food, so Carla was told to divide up the food for enough meals (mostly consisting of cold ham and canned vegetables) for a week.

"Someone's coming!" Robert said, peeking out a window in the front. "Three. No, four men. Semiautomatic weapons. One of the guys might be Chico."

"Hey! In the house!" someone outside said.

"Yeah?" Greenie called back.

"That you, Greenie?"

"Yeah! What do you want?"

"We wanna talk. Come outside."

Ricky looked at Greenie but said nothing.

"We can talk through the door!" he answered.

"C'mon, Greenie! It's me, Chico!"

"Yeah, I know. I ain't got nothing to sell, Chico. You know that. I didn't get my shipment yesterday. It's not here! Juan probably ran off with all of it. Go find *him!*"

"You got those people in there, Greenie? You know. The gray-suits?"

Everyone in the room looked at Greenie and Ricky as if to say, "Are we going to throw them out?"

Ricky shook his head no.

"No!" Greenie yelled.

"Someone thought they saw you run in here last night with some of them. You sure?"

"Chico," Ricky said through the door. "This is Raton. There's a bunch of us in here. We have Damian. If you see his family, tell them he's hurt, but he's OK. We won't come out till this is over. We don't have anything you need."

There was silence. After a few minutes, the men outside left.

"They'll be back, Ricky," Greenie said. He looked at Haynes and his three body guards. "And I have no intention of dying for you. If it's a choice between me and you, guess what? I'll just throw you right out the door and let them have you!"

The day passed slowly. Haynes and his men ate only vegetables for lunch, but didn't dare complain. Damian was holding his own. George's leg throbbed, but he seemed to be recovering. After sunset, Ricky gave the last dose of painkiller to Damian and sat in a chair between the two beds while the boy drifted off.

Ricky prayed quietly for him, then said, "Damian, be healed, in the name of Jesus. I rebuke any infection and command it to leave his body. Lord, I ask You to overshadow him with Your grace, for it's Your kindness that makes people want to change."

The room was silent for quite some time before George spoke. Ricky didn't know how long he'd been awake, or if he'd been asleep at all.

"Think those guys will come back?" George asked.

"Yeah."

"What are you going to do?"

"All I know to do is keep praying."

"How do you know what to pray for? If it's a choice between us and them, what would you choose?"

"We haven't been asked to make that choice yet. I believe God will keep us safe if we all stay in the house. He didn't give me a plan B."

"Raton!" someone whispered loudly at the end of the hall. He got up from the chair and crept down the hall, passing Robert going toward the bedroom with a gun.

"There's people outside," Greenie whispered as he got closer. "At least six we can see."

Greenie had stationed his men all over the house as lookouts. He and Ricky were alone in the living room. Haynes and company sat in the dining room with Carla. They all heard a bumping noise on the front porch, and Greenie pumped his shotgun.

Ricky put a large hand on his friend's shoulder. As soon as he did so, a figure suddenly appeared in the living room. A large glowing figure. Larger than a man. He stood in front of the door with His back to them, and He held a glowing object in his hand.

Greenie shuddered as he sucked in air and swung the barrel of the shotgun around.

Ricky quickly leaned forward and whispered in his friend's ear while keeping his eyes on the figure. "Wait, Greenie. Just stay quiet."

"Do you see it . . . ?" he whispered back, then started genuflecting over and over.

"Quiet. Hold still."

They stood for what seemed an eternity watching him. The figure kept His back to them and continually looked to the right and to the left without seeming to notice them at all. Then, as suddenly as He had appeared, He faded, and they saw Him no more.

CHAPTER SIXTY-ONE

GREENIE SAT DOWN BUT REMAINED QUIET FOR A FEW MINutes before whispering, "You saw it?"

"Yes."

"How come I could see it?"

"Maybe God wanted you to know He's on your side, that He's watching over us."

"Why would He be on *my* side?"

"Why wouldn't He be?"

"You know what I do, Ricky."

"Are you saying you know what you do is wrong?"

"Well . . . yeah."

"And so that means God hates you?"

"Yeah."

Ricky sat in a chair facing his friend. "He doesn't hate you, Greenie. You can choose to live outside His will your whole life, but He will take no pleasure in your death. Not yours. Not Haynes's death. God has always cared about you, and *He* doesn't change. . . . I think the only thing that may have changed since yesterday is that you've become more willing to admit the truth. . . . Is that so?"

"Yeah."

"In the light of that, don't you think you ought to make a change?"

"Yeah."

"Don't you think you should do it now, while you still can?"

Greenie swallowed. The dreaded decision had now come. "Yeah . . . but we can't get out of here to go to church."

"Are you sayin' that to put things off, or because you think you can only get saved at church? If you want to give your heart to God, you can do it right here in this living room. If you don't mean what you say, it won't count no matter where you are."

"What do I have to do?"

"The Bible says that if you confess with your mouth that Jesus is Lord and believe in your heart that He was raised from the dead, you are saved. Period. You need to believe in Him and say it."

"What about baptism? I was never baptized. . . . "

Ricky could see that his friend was truly concerned about this. "Baptism is you showing others you've gotten saved. Like saying it out in public, you know? When this is over, you can come with me and we'll see that you get baptized . . . but you need to get saved first, Greenie."

Until now, Greenie would have been embarrassed for anyone to know he'd even *thought* of religious things. However, as he stood in the living room watching that figure he was faced with the truth. He'd always known God was there. And now he realized that not only was there a God, but that—sooner than he'd planned—he might be standing before Him to give an account of his life. Ricky assured him that if he was sincerely sorry for his sins and was willing to turn away from them, he would be forgiven. If he accepted Jesus as his Savior, he would be saved.

Even if he died on the spot, he would appear before God in heaven clean and forgiven. He would have nothing to show for his life so far—like a man who runs out of his burning house in the middle of the night—but he would be clean. If they survived this, he would be able to build on the new foundation that he received when he got saved. If what he built on that foundation was good before God, he would have a reward in heaven.

Ricky got on his knees. "You going to do it?"

Greenie knelt in front of Ricky. "Yeah. What do I say?"

"Say the words after me . . . but only if you mean them . . . Father God," Ricky said, and Greenie echoed after him. "I come to You tonight . . . and I realize I have lived a life of sin . . . I have grieved You. I turn away from all that sin tonight . . . I see it as dirt, and I want to be made clean . . . I believe that Your Son, Jesus, came to earth and died for my sin . . . He was killed in my place . . . He was buried for my sin . . . but then He rose from the grave, and now He is alive forever. You have said that if I believe this in my heart and say it, that I will be forgiven, that I am made clean by the blood that was shed by Your Son . . . I say it right now. I say that Jesus is my Lord and my Savior. I thank You, God, for saving me. Amen."

Almost the moment they stopped praying, total war seemed to break loose outside. Several explosions ripped through the air, followed by the sound of automatic weapons. During the next two hours, they heard shouts and cries as people were hit by gunfire or attacked. At one point, they heard a woman screaming, and Ricky was tempted to run out of the house to find her. The warning he had gotten from the Lord was the only thing that kept him in the house.

Suddenly, almost all sound stopped. The silence was as frightening as the noise. After an hour of eerie quiet, they once again heard gunfire and shouting in the distance and smelled more smoke.

The rest of Sunday night passed without further threats to the house, but by morning all of Greenie's guys needed to sleep. They'd stayed awake all night on adrenaline and were exhausted. Haynes offered that he and his men should take the next watch. Greenie didn't like the idea, but he came up with a plan.

"You can stand watch, but your guys don't get any guns. If there's a problem, we'll all get up. I'll stay up with you for a few hours, then Ricky, then Robert, then Lazaro, then Juan. Carla, you yell if anyone bothers you or messes with the stuff in the kitchen, OK?"

She nodded her head and looked at Haynes and the others.

With everyone so thirsty now, it was getting harder to restrain themselves from taking more water than they should.

Ricky went back to the bedroom and found George sitting up in bed.

"Wow. You must be feeling a bit better."

"Actually, I do. You pray for me, too? The leg is really stiff, but I should probably move around. Help me over onto the chair, and we can look at Damian."

The young man had been sleeping, but he started to stir when he heard George and Ricky talking.

Ricky moved the chair close to the other bed and helped his friend onto it. George just sat with his eyes closed and his lips pressed in for a few moments, then exhaled and opened his eyes. "Man, that hurts," he said. "Now, let's see what we can do for Damian here."

Damian opened his eyes.

"How you doing today?" George asked.

"Better, I think," he said.

Ricky smiled. "Well, at least we can understand what you're saying. The swelling in your mouth must be a little better. If I got you some mashed up food, do you think you could swallow it?"

"Yeah."

A series of explosions boomed in the distance, and the house shook several times. Then three more booms, followed by more shaking.

George and Ricky looked at one another while it went on.

"Sounds as if the world is coming to an end out there," George said.

"I wonder who's doin' what to whom," Ricky said. "Maybe we can find out on the radio. Sounds at least a block or two away . . . Could be troops moving in or . . . ," he thought a moment before adding, "it could be someone's stockpile blowing up."

Ricky went to check the radio. All that was being reported was the fact that in some areas the military had established a presence and was preparing to move in.

Carla said she would feed Damian, so Ricky went to Greenie's room with a pillow and a blanket and fell asleep on the floor.

It seemed as if he'd just dozed off when someone shook him, and he sat up quickly.

"It's me. Greenie. It's your turn. Wake up Robert in three hours."

Ricky didn't say anything. He slowly got up off the floor and started out of the room.

"Hey. You forgot the shotgun."

Ricky just waved his hand and left the room. He could hear more explosions going off as he went into the kitchen, but all he could think of was how thirsty he was. He'd been dreaming of water when Greenie woke him up. Lots of water. Cold water. In his dream, he just kept drinking and drinking. Now he could actually get some, but only a small cup. It was gone all too quickly. He promised himself to drink at least two gallons nonstop when this was over. And what wouldn't he give for a toothbrush? His teeth felt as if they had sweaters on them. He went to a closet and found a clean washcloth to put on his finger and rub around in his mouth.

Carla appeared in the hall. "How's Damian? Did he eat anything?" he asked her.

"Yeah. But it made him hurt pretty bad. I had him rinse out, and I gave him some aspirin. I think he's better. At least he ate something, and he sat up for a while."

"Good. And George?"

"He's in the living room."

"Thanks," Ricky said.

She smiled.

Ricky went to the living room. Sure enough, there sat George and Mr. Haynes by the radio. It was turned down very low, and they both leaned toward it so they could hear.

"Anything new?"

"Well," George said, "they won't give locations or details so we still don't know what the explosions are."

Another explosion boomed outside. This one was closer, and the windows rattled.

"We'd better turn off the radio then," Ricky said.

Haynes snapped off the radio, and the three of them sat in silence for a while.

George spoke first. "You know, when this is over, I'm going to take the longest vacation. I'm going to take Edwina anywhere she wants to go. Just as long as it's *far* away."

"I guess some of us don't have the luxury of escaping," Haynes said.

"I've seen your house. You're not poor," Ricky responded.

"I feel an obligation to my people," Haynes said. "I can't leave just because things are going badly."

"You can't leave because you'd be arrested," Ricky said.

"Because you have falsely accused me."

George felt like he was watching a tennis match. He kept quiet and listened while the two men shot words back and forth.

"I suppose Dana beat herself senseless," Ricky said.

"She's a prostitute. One of her customers probably beat her up."

"And why would a fifteen-year-old run away from a nice home and become a prostitute?"

"She was rebellious. She wouldn't follow the rules her mother and I set."

Ricky looked Haynes in the eye. "I don't believe you. You did things to that girl. You did more than beat her."

"That's a lie!" Haynes shouted.

"Is it?"

"I swear it is."

"Sure you do," Ricky said.

"What's that supposed to mean?"

"Listen, I've been working with kids on the street for years. I know a scam when I hear one. Some of them really do falsely accuse their parents of things, but I don't think Dana's lying. Especially not now."

"Now?"

"She's changing. God is changing her. He's restoring her. I don't think she wants to tell lies anymore. She doesn't want to live them either."

Haynes looked as if he were about to explode. "See? This is all so you can ruin me. You encouraged her to lie, and now you can claim her as a convert."

Ricky nodded his head. "I see. Everything's about you, isn't it, Mr. Haynes? Everything is a conspiracy against you. We work night and day making up things to do to you and say about you."

"Well, if you're such an almighty big Christian, then why don't you just forgive me?"

"Trust me, Mr. Haynes, if I didn't know Jesus, I'd have killed you that first day I found her under the bridge. You see, when I got saved, I was in jail because I was charged with murder." He leaned toward Haynes. "I killed my stepfather."

George's mouth dropped open. Haynes looked as if he shrank a notch, and he backed a bit further.

Ricky continued. "He was a drunk, and he was molesting my sister. One night, I came home to find him beating her. We got in a fight, and he pulled out a gun and shot me. We struggled, and the gun went off two more times. . . . I spent two months in the hospital and a year in jail waiting for the trial. I was eventually found not guilty because a jury believed I was defending myself. And that's the truth. The gun went off as we struggled over it. But a greater truth is that even if he'd been running out the door, I still would have killed him. I hated him enough to kill him a thousand times . . . and if God hadn't set me free from that hate, after I found Dana like that, I'd have killed *you*. With my bare hands."

Haynes sat very still now. All of the fight seemed to have left him.

"But you know what I found out?" Ricky continued. "It isn't people who are the real enemy. It's Satan. And I want to get him where it hurts, so I try to take what he thinks is safe in his little kingdom. First that was Dana— and now, it's you."

"How dare . . . "

"That's right, Mr. Haynes, this really *is* about you. Dana *could* just say, 'I forgive you,' and let you keep doing what you're doing—if not to her, then to others. She knows you'd pay eventually. You'd go to hell. But we're not going to settle for that. We want you to be confronted with your sin here and now so that you can escape the darkness you're in. While there's still time."

"I won't listen to this!" he said. He stood and started to leave the room.

"You're a preacher's kid, aren't you?" Ricky said quickly.

He stopped and turned around. "Did she tell you that?"

"What happened to you? Were they so hard that they drove you away from the Lord? If that's so, I'm sorry. But you can't get revenge on them by resisting God. It won't work, Mr. Haynes."

"I was beaten for the smallest thing. I was forced to . . . never mind. The point is, I know all about Christianity, and I want nothing to do with it."

"So you've joined a cult where you beat people for the smallest thing and make them comply with *your* wishes. That about it?"

He stiffened. "Obviously, you haven't been enlightened."

"Yeah, right. About the Big One, sorry, I mean the Great One," Ricky said, rubbing the scab on his face. "And here I thought you enlightened me the other night."

Haynes left the room.

George looked at Ricky. "You really killed him?"

Ricky looked down. "Yeah."

"Is there anything else I don't know about you? Does Rosa know all this?"

"I've pretty much done it all, George. Yes, Rosa knows."

A large blast shook the house and woke everyone up. Carla came running out into the living room.

"You think we'll all get blown up?" she asked.

"I don't think so," said Ricky.

Within a minute, everyone had gathered in the living room, and they sent Tyrell to carry Damian in with the rest of them. He was feeling a little stronger and could sit up a while.

Few words were spoken as the house repeatedly shook and the blasts got louder.

"How long till it gets dark?" someone finally asked.

"About five hours," Greenie said. "Anyone else that wants to get some rest better do it while they can. If they can."

Haynes and two of his bodyguards started repeating a chant to the Great One.

"Just stop it! You're not going to do that in *my* house," Greenie said, standing up. "You wanna do that, go outside." He walked to the door. "I'll unlock it for you."

Haynes and the two bodyguards retreated to the dining room and huddled together. His other bodyguard, Tyrell, stayed in the living room.

Ricky went back to Greenie's room.

Robert stayed with Carla in the kitchen. She was too scared to be alone.

While the others talked quietly, George sat in silence, thinking of Edwina. He had so many regrets about things they should have done. He should have let her adopt a baby long ago. He should have cherished her more and cared less about the success of his career. He had loved her for so many years, but now all he saw were the times when he had taken her for granted. What must she be thinking now? What would she be doing? He began to pray for her, that God would somehow get her through all this. He prayed that God would forgive him for his selfishness. Sure, he had helped poor people, but wasn't his motive more to be a hero than to help others? To be admired? To have things named in his memory? He confronted all of his secret ambitions while he sat with his eyes closed. He realized George Grant wasn't such a nice guy after all.

Mr. Haynes sat in the dining room with his two remaining bodyguards. He realized that Tyrell was no longer one of them. *Just goes to show you,* he thought, *you don't know who's really on your side until you get into something like this.* They would have to censure him and publicly expel him when this was over. During the quiet spells, which sometimes lasted as long as an hour, Haynes, Richard, and Jackson put their heads together and planned. Maybe they *should* leave and take their chances outside while it was still light. Maybe they should slip away after dark. They discussed the possibilities but came to no conclusions.

Ricky prayed and thought of Rosa. His precious Rosa. At around three in the afternoon, he finally fell asleep.

CHAPTER SIXTY-TWO

IT WAS THREE-THIRTY ON MONDAY AFTERNOON. DON COLE looked out the window of the large, armor-plated helicopter. He and a camera crew from Universal Information Group were on their way to Manhattan Island with a detachment of troops. All of them wore full protective gear, and Don tried to decide which was more suffocating—the biohazard suit he'd worn in Denver or all this gear. He looked across the water and saw smoke rising in huge columns from several areas of the island and beyond.

What on earth possessed you to do this? his mind yelled. *Who do you think you are, anyway? You have a Superman complex or something? Look at all this junk you have on! If you don't suffocate, someone will get a lucky shot into your neck, and you'll spend your life in a motorized chair! At least with the virus thing, you'd have been dead in a day.* He realized he was allowing his thoughts to fill him with fear. He tried humoring himself. *Maybe this will get you an honorary membership in the Quick and the Dead! Willing to play with death . . . perhaps you can have cards printed up. Don Cole: The Man With No Brain. Will play with death. No money needed, just a good cause.* He smiled to himself. *Sure, that'll work.*

The officer next to Don pointed out the window at the escort choppers. "Don't worry, sir, those babies will do better than two hundred knots. They've got some of the most sophisticated detection devices known to man, plus 20mm cannons, machine guns, and air-to-surface missiles. Nobody in their right mind is going to mess with us."

Who said any of the people down there were in their right minds? Don thought. *Hey, maybe we can ALL have cards printed up. Save money on a bulk order.*

The meeting with Cole and the gang representatives had been postponed twice. Once because communications went down, and once because the gang leaders did not like the selected meeting site. If today's meeting, scheduled for four o'clock, was postponed, they might have to wait until tomorrow for another opportunity. Too many things could go wrong after dark. The plan was for Cole and the UIG people to meet with the gang coalition at a mutually agreed site near the Manhattan Bridge. If the time and conditions of surrender were agreed upon and broadcast, the leaders would come out of hiding and surrender at the locations specified in the agreement.

Todd had given Cole a guarantee that government forces would not attempt any type of assault during this meeting. The equipment the media brought would allow them to broadcast a live signal. The negotiations would not be open to the media, but cameras would be present to keep everyone honest. A reporter would be standing by to give frequent updates as details became available. If the signal went down for any reason, the talks were off, and UIG would be the first to cry foul.

As they neared the landing area, the helicopter slowed, then halted all forward motion. After several minutes, the officer next to Don received a message from the pilot in his headset. He leaned over to Don. "Sorry, sir, it's a 'no go.' Something has gone wrong down there, and we can't land right now."

Don noted that two of the four escort helicopters stayed behind, and only two returned with his aircraft. He hoped it was only another technical glitch and not anything of a more serious nature. All these delays were making him jittery. Suddenly, a thought occurred to him, almost as if it weren't his own, and yet it was. *Remember: No matter what it looks like, God is with you.* He began to think the delay might be in his favor. He thanked God and apologized for his flippant attitude earlier. If he were going in his own strength, he was in big trouble. But if God were with him, who could be against him?

When the helicopter landed back in New Jersey, he was told he would be briefed on the situation. The UIG people would not be part of the briefing. The chopper touched down, and Don exited the craft. As he walked, he peeled off his protective gear and handed it to one of the soldiers assigned to him and his two Secret Service men.

Don and his small entourage were taken to a large, empty conference room and told Colonel Brigham would be there shortly. One of the soldiers asked him if he needed anything.

"A cold drink would be nice."

Soon the young man returned with soft drinks for Don and the men assigned to him. As he sat there, he thought about the last twenty-four hours. After his initial conversations with Kressman and Todd, he managed to get a call through to his "twin," Josh Thornton. Within hours, Don was on a plane bound for a military base in New Jersey. This morning, he'd received another call from Kressman, who was jetting his way back to the United States from Europe. During the call, Kressman complimented what he referred to as Don's "communication skills." Yet something about Kressman's manner made Don uneasy. He couldn't quite put his finger it, but it was as if an alarm bell had gone off inside him when he heard Kressman's voice. They had agreed to sit and discuss matters later that evening if circumstances permitted. If the meeting took place, Don would be on guard.

Colonel William Brigham came through the door. Everyone stood, and the soldiers all saluted. Most of them were excused and told to wait outside the door with the Secret Service men.

"Mr. Cole," Brigham said, extending his hand.

"Colonel," Don said, shaking his hand.

"Please, be seated."

He sat down and studied Brigham for a moment. A short man with a barrel chest and light brown hair, he reminded Don of a bulldog. Even his manner was all business.

"I've been on the phone with President Todd, sir, and he's authorized me to update you on our current situation. You must understand, though, that this information is not to leave this room."

Don nodded.

"At thirteen hundred hours—one o'clock—an armored vehicle carrying live grenades, percussion grenades, rifles, special ammunition, and other gear was hijacked not far from the Manhattan Bridge."

"An *armored* vehicle? How did this happen?" Don was astounded.

"Listen, you want to chew me out—get in line. Todd's been at it for thirty minutes. We don't know how it happened yet, but trust me, we *will* find out. The vehicle was parked near a perimeter when it disappeared."

"*Disappeared*? So you have no idea where it is or who has it?"

Brigham took a deep breath. "We are making every effort to recover the vehicle. We have search helicopters in addition to ground troops involved in the operation.

Once it gets dark, we'll have infrared and heat-sensitive cameras on the job. But until we locate the materials, we can't let you into the area."

A junior officer appeared in the doorway, and Brigham motioned for him to come in. He handed the colonel an envelope and stood waiting for a response while Brigham read the single sheet of paper inside. After he scanned the page, he briefly closed his eyes and shook his head. "That will be all. There's no reply." The young officer left the room.

Brigham looked at Don. "We found the vehicle."

"Great. So the meeting's on again?"

"No . . . the vehicle is empty."

Thirty miles away from the conference room, Elder Jerome Rolle sat and surveyed his new source of power: hundreds of explosive devices, rifles, and ammo. He laughed out loud. Who would believe his incredible luck? Surely the Great One must have been with them. Only hours ago, they had been running for their lives.

As one of the elders, he had taken part in the punishment of the two young men caught vandalizing the inner sanctuary of the meeting hall and stealing the sound system two days ago. Even though they were caught red-handed, both remained defiant to the last. Jerome realized the punishment went too far, but if the young men hadn't fought back so hard, if they hadn't been so blasphemous, they would not have been punished so severely.

Once the crowd gathered outside the hall, Jerome's group knew they had bitten off more than they could chew, but how could they turn back? What was to be done? Unable to secure a place in one of the escaping cars, Jerome and twenty-two others took refuge in a house. They hid the women and children in the basement while they heard the sounds of other houses being looted and burned—some with the occupants still inside. It was a night of terror Jerome and the others would never forget.

Just before daylight came, the group barely escaped to a neighborhood service station where an old school bus, which had been purchased by the Vital Union, had been sent for repairs. They hid out in the garage as the next night passed and many of the nearby buildings were looted and burned. By dawn on Monday, they realized they would all die if they did not escape from the neighborhood. They were able to start the bus, so they opened the doors and made a run for it. Within moments, men from the neighborhood gang followed them and started firing into the bus—wounding two of Jerome's men. An accident involving one of the gang's cars at an intersection temporarily stopped their pursuit. Since anyone who was able—including the police—had evacuated the night before, the bus zoomed down empty streets. They made it into a parking garage with a ramp for oversized vehicles before the cars searching for them raced by.

Jerome and the others had holed up in the garage for several hours when a large, armored truck came down the street. A driver and two others inside had stolen the vehicle. Trying to pull the truck up the same ramp the bus had used, the driver hit the curb with his rear tire. He stalled the truck trying to ease it up and over the curb, then he restarted the engine and backed up. He was in a hurry and didn't notice the "Stop! Severe Tire Damage!" sign warning those who would try to exit the garage without paying. There was a loud pop as the rear tires deflated on racks of metal spikes. Two of the men inside jumped out of the truck and assessed the damage, yelling and cursing at each other.

Jerome and several others had been watching, and now they began to creep up on the men arguing outside the truck. They rushed forward and overpowered the men from the armored truck before they could get back into the vehicle.

Within moments, they drove the truck far enough into the garage to be out of sight. They loaded its contents onto the bus and skidded out of the garage after blowing off the gate. Another garage with a large entrance was found within a mile.

Jerome sat and considered what he would do with his newfound power. *They killed Woodsworth. They would have killed all of us. Now, it's our turn. The Great One has provided us a means of revenge.* Jerome would see that the two wounded men, the women, and the children were left where soldiers could pick them up. The rest of the men would go back to save any of the Union who were still alive and pay back the ones who started this . . . before they had time to escape. He motioned to Gerald. "Let's wait till dark, then we'll go back."

CHAPTER SIXTY-THREE

As the sky grew dark that night, Don Cole readied himself to meet E. E. Kressman. He dressed in his best suit and tie and opted to wear his good watch. It wasn't every day he met one of the richest and most powerful men on earth.

Remember, I am with you, echoed in his head. *And if I am for you, who can be against you?*

"OK, Lord," he said quietly, "I know that to You he's just a man, but down here, things look different."

It was time to go. Cole had given Avery some time off before they left for New York, so he would be taking only two Secret Service men, Reggie and Sam, to the meeting. Reggie was an OK sort of guy. Sam was more "by the book." Don was privately amused as he noted the ways they quietly irritated each other over procedures at times.

Permission had been granted for a corporate helicopter to land on the military base and pick them up. When the three of them boarded the helicopter, Don instantly noted the luxury. Nothing in the interior was overstated, but all the furnishings were the finest money could buy. The helicopter went to altitude, and the smell of smoke rising from New York reminded him that this was not merely some dinner with one of the power elite for brownie points. He needed to stay on his toes.

Although owning UIG and its subsidiaries would be enough to give anyone sizable clout in the world of politics, this was actually one of Kressman's smaller holdings. The man was a major player in corporate and political realms—even without UIG he had sizable financial, manufacturing, and property holdings around the world. He regularly met with heads of state. His slender, olive-skinned face topped with a salt-and-pepper mane of hair was recognized in almost any country. What Don would remember most about him, however, was his voice. That voice.

Within thirty minutes, they touched down at one of Kressman's corporate holdings, a black glass building set in the midst of precisely manicured acreage. Don looked out over the grounds as they settled onto the helicopter pad. *The electric bill alone must be incredible,* he thought, looking down at all the lights and fountains among the trees.

A man in a beige suit ran to open the door of the helicopter. "Welcome," he said, with a thick accent. "Please follow me."

The man led them into a spacious elevator. When the doors opened, Don and his guards were ushered down a long hall. As they walked, Don noted the pieces of art and ancient artifacts displayed in cases and on the walls. At the end of the hall their escort opened a large set of double doors and bid them to enter.

E. E. Kressman sat studying a computer monitor in the surface of a large desk. The smooth desktop reflected Kressman and the bookcase behind him like the surface of a small pond on a windless day. He touched the screen, and it went dark as Don approached. He made no attempt to rise or to shake hands across the great expanse of the desk.

"Mr. Cole. I'm pleased to finally meet you," he said, folding his hands. "Was the flight smooth?"

"Yes. The flight was fine."

"I hope you are hungry. My chef has prepared an excellent meal for us this evening. Let me just get an update on the situation in New York before we retire to the dining room," he said, picking up a small phone receiver out of a shallow drawer on his left. "Yes. What do we have in the way of an update?" he asked, then listened. "Thank you," he said, and hung up the receiver.

He looked at Don. "Well, Mr. Cole. Even though the meeting has been delayed, there seem to be some good results. As a show of goodwill, there has been a general truce so far tonight. There are fires and some shooting, but no escalation in any areas and a decrease of activities in most. Hopefully, tomorrow, if all goes well, we can have an equitable solution to the problem."

"I doubt there can be a fair solution to something that has taken such a toll already, but certainly we can hope the violence will be brought to an end."

Kressman kept him in a steady gaze. "I stand corrected. Shall we go to dinner now?"

They were shown to a small, exquisite dining room with place settings for two. Agent Reggie sat outside the door, Sam went to the kitchen. Kressman and Cole were disturbed only when servants came in to deliver food or remove dishes. Don's host had been right. The meal was excellent.

The two men briefly discussed monetary policies, the Middle East, and the election. Don chose his words carefully; Kressman revealed little of his own opinions. Finally, his host got to the heart of the matter.

"I wanted to meet you tonight," Kressman said, "because I know you will win the next election. I thought we should get together and begin our relationship before that happened."

"What makes you think I will win?" Cole asked.

"You don't think you will win?"

"Oh, yes, I do. But what makes *you* think I will?"

"Todd used poor judgment and overstepped his bounds in the Denver incident. I think it swung the pendulum in your direction. Of course, what I am doing for you now will help you as well."

Cole noted the word *incident*. Like it was a minor mishap. "Well," he said, "I *do* appreciate favorable reporting, but I want you to know up front—however this goes—I feel accurate reporting should always be your mandate."

"Come now. You and I both know any truth can be told in a manner that can help or hurt, depending on how much of it is told. . . . The fact of the matter is that I am the one who chose you to negotiate. In exchange for the brief risk, you will win the White House. I like men who are willing to take risks for what they want."

This irritated Don. Kressman wanted to make it sound as if he had just been bought—that in exchange for some minimal danger, he was offering Don the presidency.

"The truth is, Mr. Kressman, I am doing this for America. I told you at the outset that if Todd had a sensible plan, I'd support him. I meant it. Regardless of what you think, I don't have any other angles. I love this country, and I don't want to see it destroyed. If we have agreement on that point, I guess we'll work together."

Kressman's face softened into a smile. He raised his glass and said in a soothing voice, "I look forward to working with you often, Mr. Cole."

At several minutes after eleven, the visit finally drew to a close. Don, Reggie, and Sam were taken back to the helicopter. After the first few minutes of flight, Cole once again smelled smoke. He looked out the windows on the left side and was startled to see bright flashes of light in the distance coming up from the darkness below.

"Look out there," he said to the agents.

"Something's definitely going on down there," Sam said, nodding his head. "Explosions."

The helicopter suddenly banked to the right. A steward appeared and offered apologies.

"I'm sorry, sir. We've been asked to clear this airspace. We've also been informed that we cannot land at the base. We'll have to go to a nearby heliport. We've already ordered a car to take you back to the base. Again, our apologies."

Don turned and peered out at the flashes of light receding in the distance and wondered what had happened.

At that moment, with his house close to ground zero, Greenie was bargaining hard with God. What they'd heard outside before was nothing compared to what they were about to endure. If God would let him live, he promised things would be different. By midnight, the only one who believed they would see daylight again was Ricky.

CHAPTER SIXTY-FOUR

IT WAS 10:30 P.M. AS DONALD COLE DINED WITH E. E. Kressman miles away, Vital Union Elder Jerome Rolle crouched down inside the burned-out shell of a former Union house. So far, they had located only two members in the neighborhood who were still alive. One of them, however, did say that Reuben Haynes and several others had been taken hostage by a gang leader and were being held in a house nearby. Jerome now formulated a plan for rescuing those held prisoner. They had flares, live grenades, percussion grenades, and rifles with large-caliber armor-piercing shells.

Jerome's group would use the grenades to work their way to the gang leader's house, then they would demand the release of Haynes and the others. They had been told the house was well protected and had a steel door.

We'll see how long that door lasts when we shoot it with these, Jerome thought, loading the rifle with a round of shells. Each of the others loaded themselves up with weapons. They had all "procured" heavy-duty, canvas bags from a local sporting goods store to carry grenades and plenty of extra ammo.

Once they had Haynes, they would give the signal—two flares. Four men would speed the cars to a park just one block south of the house. They would rendezvous at the park and escape with Haynes to a safer area. At this point, Rolle was prepared to pay any price for his own vindication.

All was ready. They would begin moving toward the house.

At 11:30 P.M., Capt. Benjamin "Red Dog" Weir and his counterpart, Capt. Wally "Wall Eye" Dover flew their MOH-650 Talisman helicopters in tandem close to the surface of the water. Soon they would reach the reconnaissance area and split up. Weir would work his way to the northeast, Dover to the southwest.

"Wall Eye, this is Red Dog. Let's split for the first run."

"Affirmative, Red Dog."

The two helicopters separated and began to move into the targeted search areas. The Talisman was the latest in high-tech, armed-reconnaissance aircraft. Made almost entirely of radar-absorbing composite material, it had a low-noise, five-bladed rotor and could maneuver in tight areas. Operated by a three-man crew, each was equipped with infrared, low-light, and vapor-sensitive cameras with helmet-mounted displays. With triple redundant electrical and hydraulic systems, the helicopter was capable of taking several hits and continuing to operate while striking back with a small turret-mounted canon that could fire over sixteen hundred rounds per minute. In addition, the craft was equipped with three-inch rockets, air-to-surface missiles, and air-to-air missiles.

As Captain Weir made a pass through the first quadrant of his designated area, he picked up very little movement. Several small groups of people traveled on foot, and the heat-sensitive infrared cameras indicated that several vehicles had recently been moved. A small fire in a grocery store seemed to be burning itself out. They had received radio reports that multiple explosions had rocked the area within the past thirty minutes, but Weir saw no sign of current rioting. They knew someone down there had possession of a truckload of riot gear and weapons. The hijacked weapons included grenades and armor-piercing bullets, so he had been told to use extreme caution. Part of their mission for the night was to see if they could locate the people who had stolen the weapons and pinpoint their position for a strike by a response team. If it appeared that those possessing the weapons might escape and disperse, Weir and Dover had orders to use deadly force.

On the ground, Jerome Rolle and his men were nearing Greenie's house. They had just eliminated the last resistance in the area. Those who had chosen to remain in the neighborhood had already spent most of their ammunition. They had little defense against the Vital Union group. Jerome and company—drunk with their new-found power—used an excess of grenades.

In their pause to regroup, there had been a period of calm. The VU faction slowly approached the house which, they had been told, was heavily guarded. As they crept closer, Gerald managed to shoot one of them off the roof.

Inside, Greenie and his men were on full alert. The explosions had been so near the house that the furniture shook with each blast. In the quiet that followed, Robert heard Lazaro take a hit and fall from the roof.

A thud on the door was followed by the sound of small chunks of plaster hitting the floor. It took a few moments before Greenie realized something had punched right through the front door and imbedded itself in the ceiling of the living room.

Someone called into the house. It was Jerome Rolle.

"You! In the house! We know you have some of the men from the Union! Let them out now! As you can see, we can blow the door off if we want to. Let them out now, and we can talk!" This was a lie. As soon as Haynes and his men were safe, Rolle had no intention of leaving anyone in the house alive. Once Haynes was out, it would start raining grenades.

Jerome shot another hole through the front door. "Did you hear me in there? This is Elder Rolle of the Vital Union! Let Haynes and the others go! I'll give you one minute to comply, then we take down the door!"

Greenie and Ricky had been standing together near the door, but now crouched down against a side wall. Haynes and the others had been told to sit on the floor in the dining room earlier, but Haynes crawled into the living room. He heard Rolle calling to them and recognized the name.

Greenie and Ricky spoke to each other in Spanish.

"What now, Raton?"

"You know what I told you, Greenie. Don't open the door or let anyone leave. You've seen that God has kept us safe. Don't open the door. Don't let them out. They'll die."

"What do I care about them? If they want to go, I say let them go!"

"If you open that door, Greenie, we may die as well. I say wait it out."

Haynes didn't know what they were saying. He interrupted them. "Just let us go. I'll have you all on charges of kidnapping and unlawful imprisonment when this is over."

Ricky turned to face Haynes and addressed him in English. "It's not as simple as that. We're keeping you here for your own safety. If you go out that door before this is all over, you're going to die."

"Are you going to shoot us in the back?"

Ricky exhaled and shook his head. "Look. When I told you that God wanted to save you, I meant it. Even you. As long as you stay in this house with us, you are safe. I'm *asking* you to stay."

Two of Haynes' bodyguards, Richard and Jackson, belly-crawled into the living room. Haynes looked at them and then turned to face Greenie. "We want out of here. I swear you'll do prison time if you keep us here."

Ricky spoke to his friend in Spanish once again. "Please, I'm begging you not to open that door, Greenie. I would rather stand trial for kidnapping than let them out. That's how strongly I feel about this. You can say I wouldn't let you open the door. I will say it was I who insisted on holding them here. *Please*, don't open that door."

Greenie thought for a moment. In spite of what he had seen two nights before, fear gripped him. He knew the men outside had explosives as well as large fire power. They could blow the door off. He could see no way to stave off the coming attack. Although he believed Ricky was sincere, Greenie was no longer convinced they could be protected from such force. His desire to save himself and his friends surpassed his desire to save Haynes and his men. "I'm not going to jail *or* die for them, Raton, and I can't let you do it either," he said, then looked at Tyrell, who crouched in the corner with George. "How about you? Do you want to go, too?"

Tyrell shook his head no.

"We'll deal with *you* later," Haynes said to Tyrell. "But we choose to go. Are you going to hold us against our will?"

Greenie looked at everyone else and then at Ricky. "I'm not going to make 'em stay." He stood, walked to the door, and unbolted it. "You want out? Then go. No one from this house will stop you . . . Robert!" he called toward the back of the house.

"*Sí!*" came the reply.

"Robert! Tell the others! Haynes and two more are leaving. Let them go!"

Greenie stepped away from the door and then motioned to Haynes and the others with his arm. "So go!"

Haynes inched toward the door then opened it a crack and yelled to the men outside. "It's me! Haynes! I'm coming out with two others! Don't shoot!" He motioned to his men to go out first.

"It's too bad your wife isn't here. She could go before you too, you stinking coward!" Greenie spat out.

Haynes stiffened, then turned, pushed the door open wider, put his hands up, and stepped outside. The two others followed him.

Jerome and his men stood ready for any kind of trick the gang members might try to play. He couldn't imagine they would give up Haynes without resistance. He could hear the sound of a helicopter, but the noise was so soft, he figured it was at least a mile away. They saw the door swing open, and they all raised their weapons. Within moments three men emerged with their hands raised. Jerome couldn't see well enough in the dark to tell whether any of them was indeed Haynes. "Come down off the stoop!" he yelled.

Captain Benjamin Weir had picked up a large number of heat signatures in the second quadrant he flew over. He'd discovered more than twenty-seven bodies in small groups, still warm, in destroyed structures within a three-block area. He had radioed his counterpart, Captain Dover, who was now en route to Weir's location. Before his partner arrived, Weir had popped behind a building and raised up just enough to have the cameras trained on a group of men outside a house. They all held weapons, still warm from having been fired. After a few moments, the door of the house opened and three men appeared. Their hands were up, so Weir assumed they were surrendering. He had already radioed to base. Were there any troops in the area? No. Could some be sent? Yes.

Someone had systematically gone through this neighborhood and killed twenty-seven people. Weir decided to swing around closer to the action. As the three men came off the porch, some of the armed group crouched down to rummage through large duffle bags. Weir switched to infrared camera. Several of the men stood up with what appeared to be grenades.

Weir spoke to the crew of his craft. "Prepare to dust them."

His copilot responded, "Ready at your command."

Weir gave the countdown. "Three, two, one, release the tube."

A two-foot long, three-inch wide cylinder dropped silently from the undercarriage of the craft. It made contact with the ground and rolled for two seconds toward the suspects as the helicopter nosed down. A sudden, fluorescent burst of dust blew through the entire area, marking every object within a sixty-foot radius.

Jerome's men saw the fluorescent burst, felt the sting of powder blown at high velocity striking their skin and eyes, and heard a voice thundering from the sky.

"This is Captain Weir of the United States Army. I have weapons trained on you. Lay your weapons on the ground now, raise your hands, and back away ten paces."

Jerome and the others were taken completely by surprise. Within moments, another helicopter appeared. As he dove behind a car, he was sure he saw several of the men heaving grenades at one of the choppers and a response of small rockets. Plumes of fire and smoke rose in the night sky and brought what seemed the light of day and a deafening roar.

CHAPTER SIXTY-FIVE

ROSA'S EYES SNAPPED OPEN. WHAT TIME WAS IT? SHE LOOKED over at the clock and sat up. It was 11:30 P.M., Monday night. She had crawled into the bed around 7:00 P.M. hoping to get some rest. She'd heard on the news that a resolution to the problem in New York might come by the next day. Reports said that Donald Cole was negotiating with the gangs for a truce. Even after it got dark, the violence seemed to have quietened.

Rosa had slept only in short bursts since she and Edwina first got the news about the riots on Saturday night. Neither she nor Edwina had left the hotel suite, and neither of them had been able to eat much. They roamed around the suite in shifts—listening for the phone, watching the news, praying.

On Sunday, Rosa remembered something Ricky had taught her about praying from the Bible. One of the scriptures he showed her to pray if she was ever in trouble or in danger was Psalm 91. He told her she could remember it by thinking of it as a "911" call to the Lord.

Start at Psalm 91, verse one, he'd said. She found the passage and began to pray it for Ricky.

"Lord, it says here that he who dwells in the secret place of the Most High God shall abide under Your shadow. Lord, I know Ricky dwells in Your presence. He is Your own, and I ask You to keep him under Your shadow. . . . "

She continued to pray the rest of the chapter for Ricky. She shared this idea with Edwina and asked her if she'd like to pray like this for George.

"I don't know if I can . . . honestly, " Edwina said with tears. "I can't say that George even *knows* the Lord. Rosa, what can I do?"

Rosa considered this a moment. She'd had the same fears for George. . . . Suddenly the answer came to her. "Well, *you* know Lord now, don't you?

"Yes."

"Ricky and I have been reading about marriage. The Bible says that even an unbelieving spouse is sanctified through the saved one."

Edwina looked puzzled. "So what does *that* mean? Does it mean that George is saved?"

"I asked Ricky the same thing. No. But it does mean you have the authority to ask the same protection and blessing for George that you'd ask for yourself. You are one flesh. God sees you as one person. It's as if you have an umbrella over you, and as long as George is your husband, in the spirit he's next to you. He's covered by *your* umbrella. While you both are alive, he's covered by what's covering *you*. When one of you dies, you are no longer married, and he'd be on his own."

Edwina looked scared again.

"But you have every right to ask for George's safety," Rosa continued, "and to ask that, somehow, through all this, he comes to trust in the Lord for himself."

Edwina took the Bible and started to pray, then stopped. "What if I say it wrong?"

Rosa put her arms around her friend. "Remember? It's OK. He knows."

Later, when they heard about Cole, they prayed for him, too. Other times, when they watched the news, they just sat and wept, asking for God's mercy in the whole situation. They did all they knew to do.

Now, Rosa was wide awake. She felt prompted to get up immediately. "What should I do, Lord?" she asked as she stood in her room.

Nine one one, nine one one . . . nine one one.

Rosa ran to the living room. Edwina was asleep on the sofa.

"Edwina! Edwina!" Rosa said urgently, shaking her friend.

"What?" Edwina exclaimed as she sat up. "What's happened?"

"They're in danger or in trouble; I just know it. We need to pray right now."

Edwina didn't take time to argue or question. She instantly dropped to her knees from the couch.

Rosa got out her Bible and began to pray the ninety-first psalm. She went through the whole thing for Ricky and George, with Edwina saying "Yes" or "Yes, Lord" in agreement with her.

When Rosa finished, she did not feel peaceful. "I still feel uneasy. Do you feel at peace?"

"No."

"Whatever it is hasn't passed yet. Let's keep praying," she said to Edwina.

They prayed together again, this time with Edwina in the lead and Rosa in agreement.

CHAPTER SIXTY-SIX

GREENIE, RICKY, AND THE OTHERS WHO HAD GATHERED IN the living room heard Jerome Rolle tell Haynes and his men to come off the stoop of the house. A flash of fluorescent powder burst through the open door and splashed across the floor. The next thing they heard was the faint sound of a helicopter and a voice on a loudspeaker saying, "This is Captain Weir of the United States Army . . . "

Within seconds, huge explosions rocked the house. Bright flashes of light could be seen through the open door, and they could hear spurts of gunfire as the men outside attempted to fight and run.

"*Everybody!*" Ricky shouted, "To the back of the house! Quickly! Everybody!" He yanked George up from his position on the floor and sent him flying down the hall with the others. He and Greenie took up the rear as all the glass in the front of the house shattered. Ricky looked to see if Damian was in the room and then crouched in the doorway. "Stay down! Cover your heads!"

"Let me see if Robert and the others are OK!" Greenie shouted over the din.

"Stay in the back of the house!" Ricky called out, letting him crawl out the bedroom door.

Greenie could see the light from all the explosions and fire flashing through the door and reflecting down the hall in bright spurts. He was overcome with remorse that he had opened the front door and knew he must go and close it. If he didn't, the men from outside might run in and kill them all. He stood up and ran down the hall.

Ricky turned and saw the silhouette of his friend disappear into the front of the house. "Greenie! No!" He yelled and started after him.

Greenie had reached the front door. As he stepped outside to grab the knob of the door, a grenade rolled onto the threshold. With no thought for himself Greenie quickly bent down, snatched up the grenade and threw it into the street. Before he could step back into the safety of the house, a bullet shot through his midsection. The force of it propelled him back through the doorway. Ricky had reached the end of the hall. It was as if time had frozen. Greenie looked down at himself and then at Ricky. The expression on his face said, *Can you believe this?* As he started to fall, an explosion blew the door off its hinges. Ricky was blown back down the hall. When his head hit the floor, he lost consciousness.

When he woke up, one of his ears was ringing loudly. In the other, he could hear George's voice.

"Ricky? Ricky? Can you hear me? Ricky?"

He opened his eyes. George lay next to him in the hall. "Yes, George. I can hear you. At least in *this* ear I can," he said, pointing to his right ear. "What happened?"

George shined a light into Ricky's eyes. "It's over, Ricky. Soldiers are securing the area and will be back in a few minutes to take us out of here. We just need to wait for them. You feel OK?"

"Yeah," he said, then suddenly remembered how he got thrown down the hall. "Where's Greenie?"

"I had him taken to the dining room."

Ricky realized he could hear Carla crying. "Is he dead?"

"No. But it's not long. I'm sorry, Ricky. He took a shot to the gut, and it severed his spinal cord. . . . I'm sorry, Ricky."

Ricky sat up. "Help me up. I have to see him." George and Tyrell helped Ricky to his feet. He wobbled to the dining room. One of the oil lamps had been lit, and he could see Greenie stretched out on the mattress. Ricky put his back to the wall near his friend and slid down it, then scooted closer and leaned over him. Carla held Greenie's hand.

"Greenie? It's me, Raton," he said in a low voice.

"I think both his eardrums were blown out, Ricky. I don't think he can hear you," George said as Tyrell helped him sit next to Ricky.

Greenie started coughing. "Sit . . . up . . . please," he finally managed to say.

Ricky put an arm under his shoulders and slid over to sit on the mattress, holding his friend in his arms. Greenie groaned, then opened his eyes. "That you, Raton?"

Ricky nodded. "It's me."

"Raton, I'm so . . . sorry. I should have listened. I'm so sorry . . . I opened . . . the door. My fault."

Tears filled Ricky's eyes. "It's OK, Greenie."

"You know? . . . We've been trying to get . . . out of this neighborhood since we were kids. Remember?"

Ricky nodded again.

"Remember when we were both ten . . . and we thought we could run away to Texas and work on the rail-road?" Blood trickled out the corner of Greenie's mouth as he smiled. "After all that time on the road hitchhiking, and then realizing we were at the Canadian border . . . and they sent us home."

George handed Ricky a piece of gauze, and he tenderly wiped his friend's mouth. "Stop talking, Greenie. Save your strength."

"I remember the time we boosted that car. . . . and got to Maryland before they caught us. . . . and the time the LZ Posse tried to find us. Remember? They shot your finger off . . . 'cause you wouldn't tell 'em where I was. . . . You've been my only friend, Raton . . . I'm sorry I didn't listen to you."

Ricky just shook his head.

Greenie slowly put a hand on Ricky's arm. "Two hours ago, I was telling God how much I wanted to be able to escape from here . . . to be free . . . to live in a nice place . . . to rest from all this. . . . "

Ricky spoke louder. "Greenie! Stop talking! They'll be back soon, just hold on!"

Greenie spoke in Spanish now. "It's OK. . . . Let me go, my friend. I finally have a nice place to go to . . . I'm clean now, remember? . . . Thank you, Ricky . . . for coming back for me . . . I'm so tired." He closed his eyes for the last time.

Ricky held his friend close and rocked back and forth as he cried.

CHAPTER SIXTY-SEVEN

DONALD LARSON COLE SHIFTED AROUND IN HIS SEAT AT the table. It was ten o'clock on Tuesday morning, and the protective gear was making him very uncomfortable. He looked at the representatives who had gathered to negotiate with him and cleared his throat. "So, at this point, what they want is the guarantee of safety at the surrender point? They are dropping the demands for amnesty?"

Don knew there had been at least one large battle in a neighborhood the night before between Vital Union forces, gang members, and the military. He'd seen the rockets and explosions. The report he heard said that none of the Vital Union people survived. Several gang members died; some were in custody. By now, the gang leaders realized they had nothing to gain by waiting for amnesty. It just wasn't going to happen. Meanwhile, they could be killed at any moment. The firefight with the army last night had proved that. All they wanted now was the guarantee that they would not be attacked when they came out of hiding.

The man who spoke for the group, Arlis, said, "Yeah. We want a chopper with a news crew to go to each location and broadcast the surrenders. So everyone can see we didn't resist."

"Done. So how do we know where they are?"

"Each of us knows where someone is. We'll go one by one with you and the news guys to each location and then to a safe place. The word will go out once we're safe that there is a cease-fire."

"Cease-fire. You mean you won't shoot at the military or anybody else, even Vital Union?"

The men put their heads together for a few moments. The spokesman turned to Don again. "We won't shoot at anyone unless they shoot first."

Colonel Brigham had traveled with Don on this trip. Now he addressed the group of men. "We need to clarify something here. The place of surrender will have to be where the helicopter picks them up. As soon as they step out of hiding, it's over. They'll be taken to safety, but the surrender part will have already taken place. The leaders *must* understand that wherever there is a surrender for *everybody,* not just the leaders, no one can approach troops with weapons in hand or on their persons. As soon as visual contact is made, they must set *all* weapons on the ground and move away from them. It must be made absolutely clear. In order for this to work, they must agree and pass the word down."

"What if someone starts shooting after we set the guns down?" Arlis wanted to know. All the others nodded in assent.

"As long as you don't have weapons, no soldier will fire at you. If someone else starts shooting, then the troops will go after them."

Cole could tell this was not sitting well with them. "Colonel Brigham is not being unreasonable. You cannot expect to get on a helicopter with weapons."

The men looked at each other, then Arlis spoke again. "OK. But you guarantee this will be broadcast, right?"

"Yes," Cole responded and put out his hand. "If we have a deal, shake my hand."

Arlis reached out and took Cole's hand.

Miles away, Rosa and Edwina sat glued to the TV set. It had been announced that Cole was meeting with gang leaders and that a formal agreement was imminent. Once that was in place, the process of surrender and reclamation of the city, block by block, would take place. Fighting had already stopped in five other cities, and it was hoped the agreement would signal the end of all the hostilities everywhere.

The newscast made a brief mention of an incident involving two military helicopters the night before, but no details were given. UIG and most of the other networks were under a self-imposed moratorium of any reporting that might foment more unrest. The government had even asked that broadcast talk shows refrain from entertaining America with heated debates, call-in shows, or strongly opinionated guests who might inflame the situation with the riots even further. Several networks and hosts considered this an infringement of their First Amendment rights, but most voluntarily agreed to the ban.

Rosa and Edwina had prayed into the early hours of the morning and finally fallen asleep on the living room floor. When they woke up, they turned on the television to hear the first good news out of New York in days. Rosa turned the volume up.

Trisha Bledsoe was speaking from a studio outside Atlanta. "Yes," she said glancing off camera for a moment, "we have just received word. There is definite progress with the talks in New York. We now take you live to Tad Gardner at the site of the secret talks. Tad? Can you hear me?"

A young man wearing full riot gear appeared on the screen. "Yes, Trisha, we can hear you."

"Have you anything to report regarding the talks?"

"Yes. We have some of the best news we've heard in days. Donald Cole has been able to meet with gang representatives, and they have reached a final agreement. We will be traveling within a few minutes to the site of the first surrender. We will remain on the air live to record the entire event."

Rosa and Edwina hugged each other. "Hallelujah!" Rosa shouted. "O God, thank You!"

"Yes, God, thank You!" Edwina echoed.

Tad looked straight into the camera and gave an update. "We will travel in an army helicopter along with two gun ships and two helicopters carrying a contingent of soldiers. When we approach the area, one of the troop ships will land first and the soldiers will disembark. Our helicopter will land next, the other troop ship last. The two gun ships will remain airborne. Once the leaders at each location surrender and are taken aboard our craft, we'll take off again. Soldiers from the other helicopters will remain at that location to secure the area. Ground troops will then secure roads to each place to facilitate the surrender and transport of everyone else out of the area. One of the gun ships will escort us to an unnamed military base. Then we'll pick up more troops and head to the next location. I'm told this will happen as many as ten times today as long as things go smoothly."

Trisha appeared on a split screen with Tad. "And our understanding—at this point—is that *everybody* has to surrender. Even people who claim to be bystanders. Is that correct?"

"Yes it is, Trisha. There is no way of knowing who did what at this point. Everyone will have to surrender. And everyone but the leaders will be taken to a processing center to be identified and interviewed before they can be released."

Rosa and Edwina looked at each other. Did this mean they might not know about Ricky and George for days to come?

"How many processing centers are there?" Trisha asked.

"There will be over one hundred processing centers set up in New York alone. Other cities will work it the same way. The military began setting up the centers yesterday, I am told. And we have received assurances that no one will be held longer than is absolutely necessary."

"What does that mean?" Trisha said.

"Yeah," Edwina said to the TV. "What does that mean?"

Tad shrugged. "That's all the information I have at this point, Trisha. We're going to give it back to you in the studio for a few minutes until we are ready to load up and go to the first location."

A split-screen view remained on the set. Trisha filled the left half of the screen. The right half continued with live shots of preparation to move out in helicopters.

"What you see on the right half of the screen," Trisha said, "will be our continuing live coverage of the events unfolding in New York. We will stay live with this, even during commercial announcements—which will only be broadcast on the left side of your screen. I am told that President Todd is about to hold a press conference in Washington. Rene Lister is our reporter in Washington. Rene, can you hear me?"

Rene Lister's face replaced Trisha's on the left side of the screen. "Yes, Trisha," she said in a hushed tone. "We now join the president's remarks in progress."

" . . . citizens of the United States," Todd began. "It is with fervent hope of a conclusion to the events of recent days that I speak to you. I continue to ask for calm in the American people. . . .

"As some of you may already know, we have managed to effect a cease-fire in five cities—Miami, Tampa,

Chicago, Dallas, and San Diego. In New York, we have made much progress and soon hope to see an end to the tensions there as well.

"Several days ago, I called Mr. Donald Cole and asked him to join me in efforts to bring the riots in New York to a close. Even though Mr. Cole is my political rival, I felt that we should stick together in this for the sake of the country. He has represented me—and you, the American people—in these talks, which hopefully soon will result in an end to the violence in New York. While it appears the riots are coming to a rapid conclusion everywhere, we should still be grateful for Mr. Cole's efforts. This is not the time for politics. I pray the Lord will bless our efforts for peace."

Rosa and Edwina exchanged puzzled looks.

"Todd's a Christian?" Edwina said.

"Well, maybe he got saved in the middle of this," Rosa said, squeezing her friend's hand. "I bet lots of people did."

Edwina nodded and gave a little laugh. "I bet you're right."

The live shot of New York continued on the right side of the screen while Todd spoke.

"While much work remains to be done, I am grateful for the support of the American people in bringing things in the cities . . . "

The phone rang. Both women froze. It rang again. Rosa jumped up and ran to it.

"Yes?" she said.

"Is this the incredibly beautiful woman who agreed to marry Ricky Ruiz?"

"*Ricky!*" she shouted. Edwina ran to her side as Rosa blurted out a host of questions. "Praise God! Oh, Ricky! Where are you? Where's George? Is everything OK? Are the two of you OK? What happened?" She motioned for Edwina to get on the extension in the bedroom.

"We're at a military base about fifty miles from you. George is standing right here next to me. Don't tell Edwina, but he got shot in the leg."

Edwina gasped.

"Edwina's on the extension, honey."

"Oh, well. He's fine! Honest he is. He'll talk to her when I'm done."

"Are you sure he's OK?" Edwina said quickly.

"Yeah. He's right here. Say hi to your wife, George, but say it quick, cause this is *my* two minutes. You'll get yours next."

George's resonant voice came over the wire. "Hi, sweetheart, I'll talk to you in a minute, OK? I promise."

Edwina started to cry. "OK. Rosa can tell me when it's my time." She hung up her extension and got on her knees beside her bed. "Thank You, thank You . . . " was all she could say.

Rosa continued with the barrage of questions. "Are they keeping you there? When will they let you go? Can we come and get you? *You're* not hurt, are you?"

"They are almost finished interrogating all of us. We were told we'd be free to go at about two this afternoon. Please come and get us, *mi corazón.*"

Tears streamed down Rosa's face. "You just don't know. Edwina and I have been praying our hearts out for you and George."

"You *and* Edwina? How wonderful. As you can hear, it worked! Before we hang up, we have a list of things for you to bring, OK?"

"Like what?"

"Clothes and stuff."

"Did everyone else with you stay safe?"

Ricky was silent for a few moments. "No . . . we'll talk later, Rosa. . . . I'm so glad you were not here. . . . You still want to marry me?"

"With all my heart, Mr. Ruiz."

"I'll see you in four hours?"

"Yes! All I want to do is wrap my arms around you and hold on."

"Yes, please! But I'm warning you. We look terrible. We haven't shaved or anything for four days. They gave us some deodorant and some paper clothes to wear . . . but, well, you'll see. Promise me you won't laugh."

"That bad, eh?"

"Yeah. Let me put George on. He has the list of things we want. . . . I love you, Rosalinda."

When Edwina got off the phone, the two of them embraced, cried, and thanked the Lord again for sparing their men. George had told Edwina what happened to Greenie when Ricky walked away from the phone. Edwina told Rosa.

In less than two hours, Rosa and Edwina had rented a car and purchased a road map. They stopped at a nearby store to purchase some clothes and toiletries, then headed out of town on their way to the military base to pick up their men.

CHAPTER SIXTY-EIGHT

ROSA AND EDWINA TURNED INTO THE PARKING LOT FOR the Visitor's Center. They would have to go inside and request permission to enter the base. Rosa's heart pounded. What if they wouldn't let her in? What if they had changed their minds, and they weren't going to let Ricky and George go?

She looked at Edwina. "Are you scared? I'm almost shaking."

"Me, too."

They made their way into the building and stood in line for a few moments to speak to a young man in uniform behind the counter. When it was their turn, Edwina spoke first.

"Yes. We're here to pick up two men. Dr. George Grant and Enrique Ruiz . . . they were brought here last night . . . they're expecting us . . . we were told to come and get them." Edwina realized she sounded like someone giving an alibi for a crime. She took a deep breath and tried to relax.

The young man picked up a phone to relay the information, then asked them to be seated.

Rosa whispered to Edwina. "You think they'll just send Ricky and George out to us?"

Edwina shrugged. "I have no idea."

The phone rang, but the young man at the counter kept doing his paperwork. It rang three times, four times, five times . . .

Rosa wanted to jump up and yell, *Are you deaf? Answer the phone! Maybe it's about Ricky!* She decided, however, this was not a prudent thing to do. She scrunched up her hands into fists.

He finally picked up the phone and answered it with what sounded like a fifty-word greeting that included the base name, which gate the building was at, the name and number of the building, plus his name and rank.

What's wrong with 'hello?' Rosa thought. *Terrorists could take over the whole base by the time he spits all that out.*

"Yes, sir," he said and hung up the phone.

Well? Rosa's mind screamed. To her disappointment he slowly moved from the counter to retrieve papers from a file cabinet. He returned to his place behind the counter, sat down on a bar stool, and looked the papers over. At length. Just when she'd given up, he looked over at Edwina.

"Ma'am?"

"Yes?"

"If you and the other lady will fill out these forms and bring them back to me with your IDs, I'll give you badges to get on the base and directions to your destination."

It took every ounce of restraint Rosa possessed to gracefully rise and receive her forms. She wanted to snatch them out of his hand. She and Edwina quickly filled them out and handed them back along with their IDs. He methodically read each paper and inspected their

IDs. Then he went to photocopy their IDs, but the machine was out of paper. Once he found a ream of paper and loaded it, he made copies. Rosa thought she might die—or do bodily harm to the young man in the uniform. He returned to his place at the counter with the copies and slowly sorted each woman's forms into a stack before stapling them. Finally, he gave them three badges—one for Edwina, one for Rosa, one to hang from the mirror of the car—and a small map that identified the "stockade" as their destination. Rosa and Edwina said nothing but looked at each other. Once outside, they climbed in the car before speaking.

"Oh, Rosa! The stockade! Why are they in the stockade?"

"I don't know, 'Wina, but we're going to find out right now." Rosa started the car and drove to the entrance gate.

It took them ten minutes to locate the stockade and park the car. They were directed to the visitor's entrance of the building and went inside. A woman in an Military Police uniform showed them to a waiting room with a thick plexiglass partition down the middle of it. Long tables stretched across either side of the partition. Small holes had been drilled through the plexiglass so that people on either side could speak to one another.

Now the two women were shaking.

The door on the other side of the room opened. Into the room came George, on crutches, and Ricky. Both of them wore white, long-sleeved, one-piece paper overalls. Ricky's suit was not large enough for him and had torn under the arms of his large frame. George's was baggy on him. Neither had shaved in days.

Rosa and Edwina rushed to the partition and almost simultaneously raised their hands to place them on the glass. Ricky moved opposite Rosa and put his hands opposite hers. George sat down and did the same with Edwina.

"Hello, precious," Ricky said.

What if we are only going be allowed to visit them? Rosa tried not to panic. "Are you OK?"she asked.

He put his hand over his left ear. "Yeah, pretty much. . . . Can you give our things to the guard there? They need to look it over before they bring it in. After we change, they'll let us out."

Rosa burst into tears. "So they *will* let you go!"

Edwina and George stopped talking to listen to this exchange. Edwina had been experiencing the same fear.

"Yes, *mi corazón,* of course they will let us out. I told you they were releasing us."

"But you didn't say they had you in jail!"

He and George laughed. "I'm sorry," Ricky said. Neither Rosa nor Edwina thought this was terribly amusing. "Are you OK now?" he asked.

Rosa shook her head. "Not until I can get my arms around you."

He smiled again. "Well, pass our clothes to the guard there, and we'll get to it!"

She handed the bag to the guard As soon as he left the room with it, Rosa moved back to the partition and put her hand on it again. Ricky reciprocated. They stared into each other's eyes while George and Edwina talked for a couple of minutes.

"Oh, honey, look," Edwina said, once she noticed the two of them. "The lovebirds are at it again." She and George smiled and shook their heads.

The door behind the men opened, and a male military policeman called them out of the room. Ricky looked at Rosa and said, "We're going to clean up and change. We'll be out in just a few minutes. . . . You going to be all right?"

She smiled. *I can tell our children about this,* she thought. "Yes."

When the men first entered the room, Rosa was so happy to see Ricky that she hadn't paid much attention to the way he looked. Now when he stood she noticed the ripped armpits in the suit, and as he turned to leave, the pant legs that were at least four inches too short. She burst into laughter. Ricky's back was to her, but as soon as he heard the laughter, his head slumped.

He turned slowly and said, "You promised you wouldn't laugh."

She covered her mouth and finally managed to say, "I'm sorry, sweetheart, but if you could just *see* yourself!"

Now Edwina was laughing, too.

He nodded and said, "Thank you, ladies," and then left the room.

Rosa was grateful for the comic relief, but still nervous. All she wanted was to escape this place with Ricky. She and Edwina tried to make conversation for what seemed the longest twenty minutes of her life.

The door to the waiting room finally opened, and they turned to look. George hobbled in first, followed by Ricky. Both men were freshly shaven and wearing their new clothes.

Rosa flew off her chair and threw her arms around Ricky, almost knocking him over. He couldn't believe she was capable of squeezing anyone that hard. "Does this mean you still love me?" he asked, grinning.

Edwina put her arms around her husband and cried. "Don't you ever leave me again as long as you live, George Grant."

"Don't worry," he said in a shaky voice. "I'm not capable of getting anywhere too quickly. I'm certain you could catch me before I got too far." He pulled her chin up so he could look her in the eyes. "I love you, 'Wina. I'm so grateful to be alive and to still have you." He kissed her.

When they looked over, Ricky had pried Rosa loose long enough to pick her up off the floor and kiss her.

"Let's get out of here," George said.

"I'm in favor of that!" Edwina exclaimed.

Ricky set Rosa down. "Let's go."

After stopping at the base gate long enough to return the badges, they got on the road to the spa. Ricky and George were starving, so they decided to stop at a restaurant along the way.

"What are you hungry for?" Edwina asked George over her menu.

"Anything but ham."

She gave him a puzzled look.

"That's all we've eaten for days. Oh. And we had powdered eggs for breakfast this morning." He looked at Ricky. "Do powdered eggs qualify as food?"

"Yeah. I think they're in the 'powder' food group."

The waitress came to the table. "You ready to order?"

"First, I want three large glasses of water, no ice . . . " Ricky said.

The two men gobbled down huge meals; Rosa and Edwina ate salads. George and Ricky topped lunch off with large desserts.

"I sure hope you don't get sick on all this," Edwina said, eyeing the empty banana split bowl in front of George. "We're riding in a rental car, you know."

"That's what I really love about you," he said, kissing her on the forehead. "You're just so . . . practical."

Ricky spooned the last bite of ice cream into Rosa's mouth.

She smiled at him and looked in his eyes.

"Oh, no. They're starting it again, 'Wina," George said. "We'd better get going before they get into that mutual-catatonic thing."

Ricky held Rosa's gaze and said, "You have ravished my heart, my sister, my bride, you have ravished my heart with a glance of your eyes."

"Whoa," Edwina said. "You just make that up?"

"No," he replied, still looking at Rosa, "It's a verse of Scripture. From Song of Solomon."

"You know, that's not half bad, George," Edwina said, looking at him over her coffee cup.

George wiggled his eyebrows. "Well, honey," he said, "you can peer into my eyes and steal my heart when we get in the car on the way to the spa."

While George was trying to scoot out of the booth, Ricky pulled Rosa close. "You OK?"

"Now I am."

Miles away, Donald Larson Cole sat with a driver and his two Secret Service men in a military van at a checkpoint. Having finished the negotiations, he was officially excused. He was told he would be taken anywhere he wanted to go, but he was asked to remain "in the area—just in case."

At Don's request, Colonel Brigham sent soldiers to Josh Thornton's house to see if he were home and to relay a message to him. Josh was there when the soldiers arrived, and they allowed him to speak to Don by radio. He said the house was not in an area where there had been rioting, but that the power and phone service had been cut off and there was little hope they'd be restored quickly. However, the house *did* have water and a gas grill. Josh told Don he could bring his two agents and enjoy the Thornton's hospitality—if he thought he could find a way to get there. Don intended to take him up on the offer. After all, he and Josh had gone through worse things together. It would be like old times.

Reggie and Sam were in the van with Don. Reggie was taking it all in stride. Sam, the "rules freak," as he'd heard Reggie call him in a quiet exchange of temper, thought this was a very unwise move. He much preferred keeping the candidate for president in the safety of a military base. Don, on the other hand, figured that with all the troops in the city, New York would be safer now than it had been in years.

Don also knew that if electricity were not restored soon, the military would have to set up distribution tents for government and volunteer agencies to give out food and vital supplies in each neighborhood. With no power, there would be no traffic signals, and traffic would be a nightmare. And even the luxury of driving would be reserved for those who had, prior to the loss of electricity, put enough gas in their cars to get someplace before the sunset curfew.

It would probably be days before most grocery stores and gas stations re-opened. A few enterprising business owners would obtain generators and manage to stay open during daylight hours, until people ran out of cash. Banks and automated tellers would be closed. There would be no phone lines to obtain approval of credit cards, and only the foolish would accept checks during this time. Within a week, if there was still no electricity, the military would have to serve as armed guards for banking to be done.

Don thought about what he could take to Josh's house. He knew just what to get. The back of the van contained ice in two large ice chests, several boxes of non-perishable groceries, cheap flashlights, plenty of batteries in all sizes, first aid supplies, and a small radio. Most people had high-tech, integrated sound systems, but few people had small radios anymore. Don didn't know if Josh had one, so he went ahead and got it.

He'd always known his experiences in Denver would benefit him, but he hadn't planned on it being this soon.

As they drove past military checkpoints, Don looked out at the various neighborhoods. Some looked unscathed, some showed signs of looting, others were charred rubble. He found himself comparing everything with Denver. This neighborhood looked OK, compared to Denver, that one looked as bad as Denver. People on the streets looked scared, tired, and worried. His heart went out to them because he knew how they felt.

When he arrived at Josh's house, Don felt as if he were home. He'd met Josh's wife, Carol, on his previous trip. Now he was introduced to Josh's children: Amy, 14; Elijah, 10; and Paul, 7. Josh had spoken of them so often that Don felt as if he already knew them.

They all snacked on some of the cookies he brought, and the children talked the adults into a board game. Eventually, Elijah won. Don was enjoying himself. It was so good to be able to relax. *This is what it must be like to have a brother, a sister-in-law, nephews, a niece,* he thought. Belonging to a family was something he'd forgotten about. Something he hadn't realized how much he missed until that evening.

Later, as they sat in lawn chairs outside and listened to the latest happenings on the radio, Don and Josh heard a replay of the speech Todd gave earlier in the day. He heard Todd mention the Lord.

"You think Todd's a Christian?"

Josh's eyes widened as if it were a shocking possibility to him.

"My thinking exactly."

"Well, wait," Josh said. "Let me retract that look. Even though it doesn't seem likely, in all fairness, I must say that it is possible for *anybody* to get saved. Even Todd. Who knows? Something may have turned him around. A lot of people have been praying for him. Especially this week. You may not know it, but since this started, thousands of churches across the country have been open twenty-four hours a day for prayer."

"If God's purpose is to get people to turn around, and they do, will these atrocities stop? And when I'm elected, if I continue to seek God, won't there be a good result? Can't I ask God to bless us again?"

Josh's lawn chair creaked as he leaned back in it. "You can ask, but that doesn't guarantee bad things will stop happening, Don."

"You think maybe we've already gone too far? Past a point of no return?"

Josh put his hands behind his head and looked up at the multitude of stars. "Let me explain it this way. There are some things that God says we *can* change by seeking Him—like circumstances that will lead others to Jesus, sickness, persecution—even the outcome of wars. But there are other things that *cannot* be changed—the one-time-payment for the sins of all mankind by Jesus at the cross, God's ultimate plan for the believer or history, the appearance of the Antichrist, the resurrection and reward of the just, the punishment of the wicked, and the defeat of Satan and his angels. Those things will never change, and they have happened or will happen at exactly the time God appointed for them."

Josh leaned forward again and made a sweeping gesture with his hand. "You may see this whole country turn around and be blessed, Don . . . but, *if* these are indeed the last days as so many think, what happens here might be unpleasant but unavoidable. In the larger scheme, you may be bumping into some of the things that *cannot* be changed. I believe that God wants to save the American people, but that doesn't guarantee He will preserve our country as we now know it. What you do, and what we choose as a people, may result in the salvation of many, but it may not prevent the country from being removed as a world power, or even decimated and overtaken by others."

Don broke in. "But isn't Jesus going to come and take us away before all that happens? That's what I've always heard."

"Yes, Don, that's the prevailing view, but Scripture makes a distinction between correction and wrath. God chastens those He loves. Look what God allowed to happen to Israel when they sinned against Him. Read the warnings He gave to the *churches* in the Book of Revelation! It's sobering!

"What we've experienced in the last few years still doesn't begin to compare with what some Christians and Jews in other countries have suffered! Why is it that God's people everywhere *else* can suffer *unspeakable* things . . . can be tortured and killed with barely a notice from us . . . yet we cling to the belief that God would come and get the *American* Christians before anything really bad happens? What horrible conceit! What it boils down to is the fact that our relationship with God has been totally dependent on getting our own way. We want to think of ourselves as the center of the Christian universe. We want to define God's whole timetable for the last days by what happens to American believers. Yet, we don't follow hard after God. We want the abundant life but not the responsibility of it. We have forgotten that the Word says 'judgment begins in the household of faith.'"

Don frowned. "But I thought . . . well, I guess I never really thought we'd be here for God's judgment. I thought all the real destruction would happen after we were gone."

"Jesus may return very soon, Don. He's giving us an opportunity to stop doing those things we'll be ashamed of when the records are opened. He's giving us a chance to be renewed, to become wise, to do exploits in His name, to be faithful with what He's entrusted to us. . . . He's shaking us to wake us up. But there will come a day when that last call is given . . . and no matter what has happened to God's people, it won't begin to compare with what will happen to those who chose to ignore the calls of the Lord, those who hated Him and His people, those who shed the blood of the righteous. . . . In that day, a different judgment will come upon the whole earth. It will be the wrath of God. And there will be no stopping the destruction it brings."

Don got a chill.

Carol opened the back door and peered out. "You going to start dinner, or just sit there and talk all evening?"

"I guess I got to preaching and the time got away from me!" Josh said.

"I'm sorry," his wife said. "I thought you were just talking 'guy stuff' out here. Dinner can wait a while longer."

"No. That's OK, Carol. You know me and captive audiences. . . . What's on the menu for tonight?"

"I saw some cans of chili and crackers in the things Don brought."

"Ahhhh! Chili—cooked on the barbeque. And with fresh crackers. Yes, that sounds marvelous. . . . Will you find my apron?" She went back inside, and Josh whispered to Don, "She thinks all outdoor cooking is my domain. I'm humoring her. . . . "

At ten o'clock that evening, two hundred miles away, President Todd sat with his wife, Edith, and Raiza, the advisor, in the private quarters of the White House. He had many questions to ask.

"I have to say," he began, "that I felt energized from the first moments we spent together last night. But then I couldn't sleep for a long time. When I finally did get to sleep, I had terrible nightmares. Why is that?"

A knowing smile came to Raiza's face. "Yes," she nodded. "This happens to many people. Especially the ones who have a great call." She patted his hand. "Your aura shows you are a man of great power. What you were sensing was the tremendous warfare over you. It's been there before, but now that you are becoming enlightened, you can really see the negative forces coming against you. This is why you *must* spend time in meditation.

Trust me, if you meditate, this sense of fear will eventually stop, and you will know peace." She looked over his head. "Even now, I sense an empowerment of light coming to fill you."

Todd felt a physical sensation of being touched on the back of his neck. A horrible feeling shot through him. "That's just what I mean," he said, "I *feel* something touching me, and I don't like it."

Edith frowned. She hoped he wasn't going to make Raiza angry.

"Press in," Raiza said, reaching over and holding his hand, "just empty your mind. Surrender, and the feeling will pass."

Raiza was so much better at this than Edith had expected. She was almost glad Tony was out of pocket. Surely fate had brought Raiza here instead.

The phone rang. *No!* Edith thought. *Just when we were making progress.*

"I need to answer that," Todd said. He rose and went to the phone. "Hello?" He listened for a few moments, then put his hand on the receiver and turned to face Edith and Raiza. "If you ladies will excuse me, this is important."

His wife and the guest left the room. Todd took his hand off the mouthpiece, "Yes. Put him on. . . . Mr. Kressman? Thank you for calling me back. I know it's late, so I'll get right to the point. I wanted to set up some meetings with you this week, or even over the weekend if your schedule will permit."

"Really?" Kressman said. "What did you have in mind?"

"Well, first of all, I wanted to thank you for your help in recent days. I'm grateful you were so willing to work behind the scenes to get things accomplished."

"Thank you," Kressman said in a soft voice. "You know I am always willing to be of service."

"Yes. I know. And really, that's why I called you, Mr. Kressman. . . . Having so many media, business, and political connections, I'm sure that the new situation developing in the Middle East has not escaped your attention."

"No, it has not."

"That's what I would like to talk to you about. . . . I know you're a man who wishes to stay out of the spotlight. I also know you possess considerable negotiating skills and have numerous alliances with the governments in the Middle East." Todd paused for a response, but the line remained still silent, so he went on. "I believe I have discerned, in our past dealings, that you share my views for the region. And I sense that you also desire to see lasting peace in that part of the world. Peace that can only be brought about if we stop catering to fanatical religious beliefs that only foment problems. . . . America needs someone with balance, power, and political skill to oversee our role there, to make our position clear. . . . Mr. Kressman, I believe that man is you."

As if he had already given the matter consideration, Kressman said, "You know, there are many ignorant people who would not understand our view. Be aware, Mr. President, that many in this country would criticize you for selecting me. Unless, of course, my role is a secret one . . . even so, you'd be taking a risk here."

"We can get together and discuss the matter then?"

"By all means. . . . I like a man who is willing to take risks."

By the time Edith and Raiza were allowed back into the room, Todd was ecstatic. He hugged his wife and grabbed Raiza's hand. "You know, it worked, it really worked. I can't tell you what happened, but I want you to know, it worked."

Edith smiled. She knew nothing would stop her husband from moving forward into his destiny now.

CHAPTER SIXTY-NINE

DUE TO THE OVERFLOW FROM THE DISASTROUS EVENTS IN New York, vacant hotel rooms within a fifty-mile radius could not be found. Ricky would have to sleep in the living room of the spa suite. He removed his shoes and, after realizing the sofa was too short, spread his blanket on the floor and lay down. He was so exhausted that, in spite of the discomfort, he was soon sound asleep.

Hours later, Rosa woke up and looked at her clock again. It was five-thirty in the morning. She thought she'd heard a sound.

Was Ricky awake?

She looked over toward the living room and could see a slice of light at the bottom of the door. She rose and dressed, then knocked quietly and opened the door a crack.

"Can I come in?" she asked.

"Sure you can," came the response.

She opened the door and looked around the room. Ricky sat on a blanket in the corner of the room with his

Bible on his lap. He patted the spot next to him, and Rosa happily complied.

"What are you doing up so early, honey?" he asked, as she rested her head on his shoulder.

"I could barely sleep. I kept thinking you'd wake up and leave me before I got up. I'm sorry I disturbed you."

"You aren't disturbing me. What time is it?" he asked.

She looked at her watch. "It's twenty minutes till six."

He pulled her close and closed his eyes. "Good morning, Lord. Rosa and I are here, ready to start our day. We give You all our plans, all our hopes for the day. Help us to make good choices in all that we do. We love You, Father . . . "

She smiled. "Oh, yes, Lord. We love You. Thank You for bringing Ricky and George back safely to Edwina and me. Thank You for a new day. . . . "

They sat in silence for a few moments before Ricky said *Amen*, and stood up. Once he was on his feet, he offered her a hand up. "I wouldn't have left you without saying good-bye, Rosa."

Her eyes filled with tears. "I just can't bear to *not* be near you. Please don't leave me."

He hugged her. "I'm not leaving you; I'm going away for the day," he said. "So are you going to propose to me now?"

She put her head against his chest. "Will you marry me, Ricky?"

"Well, let me see . . . " he said, looking at the ceiling then down at her. "OK! . . . I love you."

The door to Edwina and George's bedroom opened, and Edwina emerged in a housecoat, rubbing her eyes. "Goodness. I thought I was the early bird this morning. I already called for coffee and was going to answer the door before they made noise and woke you up. But here you are, up and dressed already!"

"Yeah," Ricky said, still hugging Rosa and smiling. "She was just proposing to me."

A knock came at the door. Edwina opened it and let a young man with a large tray in the room. She tipped him as he left.

"Anyone for coffee? Danish? Juice?" she asked.

"Yes," Ricky and Rosa said simultaneously.

"Well, I know you probably want me to stay and make snappy morning conversation with you, but I'm taking George's breakfast to him. Bye." With that, Edwina set half the things from the tray on the coffee table, picked up the tray, and disappeared into her room.

"Here," Rosa said, seating herself on the couch, "sit down."

"In a moment. I want the luxury of brushing my teeth first. Be right back."

Edwina closed the door and set the tray on her corner of the bed. "Breakfast, dear. Want to sit up?"

George didn't open his eyes, but he did nod and move his pillow against the headboard. Gradually, he pulled himself to a sitting position and scooted back to the headboard. He opened his eyes.

"Ready?"

He nodded. She brought him a cup of coffee, a danish, and a napkin. He cleared his throat. "Seen the lovebirds yet?"

"Oh, yeah. They're already up and proposing to each other."

George took a sip of coffee. "Have I told you how much I adore you yet today?"

"Were you going to say something nice, or did you just want to know if you had?"

He set his coffee down and smiled at her. "Come here."

She moved the tray to the dresser and slid in next to him. He leaned over and put his head against hers. "Edwina Grant, I love you more than I ever have before."

"Sure you do," she laughed.

He sat up and looked at her. "No, 'Wina. I'm not being silly. I never realized just how much I loved you until three days ago. I have been so selfish. I can't tell you how sorry I am for the way I've been."

She pulled up her legs and turned to face him. "You make it sound like you've kept me in the basement and beat me regularly."

He gently put his hand on her mouth. "No. Let me say it. You have put so many things in your life on hold for me. What I wanted came first. . . . When I thought I might die, I realized how much of our lives I've wasted pursuing a name for myself. And wealth . . . I've talked to Ricky a lot lately, especially while we were in the stockade. He says I can have a clean slate to start over, and I'm taking it. I've given my life to the Lord, Edwina, and now I'm asking you to marry me again. The first time I made those promises, they didn't mean to me what they do now . . . and the new George wants to make those promises again. . . . "

Rosa and Ricky ate quietly for a few minutes. She put the cup back on the saucer and set it on the table. "Please don't go. Not today."

"We went over this last night, *mi corazón*. I must find out how my family and Daniel are and let them know I am all right. You've talked to *your* family. You know how they are, and they know that you are safe. I must do that, too. While I am there, I'll see if I can check on the clinic and maybe our apartments. All I have is my jacket and the clothes on my back. I don't even have my checkbook! I need to go, Rosa, but I promise, if at all possible, I will be back tonight. If not tonight, first thing in the morning."

She kept looking away from him and wiping her eyes. "Then why can't I come with you?"

TERRY L. CRAIG\hfill \481

He sighed. "Please don't hurt me like this. I won't take you till I know it's safe."

She moved closer and hugged him tightly. "I'm sorry. But what if it is dangerous? Something could happen to you."

"Did God keep me through four days of the worst of it?"

"Yes."

"Can He keep me safe today?"

"Yes," she said.

"Well?"

"You promise me you'll come back tonight?"

"If at all possible. And if I can't make it, I'll try to get word to you somehow."

"Will you promise me you won't take any unnecessary chances? You won't go on rescue missions or anything? No hero stuff?"

"I promise. I'll be a little mouse," he said, holding his thumb and finger about an inch apart in front of her face. "A little *raton*. Like this. I'll go check on everybody, maybe get some of my cheese, and get out." He raised his eyebrows, smiled, and looked at her as if to say, *Well, what about it?*

Almost against her will, she smiled.

"Besides," he added, "Edwina told me she's taking you on a wild shopping spree today. Can you get me a few things, too, in case I can't get to my apartment? The time will fly, and then I'll be back. OK?"

"OK."

Trains to the city were running during the day on a limited schedule. Rosa dropped Ricky at the station and tried not to cry again as she watched him disappear into the throng of people. "O Lord," she whispered, "please keep him safe and bring him back to me."

In the afternoon, once Edwina was satisfied that George could be left alone for a while, she and Rosa went shopping. The first part of the afternoon went faster than

Rosa anticipated. She and Edwina had a lot to talk about. Edwina told Rosa about George giving his heart to the Lord and proposing to her. Rosa was thrilled at the news.

At the mall, Edwina talked Rosa into buying a lovely dress to wear to dinner that evening. She said George wanted to go out for the "ultimate dinner." Then Edwina took Rosa to a tall shop and helped pick out a nice suit and a few other clothes for Ricky. She paid for them, saying that they had not been able to give Ricky his last paycheck yet.

Rosa began to miss Ricky, but there was still more to do. They needed to get clothes for George and a nice dress for Edwina. By six o'clock, when they were getting in the car, Rosa was exhausted. She wasn't sure she'd be able to go out for a big dinner. Before she started the engine, her beeper went off. She tore open her purse and pushed the button on the device to read the message:

"Sorry! Got delayed past the last train. Am safe! Got some cheese, too! I love you! Ricky."

Rosa slowly put the beeper back in her purse. *You're not going to get hysterical over this,* she told herself. *He'll be here first thing in the morning. He said he was safe. Don't be a baby!*

"What's wrong, Rosa?"

"Ricky missed the last train. He's not going to be here tonight," she said, looking away.

"I'm so sorry," Edwina said, patting her arm. "We'll still make a night of it if you'd like. You'll see. It'll be morning before you know it!"

They drove back to the spa and found George in the living room, watching television. He was a king in his glory, foot up on a pillow, TV remote in his hand.

Rosa said hello to him and headed straight to her room.

"She got a message from Ricky?" George surmised.

"Yep."

He motioned to Edwina to come closer. When she was seated next to him, he whispered. "He called here, too. Don't worry. It's still going to happen."

Edwina hugged her husband. "You get the reservations?"

"Yeah. It took me half the day, but I finally found a really nice cabin in the hills. It's got a fireplace and everything."

"Really? Wonderful!"

Rosa had come back into the living room. Edwina looked up and saw her. "Oh, Rosa. George found a cabin in the hills—with a fireplace!"

"What for?" she asked, absently.

"We decided it was time for a honeymoon," George said, smiling.

"Oh," Rosa responded, then was ashamed of her attitude. *What's wrong with you?* she chided herself. *How do you feel when something good happens for you, and your friends are either jealous or can only think they wished it happened for them?* With all the graciousness she could muster she said, "That's really sweet, George! I hope you have a great time. . . . I'm sorry, I didn't even ask earlier. Is your leg any better today?"

"Much better, thanks. . . . Ready to go to dinner? Since Ricky's not here, we can do the ultimate dinner thing tomorrow, but we can still have a nice dinner tonight. What would you like to eat, Rosa?"

"Thanks for the offer, George, but I'm really tired. I think I'll just skip dinner and go to bed. I didn't sleep well last night anyway. This way I can look good for Ricky in the morning."

George and Edwina exchanged looks before Edwina spoke. "You sure?"

"Yes."

"Well, then maybe we'll just have dinner in the room tonight. What do you say, Dr. Grant?"

"Works for me."

Rosa excused herself and went back to her room.

Later, when Edwina was close to Rosa's door, she could hear Rosa crying.

"Oh, George," Edwina said. "This is just awful. She's crying her eyes out in there. Maybe we should tell her."

"You'll do no such thing. Ricky and I have worked very hard on this. She'll be just fine soon."

Hours later, Rosa rolled over. She had been in a sound sleep. Had someone knocked on her door? She heard the sound again, and Edwina was calling her name.

"Rosa?"

"Come in."

The light from the living room blinded her. Rosa put a hand over her eyes until the door closed again. "What do you need, Edwina?"

Edwina sat on her bed. "You need to get up and get dressed."

"Huh?" Rosa squinted at her clock. "Edwina, it's still night."

"I know. And Ricky's here for you."

"*What?*" Rosa said, jumping up.

"Yep. Ricky's here. Brought a judge *and* a preacher. Good thing you bought a nice dress today. I'd hate to see you get married in blue jeans."

Rosa stared at Edwina. "This isn't some sort of joke, is it? You aren't kidding, are you?"

"No, he's really here. *They're* really here. You want help getting dressed?"

There was another knock on the door. "Rosa?"

It was Ricky. She ran to the door and spoke through it. "Ricky?"

"It's me, beloved. Are you going to come out here and marry me? Remember, you proposed to me just this morning!"

"I'll be right out!" she said.

"I take it that's a yes."

"Yes!"

Rosa fumbled into her dress. Edwina helped her with her hair and makeup. When they were finished, Edwina looked at her and said, "I thought my pearls would look nice with this dress. What do you think?"

"Oh, they would! May I borrow them?"

Edwina got them out of her pocket, put them around her friend's neck, and stopped to admire them. "Perfect! They're my wedding gift to you."

"'Wina, I don't know what to say!" Rosa embraced her. "You are the most wonderful friend. Thank you."

"Just don't start crying! You'll ruin the makeup!"

Rosa let out a small laugh. "I've cried so much, I don't think I've got any tears left!"

"Let's go! Your groom awaits."

Edwina came out of the room first. Ricky and the others stood up and watched Rosa come into the room. He thought she was the most beautiful woman he'd ever seen. She noticed he was wearing the suit she had chosen for him that afternoon. He walked over and took her hand. "Rosa, this is Judge Palmer. You know Pastor Dan and his wife, Anne." They all exchanged greetings.

Ricky had gone to New York to find Daniel. When they talked, Daniel agreed to come to the wedding. He could not legally marry them at the hotel, but would read the Scriptures for them. He would come with his wife for the night and return to the city in the morning. Anne was excited about the wedding—and the added bonus of electricity and a hot bath. George had arranged for a local judge to meet them all at the spa. The judge would do the legal part. In addition to Ricky and Rosa getting married, George and Edwina planned to renew their vows.

George had rented a small meeting room at the spa for the wedding. The management provided some decorations and set up a table with cake.

The seven of them gathered in the room for the simple ceremony. Rosa still had more tears, but Ricky cried, too.

After they said their vows, Daniel prayed for the couples and blessed them.

As they nibbled on the cake, Edwina moved close to Rosa. "You'd better hurry and finish packing your bags, girl. I tried to throw most of your things together, but you'd better finish the job."

"What do you mean?"

"You don't really want to spend your wedding night with me and George, do you? Besides, you know there's no more hotel rooms around here. Pastor and his wife will have to sleep in your room."

"Where am I going?" Rosa said as Ricky came near.

Edwina smiled. "A cabin. In the hills. With a fireplace. Remember? George said it was for a honeymoon. He just didn't say *whose* honeymoon. And he even found a limo to take you there!"

Rosa threw her arms around George and kissed him on the cheek. "Careful! Don't damage me!" George said, holding on to his crutches for dear life.

When Rosa let go, Edwina took a turn at hugging him. "Isn't my George the best?"

Rosa looked into her own husband's eyes. "Well, almost."

CHAPTER SEVENTY

THREE WEEKS HAD PASSED SINCE THE RIOTS, AND THE DAY of the presidential election had arrived. Even though the damage would take months to repair, order had been restored. Five cities—New York, Los Angeles, Detroit, Philadelphia, and Baltimore—had sustained major damage. In spite of this, the election would be held on time.

Since the riots, most news reports on Todd were surprisingly favorable. UIG had been the most complimentary, Banner Network the least. Polls that morning showed Todd and Cole in a dead heat. Todd had sent in his absentee ballot a week ago. Spending time and taxpayer money to fly back to his home state and vote would have seemed imprudent, given the current problems at hand. The press was told he had decided to spend the day in his office and then have a quiet dinner with family. Later, after the polls in California had closed, he planned to arrive at the hall where the celebration in his honor would begin. He would stay in a group of rooms reserved for him and his upper echelon until it was time to make an official appearance. If he won, he would give his acceptance speech, then travel to several other locations where supporters had gathered, briefly thanking them for their help. The only problem was, the race was so close the victor might not be known until the following day.

Don voted early in the morning, then he camped out in his condominium with campaign workers and friends. Josh and Carol Thornton were flying in and would arrive in the afternoon. His mother would arrive in the early evening.

Don sat in front of the television for a few minutes to watch exit polls. He decided not to watch anymore when one girl in her early twenties was interviewed and said she voted for Don because he was "so cute."

"Now *there's* an intelligent voter!" Bob Post laughed.

"That's it. I'm leaving," Don said, taking his glass with him. He squeezed by several people in the hallway and escaped to the kitchen. He set his glass on the counter and got out the milk.

"Want some cookies with that?"

He turned to see Trina waving a bag of fresh ones.

"Depends. Do I have to make you Secretary of State or anything?"

"No. Ambassador to Tahiti will do."

He grabbed the cookies and inspected them. "Aha!" he said, pulling out half a cookie.

"Told you. You want three full cookies, send Avery. He doesn't like sweets. I, on the other hand, charge a fee."

"But I didn't *send* you for these."

She gave him the look. "You want the cookies or not?"

He glanced at her as he ate the cookie half. She looked like a fashion model. "You know, stealing is a nasty habit. You'll have to reform or learn to blame others if you plan a Washington career."

She smacked him on the arm.

"Hey! Let's not be assaulting the future president of the United States," Avery said, entering the kitchen.

"Want a cookie?" Don offered.

"Nah."

"He knew you wouldn't want it. He was just *pretending* to be nice," Trina said, smiling.

Jason came into the kitchen. "This a last-minute strategy session going on in here?"

"As a matter of fact," Don said in a confidential tone, "Trina was telling me the two of you were going to run out and do some last-minute shopping for me."

Both Avery and Jason left the kitchen with no further comment.

Trina laughed. "I'll give you one thing, Mr. President, you sure know how to empty a room."

He looked at his watch. "Are you going to be around for a while?"

"Why do you ask?" she said, suspiciously.

"Well, I guess I could do it right now."

"Do what?"

"I wanted to thank each of you personally for sticking with me and for working so hard. You, especially. You've worked as hard or harder than anyone else, and I haven't said thank you very many times, so I wanted so say it now. If you should ever want to work for anyone else, you will get my highest recommendation."

Though kind, his words saddened her a bit. Was he dismissing her in a nice way?

In his own way, Don really *was* dismissing her. He could sense a change in her demeanor toward him, and he wanted to be sure their relationship remained a business one. Friendly, but businesslike. He had made this decision several other times in his life and saw no reason to change it now. Don knew himself—a person who became totally absorbed in whatever he was doing. His duties could take all of his attention for days or weeks, and he wouldn't care about anything else. In his new job, the ability to focus all his energies on the work at hand would be essential. Many things were in total disarray. He knew God had called him to begin setting things in order, and he looked forward to getting at it as soon as possible.

Trina was a good woman, but he knew it wasn't meant to be. Don wanted her to know exactly where she stood. It was only fair. If she wanted to stay under those terms, she would be welcome to stay on his staff.

Almost two thousand miles away, in New York, Edwina Grant knocked on the door to Rosa's apartment. Ricky opened the door.

"Hey! Come on in!" he said, giving her a small hug. "It's pretty messy, but you know how it is." He turned and yelled, "Rosa! We have company!"

Edwina looked around the apartment and sighed. Boxes were stacked everywhere. Ricky's replacement at the clinic, Bobby Landis, had gladly taken Ricky's old apartment. Ricky packed up his household goods and moved them to Rosa's but left most of them in the boxes. In two months, they would be moving to Oklahoma. Ricky had delayed their move by a month so he could help George get the clinic up and running again. It had been looted and damaged severely in the riots.

Two days after the wedding, the Grants had gone on a short honeymoon of their own. George and Edwina were no longer sure they wanted to stay in New York either, but they would have to repair the clinic to be able to use it *or* sell it. They still had the van, and they found it ideal for the kinds of things needed in many neighborhoods— tetanus shots, suturing cuts, and dispensing antibiotics.

Rosa came out of the kitchen. "'Wina!" she exclaimed, and gave her friend a big squeeze. "What a great surprise! Isn't life without a phone weird? But at least we've got electricity! Come in the kitchen with me, and I'll fix you something hot to drink."

The two women hurried to the kitchen to talk.

"So. How do you like him, Mrs. Ruiz?"

"Oh, Edwina," she said, with a sigh. "I'm so happy."

"The first night you met him, I knew that was it. I'd never seen you get so annoyed with anyone before. You'd have slapped the man's face clean off if you could have!"

Rosa blushed, then peeked into the living room to see if Ricky could hear them. "Shhhh!"

"I just want you to remember how hard I worked for this! And in the end, I suppose George did his share, too. He was a reluctant participant at first, but eventually he got into it."

They heard Ricky singing and humming something in the other room. Rosa blushed again. This made Edwina curious, so she moved closer to the doorway. He was singing in Spanish so she could only pick up two words, "Rosa" and "*esposa.*"

"What's he singing?" Edwina asked.

Rosa's face turned red. "It's just a song he made up. This is really embarrassing. It's about me. You know, things like he thinks I'm lovely, etc., etc., etc.," her voice trailed off at the end.

"Why are you so embarrassed? I think that's sweet!"

Rosa leaned close to her friend. "Well, it's just that he sings it all the time. And you know how badly he sings . . . and the terrible rhymes . . . "

"Well, like what, for instance?"

"It's just that my name happens to rhyme with lots of things in Spanish. Like wife, and beautiful, and marvelous, and butterfly . . . "

Edwina laughed. "How adorable!"

"How would you like it if George went everywhere," she paused and lowered her voice again, "singing something—badly, mind you—like, 'Oh, my Edwina, you've never seena, one so lovely as Edwina. . . . She's my

queena. I'll take her to North Caroleeeena, my Edwina!
I'd rather remove my own spleeena than lose my
Edwina!' . . . You get the idea, don't you?"

By now, Edwina couldn't catch her breath from
laughing.

Ricky poked his head into the kitchen. "What's going
on?"

"I was just watching your bride blush at the sound of a
love song."

"Oh! That!" he said, and began to sing it proudly. *"O
Rosa, mi esposa! . . . Mi mariposa, cuan hermosa es mi
esposa, Rosa! . . ."*

Edwina clapped her hands. "That's so sweet. If I could
remember any Spanish, I'd help you out!"

"Stop encouraging him!" Rosa insisted, but her eyes
said she loved it.

She threw a dish towel at Ricky. He ducked and sang,
"Cuan peligrosa, es mi Rosa!" He then retreated to the
other room, still humming the song.

Edwina gave Rosa a questioning look.

"Now he's saying I'm 'dangerous!'" Rosa said,
pointing a finger at her friend with pretended anger.
"And I'm going to get even with *you*, too, if you don't
quit!"

"Oh yeah?" Edwina said, her voice growing serious.
"You're already moving away and breaking my heart. And
George doesn't know *what* he'll do without Ricky."

"That reminds me," Rosa said trying to divert the conversation, "do you know anyone who wants to buy my
furniture?"

"You just bought it, and you're not taking it with
you?"

"When I bought those beautiful little cream-colored,
French provincial things, I didn't have two hundred forty
pounds of Ricky. Look at that big, ugly leather recliner of
his in there. It's the only thing he'll sit on. He gingerly
perches on everything else as if it's going to turn to

toothpicks under him. And the bed is too short. I never realized how awful life could be for tall people till I met Ricky. On the bright side, when we get to Oklahoma we'll get to decorate together. It'll be fun."

Edwina sighed. "Oh, Rosa. I hope you are blessed wherever you are, but I'm sure going to miss you."

"I'll miss you, too."

Ricky popped back into the kitchen. "Excuse me, but Rosa, if you want to vote, we need to go soon. Edwina can come with us, and we'll find hot dogs or something really nutritious to snort down. How about it?"

"Actually, I came to invite the two of you to dinner," Edwina said. "How about if I take you to vote, then you come home with me for dinner."

"What about curfew?" Rosa said.

"You can bring a few things and spend the night in the guest room. What'd you say, Mr. Ruiz?" she looked at him. "George bought himself a Bible today. You might need to show him how it works!"

"This woman would say anything to get us to dinner, wouldn't she?" Ricky said to Rosa. "OK, it's a deal."

When Ricky, Rosa, and Edwina arrived at the apartment, George was ecstatic. He still walked with a slight limp, but he needed no crutches or cane. "Oh, 'Wina!" he said rushing to the door. "We have cable again!"

Rosa and Edwina gave each other a look that said *big deal*.

"No really, honey. We do." Then noting his wife's lack of enthusiasm, he turned to Ricky. "We can catch a game tonight!"

"Great!" Ricky said.

"There's a game on election night?" Edwina said.

"East Coast, honey. East Coast. Polls will be closed by then."

The women rolled their eyes and left the men to themselves for a while.

The two couples stayed up late, talking and laughing, occasionally looking at sports or election updates. By the time they went to bed, Cole had pulled ahead, but the results of the election were still in the balance.

At 4:00 A.M. Mountain Standard Time, the news declared Cole the official winner of the presidential election. Although everyone in the Cole camp was elated about the win, they were also exhausted. He knew that few were still up watching television, so he kept his acceptance speech short. He'd save the best material for the next day when everyone was awake.

Todd had spent election day in his office, and then he had gone to his private quarter where he ate alone. He and Edith had reached an impasse. He'd really tried to get "enlightened," but after two weeks, he was a nervous wreck. He kept seeing things move in the corner of his eye, only to turn and find nothing there. He would wake up in the middle of the night and feel an ominous presence. Edith and her friend seemed to think it was "marvelous" that he was sensing "visitations" so quickly in his new walk, but all he felt was scared. He told Edith she could do what she wanted, but he had no more desire to get any further involved with Raiza and her "visitors."

When it was time to leave for the festivities, he went to Edith's room to make sure she was ready to go. She was cordial but cool. They rode to the hall together and ended up spending the entire night in the private rooms reserved for his inner circle. By 6:00 A.M. Eastern Standard Time, his defeat was confirmed. He didn't bother to address the few people who remained in the hall. He wanted to go back to the White House and pack for Camp David. He needed to take a day or two to consider life outside the Oval Office.

He had previously threatened to line-item-veto parts of a defense spending bill, but Yosef had talked him out of it. The mere threat of the vetoes had worked; the corporations decided to continue to support him until election day. He'd even gotten good press coverage. Given these things, he should have won. He'd always won this way before. But this time, he lost. It could only be blamed on the fact that he was not popular with ordinary people—most of whom voted. This was a bitter pill for him to swallow. Even though Yosef promised him that life in the business world would be "satisfying and lucrative" if he lost the election, he couldn't get over the fact that he'd been rejected.

Later that day, Todd waited at Camp David for the call saying that Secretary of Defense Ernie Schollet was on his way into the compound. The call came, and Todd went outside to meet him. Having Yosef or Ernie near his wife made him nervous for some reason. Was it because he was afraid she would get curious about them? Although he felt his personal logs were enough to protect his wife and adult daughter from the threat of harm, he still wanted to keep his dealings with the two men far removed from his family.

What Sonny Todd did not know was that Yosef had already located two of his three personal logs and was hours away from confiscating the third. Schollet had agreed with Yosef that Todd was no longer a viable work partner. Schollet knew that Todd, who was beginning to exhibit stranger behavior every day, might snap at any second, and they'd all get thrown into prison. He made a deal while he still could.

The call came in, and Sonny told Edith that he and Ernie would be going for a walk.

"Will he be staying for a meal? A drink? Anything?" she asked.

"No. We have some things to talk over, and then he's got to head back to D.C. He's just stopping by for a few minutes. I'll be back soon," he said as he left the house.

The car pulled into the drive, and he went out with the agents to meet it. The Secretary of Defense got out and shook his hand. The day was unusually cool, and Ernie wore gloves. When they shook hands, Todd got a strange feeling. There was something different about his friend today. Perhaps if he'd known that the Secretary had just been to see Yosef, he wouldn't have been so quickly distracted from the disquiet he felt. But Ernie said he was in a hurry to catch a flight, and the urgency of his statement caused Todd to jump right into the business at hand. As they began walking down the road, the agents "fell back" as requested, and they watched from a distance. The entire area was cordoned off and would be safe for a walk.

Ernie lost no time once they were out of earshot. "I have a list of your possibilities and some of the figures involved." He pulled an envelope from his coat pocket and handed it to Todd, who tore it open to read the list.

"If you look at the figures here . . . " Ernie said, suddenly pulling the paper out of Todd's hand.

Todd jumped as the edge of the paper cut the skin between his thumb and forefinger.

"Oh, so sorry," Ernie said. "I hate it when that happens to me."

Todd sucked on the spot. "Yeah. That really hurts. Funny how we can tough out big things, but a paper cut is almost unbearable."

They both chuckled.

Ernie pointed to the figures he wanted to show Todd, then carefully placed the paper back in the envelope and tucked it in his pocket. The entire exchange took less than two minutes.

By the next morning Sonny was beginning to feel a bit under the weather. Two days later, as he sat in the Oval Office, Sonny Todd slumped over his desk and died.

News of his death shocked the nation. Only fifty-four, Sonny had received a clean bill of health at his last physical. An autopsy revealed that he'd suffered a massive stroke and died almost instantly.

Within hours of Todd's death, Victor Bartlett was sworn in as president of the United States. Five hours after being sworn in, he met with Ernie Schollet and Yosef, and they assured him of their full support. They told him of their constant desire to keep him "in" on things before Todd's death. Of course, *now* they could see that Todd's irrational suspicion of Victor and his insistence on keeping the vice president out of the loop were due to his physical and mental health problems. But at the time, what could they have done? After all, Todd was the president, and he called the shots. Now that Victor was president, they were completely behind him. He thanked them and ended the meeting.

Victor wasn't convinced. He was relatively certain he couldn't trust them anymore but had little choice in the matter. What could he do? Before the day was over, an urgent situation had already presented itself. On the first day of the riots, an anonymous tip had come into the office of the National Security Agency regarding two nuclear devices that had been tracked from France to New York. Victor figured that they were, in all likelihood, the two ERWs stolen during the botched plan in Africa.

Victor recalled the Secretary of Defense to his office to discuss their next move. As soon as the door was closed, he launched into a twenty-minute tirade about the state of affairs were in when Todd died. Finally, he got to the topic of the weapons.

"How could this have happened? They got a report of transportable *nuclear devices* in an American city and *forgot* about it? Or they *lost* it? What's *wrong* with these people? Riot or no riot, there's no excuse for misplacing a lead about something of this magnitude! And apparently, the trail is totally cold. *Nobody* knows where the cursed things are now! I should fire the Chief of the Agency! Even if someone *finds* the weapons, the worst part is they'll see the devices are *ours*. We're really up a creek here, Ernie."

Ernie advised Victor to remain calm. Hasty actions could draw unwanted attention to the situation. He and

Ernie spent time devising a plan. They would let the whole issue of the initial report get "lost" once again, this time in the "crank calls" file of the Agency. Next, they would send their *own* special agents to look into the problem. Lastly, they would hope everyone else remained unaware of their predicament. This was one piece of information they had no intention of transferring to the new president.

CHAPTER SEVENTY-ONE

DONALD LARSON COLE FINISHED BUTTONING HIS TOP-coat. It was the day he had waited for. A day he felt he'd been born for. The morning had dawned crisp and bright, and he was about to be sworn in as president of the United Sates of America.

Don was alone in his room, and he wanted to linger there a little longer. To savor his last few moments of privacy. The last few moments he would be responsible only for himself. He looked up.

"I'm almost ready. I wanted to say thanks, again. I know You are calling me to a hard place, but I'll try to do my best for you. I'm still so new at this. Help me never to step back or step down until You want me to. Help me to stand. . . . God, as I sought You for the words to say today, I believe You gave me wisdom. . . . Now I ask that You help people to hear what I say. . . . Amen."

Don walked to the door, took one deep breath, and stepped out into the crowd of people gathered in the suite. A small army of Secret Service men filled the room.

Reggie, one of his favorites, was there at Don's request. His mother stepped up and gave him a kiss. Bob, Trina, Avery, and many others from his staff had agreed to stay on with him and had also gathered in the room along with Josh and Carol Thornton, who were like family to him.

As the agents made preparations to transport Cole and his entourage, Victor Bartlett and others from the Todd administration said their farewells. They would remain edgy until enough time and space had elapsed to know all the incriminating evidence of their endeavors had been sufficiently covered. They had not managed to locate the ERWs, but neither had they informed Cole of the problem. In fact, they reasoned, once they were safely out of Washington, why not continue the search for the weapons? If their own agents found the ERWs, there would be no need to publicize the recovery *or* to give them back to the government. Once they secured Yosef's promise that the weapons would not be used in the United States, they were open to discuss business terms. Victor was still leery of the others, but he had begun to lower his guard once he'd found out how lucrative working with them could be.

In New York City, Ricky and Rosa sat in the Grants' apartment watching television on their last day in New York. They had finished packing all their belongings the day before and sent them on by truck to Oklahoma. They would spend their last New York night in George and Edwina's guest room. George had taken the day off, and they planned on having a small going away party for "the lovebirds" later that evening.

The previous Sunday, the Grants made their third trip to church with Ricky and Rosa. The pastors had called the young couple up onto the platform and prayed for them, amid many tears and hugs. Obviously George and Edwina weren't the only ones who would miss them. Despite the sad good-byes, the Grants enjoyed the service and thought they might visit again the following weekend. This, of course, made Ricky very happy. He wanted to think he was leaving George and Edwina in good hands.

The inauguration hadn't started yet. The commentator on one channel, Lester McGrath, was giving a "warm up" for the event.

"We have been told that Mr. Cole insisted on writing his own address for today and has spent a great deal of time laboring over the words he will be delivering to the American people. He has developed several initiatives for financial recovery in the hard-hit cities, has come up with some tax reform ideas, and even has new disaster relief plans. Whether he will speak about one or all of these issues remains to be . . . "

George flipped from channel to channel with the remote. Ricky didn't seem to notice. This was driving the two women crazy, so they decided to go have some tea in the kitchen. Rosa looked at her husband and winked before leaving the room.

"What kind do you want?" Edwina said, surveying her cupboard. "Cinnamon? Peach? . . . Mint?" There was no response, so she looked over at Rosa, who was growing pale.

"Maybe I'll just have water."

"Are you ill?" Edwina asked.

"Well, no." Rosa said, getting back a little color. "I've wanted to tell you for a couple of weeks. So far, only Ricky and I know it, but . . . we wanted to tell you guys before we left . . . we owe the two of you so much and . . . we're going to have a baby."

"*What?* Rosa!" Edwina rushed over and hugged her. "I'm so happy for you!" She let go and looked at her. "Are *you* happy for you?"

"Oh, yes! We really want a baby. We can't wait. Ricky is beside himself! He's already talking to her. He's probably making up a song already!"

Edwina reflected a moment. Yes, Ricky had appeared unusually perky the last few days, even for Ricky. "Her? He wants a girl?"

"He says he feels that it's a girl."

Edwina hugged her again. "Does George know?"

"No. I wanted to tell you first. . . . It's just, well . . . I haven't known how to tell you. I know how much you've wanted a baby, 'Wina. I knew you'd be happy for me, but . . . "

"I'm OK," she smiled. "Really I am. George and I have done a lot more talking about it lately. It used to be that I talked—make that begged—and he stalled. Now he's ready to go, and *I'm* stalling! Isn't that funny? The thing I thought I wanted most, and now that I can have it, I'm a little uncertain."

"How come?" Rosa asked.

"We don't even know if we're going to stay here in New York. We're leaning toward it, but we're not sure. We see a bigger need than ever for our services in the neighborhoods, and I have to admit that part is very satisfying. I just want to be more settled, I guess . . . and . . . "

Rosa looked directly at Edwina. "And what?"

"Things in the world are so scary right now. Are we sure we want children in the middle of all this?"

Rosa smiled. "I'm sure. Listen, 'Wina, people have been saying that it's a bad time to have kids since time began. Ricky and I prayed about this even before we were married, and we decided we would have children unless God told us not to. . . . You can't let fear make your decisions in life, or you'll never live it! If I'm ever afraid of what might happen to this precious one," she said, placing a hand on her stomach, "I'll have to remind myself that however long she lives on this earth, whether that's three weeks or a ninety-nine years, I'll have her forever in heaven! We've brought someone into being that will live on and on, beyond any sorrow or suffering on this earth. Look at things through God's eyes, 'Wina." She put Edwina's hand under her own. "Edwina, this is your niece—or nephew, if Ricky is wrong."

"Hey!" George shouted from the living room. "It's on!"

"Let me tell him later tonight," Edwina said.

"OK, as long as I can get to Ricky first. He's just bursting to tell George."

They went into the living room. Rosa gave Ricky the I-want-to-see-you-in-the-other-room look. He finally caught on and followed her to the bedroom.

He put his arms around her and smiled. "What do you want, *Mami?*"

"I told Edwina."

"Oh! Can I tell George now?"

She had to laugh. He was just like a kid sometimes. "Well, honey, Edwina wanted to know if she could tell him."

"How come? Was she really depressed?"

"Oh, no. That's the funny part. Apparently *he* wants one now, and *she's* not sure!"

"You're kidding?"

"Nope."

"If I live to be a hundred, I'll never understand women," he said, shaking his head.

"Better get used to it, *Papi,*" she said, poking a finger in his chest, "'cause there may be two of them in your household soon!"

He beamed at her.

They went back to the living room, and Rosa gave Edwina a little nod.

The inauguration was starting. Donald Larson Cole placed his hand on a Bible and took the oath of office.

Ricky found out that Cole had become the friend of one of his pastors, Josh Thornton, and that he'd let both Josh and Daniel pray with him. Although Josh intended to keep his ongoing relationship with Don confidential (turning down several interviews with the press), he had shared one thing with Ricky. Josh said that Cole was not a Christian in the only-on-Sunday sense, but he had become someone who fully intended to seek God's wisdom in all that he did. This made watching the ceremonies much more meaningful to Ricky, who hadn't paid much attention to political things before. As he watched Cole take his oath, he regretted he'd never taken it seriously until now.

When it came time for Cole's address, they all listened intently to his words.

Donald Cole stood at the podium. He'd spent weeks thinking and praying about what he would say. The time had finally come.

"My fellow Americans. It is with a humble heart that I address you today. I thought about many things as I prepared to make this address. I had so much that I had wanted to communicate to you concerning plans, programs, and ideas. But while I was looking for just the right words, I heard this story, and I want to share it with you.

"There was a man who had a beautiful daughter. From the day she was born she was his delight. When she was small, she depended on him, she looked up to him, she trusted him, and he gave her every good thing. Even when he disciplined her, he did it with love.

"The little girl grew up to womanhood, and the father thought about what sort of man he would want his daughter to marry. He wanted only the best for his daughter. He wanted the perfect husband for her, one who would love her and never abuse her, one who would see her many talents and praise her as she put them to work for their mutual benefit . . . a man who would honor and respect her, who would share all that he had with her. This is what the father longed for.

"But as his daughter came of age, she began to do rebellious things. She began to abuse the trust her father had given her. She found odd friends, she adopted all their ways of dress and speech. She stayed out late at night with these friends and then slept during the day. This behavior concerned her father. He tried to speak to her, but she wouldn't listen. She was old enough to make her own decisions now. She was free to do as she pleased—and it pleased her to look the way she did and go where she wanted. She was only 'having a little fun.'

"The father was upset by this, but he hoped that it was just a phase she was going through. He became even more concerned, however, when he learned how she was spending the money he'd given her. She was using it for more clothes than she could possibly wear, for wild parties with her friends, and for drugs.

"He'd put few conditions on what he'd given her. He asked that she spend it wisely and that she give a portion of it to those who were in need. Instead, she spent it all, and more, upon herself. She seemed to take perverse pleasure in driving her luxury car past those who had nothing. It gave her a sense of power, of being better. Whenever she fell short of cash, she just borrowed from others. She'd pay it back. Someday.

"Meanwhile, the poor people in her community began to feel animosity toward her. She treated them like dirt and laughed at their needs while she squandered her fortune on herself. Many of the children she passed on the street would have gladly eaten what she threw away or happily worn the clothes that she carelessly tossed on the floor of her room. Many of them would have given all they possessed to spend time with a loving father like the one she was ashamed to have known.

"The father of this young woman sat at home, grieved. He asked himself, 'How could I have raised such a girl?'

"A cold shiver ran through him when he watched the news that night. A stalker was loose in the community. He was preying on young women who traveled alone at night. When his daughter came home, just before dawn, he felt torn. Was he glad she was safe or angry at her foolishness?

"In the coming weeks he warned her often of the dangers with which she flirted. She called him 'old fashioned' and 'paranoid.' One evening, as she was leaving, she told him she'd been thinking of moving out of his house altogether. Some of her friends didn't feel comfortable there. Besides, she needed more space, wanted more freedom.

"That night, the dreaded call came to her father's house from the hospital. His daughter had been found on a street in a slum, left for dead. What the stalker didn't take, the neighborhood people carried away with no pity. The father rushed to the hospital and ran to her room. There, in the bed, covered with tubes and wires, lay a distorted figure. Surely this couldn't be his beautiful daughter. There must be some mistake. But no, they were certain. It was his daughter.

"The father looked again at the one in the bed. He looked at the blackened eyes, the horrible slashes and deep wounds, the crushed hand that he'd always hoped would wear the ring of the perfect husband. Would she even live?

"The physician came and stood by the father. He said he would do all he could for the young woman, but that part of the recovery was up to her. She had to want to live. And even if she did, there would be a long period of recuperation . . . if all went well, perhaps some of her former beauty could be restored, in time.

"Her father knew that even if she recovered, she would have to choose once again how she would live. Would she have learned from the horrible price she paid, or would she sink back into her former life?"

Don Cole paused a moment and surveyed those who had gathered to hear the speech. "That's as much as I've heard of the story so far. It's a sad story, isn't it? I dare to say there are some of you within the sound of my voice who have lived through similar nightmares with your own children and have known that awful pain.

"Today, I stand here and tell you that when this nation was born, she was birthed to Father God. He gave her life and freedom. When she was young, she depended on Him, she looked up to Him, she trusted His wisdom, and He gave her every good blessing.

"But she came of age and started making her own decisions. She took advantage of the trust and the liberty God gave her. She ground down the face of the poor with her heel and left the safety of her Father's house to roam wherever she pleased and do what she liked, calling it freedom. When she ran out of money, she just borrowed some. When people tried to remind her of who her Father was, she despised them, and even took them to court for saying hateful things and lies about her, because she was ashamed that she'd ever known Him.

"Many stalked her with the intent of killing her and stripping her of her goods, but she laughed at warnings about them, saying, 'Surely, no harm will come to me. Look who I am! Who would dare to harm me?'

"But I stand here today to tell you that this woman—America—was recently caught by some of those who hate her, and she was beaten within an inch of her life. She's been taken to the hospital. . . .

"I want you to know her Father has been called. . . . She's out of immediate danger, but if care isn't taken, she could still die. I believe I have been selected as the physician over this battered patient, but I have come to the humbling conclusion that I am only one man. I may have the skill to fix some of the things that are broken, but I cannot make this patient well. . . . Part of it is up to her. She has to want to live. Her recovery could be slow, and when she is better, she will have to make some choices regarding how she lives.

"If you, like me, have been alarmed by the recent events that have taken place in this country, then it's time to pay attention. We are at a crossroads in our history. You, the American people, have to decide if you want the country to go back to the house from which she came, or back to the dark streets of 'no restraint, anything goes.'

"If you, like me, are horrified by the prospect of having your every move and thought regulated, then we had better *re*-learn the lessons of *self*-restraint, or we will pay the ultimate price. Because a people who won't restrain themselves *will* be overtaken by those who will enslave them, or beat them, strip them of their goods, and leave them for dead. It's a choice you still have the God-given freedom to make. Choose well.

"I invite you to look around the globe today and even throughout recorded history. Those countries who have called upon the living God have been blessed. Those who sought other gods—whether they be men, or pleasure, or idols—have reaped oppression, poverty, and pestilence. Again, it's a choice you still have the God-given freedom to make. Choose well.

"I could have spent the time I had on this stage tickling your ears with many smooth and flattering words. I could have set forth a ten-point plan 'to move the nation forward,' which you probably would have forgotten by dinner time. Instead, I wanted to give you this honest assessment of our nation—and hope that it will haunt all of you the way it has haunted me.

"I am a man who is given to action. But I realize we cannot fix these problems with mere activity. There must be wisdom to know what to do and when to do it.

"I stand here as president, and I am asking for the prayers of the American people. Not just for me but for yourselves. I am asking that, starting this Sunday, every one of you begin a forty-day season of seeking the Father of this nation. I'm asking that every one of you would fast—would restrain yourself from something, whether that be your lunch every day, or meat, or television, or anything that means something to you, and that you would seek God on behalf of this country.

"I realize that some may be offended by this request, but that is all it is. A request. You choose what you will do. It's a choice you still have the God-given freedom to make. Choose well.

"Scripture says that God's mercy is new every morning. It also says that it is wise to seek Him while He can be found. May God's mercy be extended to this country this morning, and may we know His blessing once again. . . . I thank you."

President Donald Cole stepped away from the podium.

At first the media, rarely at a loss for words, were caught off guard by the topic of the speech. But within days, thousands of words of commentary would be written and spoken about this inaugural address. Many would have heard what Cole said and, for a season, the course of the nation would be changed.